SHATTERED TRUTHS

New York Times Bestselling Author **HELENA HUNTING**
writing as

H. HUNTING

SHATTERED TRUTHS

The first time I met Winter Marks, I almost took her out with my Jeep.

To be fair, she came out of nowhere.

I flirted with her, and she flipped me off and disappeared into the woods on her bike.

But she left me a souvenir: a single hockey skate.

Seemed to me that divine intervention shouldn't be ignored.

She was my icy Cinderella and I would be her Prince Not-So-Charming.

Winter was more than just a sassy, badass hockey-playing hottie.

She's stuck in a prison of a life. And I'm the perfect escape.

Neither of us expected to fall.

Or for the truth to shatter us.

SHATTERED TRUTHS

For the caretakers and the shields.

ACKNOWLEDGMENTS

This book.

If ever this was a story that was hard fought for, it's this one. Having written it not once, but twice, I'm doubly grateful for the amazing people in my life who held me up and handed me tissues when I stepped into rewrites, and started over again with these characters until I had their story exactly how it was meant to be. Hubs and kidlet, thank you for being the most amazing support system, for hugging me when I needed it, for cheering me on when I was fighting to get to the end, again, and for always being my sunshine and my rainbow. I adore you.

Deb, you are a rare gem and I'm so grateful for your friendship. Thank you for being the Pepper to my Salt.

Kimberly, thank you for all the time, conversations and brainstorming that took place as we wrangled this book into submission. It wasn't easy, but it also wouldn't have become the story I needed it to without your support.

Jessica, Christa, Julia, Amanda, thank you so much for working through this one with me. I'm so fortunate to have such an incredible team of women to help make this book shine.

Hang, you create the most amazing covers. Your art is a gift.

Sarah Pie, you are such a rock and a wonderful friend and I am ever grateful to have you on my side.

Hustlers, thank you for being my team, for having my back

and for lifting me up when I need it the most. I'm so thankful for all of you.

My SS team, you are beyond fabulous and your support and attention to detail are so greatly appreciated.

Sarah and Gel, thank you for being graphic gurus. Your incredible talent never ceases to amaze me.

Beavers, thank you for giving me a safe place to land, and for always being excited about what's next.

Deb, Tijan, Sarah, Melissa, Heather, Kat, Marnie and Krystin, you are some boss level women and I'm so lucky to have you in my life.

Readers, bloggers, bookstagrammers and booktokers, your passion for love stories is unparalleled, thank you for all that you do for the reading community.

SHATTERED TRUTHS CAST

BJ BALLISTIC
Parents
RANDY AND LILY BALLISTIC
PUCKED SERIES: PUCKED OVER/UNDER
(BEST FRIEND/FRIENDS WITH WINTER)
Siblings
LOGAN
LIAM & LANE
LAUGHLIN
LACEY (TWIN)

LOVEY BUTTERSON
Parents
SUNNY AND MILLER
PUCKED SERIES: PUCKED UP

ADELE
BJ'S PAIR'S PARTNER

QUINN ROMERO
TEAMMATE/HOUSEMATE TO BJ & ROSE
Siblings
CELESTE
HEATHER
Parents
LANCE & POPPY ROMERO
PUCKED SERIES: PUCKED OFF

MAVERICK, RIVER AND LAVENDER WATERS
BJ'S COUSINS (MOTHER'S ARE HALF SISTERS)
LIES, HEARTS & TRUTHS SERIES: BITTER SWEET HEART & LITTLE LIES
Parents
ALEX & VIOLET WATERS
PUCKED SERIES: PUCKED/FOREVER PUCKED

WINTER MARKS
Parents
LUCY AND CLAYTON MARKS

ROSE WESTINGHOUSE
WORKS WITH WINTER AT BOONES
MUTUAL FRIEND OF BJ'S
BJ AND QUINN'S HOUSEMATE
Parents
DARREN AND CHARLENE WESTINGHOUSE
PUCKED SERIES: PUCKED LOVE

CLOVER SWEET
MAVERICK'S GIRLFRIEND
WORKS AT LOCAL LIBRARY/FRIEND
LIES, HEARTS & TRUTHS SERIES: BITTER SWEET HEART

FERN HARMER
HOCKEY TEAMMATE

1

Near Miss

BJ

"I'M HEADING TO THE ARENA." I grab an apple from the fruit bowl and kiss my mom on the cheek.

She glances at the clock on the stove. "I thought you didn't have practice with Adele until ten."

"I don't. Just getting in some solo ice time." I take a bite out of the apple while I fill my travel mug with coffee.

"Don't forget we have a free skate tonight," Dad says as he slathers butter on toast.

"Looking forward to it." I put the lid on my coffee and head for the door.

"An apple won't cut it for breakfast, Randall. You need protein!" Mom calls after me.

"I've got bars in my bag. See you at the rink!" I shove my feet into my slides, grab the keys to my Jeep, and bust my ass out the door before my mom tries to sit me down for a seven-course meal. Skating on an overly full stomach isn't my favorite.

A minute later, I'm pulling out of the driveway and onto the packed-gravel road, stones spitting from beneath my tires. I slow down at the T-intersection, glancing in both directions before I pull onto the main road that leads to town. As I accelerate, a person on a bike comes shooting out of the wooded trail that runs perpendicular to the road. I hit the brakes and the tires squeal, leaving rubber behind me.

My heart is in my throat as I make eye contact with the girl on the bike. She's wearing a helmet, thank God. Her eyes are wide with shock as she attempts to course correct, and her lips form the word *fuck* as she turns the handlebars. I'm sure we're about to collide, but she manages the turn, though she nearly skids out as she avoids slamming into the side of my Jeep.

"The fuck, dude?" She grabs the edge of my door to steady herself. "It's called a goddamn stop sign for a reason, not a fucking pause-and-keep-on-rolling sign."

In the brief moment when our faces are less than half a foot apart, I notice a lot of things—the first being that she's smoking hot, in an unconventional way. Her face is all angles and sharp lines, and her eyes are the color of a stormy sky, but her lips are full and pouty, softening her features, and her chin tapers, giving her face a heart shape. There's a jagged horizontal scar in the center of her chin, and freckles dot the bridge of her nose. Her long, dark hair is pulled back in a braid that hangs nearly to her waist, and there's a hockey bag strapped to the back of her bike.

"Your reaction time is incredible," I say, like an idiot.

"Seriously? You're lucky I didn't dent your Jeep, asshole."

The last thing I should do is smile, but I can't help it. "Damn. You're gorgeous, with a sharp tongue, and you play hockey? This is divine intervention. You're basically the woman of my dreams."

She looks at me like I have two heads, then purses her lips and pushes off the side of the Jeep. She rounds the hood while firing the bird at the windshield. "I hope you don't fuck like you drive," she yells.

As she navigates the steep slope that leads to the trail on the opposite side of the road, her back tire skids on the fresh gravel and she goes down.

"Shit." I flick on my hazard lights, pull onto the soft shoulder, and hop out of the Jeep. By the time I reach the bumper, she's already back on her bike, disappearing into the forest. But not before I notice the Boones logo on the back of her shirt. It's a local bakery that makes the most amazing fried apple fritter rings. Everyone I know is addicted to them, including me.

A skid mark from her tires mars the gravel where she wiped out, and something glints from the wildflowers that line the road. I crouch to get a better look. It's a hockey skate with MARKS Sharpied on the tongue.

I pick it up and smile. Looks like I'm making a pit stop before I hit the ice.

Cinderella on Blades

WINTER

I MAKE it to Boones with ten minutes to spare, which is good because my elbow is bleeding and so is my knee, and the back of my right thigh has some serious road rash.

This morning has been a clusterfuck of epic proportions. It started with the timer going off on the toaster oven and waking my dad. He's an asshole on a good day, let alone when he's woken up by something other than his alarm. My usefulness as a human being was called into question. Not the ideal way to start things off.

I lock up my bike and lug my hockey bag into Boones through the back entrance. I feel bad about storing it in the break room, because it takes up so much space, but leaving it outside is begging for it to be stolen.

I key in my employee number to unlock the back door, and it dings, signaling my arrival. A petite, auburn-haired girl pokes her head through the door that connects the kitchen to the bakery. "Hey! You must be Winter."

I nod. "That's me." I started last week, but now that I'm finished training, I no longer need to be scheduled with Tracey Lynn, the manager and daughter of the owner.

"I'm Rose." She pops a pink bubble as her gaze moves over me, pausing at the hockey bag slung over my shoulder. It's hard to miss since it's huge and weighs a good fifty pounds. Her eyes widen when she gets to my bloody knee. "Oh shit. You're bleeding." She rolls her eyes. "Which I'm sure you already know. Are you okay? What happened?"

"I'm fine. Some douche in a Jeep almost ran me over." *And then tried to flirt with me.* I point to my knee. "Just gonna clean this up real quick and I'll be right out."

"Want me to put your hockey bag in the staff room?" she offers.

"It's heavy," I warn.

"I'm stronger than I look." She flexes a thin arm, her biceps popping.

"Thanks. I swear I'm not always this much of a hot mess." I set the bag on the floor and pull on the handle, but it only comes out halfway. "One of the wheels is broken."

"You're fine. It's quiet right now." She makes a face when she gets a load of the road rash on my leg. "Yeesh. That looks rough."

"I've had worse. I'll just be a minute." I grab the first aid kit from the wall and rush to the bathroom, calling a quick hello to Scottie, who works in the kitchen prepping the apples for fritters, and salads and sandwiches for the lunch rush.

It doesn't take long to clean and dress the cut on my knee. The road rash is red and ugly, but not a big deal. My elbow could be worse. As a hockey player, I'm used to bruises, scrapes, and even stitches, but starting my shift bleeding isn't exactly appealing to customers. I slap on bandages to cover the worst of it and push through the door to the bakery at 7:58.

Rose is leaning against the counter, phone in one hand and a coffee in the other, snapping selfies, if I had to guess. Her auburn hair is pulled through the snapback of a red Boones ball cap and twisted into a bun that's covered with a hairnet.

"Sorry about that. I'm ready to get to work. What can I do?" I run my damp palms over my thighs. I'm all adrenaline this morning.

"Tracey Lynn won't be in for two more hours, so you can take the eager beaver down a couple of notches." She drags her eyes away from her phone and motions to the espresso machine. "Make yourself a coffee, or a latte, or a cappuccino. Take a breath. Maybe give yourself a minute to get over almost getting hit by a Jeep."

The regular drip coffee is free for us, so I pour myself a cup and add a healthy dose of cream and two sugar packets. "It's been a weird morning."

The bell on the door tinkles, signaling a new customer. I set my coffee on the counter and turn around.

Standing in a beam of sunlight is the Jeep-driving douche. I didn't have much of a chance to appreciate his appearance while I was trying not to collide with the side of his vehicle, but he's hot...and vaguely familiar for reasons I can't put my finger on.

Now that I can see all of him, it's hella hard not to admire the view. He's tall and lean, with dark hair—shaved at the sides, the top long enough to pull back with a hot pink spiral hair tie. His short beard is neatly groomed, and his whiskey-brown eyes are framed with thick lashes the rich girls on the lake pay money for. But it's the sleeve running the length of his right arm, a vibrant burst of watercolor flowers, that really commands attention. His left arm has more artwork that ends at his elbow. That's a lot of hours under a needle. On a scale of one to spontaneous orgasm, he's a bean-flicking dream.

"Oh fuck," I mutter.

Rose glances from me to the guy. Her eyes light up. "Oh. No way. Is *he* the douche who almost hit you?"

This is going to get super awkward in a hurry. "Maybe."

"Oh, this is gonna be awesome. I wish I had popcorn." She spins to face the hot douche. "BJ. So wild, we were *just* talking about you."

My stomach sinks and twists as realization dawns. "Oh my God, you *know* him?"

"Hey, Rose. Enjoying your summer punishment?" His eyes move over me on a slow, assessing sweep.

"It just got a million times better." She slings her arm over my shoulder, which must be awkward for her, since she's a good four inches shorter than me. "I'd like to introduce you to Winter, who you apparently tried to run over this morning."

"Well, I wouldn't say he *tried* to run me over." *Why am I defending this guy?* "He just failed to obey basic traffic laws, and I nearly launched myself through his driver's side window." Ah, there's my barbed tongue.

One side of his mouth quirks up in an annoyingly attractive half-smile. "Your reaction time is a turn-on."

Rose throws her head back and laughs. "Oh, this is magic."

I cross my arms, determined not to be affected by the pretty. "Almost taking out a woman with your custom-paint-job Jeep turns you on?"

"Not in the slightest. The fact that you had to have been going twenty-five miles an hour, managed to stop without going over your handlebars, *and* still gave me shit for not paying attention to the road is a turn-on." He rubs his bottom lip with his thumb. "And I did stop to see if you were okay, but you seemed to be in a hurry."

"I didn't want to be late for work."

"This is like watching verbal foreplay, and I'm here for it." Rose hops up on the counter and crosses her legs.

"Are you okay?" he asks.

"I'm fine."

"You are totally not fine." Rose jumps down and spins me around. My braid whips out and slaps her arm. "Look at this!" I assume she's pointing at the road rash, which happens to be located just below where my shorts end.

BJ sucks in a breath.

"And that's not even the worst of it!" Rose declares.

I turn around. "I'm really fine. It looks worse than it is."

"That's not going to feel good when you're on the ice later," he murmurs.

I frown. "How do you know I'm going to be on the ice later?"

"You had a hockey bag strapped to your bike."

"Right. Yeah." Logic implies that his assumption is accurate, but my hockey bag is currently full of dirty clothes I'm taking to the laundromat after my shift. "A couple of scrapes will hardly slow me down."

A full smile spreads across his face, and as much as I don't want to admit it, all it does is make him hotter. "I was hoping you'd say that."

"Oh. Oh yes. I know what's coming! This is so happening." Rose claps enthusiastically.

I give her a look. She's a weird one for sure. She just grins and moves over to the fritter fryer to drop a few in the oil, making it hiss and bubble.

"There's a free skate at the arena tonight," BJ says.

I frown. "The new one or the old one?" It's been around several years, but locals still call it the new arena to differentiate it from the one built more than fifty years ago.

"The new one."

"I didn't see it posted." I always keep tabs on the free skates. They advertise them at the local library on the community board. I was there yesterday, and the next one isn't supposed to be until tomorrow, but I'll be working so I can't make it.

"We have the ice from seven to nine."

Rose siphons out the fritters and drops them into the cinnamon-sugar bowl, coating them before she puts them in a paper-lined box.

Two hours of free ice time is a dream. And the new arena is amazing. "I'm supposed to play pick-up at the old arena later."

"Might be tough with one skate," BJ says.

"What?" Rose passes me the box of fritters, and I hand them to BJ.

He drops a ten-dollar bill on the counter and steps back.

"I think you might have lost one of yours. You should check your bag, make sure you have both." He moves toward the entrance. "If you're missing one, you know where you can find it. Hopefully I'll see you later tonight. Rink three. Seven o'clock."

"Wait, what?" I don't even know what's happening.

He pushes through the door. "It was nice to meet you, Winter. I'm sorry about earlier."

I hold up the ten. A six-pack costs eight bucks. "What about your change?"

"It's cool. Keep it."

The door closes, and I watch him pass the front window and hop into his Jeep. I'm still stunned. "What the hell just happened?"

"BJ happened." Rose sips her coffee.

"I need to check something." I rush to the back room to look in my hockey bag. If I had enough time, I'd planned to get my skates sharpened this afternoon. I rummage through the contents and come up with only one skate. He was telling the truth.

I return to the front of the store, where Rose is back to looking at her phone.

"I think he might be holding my skate hostage."

She pockets her phone. "Seems like something BJ would do. I can probably get it back for you if you don't want to come to free skate, but I'm going, and it's loads of fun. Half the time they use the first hour for a free skate, and if there are enough players, they have a game of pick-up after."

"Really?" An hour of ice time and a game of pick-up for free. At the new arena.

Rose's eyes are lit up like a kid at Christmas. "You're coming, aren't you?"

"Maybe." It's an opportunity I'm not sure I want to pass up. "What's BJ's deal? How do you know each other?"

She gives me a curious look. "Our families have been friends my whole life. He's a relentless flirt, but a good guy."

"So take all the nonsense about me being the woman of his dreams with a bucket of salt?" I mutter.

Rose shrugs. "Hard to say. BJ isn't the type to throw around words if they don't mean anything."

"Huh."

The bell over the door tinkles again, and a group of summer teens comes in. It gets busy after that, so I don't have a whole lot of opportunity to ask Rose questions. I'm too focused on making fritters. It stays steady all the way through until the end of her shift at noon. We exchange phone numbers before she leaves, and she offers to pick me up if I'm serious about coming to this free skate.

I'm still on the fence as to whether it's a good idea, but I'm leaning toward going. Free is hard to pass up.

3

It's a Hard-Knock Life

WINTER

WHEN MY SHIFT at Boones finishes, Tracey Lynn gives me a six-pack of fritters to take home. She's aware that my family's financial situation isn't the best. Staying anonymous in a small town is tough, and while charity can be a hard pill to swallow, food is a gift I can't and won't say no to.

I strap my hockey bag to my bike and pedal to the laundromat. There's a washing machine at the cabin, but it's broken, and getting someone to look at it costs fifty bucks. So until I teach myself how to fix a washing machine, this is my plan. I'm used to that anyway.

As I empty the bag into the washing machine, I discover a hole in the bottom, which explains how I lost my skate this morning. In a way, I'm lucky BJ found it. Otherwise I'd have to use money from my secret tuition stash to buy a new pair.

It's already closing in on five thirty by the time I get home. I have a message from my mom that she's staying to work the dinner shift at the diner. She used to work at the one in Lake Geneva, back when we were living in the trailer park on the edge of town, but it's too far to bike all the way there, so she works at Tom's Diner in town now. She'll be exhausted by the time she gets home. Last night she and my dad were arguing until well after midnight, and then I accidentally woke him up with the toaster oven this morning, so she ended and started her day with his bad mood. It's not uncommon, but it still sucks.

I hang most of the laundry on the line, then head for the deck so I can drape the rest over the railing. The cabin is perched on a bluff, and the railing is the only thing between me and a two-story drop to the moss-covered rocks below. It's wobbly in places, and most of it needs replacing, but it's a huge step up from the trailer park where we sometimes have to live. Technically, I can move out if I want, since I'm nineteen, but my part-time job helps with bills my parents won't be able to cover otherwise.

I do the dishes from this morning so the sink is clean, then make myself two peanut butter sandwiches, scarf them down, and make a third to take with me to the arena.

When everything else is taken care of, I hop into the shower to rinse off. It's kind of pointless since I'll get sweaty all over again on the way to the arena, but the novelty of having our own shower hasn't worn off yet.

Even though a helmet and hockey gear don't scream sexy, I rim my eyes with dark liner, throw on a coat of clear mascara, and rebraid my hair.

By the time I'm finished, it's closing in on six thirty. The bike ride to the arena takes about twenty minutes. Rose messaged half an hour ago asking if I wanted her to pick me up. But that would mean giving her my address, and I don't want her to see where I live. Not now, probably not ever. So I tell her I'll meet her there. She responds with at least half a dozen gifs ranging from excitement to a girl shoveling popcorn into her face. I think I'm going to like Rose.

I grab my hockey gear from the railing. It's still damp, but it'll have to do. I make sure the hole in my bag is covered with a piece of cardboard before I jam in all my equipment and my single skate. I find my stick and secure it all to my bike with bungee cords. I'm about to head out when my dad's rusted-out Buick comes chugging down the driveway. The driver's side window is rolled down, and a cigarette dangles from his yellow-stained fingers.

We can barely afford basic groceries, but there's always money for smokes and beer.

"Where the hell do you think you're going?" Dad steps out of the car, an open can already in his hand. I'm sure he cracked it once he was off the main drag.

I bite back a sarcastic response, since I think it's obvious, and tap the end of my stick instead. The tape needs replacing, but I ran out last week and haven't had time to pick up more. "I got invited to play with some friends."

"The lawn needs to be mowed." He chugs his beer, throat bobbing as he drains the can, and tosses the empty toward the recycle bin. But he misses, and it rolls under the deck.

"The mower needs oil. I'll pick some up on my way to the arena so I can take care of it after my shift tomorrow." That was not at all my plan, but I don't want my dad to hijack my night with more household chores. And if I tackle the lawn now, I won't make ice time.

For the first time he looks directly at me. His eyes narrow and his nose wrinkles. "What the fuck is on your face?"

"It's called eyeliner." I internally cringe at my patronizing tone. My dad's sharp tongue is something I'm accustomed to, but I'm not always immune to the sting.

"You look like you belong on a stripper pole." His gaze

rakes over me, pausing at my bandaged knee. "Except no one would pay money to see you without clothes since you're built like a boy and you act like one too." He pulls his cigarettes out of his pocket and taps one free. "Pick me up a pack of smokes on your way home." He turns and walks away.

Our life would be a hell of a lot easier if my dad's vices didn't eat half his paychecks.

I shake off his shitty words and push away on my bike. Once I'm on the dirt road that will take me to the arena, I allow the excitement to set in.

By the time I reach the main road, I only have twenty minutes to get there, and it'll be faster to take the road instead of the trail. I pedal hard, gaining speed as I race down the hill, needing momentum to get up the next one. My thighs burn as I downshift, pushing hard to keep my speed from waning. Once I reach the top, it's downhill and then flat for about a mile or so.

I'm a few miles from the arena when the hum of an engine signals a vehicle approaching from behind. I hug the edge of the asphalt, not interested in taking another tumble today. A familiar metallic blue Jeep passes, giving me extra room. The brake lights flash, then stay lit as the Jeep comes to a stop in the middle of the road. My stomach does a flip as I slow my approach, hitting the brakes and dropping my foot to steady myself as I reach the open passenger-side window.

BJ's hand rests casually on the steering wheel. His smile is easy, eyes warm. "Hey, Winter. This seems like divine intervention once again. You on your way to the arena?"

I arch a brow. "Divine intervention is a bit of a stretch since this is the only way to get my skate back."

He taps the steering wheel, grin widening. "I would have brought it to Boones for you tomorrow if you didn't show tonight. You want a ride the rest of the way?" He points to the roof. "I got a bike rack. It'll only take a second to clip it in."

I bite my lip, considering. Rose seems nice, and BJ seems genuinely apologetic about almost hitting me today. A ride in will save my legs and get me to the arena on time. Plus he's damn nice to look at. "Yeah. Sure. Thanks."

"Great." He inclines his head toward the shoulder. "I'll pull over."

"Sounds good."

BJ pulls ahead, puts the Jeep in park, and hops out as I detach my hockey bag. While he secures my bike on the rack, I toss my bag and stick into the trunk alongside his. I follow him to the passenger side and am momentarily perplexed when he opens the door. Then I realize he's being polite.

"Oh, uh, thanks." I'm not used to guys with manners.

He grins, his smile both disarming and lopsided. "No problem. Hop on in."

I climb up and settle into the passenger seat, breathing the scent of his cologne and something vaguely cinnamon-y as I fasten my belt.

BJ rounds the hood and waits while an approaching truck passes before he takes his place behind the wheel.

"Thanks for the ride." I run my hands down my thighs, feeling awkward.

"It's my pleasure, and I owe you after this morning. I really am sorry." He gives me a chagrined smile and checks his mirrors before he pulls onto the road.

I steal furtive glances, checking out the pretty art decorating his right arm.

"How's the knee and the road rash?"

"It's fine." I washed and dressed it all after my shower. My knee is banged up, and the back of my leg is raw, but it'll scab over in a day or two.

He glances at me before refocusing his attention on the

road ahead of him. "Fine is usually what people say when they're the opposite."

"I play hockey. I've had worse injuries." I tap the scar on my chin and change the subject. "So is BJ short for something?"

He grins. "It is."

I wait for him to elaborate, but he doesn't. "You gonna tell me what it stands for, or am I supposed to guess?"

His smile widens. "Depends on whether you want a direct answer or the fun of trying to figure it out."

"Should I assume your parents aren't assholes and it isn't short for blow job?" I slap a hand over my mouth, wishing I could shove those back in my stupid word hole.

BJ throws his head back and laughs. "You would be correct. My parents aren't assholes, and you aren't the first or the last person to say that, so you can stop being mortified. I hang out with a lot of hockey-playing dudes, and their brains reside in their jockstraps."

I chuckle, shifting in my seat so I'm angled toward him. "Okay, does the J stand for Junior, or is it a hyphenated name?"

That earns me another lopsided grin. "Well-played. The J is for Junior."

"Okay, cool. Well, that narrows things down to names that start with B. What about Brad?"

"Nope."

"Brent? Bill? Bernard? Bobby?"

"All nopes."

"Bartholomew? Brandon? Brayden?"

He shakes his head.

I continue to lob B names at him, but none of them hits the mark.

He tosses me a hint. "Remember I said I spend a lot of time with hockey players."

I tap my lip. "Oh wait! Is the B your last name, not your first?"

"You got it."

I fire off a bunch of last names, but all of them are wrong. There are a lot of hockey families in the area, many of them retired NHL players. The new arena was funded by some of the most legendary players in the league, including Alex Waters and Rook Bowman—his son got called up to play for Philly in June. There's even a program called the Hockey Academy that every up-and-coming player in the state wants to be part of.

"You're not a Butterson, are you?" I'm mostly being tongue in cheek. I know one of the Butterson girls. Lovey works at the foodbank and the Salvation Army, both of which I frequent on the regular. She has four brothers and a twin sister.

"You're getting closer."

"Seriously?" I take in his profile. He's so familiar, and I don't think it's because I've run into him before today. "You're not a Ballistic, are you?"

BJ's eyebrows lift and lower in time with his reply. "Ding, ding, ding."

I let that sink in. "Hold the fuck on. Does that mean Randy Ballistic is your...dad?" I try to keep my voice from getting pitchy at the end, but I don't think I'm successful. Living in the lake district means I'm aware of the retired hockey players who've made it their home. But knowing they're around and actually seeing them up close and personal is a whole different story.

"He is." BJ glances at me again, maybe trying to gauge my response.

I really need to *not* fangirl, but holy shit, I'm about to get on the ice with the son of a hockey legend. It's a bit of a mindfuck. I nod a couple of times, tapping on the armrest. "Cool." And then I absorb the reality of his name. "Wait, you go by Ballistic Junior?"

"Balls Junior, actually."

I frown. "But why?"

He shrugs and chuckles. "That's what my friends have called me for years, and it stuck. My actual name is Randall Ballistic the third, but that sounds pretentious and douchey. My parents call me Randall, and my friends call me BJ. I think it's partly because my dad's best friend used to call him Randy Balls, and my aunt Violet dubbed him Horny Nutsack."

I blink a few times. "I'm sorry, did you say *horny nutsack?*"

"Sure did." He's grinning again. "My aunt is a total weirdo. She has zero verbal filter. Anyway, I became Balls Junior; BJ for short."

"Huh, that's...interesting."

"My family is a little quirky."

I won't argue with that. "They sound entertaining."

"They can be when they're not embarrassing the hell out of me." BJ makes a left into the parking lot at the arena. He's still smiling, so I can't tell if he's being serious.

"Does that happen often? Your family embarrassing you?"

He shrugs. "It's a fairly regular occurrence, but it's all in good fun."

The embarrassment he endures is probably a lot different than the kind I do at the expense of my family. I've had to bike out to the Town Pub and drive the car home for my dad when he's too wasted to function. It's a risk with me not being insured, but it's better than him getting a DUI.

BJ parks in a spot near the front doors, and we hop out of the Jeep. I meet him at the back bumper so we can grab our hockey bags and sticks from the trunk. When he tries to roll mine over, it makes an obnoxious scraping sound.

"Oh shit. You lost a wheel. That's no good." He scans the ground, searching for it.

"I know. I need to replace the bag, but I haven't had a chance," I lie as I reach for the handle.

"Why don't you take mine, and I'll carry yours?" He offers me the handle of his bag.

"It's cool. I got it." I slide the handle back in, which takes a couple of tries, because it's prone to jamming, then thread my arms through the straps and hoist it up, carrying it like a backpack.

On the way in, I check my phone. "Shoot. It's already five to seven. Sorry we're gonna be a little late."

BJ lopes along beside me, his strides measured and casual, clearly in no hurry. "It's okay. We've got two hours of ice time."

We stop at the women's change room. "You can leave your bag in there. It'll be safe since the rink is ours tonight. I'll meet you out here in a few, yeah?"

"Sure, sounds good." I take a step toward the change room.

"Winter?"

"Yeah?" I glance over my shoulder.

"I'm glad you came tonight." His smile makes my heart stutter. He's so hot it should be illegal.

"Me too." I disappear inside. It's empty and a million times nicer than the one at the old rink.

I quickly change into my hockey gear, but don't put on my pads since we'll be free skating for the first while. It isn't until I put on my left skate that I remember BJ still has the right. I hobble into the hallway and find him leaning against the wall, a jersey slung over his shoulder, his helmet tucked under his arm, and my other skate in his hand. He's wearing an athletic shirt that conforms to his long, lean, toned torso. I try not to be obvious about checking him out.

His head lifts as I approach. "Damn. Why you gotta be so beautiful?"

I bark out a laugh. "The compression pants really do it for you, huh?"

"You're a badass. It's hot." He holds up my skate. "And I forgot to give you this."

I reach for it, but BJ tips his chin toward the bench beside the locker room. "Have a seat for a sec."

I give him a questioning look, but do as he asks, mostly out of curiosity. Instead of handing me my skate, BJ drops to one knee in front of me.

I frown. "What're you doing?"

"Checking to make sure it's the right skate." He compares it to the one I'm already wearing. "Looks good to me."

"It should, unless you make a habit of holding girls' hockey skates hostage."

"Nope. You're a snowflake."

"A snowflake?"

His hand wraps around the back of my calf. It should not feel intimate. It should also not make my stomach flip or my nipples perk up, or everything below the waist clench. And yet...

His whiskey gaze lifts, and a smile tips one corner of his mouth. "One of a kind. An original."

More stomach flutters. "Wow. How many times have you used that line?"

His eyes crinkle in the corners when he laughs. "Fuck, I like you." He taps the top of my foot and holds the tongue back.

"I'm not Cinderella. I can put my own skate on, you know." But I can't say I dislike this style of flirting. It's different from what I'm used to.

"Cinderella was willfully oblivious, and a pushover, which

you are not. And I know you can put your own skate on, but I wanted a minute with you before I introduce you to everyone."

"So you could get your flirt on?"

"Basically, yeah." His grin is cheeky as he holds my skate steady. "I probably should have asked you for coffee or ice cream, huh?"

I laugh and lean forward so I can grip the tendon guard. The skate is half a size too small, but they're good quality, and I got them used for forty bucks, so I suffer through the cramped toes. I wiggle my foot in, trying not to appreciate how good he smells, or how close he is.

My cheek brushes his hair as I lift my head. "I would've said no to coffee or ice cream." Our faces are only inches apart, and for a moment I wonder what it would be like to go on a date with someone like him. Would we go to the diner? Or the pier? Would he try to kiss me at the end? Would we end up making out in the back of his Jeep? He's got all the lines, and the chemistry between us is hard to ignore.

He chuckles. "Because I need driving lessons, or because you don't like coffee or ice cream?"

I drop my head and focus on tightening my laces. "Because I thought you were an asshole."

"You're using past tense. That's good news for me." He's still on his knees in front of me, only a sliver of his artwork peeking out from under the sleeve of his shirt.

I push on his shoulder as I straighten. "Get off your knees, Ballistic."

He rises gracefully, his hand covering his heart. "Oh man, you're last-naming me? Kiss of death, right there."

I laugh and stand. I don't want to like this guy, but I think I do.

He tips his head. "Ready to get your skate on?"

I grab my helmet, gloves and stick, pads and jersey, and we clomp down the hallway together.

A rush of excitement hits me. It's partly connected to the hot guy currently flirting with me, but also to the fact that I'm about to get on the ice. It's my favorite place to be.

The rink is already full of big bodies, many of them in hockey gear, minus helmets. There are a few girls in street clothes. I spot Rose with a blond girl, lapping the rink and heading our way.

"You can leave your hockey stuff here." BJ motions to the bench lined with helmets and gloves.

I set mine at the end as Rose and the blonde approach the gate.

It takes real effort not to let my smile fade when I realize Rose's face isn't the only familiar one.

"Winter! Yes! I'm so glad you made it!" Rose grabs the sill to prevent her from sliding past the gate.

I recognize the blond girl behind her as Lovey. I met her at the beginning of May, shortly after we moved to the cabin where we're living. "Winter? Holy crap! Small world!" She looks between me and BJ, questions on her face. "You two know each other?"

"Uh, yeah. We just met today." This is so awkward.

"When BJ almost ran her over with his Jeep," Rose announces.

"What?" Lovey looks horrified.

"And then he held her skate hostage so she would come skating tonight. And it worked." Rose grins.

"I'm so confused," Lovey says.

"I'll explain later," BJ tells her.

"Yeah, you sure will." She turns to me, her smile warm and inviting. "It's so cool that you're here."

"How do you two know each other, anyway?" BJ motions between me and Lovey.

Lovey glances at me and waves a hand in the air. "Oh, you know, from all the volunteering."

I'm grateful it seems to be enough of an explanation. And I'm especially grateful when another couple skates over. But for the second time in two minutes, my stomach sinks.

"BJ, fashionably late as ever." The dark-haired guy, who is strangely familiar, arches an eyebrow and looks at me. "And you brought a friend."

"Winter? Hey! I had no idea you were coming tonight!" Clover Sweet—it's her real name—pushes past the dark-haired guy and hops off the ice, pulling me into a hug.

"You know everyone," BJ says with a curious smile.

"This is a six-degrees-of-separation convention." Rose motions between me and Clover. "How do you two know each other?"

Clover hugs my arm. "From the library. We bonded over our mutual appreciation of hockey."

The first time I met Clover, she was standing in the stacks, simultaneously shelving books and trying to read. The second time I met her, I was working on an assignment for my online college course and fell asleep in one of the comfy chairs. She had to wake me because the library was closing. My feet had been propped up on my hockey bag. She helped me gather my things and made small talk, mentioning that her boyfriend coaches here. Since then, we always chat when I come in, so she's aware that I moved here recently and that I've started working at Boones.

The dark-haired guy smirks. "You mean your appreciation of hockey romance?"

"I had no idea that was a thing until I met Clover," I admit with a grin.

"It's all about the stamina." She winks and motions to the dark-haired guy. "Winter, this is my boyfriend, Maverick."

"Hey. Nice to meet you."

His eyes light up. "Clover's mentioned you before, I think. You play hockey?"

"Mostly pick-up, but yeah."

"Awesome. We'll scrimmage later. It'll be fun to have you on the ice with us."

I'm amazed by how welcoming everyone is—and grateful that Lovey hasn't said anything about how we know each other. There's always a level of discomfort when people who know about my circumstances are also familiar with one another. It's hard not to wonder if they'll gossip later. The only thing I loathe more than my father's sharp words is pity.

BJ nudges me. "Come on, let me introduce you to everyone."

"Sure. Yeah. Okay." The girls give us room to get on the ice, and I follow BJ across the rink to a group of older, dad-aged guys.

BJ does some kind of spin thing and skates a circle around me.

He must have taken some figure-skating lessons along the way to hone his skills on the ice. "You showing off?"

He winks. "Maybe a little."

He stops when we reach the group of men gathered in a semicircle. I recognize his dad right away. It makes sense now that BJ seemed familiar when I first met him, because he looks a lot like Randy Ballistic, the former NHL star. Who I'm about to meet.

If I don't faint first.

"Hey, Dad, I wanted to introduce you to Winter. She works at Boones with Rose, *and* she's a hockey player."

The conversation amongst the dads stops, and every head turns our way.

It's a moment that will 1000 percent go down in my top-five most memorable. Because I'm in the presence of some of the greatest retired players in the league.

I raise a hand in a wave and am impressed when my voice doesn't come out seven octaves too high. "I usually play pick-up at the old town rink."

"Winter, this is my dad, Randy." BJ motions to his father. "And this is my uncle, Alex Waters; Rose's dad, Darren Westinghouse; Lovey's dad, Miller Butterson; and her brother Logan."

The puzzle pieces start falling into place. All these people I've been running into are connected to one another through their hockey-legend fathers. It's a freaking trip and a half.

I also recognize Logan. He's local law enforcement. He's stopped by the trailer park on occasion to deal with domestics or issue drunk-and-disorderly charges. If he recognizes me, he doesn't show it.

I shake their hands and try not to pass out from the thrill of it all. "It's an honor to meet you. All of you. You're like, legends." Yeah. I'm totally fangirling.

"We're very excited that you're here." Alex Waters gives me a warm smile.

"Yeah, me too." I nod a bunch of times and am grateful when BJ suggests we warm up.

He nudges me with his elbow. "You all right? You're looking a little shell-shocked."

"I have an Alex Waters rookie card. I'm low-level freaking out." I found it at a garage sale. The person getting rid of it had no idea what they were parting with.

He shifts to skate backwards in front of me. "They're glad

you're here. And so am I. Just have fun with me, Winter." He skates a circle around me and follows it with a pirouette.

"What the?"

He does some kind of jump thing. "I might have forgotten to mention that I'm not a hockey player. I'm a figure skater."

I bite my lip. A tattooed, bearded figure skater. Why does that up his hotness level? "You're full of surprises, aren't you?"

For the next forty-five minutes, we skate and talk. I find out that most of this group goes to college together in Chicago, and that Rose is moving in with Lovey and her twin sister, Lacey, and their cousin River, who is Maverick's brother. It finally clicked that Maverick is Alex's son. I also find out that Lovey is BJ's best friend, which is...interesting. Lovey is gorgeous in that all-American-girl way: tall, willowy, fair-haired with tan skin. She looks like she could be captain of the cheer squad, and she has a gentle, kind personality. I also learn that the foodbank isn't the only place Lovey volunteers, but I don't correct him when he makes the assumption that we volunteer there together.

While we chat and circle the rink, BJ twirls and jumps and spins around everyone. It's unexpected and impressive. My skates are definitely on the dull side, so I'm extra careful on the turns, not wanting to wipe out, especially in front of all these former NHL stars.

At eight, the scoreboard lights up with ten minutes on the clock, and Rose, Lovey, and Clover glide toward the gate.

BJ skates a wide circle around me, eyes lit up. "You're gonna scrimmage with us, yeah?"

"If that's okay." I'm nervous, but excited. This is a once-in-a-lifetime opportunity. I just hope I can keep up.

"It's more than okay. Come on." BJ inclines his head to where the dads are standing by the bench. "We're about to pick teams, and I want you on mine."

I grab my gear, and we skate over to the rest of the group.

"We gonna go four-on-four? Split it two old-timers and two youngins?" Maverick asks.

Four-on-four means fast play. It'll be a challenge.

His dad—Alex freaking Waters OMG—shoots him a look. "We're veteran players, not old-timers."

"Sorry, Dad. I forget how much you hate to be reminded that you're not in your twenties anymore." Maverick sends a wink my way.

Instead of schoolyard pick, which BJ votes for, we draw pieces of paper with either a red or black dot in the center from a small box. I end up on a team with Maverick, Darren Westinghouse—he's intimidating—and BJ's dad.

Alex, Miller, Logan, and BJ form the other team.

"What position do you usually play, Winter?" Randy asks.

"I'm pretty versatile. I play right wing, but sometimes defense."

"You have a preference tonight?"

"Nope. You can put me where you need me." Defense could be tough because of tight turns in the crease, especially with dull skates.

"Let's start you on right wing, then."

"Sure. Sounds good." I'm a jumble of nerves as I take my place to the right of Randy, with BJ across from me. The easy mood turns serious, which makes sense because these guys, retired or not, are still competitive hockey players.

Clover skates in and drops the puck. There's a flurry of action as it hits the ice. Randy snags it, and then we're all barreling toward the net.

I manage an assist in the first five minutes of play, and Randy pats me on the shoulder, his smile wide. "Nice play, Winter."

"Thanks."

I'm buzzing from the praise and riding a natural high as we face off again. This time BJ's team gains control of the puck. I nearly trip as I change course, chasing BJ down the ice. I'm so focused on the puck, and trying to steal it, that I don't consider my speed, or the tight turn I'll need to make. Thanks to my dull blades, I lose my footing, careening into BJ and sending us into the boards.

I try to roll away from him, so we don't end up in a heap on the ice, but somehow, I end up under him anyway.

4

Zing

BJ

ONE SECOND I have the puck, the next I'm hitting the boards and going down. I push up on my arms, ready to give whoever checked me a shot to the kidneys, until I realize it isn't my dad or Mav who hit me.

It's Winter.

And I'm lying on top of her.

Just like this morning when she nearly skidded into the side of my Jeep, time suspends. Everything ceases to exist except her and me.

It's fucking weird. And unnerving, to be honest, but it also intrigues the hell out of me. *She* intrigues the hell out of me.

Also, getting taken down by a woman I outweigh by forty pounds is hot. And stimulating in an inconvenient way when I'm wearing a cup.

A whistle blows and time moves again. I'm still doing a

push-up on top of her. "Shit. Are you okay? I don't even know what happened there."

"I'm fine. Are you okay?" Her gaze drops from my eyes to my mouth, but darts back up again.

"You're a hell of a lot more than fine."

"How are you flirting with me right now?"

"It's a compulsion. I can't help myself."

She snorts. "Is this how you thought a coffee date would end, then?" At my confused expression, she adds, "With me underneath you?"

I laugh. "Who's flirting with who now?"

One second our faces are inches apart, and the next someone is grabbing the back of my jersey. "Dude, get a grip on your hormones," Mav mutters as he yanks me to my feet.

Uncle Alex moves in, holding out a hand to keep everyone at bay. He drops to one knee beside Winter who's still sprawled on the ice. "Did you hit your head?"

She props herself on her elbow. Her cheeks are flushed. Possibly she's embarrassed by all the eyes on her, or maybe it's my cheesy lines. "I don't think so."

"What the hell happened there, Randall?" Dad asks, coming up behind me and Mav.

"Dunno. One second I was on my feet, the next I was eating the boards."

"Girl can skate; that's for sure," Mav says.

"Damn right," Dad agrees.

"Anything hurt?" Uncle Alex asks, glancing over his shoulder and arching a disapproving brow before he turns back to Winter. "That was a hard hit you both took."

She sits up. "I'm good. More embarrassed than anything."

"Nothing to be embarrassed about. You took down a guy who's more than half a foot taller and outweighs you by a significant margin." Uncle Alex stands, seeming satisfied that she's telling the truth, and extends a hand. "Let's make sure you're concussion-free before we resume play, eh?"

"I'm really okay," she says.

"I'm sure you are, but it's for my peace of mind."

She lets him help her to her feet. I should've been the one to do that, but I was too busy flirting. Miller and Uncle Alex flank her as she skates over to the bench. My dad and I grab the sticks scattered across the ice.

"I know what the issue is." Mav tips his head in her direction. "Her skates need sharpening. Her feet keep slipping."

Dad squints and watches her glide across the rink. "You're right." He turns to me. "I'll find out what size she wears, and we can get her a loaner pair."

"Seven men's, nine women's," I tell him. "I'll get Lovey to grab them."

He arches a brow, but doesn't ask how I know this.

I break away from Mav and Logan, skating to where Lovey, Rose, and Clover sit in the stands.

"What happened? Is Winter okay?" Lovey's eyes are wide with worry as she twists the end of her ponytail.

"She's all right. Her skates need sharpening. You mind grabbing her a pair from the rental stands?" I tell her Winter's size, and she disappears down the hall.

I skate over to the bench to make sure Winter really is fine.

"Oh. It's okay. I don't have cash on me, and I forgot to bring my debit card." Winter chews on the corner of her lip, cheeks flushed all over again.

"There's no rental fee for the skates or the sharpening," Uncle Alex says.

"Lovey's gone to get a loaner pair," I tell them.

"Thanks. I feel bad. I didn't realize how dull my blades were." Winter's gaze shifts to me, then away, cheeks flushing an even deeper pink.

"It happens to the best of us. Don't worry about it," Uncle Alex reassures her.

A minute later, Lovey returns with a pair of skates in Winter's size. She passes hers back to Lovey so we can have them sharpened while we're on the ice.

If we thought Winter was a good player before, she's amazing with a pair of sharp blades. The only thing that trips her up are the tight turns in the crease, but that's nothing a few lessons with me wouldn't fix.

My dad and Uncle Alex exchange a look when she scores a goal. I can see their wheels turning. There's still a handful of weeks left in the summer program. She could be a huge asset to the women's team.

Winter's team ends up winning the scrimmage by one goal. We all pat one another on the back, and Winter gets a ton of praise. My dad and Uncle Alex take her aside as the rest of us head for the locker rooms to shower and change.

"I would bet my left nut our dads are trying to recruit her," Mav says as he pulls his jersey over his head and removes his pads. He was offered an NHL contract this year, but he turned it down. To anyone on the outside, it probably seems like a mistake, but Mav isn't obsessed enough with hockey to make it his career. It wouldn't have made him happy. Not the way teaching seems to.

"Girl's got skills." Logan unlaces his skates. "How do you know her, anyway?"

"Rose works with her at Boones, she knows Clover from the library, and Lovey knows her from the foodbank. I think they volunteer there together or something." I conveniently leave out the fact that I almost took her out with my Jeep this morning.

Logan pauses, brows pulling together. "Is that what she said? That she volunteers with Lovey?"

32

"Well, she said she knows her from the foodbank." I rid myself of my jersey and shoulder pads before I get to work on my skates.

The furrow in Logan's brow smooths out, and his face goes carefully blank as he unclips his shoulder pads. "Her last name is Marks, yeah?"

It was on the back of her jersey and inside her skate. "Seems that way. Why?"

"Just curious."

"You're never just curious."

"She's a new face." He pulls his undershirt over his head. "I gotta hit the showers. I'm on night shift this week."

We're quick to shower and change, and we drop our equipment off to be cleaned. The girls are already in the lobby when we get there. Winter's back in her leggings and T-shirt, her long, dark hair wet and hanging over her shoulder. She's built like a hockey player, with strong legs and a serious butt. I try to be subtle about checking her out.

"You guys want to grab a bite at the diner?" Lovey asks. "It's still open for another hour."

"Sure, sounds good." I can always eat. Even in my sleep.

Lovey turns to Winter. "You'll come too?"

Winter tugs on the end of her hair. "Oh, uh, I don't have my debit card, and I forgot to bring cash."

"I got you covered. I owe you for this morning," I say.

Her grin turns wry. "Pretty sure I evened things up when I took *you* down on the ice." She looks away. "I should head home. I have an early shift at Boones. Maybe next time." She turns toward the parking lot. The sun has already set, so she'll have to ride home in the dark.

I break rank from the group. "I'll give you a lift."

"It's okay. You don't need to do that." She adjusts her grip on her hockey stick. The tape needs replacing.

"I don't mind. I gotta be up early for skate practice anyway." When I picked her up, we were still a few miles out from the arena. A half-hour bike ride in the dark isn't the safest.

Seems like she's on the fence, but when lightning streaks across the sky, she relents. "Yeah. Okay. Thanks. That'd be great."

Lovey starts the hug train with Winter before she moves to me, whispering that we'll talk later. For sure she has questions. Winter and I load our bags in the back of the Jeep and climb inside. The temperature has dropped, and the promise of a summer storm makes the air feel electric.

"I'm sorry I'm taking you away from your friends. And I'm really sorry about what happened on the ice earlier. That was all me." Winter clasps and unclasps her hands, like she isn't quite sure what to do with them.

"Eh, don't feel bad. Hits happen on the ice, especially when you're playing with a bunch of retired professionals. As for my friends, I see them all the time, and I do have to be up early, so it was a good excuse to get out of there. Otherwise, I'd be up until midnight and feel like a bag of ass in the morning. Should I head toward where I picked you up?"

"Yeah, I'm not too far from there."

I pull out of the spot and turn on to the road that leads to the lakeside cottages. "Did you have fun tonight?"

"I'm still kind of reeling that I got to play hockey with all these legends. So surreal. And you being a figure skater also threw me for a loop." She gives me a sidelong glance.

"I don't fit the profile." The beard I lose for competitions, but I don't have one for a few more weeks. "Did my dad try to recruit you to his women's team?"

"He mentioned the program they run at the arena, and he gave me a bunch of pamphlets." She runs her hands over her thighs. "Hockey's expensive, though."

"Yeah. It can be. Figure skating is the same." Between the ice time, costumes, and lessons, it can cost tens of thousands a year, especially at a competitive level.

"How'd you get into figure skating when your dad is a hockey player?"

"My mom's the figure skater."

"You were destined for a life on blades." Winter shifts so she's looking at me instead of the road. "It's kinda cool that you went the figure-skater route."

"I grew up in a world full of hockey, surrounded by professionals. Maybe the natural inclination should have been to step into my dad's shoes, but he's a legend in his sport. My mom didn't get the chance to do that in hers, even though she had the ability and the passion for figure skating. So I went left instead of right." It's a tidy explanation for why I chose door B.

Winter fingers the end of her braid. "Why didn't your mom get the chance? Did she hurt herself or something?"

"No." I tap the wheel. "Financial constraints."

"Oh." Her tone implies surprise. "That's shitty."

"She didn't let it hold her back. And it tipped the scales in her favor when I was deciding between hockey and figure skating. Besides, living in the shadow of my dad and all his friends seemed like an unforgiving path. Sometimes the road less traveled is the better one."

"Less potholes?"

I glance over and find her eyes fixed on me. "Something like that, yeah."

She points to the windshield. "You can turn right at the T-intersection."

I flick on my blinker and slow the Jeep. "You must live close to the Kingstons. They're on this road too."

"I haven't had a chance to meet many of the neighbors yet." She smiles, but it looks strained.

"You will if you play with us again." Which I hope will happen sooner rather than later.

"That'd be cool." She taps restlessly on her knee. "You can pull over here."

We're in the middle of a dark stretch of road. It's packed gravel, off the main road that connects one side of the lake to the other. "Where's your driveway?"

"Just up there. It's narrow, though, and the trees need to be trimmed back. I don't want you to get stuck. Plus with my bike on the roof rack, it'll make all kinds of noise, and my mom has to get up early for work."

"Gotcha." I pull over so I'm not in the middle of the road.

She unbuckles her seat belt. "Thanks again for the ride, both ways. And the invitation to play."

"I'm glad you came."

"Had to get my skate back." She reaches for the door handle.

"Before you go, you think I could get your number? Or I can give you mine? In case you want to come play with us again. Or you change your mind about that ice cream."

Her fingers go to her lips, like she's conflicted.

"You had fun tonight, didn't you?" I ask.

She releases a long breath and nods. "Yeah. I had fun. A lot of fun."

"So why you over there sitting on the fence, Snowflake?"

She drops her head and rubs the space between her eyes, but she's smiling.

I don't know how to read her. Not yet. "I believe everything happens for a reason—the good, the bad, and mundane. There's always a purpose," I tell her. "Think about all the ways we're connected already. You play hockey, you work with Rose, you volunteer with my bestie, you and my cousin's girlfriend like the same books."

She side-eyes me. "The only hockey books I read are biographies."

"Whatever. Not the point." I motion between us. "We're destined to know each other. I like you. I think you're fucking gorgeous. I want your digits so I can tell you that in awkward text messages."

She laughs, and it's the sound of victory. "Fuck it. Yeah. You can give me your number." She passes over her phone, and I key in my number, then send myself a text.

My phone dings in my pocket.

"And now I have yours." I need to mine Lovey and Rose for info. Winter is definitely guarded.

"Well-played." She reaches for the door handle, and I do the same.

She heads for the trunk while I unfasten her bike from the roof rack. I've just set it on the ground when headlights appear in the driveway I'm parked across from. I raise my hand to shield my eyes.

"Fuck," Winter mutters.

Gravel crunches as the car pulls onto the road. The window descends, and a plume of smoke furls into the air. It's an old car, and based on the rumble of the engine, it's struggling to do its job. It's too dark to make out much of the figure behind the wheel until a crack of lightning illuminates him.

He looks tired, like life is wearing him down. And angry, like everything pisses him off.

"Who's this?" He tips his chin at me but doesn't look my way. "I thought you said you were playing hockey."

"I was. This is BJ. His dad coaches at the new arena."

He looks me over, eyes narrowed and assessing, especially as he takes in my sleeve of tattoos. "Is that right?"

"BJ, this is my dad, Clayton Marks." Her tight smile wavers.

"Nice to meet you, Mr. Marks." I hold out my hand, but he just looks at it, returning his attention to Winter.

"You get oil and a pack of smokes like I told you?"

She grimaces, and her shoulders tense. "I didn't have my debit card, and I forgot to bring cash with me."

It's the third time I've heard her say that. It's starting to sound like a script.

Her dad scoffs and flicks ash on the ground at her feet. "Of course you didn't." He mumbles something I don't catch that makes her flinch. Then he drives away, leaving us standing in exhaust fumes and dust.

It all clicks into place.

The dull skates, the no-debit-card-and-no-cash mantra, biking to the arena, the hockey bag with a missing wheel and a hole in it, saying no to the diner after, wanting me to drop her off at the end of her driveway, Lovey knowing her from the foodbank, Logan asking for clarification about that, and now meeting this dickbag of a father who treats her like garbage.

Winter doesn't have it easy.

And I'm over here with my retired-NHL-player dad, driving around in a flashy Jeep, never worrying about money. It seems like maybe she is. Some of the places around here are still the original cabins, not fancy new builds.

She turns to me on a resigned sigh. "I can *hear* your gears turning, and you'll find out eventually because this whole town is six degrees of separation." She shoulders her hockey bag and steps back, preparing for her exit. "My family's financial situation sucks a bag of dicks. I don't volunteer with Lovey. I use the foodbank when things get tight between paychecks. I hate when people feel sorry for me or treat me differently when they find out. It fucking sucks. And not for any of the reasons you probably think. Or maybe for all the reasons you probably think." She tips her chin up as the first drops of rain fall and another bolt of lightning streaks across the sky.

"I thought you were brave and a badass, but maybe I got you wrong," I say.

Her head drops forward, her expression reflecting confusion. "What?"

"Up until you gave that speech, I thought you were this take-no-shit, hockey-playing hottie with a sharp tongue and mad skills on the ice." I step forward, into her personal space. "I feel a lot of things, Snowflake, but sorry for you isn't one of them. And unless I'm reading things wrong, there's some mutual attraction here." I motion between us. "I thought we were making headway with the awkward number exchange, but it feels like you just threw up some walls to shut me out before I've even had a chance to send you cringey messages asking when I can see you again."

She bites her plush bottom lip. "Are you always like this?"

"I usually tell it like I see it, if that's what you mean." I pluck a dandelion fluff from her hair, holding it out for her to see. "Make a wish."

"Wishes lead to disappointment."

"Wishes are hope with wings," I counter. "Make one."

She shakes her head and smiles, then closes her eyes and blows on the palm of my hand. When she opens her eyes, they lift to mine. Drops of rain patter the ground around us. "I had a lot of fun tonight," she says. "It's probably going down as one of the coolest experiences of my life. Thank you for taking my skate hostage. It was worth it. I should go before I get soaked." She grabs her bike handles.

I tuck a hand in my pocket. "I'm glad the universe decided our paths should cross."

"Yeah. Me too. I think." She steers her bike toward the dark opening between the trees.

"Snowflake," I call when she reaches the mouth of her driveway.

She looks over her shoulder.

"If I text you, will you text back?"

"I guess there's only one way to find out." And with that, she disappears into the darkness.

5

The Ups and Downs of it All

WINTER

TIMING REALLY IS EVERYTHING.

If I'd been faster getting out the door this morning, BJ and I might not have almost collided. If my reaction time had been slower, his side panel might have a me-shaped dent.

If I'd been less on the fence about giving him my number, he might have been gone by the time my dad came down the driveway. Or conversely, if I'd said yes to the diner, I could have avoided my dad altogether. Though then I might have been served by my mom, depending on how late she worked. No one needs that level of awkward.

Hanging out with rich kids is already conflicting. Did I have fun? Absolutely. Do I want to do it again? For sure. Is it a good idea? I don't know. In the moment it's awesome, but afterward I go back to not having enough, which makes me wish what they have could be mine for more than a couple of hours at a time.

And BJ? Well, he makes me want a lot of things.

The rain picks up as I reach the garage. I slip in and turn on the light. The space is a disorganized mess of dump worthy items, and it smells like stale beer, cigarettes, and mold. There are several clear garbage bags full of empties.

I hang my bike on the hook, so my dad doesn't get pissed about it taking up too much space, and lay my equipment out to dry, peppering them with dryer sheets to keep them fresh between washings.

I'm on edge when I enter the house, unsure what I'm going to find. My dad going out at this time of night isn't unheard of, but it's often precipitated by a fight. My mom must have come home after the dinner rush, because she's sitting on the couch with a two-liter bottle of diet cola—the no-name brand—and a cigarette dangling from her fingers. She'll quit for a while, but she starts up again whenever she's stressed. Seems like we're back in the death-dart cycle.

She glances over when I walk through the door. Her eyes are red, and a pile of tissues sits beside her on the ancient, threadbare couch. Her expression shifts from sadness to guilt as she taps the cigarette, ash landing in the disposable metal tart shell.

"I'm not starting again. I just needed to take the edge off." The end flares red as she takes a deep haul.

I hate that they smoke in the house. I put dryer sheets in my dresser drawers and shove a towel under my door at night to keep the smell out of my clothes as much as possible.

"Was he shitty because the lawn needs mowing?" I ask.

She shrugs. "He was in a mood. Didn't like what I brought home for dinner. I don't know why I bother trying. I should just leave, see how he manages without me."

It's an empty threat. One she makes occasionally, but only when she's annoyed with dad and only to me. "Or you could kick him out. The trailer is an option." A girl can dream.

"He won't survive on his own. The only can that man knows how to open is the kind that's full of beer." She takes another pull from her cigarette and hugs a pillow to her chest.

I lean against the edge of the kitchen counter, close to the open screen door, where I can breathe fresh air. This topic is going nowhere good, and I know better than to put too many ideas in my mother's head. Otherwise I'm liable to get thrown under the bus. Not intentionally, but sometimes she runs her mouth to my dad without thinking things through.

"I bought a pound of ground beef today with my tips," I say. "It's in the fridge behind the coleslaw mix. I'll soak kidney beans and make chili tomorrow night, if you want. I made sure we have everything we need."

Her eyes light up. "That would be amazing. Maybe we can grab a bag of tortilla chips and some cheese. That'll almost be like nachos, and it'll go further."

That's always the goal with protein—make it last as long as possible since we often can't afford it. "I can pick up a bag tomorrow. See if maybe there's a sale." My stomach rumbles, the energy I expended on the ice catching up with me.

"That sounds good." She nods absently, takes one last drag on her cigarette before she butts it out.

I put the beans in a pot to soak and pull the loaf of whole grain bread from the freezer. My dad won't touch the stuff, mostly because he has the taste buds of a three-year-old and only likes meat, potatoes, white bread, and cheese.

"You hungry for cheese toast?"

She shakes her head.

I pull out three slices. She often changes her mind once the smell of food hits her. "You sure?"

She waves a hand. "Go on then."

I top the bread with cheese and broil them in the toaster oven. Once they're done, I cut them in half, top them with a thin slice of fresh tomato, and finish with a sprinkle of salt and pepper.

"How was pick-up hockey? Did you have fun?" I hear all the unasked questions in her worried tone, like, *how much did it cost?*

I hand her a plate and sit at the other end of the couch. "Yeah. It was free, and it was at the new arena. You know the one the retired hockey players built?"

Her eyes flare. "You mean the real nice one on the edge of town?"

"Yeah, that's the one. Got my skates sharpened for free and everything."

She nibbles on the edge of her toast, expression growing pinched. "You didn't tell them you couldn't afford it, did you?"

"No, Mom. It's just the way they run things there. You remember the lady I told you about who works at the library? Clover? She runs the literacy program attached to the shelter. She's new, though." I take a bite of the cheese toast, chewing slowly to savor it.

She makes a face. "Doesn't matter if she's new. She still probably thinks she knows stuff about our family."

"They're not allowed to talk about the families who use the shelter, Mom." June and July can be bad for thunderstorms around here. Sometimes we had to leave the trailer for a couple of days when the rain washed us out. Then it took a few days for everything to dry afterward. Dad never came with us, opting to crash on a friend's couch instead. But since my grandma passed away and left Mom the cabin, we won't have to do that anymore.

We won't have to worry about ending up in the trailer for missing rent too many times either, since the cabin is paid for, and it's in my mom's name. Grandma wasn't fond of my dad. But we have to stay on top of the property taxes and the electric bill so we don't lose hot water or heat in the winter. There's a wood-burning fireplace, though, so at least we'll always have some warmth. Mom was able to cover the property taxes for the year with the little my grandma had in savings, so we have until January before we have to worry about that again.

"Just because they're not allowed doesn't mean they don't."

"Anyway," I redirect the conversation. "Her boyfriend coaches over at the new arena. His name is Maverick, and his dad is one of the retired hockey players. I met him tonight."

"Oh yeah?" Her eyes narrow, and jealousy leaches into her tone. "Those guys are made of money. Always driving brand-new cars and riding around the lake in fancy boats."

She would shit a brick if she knew how close I'd been to denting one of those fancy cars. "I guess when you have a lot of disposable income, you can do that kind of thing." I swallow, nervous about this next part. "Anyway, I shot the puck with them tonight, the retired players. It was really cool."

Her jealousy turns to worry. "Be careful hanging out with those people, Winter. You'll start wanting things you can't have. We can't afford hockey right now. It's too expensive. We're barely getting by as it is."

"Yeah, I know, Mom." I take another bite of my toast and swallow the rest of my words. I already want things I shouldn't —one of them being BJ. Another is to play hockey with them again.

It doesn't matter what I say or how I say it, to her and my dad, hockey is an expensive waste of time. So I keep the biggest news to myself: that Alex Waters and Randy Ballistic offered me an opportunity to try out for a spot in their program, that they see real potential in me. That it's subsidized.

That's the part I need to find out more about. Because even

if I don't have to pay for the things I can't afford, hockey takes up a lot of time, and there are only so many hours in a day. I still have school and work, and those are my top priorities.

I finish my toast while Mom tells me about her shift at the diner. It's always the same. The teenagers are rude, and half the time they don't tip. I hope Lovey and Rose don't fit into that category. Although, mom was already home by the time they got to the diner.

When she's gotten it all out, I excuse myself to my room and get ready for bed. When I put my phone on the charger, I notice new messages. There's one from Rose telling me she'll see me at Boones in the morning and she's glad I came out tonight.

Under that are several from BJ. My stomach does a somersault and my throat tightens as I open the thread.

> Hey, Snowflake.

It's followed by several more:

> I have private ice time tomorrow afternoon.

> Four o'clock. Same rink as tonight.

A gif of a guy getting checked into the boards follows. And then:

> I'd love it if you'd join me. 😏

A grin forms. I don't answer his messages, even though my thumbs are itching to. Better to wait until morning, give him time to stew in his uncertainty and me to marinate in mine.

6

Persistence and Payoff

BJ

I'M LYING in bed with my phone on my chest, half asleep, when there's a rap on my sliding door.

"Come in," I call.

Lovey steps inside and kicks off her sandals. She crosses the room and flops down beside me on the bed. "Hey."

We've been best friends for a lot of years. Many people wonder if there's more between us, but there isn't. Although, I'm partly to blame for that since sometimes I flirt with her when I want to avoid awkward interactions with previous hookups. Only once in all our years of friendship did we cross the line. It involved a game of spin the bottle when we were fourteen. Far too many of us were related to each other for it to be anything but awkward and incest-y. And when Lovey and I had to kiss, it cemented our friends-for-life-and-nothing-more status.

"Hey yourself." I move my phone to the nightstand and fold an arm behind my head.

She rolls to her side and props her cheek on her fist. "Give me the deets on the Winter situation. Rose shared her version of events, but she's good at embellishing for the sake of an exciting story."

I explain what happened, from the near miss this morning to inviting Winter to free skate.

She lets out a low whistle. "Wow. Rose wasn't wrong about the six degrees of separation."

"A lot of threads pulling us all together," I agree.

"What happened when you dropped her off?" Lovey asks.

"I met her dad."

Her eyes widen. "You did? What's he like?"

"An asshole, as far as I can tell. And she had me drop her at the end of her driveway. She's close to the Kingstons' place, but I didn't even realize there was a house there. It's kinda hidden. She told me she doesn't volunteer at the foodbank."

Lovey nods. "I think her life is pretty hard. She's a regular at the foodbank. Everyone who volunteers there knows her."

"Interesting that her dad can afford cigarettes, but they can't keep food on the table," I muse. "It must be frustrating to watch someone literally burn away your grocery money."

"Logan said her last name was familiar," Lovey murmurs.

After meeting her dad, that's not hard to believe. "I'm guessing it's not for their community involvement."

"He didn't elaborate, but his facial expression said it all." She rolls onto her back. "Clover says she's at the library a lot and uses the computers. And with what I know, it all seems to add up to things being tough."

"Yeah. I got that impression."

"So maybe don't go pulling your usual routine with her."

I look at her out of the corner of my eye. "What routine is that?"

She pokes me in the ribs. "Don't act like you're clueless. Normally you're the king of random hookups, and then you pull the let's-be-friends card. But you also usually save that for when we're in Chicago and steer clear in the summer."

"Yeah. Because I'm too busy for them." My summers are dedicated to skating, teaching lessons, and hanging out with friends. I also avoid hookups because I learned the hard way that Pearl Lake is small and everyone knows everyone.

"So Winter's what? An anomaly?"

"I don't know how to explain it. I feel like I'm supposed to know her."

She grins knowingly. "Really? So you like her. Remember, Rose works with her, Clover and I both know her, and our dads are pretty excited about her. If ever there was a time to change how you do things, this might be it."

"Agreed. I got her number tonight."

"Unsurprising. You message her yet?"

"Yup."

"Has she messaged you back?"

"Nope."

"Good. I hope she keeps you on your toes."

THE FIRST THING I do when I wake up the next morning is roll over and reach for my phone. Still nothing from Winter.

The wave of disappointment is new and foreign. I want an excuse to hang out with her again. I consider sending another message, but I've never been *that* guy. Besides, she's working again today, so I can stop by and charm her into skating with me later.

I drag my ass out of bed and hop in the shower. Fifteen minutes later, I'm clean, my morning wood has been handled, and I'm dressed.

Mom is in multitasking mode when I reach the kitchen. She alternates between flipping pancakes and arranging cut fruit on a platter. "Morning, kiddo." She checks the pancakes and deems them flip-ready. "You sleep okay?"

"Like the dead. You need any help?"

"The pancakes are almost done. Can you grab plates?"

My phone buzzes as I pull three plates from the cupboard. Another pang of disappointment hits when I check and find Adele, my skating partner's name, flashing across the screen.

"Everything okay?" Mom asks.

"Yeah. It's Adele. She's probably messaging to tell me she'll be late." Adele is rarely punctual.

Mom frowns. "I wish she would be more respectful of your time."

"It gives me a chance to warm up." I turn my phone to silent and set it facedown on the counter.

Mom makes an annoyed sound. "I have one to three blocked off for you two. Will that be enough time?" She doesn't comment further on Adele's lateness. We're both used to it. My mom is my skating coach and has been since Adele and I started skating together.

"It should be. I have us booked in from nine to eleven thirty. Then a break for lunch before we get back on the ice with you."

"Does she have the rotation and the angle down with the triple twist?"

I lean against the counter. "She's about fifty-fifty. Sometimes she touches me as I catch her because she's off-balance. It may be too much, but we really need to up the complexity of our routine for this competition. We're going against some of the best pairs in the country."

She gives me a patient smile. "I agree, but if she's still struggling by the end of the week, we may want to swap the move. We don't want this to affect her confidence with the rest of the routine."

"Yeah, I've thought the same thing." I pop a grape into my mouth. "We've got a few weeks before the competition, so we still have time to adjust."

She plates the pancakes. "Do you want me to broach the subject with her today, feel it out?"

"It's probably better coming from you than me."

The triple twist is a tricky move. It requires a lot of skill and confidence, and sometimes Adele lacks the latter. Shifting the routine and incorporating a lift she feels confident about could be the answer, but we need to place at least third to move on to the next round.

Mom smiles and squeezes my arm. "Sounds good. I know she doesn't like to disappoint you on the ice, and if I bring it up, it'll be easier on both of you."

Dad comes in with a tray of fresh bacon, and we bring the food to the table and take our seats.

"You drove the Marks girl home last night?" He passes me the bacon.

"I did, yeah."

"She'd make a great addition to the women's team," he says.

"I think so too. She said you mentioned the program. She's working at Boones today with Rose. I plan to invite her to skate with me this afternoon since I have an hour of ice time booked at four. I can mention it again and suggest she stop by your practice after, if you want."

"That'd be great."

After breakfast, I grab my backpack and head out to start my day. I still don't have a message from Winter, but Adele has sent five more. As expected, she'll be twenty minutes late. She's sorry, and she'll make it up during practice. I send a thumbs-up in return so she doesn't message me relentlessly until I respond.

Less than ten minutes later, I arrive at Boones. The mouth-watering scent of fried dough, apple, and cinnamon sugar hits me as I step inside. When my gaze lands on Winter, my mouth waters for a whole different reason.

She's standing in front of the fryer, her back to me. She's wearing the customary Boones T-shirt and a pair of black shorts. They're basic athletic shorts, the kind someone might wear running. Under them is a second pair of shorts, made of legging material, which end mid-thigh. They cover yesterday's road rash.

Rose is behind the cash register. "You're about as subtle as a fart in an elevator." She slides her phone into her apron and arches a brow. "Wanna throw another half dozen fritters in the fryer, Winter?"

"Sure thing." Winter glances over her shoulder at me. A small smile appears, but she quickly schools it and turns back to the fritters.

Once the customer ahead of me pays for her order, Rose rings me through. "I'm going to flirt with Scottie in the kitchen and give you two a minute to be awkward together." She disappears into the back room, leaving us alone.

I lean on the counter. "You haven't answered my texts."

Winter lifts the basket of fritters from the fryer and sets it in the rack to drain. She turns and crosses her arms. "That's because I haven't made a decision yet."

"What's holding you back?"

"I'm supposed to mow the lawn after work."

"What time do you finish here?"

52

Rose pokes her head through the doorway. "One! She finishes at one!"

Winter shoots her a look. "Seriously? I thought you were giving us time to be awkward without an audience."

Rose gives her a cheeky grin. "I'm listening, not watching." She disappears again.

"You think that's enough time for you to mow the lawn and make it back to the arena at four?" I ask.

She grips the edge of the counter. "I've gotta run a couple of errands too."

"I could pick you up, if that would help you lean in my favor. Say three forty-five at the end of your driveway?" I do the thing that annoys Lovey because she says it makes me impossible to say no to. I look up at Winter from under my lashes and bite my lip. Then just in case, I also appeal to her competitive side. "Think about it. An hour on a rink, just you and me. We can run skate drills. And I'll give you a few pointers on how to tighten your turns."

Her eyes narrow. "Who said I need to tighten my turns?"

"You're confident on breakaways, but you falter in the crease. One lesson and I promise you'll have it down."

She adjusts her ball cap. "Are you always this persistent?"

That's close to a yes. "Only when I think it's worth the effort." I wink and head for the door. "Three forty-five. End of your driveway. Looking forward to getting back on the ice with you."

"Hey! What about your fritters?"

"Bring them to the arena. And I like all the toppings, so you can surprise me."

I leave before she can stop me, or change her mind.

Take a Chance

WINTER

I FINISH my shift at Boones and stop at the grocery store to pick up tortilla chips, sour cream, and a block of old cheddar that's been marked down. They'll complement the crockpot of chili I put on this morning. I stop for oil at Harry's Hardware and grab my dad a pack of smokes at the corner store, annoyed that a chunk of my tip money goes to his bad habit instead of things we need, like fresh fruit and vegetables, or to pay bills. But I know better than to forget two days in a row. It's not worth pissing him off.

I bust my ass home and tackle the lawn before I have a quick rinse off. It's wildly hot this afternoon, and we don't have the luxury of air-conditioning, so a cold shower is where it's at. Then I test the chili and find it's done enough to have a bowl. I use whole grain bread slathered in margarine to wipe the bowl clean and barely resist going back for seconds.

I toss a couple of dryer sheets into my hockey bag to help

with freshness. It's only three, so I message BJ to let him know he doesn't need to pick me up. Better to avoid him coming here if I can help it.

I leave a note for my mom and do something I normally wouldn't: lie.

I say I'm hitting the library to work on an assignment and not to wait on me for dinner. The guilt makes my stomach tight as I pedal to the arena. I arrive forty minutes early, which gives me time to catch my breath and manage my nerves. I lock up my bike and slide my arms through the straps of my hockey bag.

BJ mentioned teaching me how to tighten my turns. I wasn't sure if I would need my hockey equipment for that, so I brought everything. If I have time, I'll stop at the laundromat on the way home.

Once I'm inside, I make my way to rink three. Muffled music with a heavy bass backbeat filters through the door. I peek through the window and smile as I spot the artwork spanning the skater's right arm. I've seen BJ in full hockey gear doing pirouettes, but this is different. He's wearing a pair of black jogging pants and a black T-shirt. His hair is pulled back with a vibrant yellow tie.

There's a girl with him on the ice. Like most figure skaters, she's compact and doesn't even reach BJ's shoulder. Unlike BJ, his partner wears black leggings, a black sleeveless leotard, and one of those skirts that's more decoration than clothing. When he said he was a figure skater, I didn't consider that he might skate pairs.

They circle the rink, his expression serious, and he talks with hand gestures. She nods, listening intently. On the next trip around, their fingers link, bodies converging before they diverge again. Everything about the way they move seems effortless.

I wonder what it's like to be so in tune with someone that to everyone on the outside, you appear to be an extension of each other. His head bobs with the rhythm, and I can see his lips moving, counting beats of four. She moves in, and his hands curve around her waist. He lifts her with ease, her body a graceful arc, balanced in his palms. And then he spins, gaining speed.

I hold my breath, awestruck by the level of trust this kind of routine requires. My heart lodges in my throat as she falters, one hand lowering. It sets them off-balance, and BJ loses momentum. He quickly corrects his hold, lowering her to the ice. I see defeat written on his face, but it's only there for a second before it's gone.

When he cuts the music, I push through the doors. His partner notices me first. Her brows pull together and BJ glances over his shoulder, a smile softening his features. He leaves her in the middle of the rink and skates over, spraying ice when he stops inches from the boards.

"Super excited to see your beautiful face." His grin and his compliment do silly things to my insides.

"Sorry I'm early. I didn't mean to interrupt your practice. I figured I'd drop my bag and fill my water bottle."

"Don't apologize. We're half an hour over our practice time and not nailing the lifts anymore. I need a reason to call it a day and switch gears, so your timing is perfect. And there's a fountain right there." He points to the water station thirty feet away.

His partner skates over and threads her arm through his. "I didn't see a lesson on your schedule."

"It's not an official one so I didn't add it. Winter, this is Adele, my pairs partner. Adele, this is Winter. She's a badass hockey player, and she works at Boones."

I wave. "Hey! Nice to meet you."

"You too." Adele smiles, but she's stiffer than a corpse. She turns her attention back to BJ. "Should we run through the routine once more?"

"The lifts are getting sloppy, and my arms are tired. We'll start fresh tomorrow. It'd be awesome if you got here close to on time."

And now it's getting awkward.

Her nose scrunches, and she ducks her head. "I'm sorry. I'll set an extra alarm."

"Maybe set two." He extracts his arm from hers. "I'll see you tomorrow morning."

"Sure. Okay." She gives me another tight smile. "Have fun with BJ. He's a great teacher."

"Thanks." I wait until she's off the ice before I speak. "I didn't picture you as a pairs skater, but maybe I should have."

"Choreography can be more dynamic with pairs."

"You look good out there together." Aside from the flub at the end, they were in sync.

"Thanks." He pulls the tie from his hair and gathers it up again, refastening it. "We've been at it for hours, though, and sometimes you gotta know when to call it quits."

"Do you need a break? I brought the fritters." It was hard not to eat one before I arrived. Boones employees get to take leftovers home with us, and deli items are 50 percent off at the end of the day.

"We can save those for after we skate, if that's all right with you?"

"Sure. Sounds good."

"I'm gonna refill my water. Why don't you put your skates on and we can warm up?"

"Yeah. Perfect." I lace up while BJ fills our water bottles, and then I join him on the ice.

He matches his strides to mine as we circle the rink. "How long have you and Adele been skating together?" I ask.

"A little over four years." He does a two-foot turn so he's skating backwards, facing me.

"Is she your first pairs partner?"

He tips his head a little, his easy smile faltering. "I had a different partner in high school. We started skating together when we were thirteen. But, uh, things got complicated."

"Sounds like there's a story in there."

"There is." He skates away from me and does a spin.

I never realized figure skaters could be so damn hot. "But you're not going to tell me?"

"Not today. It's a downer, and we can't go back and change the past. All we can do is learn from our mistakes and try not to make the same ones twice." He skates a circle around me. "What about you? How long have you been playing hockey?"

I shrug. "Since I learned how to skate, I guess. When I was a kid, we had this neighbor with five sons. As soon as the lake froze, they would set up nets and play. I ended up with their hand-me-down skates and fell in love with the sport. It's my happy place. My escape." I motion to the empty rink. "Why don't you show me your best moves?"

"I can't show them all to you at once. Then how will I entice you back onto the ice with me?" His eyebrows dance on his forehead, but he breaks away and skates down the ice, gaining speed. I don't know the names of the moves, but I've watched enough skating competitions over the years to know he's damn good. He does the splits in midair, then finishes with a backflip.

I break into applause, bringing my fingers to my lips and whistling my appreciation. He skates back to me, bowing on the way. Then he snags my hand and wraps an arm around my waist, twirling me around the ice before he stops in the center of the rink.

"How was that?" he asks, breath coming in pants.

His arm still circles my waist, our other hands clasped. There's no space between our bodies. I'm damn glad we're not wearing hockey equipment, because it means I feel all those hard lines pressed against mine. His eyes move over my face, his smile warm and real and infectious. A lock of hair has escaped his topknot, and it skims his cheek.

"You put the x in sexy."

His smile widens. "I'm sweaty, and I probably smell bad."

I point to my chest. "Hockey player. Nothing beats the funk of dirty hockey equipment."

"That's the truth." His gaze drops to my mouth. "If I wasn't disgusting right now, I'd think about kissing you. Well, I'm already thinking about kissing you, but my current state keeps me from acting on that impulse." His fingers flex on my waist.

Butterflies unleash in my stomach. It's been a while since I've been kissed. And I don't think I've ever felt this kind of magnetic attraction to someone. I don't really know BJ—don't know what makes him tick apart from skating—but the chemistry we share is hard to ignore. "What if I don't care about your current state?"

His tongue sweeps along his bottom lip. "I had this all planned out in my head, you know."

"Oh? How did it go in your head?"

"We'd have a great time on the ice together. And every time you'd smile"—he bites his lip—"it would give me an emotional boner."

I bark out a laugh and shove his chest, but he captures my hand in his. "What the hell is an emotional boner?"

"It's a real thing. It's how I feel every time I make you smile or laugh. Like my emotions are all excited and can't be contained."

"You're ridiculous."

"I find you fascinating. You scramble my brain and make

me say ridiculous things like emotional boner." He brushes his lips over my knuckles.

How that simple contact makes all the important, needy parts of my body zing when he's talking about boners is a wonder. But I can't stop smiling, and all I want is for him to keep touching me and talking. Even if it's about nonsense.

"Hey, Balls! I thought you were done at three!" a male voice booms across the ice.

"Fuck a duck." BJ purses his lips. "I'm going to shave a horseshoe into his head."

He kisses the back of my hand one last time before he releases me. He looks down and makes a face. "Good thing I didn't wear gray sweats or this would be embarrassing." He spins around. "Hey, Mav. Anyone ever tell you that you have impeccably bad timing?"

Maverick's eyes widen as BJ moves to the right and I come into view.

I can't even imagine what my expression must be. My face feels hot. Along with other parts.

Maverick grins, apparently oblivious to the tension. "Hey, Winter! Are your ears burning?"

I touch my right ear. "Huh?"

"My dad and my uncle were just talking about you." He thumbs over his shoulder. "Does this mean you're coming to the women's team practice tonight?"

BJ holds up a hand. "I was getting there. Trying to ease it into conversation, if you will."

"Oh really?" Conversation was the last thing on my mind a minute ago.

"I got sidetracked. But eventually I was going to ease it into conversation."

"Woulda been hard to do with your tongue in my mouth," I mutter.

He grins down at me. "Damn, that mouth of yours is saucy." He skates over to Maverick so we don't have to shout. "We're working on tightening Winter's turns."

"Cool. BJ's an excellent teacher when he's not busy showing off." He taps the boards. "I'm sure you'll have it down before practice starts. Rink five at five. Looking forward to seeing you there." Maverick gives me the thumbs-up. "I'll leave you to it."

I wait until he's out the door before I turn to BJ. "Was that part of your plan? Distract me by kissing me and then try to coerce me into going to a team practice?"

"No. I mean, yes, I planned to try to coerce you into going to a practice, but the kiss is its own separate entity. Those two things don't intersect in any way. My being attracted to you and wanting you to try out for the team are parallel but independent of each other." He pulls his spiral tie free and his hair falls, framing his face. "I hadn't planned to move in for a kiss until like...later. But then hormones took over, and I stopped being able to think rationally and shot my plan to shit. Then Mav showed up and cockblocked the kiss."

I bite my lips together and fight a smile.

He has the audacity to look cute when he ducks his head and gives me a lopsided grin. "So back to the women's team practice. I think you should check it out."

I blow out a breath. "I don't know that I'm good enough to make the team."

"The retired hockey players who coach them seem to think you are, and I'd have to agree."

"You've seen me play once."

"Why are you fighting this? What's holding you back?" He gathers his hair back up and secures it.

As unnerving as his directness is, I like that he doesn't back down. "Hockey is expensive."

"The women's program works on a sliding scale, and it can be fully subsidized."

"Even if it's subsidized, I can't afford lessons or equipment."

"All of that is covered."

I rub my temple. "It's not just money, though. Hockey takes time, and those are hours that could be spent working, making money to help support my family and pay for my college courses."

"Half the women on the team are on full scholarship because they're high-level players," he argues.

"You have an answer for everything, don't you?" I drop my head and say the thing that scares me most. "What if I'm not good enough? What if I go to this practice and I choke?"

"Let's break this down and sort logic from nerves. You played hockey with four retired NHL players yesterday on skates so dull they couldn't cut a freaking tomato. You impressed them so much that you were the first person my dad mentioned at breakfast this morning. Hell, he came home last night and talked to my mom about you, and he's pretty good at leaving work at work. This program gets thousands of applications every year. They don't need to chase talent; it comes to them. But they see the talent in you, and frankly so do I."

I scrub a hand over my face. "Hope is a dangerous emotion."

"It can be when it's misplaced, but I don't think your hope fits into that category. Spend the next half hour working on tightening your turns with me. Then let's assess where your head is. But if you don't at least give it a shot, you'll never know. And isn't that worse? The never knowing what could have been if you'd just taken a chance? Fear is hope's nemesis. It doesn't belong in this battle."

I roll my eyes, but BJ and I spend the next half hour working on my turns, particularly in the crease, which he uses pylons to mimic the net. We also flirt like it's our second job. All the innocent touches make me feel like I'm about to spontaneously combust. And I ask him to repeat himself a few times, because I keep staring at his mouth, getting lost in what could have happened if Maverick hadn't shown up.

At four twenty, BJ calls a timeout. "As much as I'd love to keep doing this for the next two hours, you're killing the turns, women's practice starts in a little more than half an hour, and we still need to eat fritters."

We leave the ice, and I take my skates off and put on my running shoes, relieved that my toes are no longer scrunched up. Instead of sitting at one of the tables by the concession stand, BJ takes me through to the offices, where there's a staff room. It's complete with a huge conference table and a fully equipped kitchen with a stove, two fridges, a dishwasher, a microwave, and a toaster oven.

I line the metal tray for the toaster oven with foil and arrange the fritters in two rows, warming them while BJ rummages in the beverage fridge. "You want a Vitamin Water?"

"I can just have tap water." I search the cupboards for plates.

"There's no charge for them. Orange, strawberry-kiwi, or lemon-lime?"

I appreciate that he addresses my concerns without making it a big deal. "Lemon-lime, please."

He moves to the big fridge and pulls out a canister of spray whipped cream, plus a tub of vanilla ice cream from the freezer —and not the no-name kind, but the full-fat, creamery-style stuff. When the fritters are ready, I split them between two plates, BJ tops them with ice cream and whipped cream, and we sit at the table to eat.

"Thanks for the lesson today. Maverick and Adele are right. You're an awesome teacher." I slide my fork through the crispy dough, gather some melting ice cream, and take my first bite, groaning as the flavors hit my mouth. Sweet, creamy, and damn well delicious.

"It's easy to be a good teacher when I'm working with someone who's naturally gifted on the ice. Have you ever had lessons before?"

I shake my head, swallowing the bite before I answer. "I played for my high school team for a while, but mostly it's been pick-up or outdoor-rink games."

"We can keep doing this, if you want." He motions between us. "I'm always available from three to five."

"I don't want to monopolize your time like that."

"It's only monopolizing if I'm not willing, and I wouldn't offer if I didn't want to do it."

I lift my gaze.

"And we get to hang out. All wins, as far as I'm concerned." He stabs an entire fritter with his fork and takes a huge bite.

"I'll have to check my hours, see if it works." Free lessons with a hot, tattooed figure skater aren't something I want to pass up, but my hours at Boones come first. I need the money for fall tuition.

"For sure. Just know I can get us ice time five days a week if there are things you want to work on."

BJ finishes his fritters long before me. I'm trying my best to savor, while also being mindful of the time. At four fifty-two I polish off the last bite, and BJ rinses our dishes and loads them in the dishwasher.

I wipe my hands on my thighs, nervous as we leave the staff room. I'm half regretting those fritters with the way my stomach is kicking up a fuss.

"Hey." BJ tugs on my sleeve.

I realize he's stopped walking because we've reached rink five.

His eyes move over my face. "You all right?"

"Yeah. No. I'm nervous. This feels like a high-pressure interview."

He takes me by the shoulders. "Repeat after me."

"Repeat after me," I deadpan.

He grins and bites his lip. "So fucking saucy. I love it."

I fight my own smile.

"I'm a badass hockey player, and any team would be lucky to have me."

I make a face.

He arches a brow. "Seriously? Don't you give yourself pep talks before you get on the ice, or do something new? I mean, I do it all the time. Like, on the way to Boones this morning, I rehearsed the fuck out of what I was going to say to you."

I arch a skeptical brow. "You did not."

"I absolutely did. Fake it till you make it, if you need to." He thumbs over his shoulder. "But they *want* you here. Remember that. This is a tryout for a spot that's already yours. Take the leap, Winter. I promise the landing is soft on this one."

"You're hired as my personal cheerleader."

"You got this." He squeezes my shoulders. "One question before I send you in there. Two, actually."

"Okay."

"First, can I hug you?"

I'm momentarily stunned, so it takes a few seconds for me to respond. "Um, yes?"

"No pressure if you're not a hugger."

"I like hugs."

"Excellent. Me too." He envelops me with his arms.

It feels...nice. Good. And he still smells good, even though he's been skating his ass off for hours. Like cologne and deodorant, fresh laundry, and man-boy sweat.

It's over far too soon.

"Question two, can I stick around and drive you home? Or as close to home as you're okay with?"

"You don't have to do that."

"I know. I want to. Besides, I never finished telling you about the rest of my master plan that was foiled thanks to Mav's awful timing."

"Right. How could I forget about that? Sure. If you want to stick around, that's cool with me."

"Awesome. I teach until seven. Team practices run about the same, so I'll catch up with you after." He kisses me on the cheek. "I gotta run. Knock 'em dead."

He walks away, leaving me entirely discombobulated in the best way possible.

8

All the Good Things

WINTER

IT TAKES LESS than five seconds for Alex Waters to notice me when I enter rink five. Part of it might be because I'm not suited up or wearing a team jersey.

Alex Waters is a big man—well over six feet, with broad shoulders, a thick head of dark brown hair, gray flirting at the temples. He should be intimidating, but his wide, friendly smile immediately puts me at ease. "We were hoping you'd come out today. Why don't you lace up and I'll grab you a temporary jersey. Randy will introduce you to the team." He brings his fingers to his lips and whistles shrilly.

Randy Ballistic glances over his shoulder, and as soon as he sees me, he gives the players instructions and skates over, wearing the same wide grin as Alex. "Very happy to see you here today, Winter."

"BJ convinced me it was a good idea."

"He's got persuasion down to an art," his dad says.

67

"I'll grab Winter a jersey while you introduce her to the team, eh?" Alex asks.

"Absolutely. Let's get you on the ice," BJ's dad says.

I jam my feet back into my skates, my toes protesting the return to their cramped prison. Alex reappears as I finish lacing up and hands me a jersey. "If you decide you want to play for the team, we'll get you a number and set you up with new gear."

"Right, okay. Thank you." I have a million questions, mainly pertaining to costs and what playing on this team will look like, but for now I table them and give myself permission to enjoy this opportunity. The Hockey Academy's women's team is number one in the state, and their captain has broken scoring records this season.

There's a round of introductions, and I'm grateful everyone's last name is on their jersey. We spend the first hour running drills, and then we're divided into two teams so we can scrimmage. Despite my lack of formal training, I keep up with the rest of the players for the most part. And thanks to my lesson from BJ today, I'm more confident in the crease. I manage an assist and a goal for my team, which earns me praise from both sides.

At the end of practice, Coach Waters pulls me aside. "You were great out there, Winter."

"Thanks. I had so much fun."

He smiles. "I'm glad to hear that." He passes me what looks like a coupon. "Once you're showered and changed, you can join the team in Iced Out, our cafeteria. There's a buffet. Just give the hostess that ticket because they comp our players. If you decide you want a place on the team, you'll get an ID card and the coupon won't be necessary."

I frown at the paper. "You feed us after practice?"

"It's all part of the program, which I'll explain after you've had a chance to eat with the team."

"Right. Okay. Thanks." I grab my hockey bag and go to the locker room.

Fern Harmer, the team captain, sets me up with an empty cubby. "Girl, you're all the buzz. Where the heck did you come from, and why haven't I seen you on the ice before?"

I strip out of my jersey and unfasten my pads. "We just moved to Pearl Lake a couple of months ago. Before that, I played pick-up at the old arena because it was closer to home."

"Ah, that makes sense. Welcome to the team." She squeezes my shoulder. "We're gonna love having you here."

"Thanks."

Other players compliment me on my playing on their way to the showers. When I start stuffing my gear back in my hockey bag, Fern holds up a hand. "Just leave it in your cubby. They'll have it all cleaned for tomorrow's practice."

I freeze. "Seriously?"

"Yup. This team functions the same way as college teams, so all your equipment stays at the rink."

"Right. Okay." This is all new information for me.

We hit the showers, and I luxuriate in the pounding of water on my back. Each stall has body wash, shampoo, and conditioner that smell like eucalyptus and green tea. My whole life we've used whatever was in the clearance section, and we water down the conditioner so it lasts longer.

I don't want to get used to this if it's only going to be temporary, but tonight I'll indulge. After my shower, I slide my underwear up my legs quickly, then pull on my leggings. It's not about modesty; it's about hiding my ancient, once-white-now-gray underwear from my teammates. My sports bra is black, so it's harder to see how ratty it is. Once I'm dressed and my hair is braided, I join Fern and the rest of the team in Iced Out. I hand over my coupon and follow my teammates to the buffet.

For a moment I'm unable to move as I take in the volume of food. There are two types of salad, roasted vegetables and potatoes, chicken breasts, a pasta bar, and an entire dessert bar. Some of the other girls are already picking up plates and filing down the line.

"I was overwhelmed at first too. It was hard to wrap my head around all the options when usually mine were limited to peanut butter and jam or mac and cheese." Fern gives me a small, understanding smile and hands me a plate. "You can go up as many times as you want."

The first round, I fill my plate with salad and vegetables and chicken. I'm desperate for protein, and the only chicken we can usually afford is frozen or sometimes thighs when they're on sale. My second course is pasta with three different sauces. I go back for more salad. And I finish with an ice cream sundae and a piece of chocolate cake.

Guilt makes my gut churn—that I get to eat all this amazing food while my mom eats crockpot chili makes me feel shitty. But then come the takeout containers. We're all allowed one, but only about half the team picks up a container.

"What happens to the rest of the food?" I ask Fern.

"It goes to the foodbank for tomorrow."

I remember getting a fully packaged family meal a few times when I arrived early enough at the foodbank. Everything about this program is designed to give back, to help the community, to give opportunity to people who otherwise wouldn't have it. I fill my container to take home.

I'm so full, my stomach hurts, but I'll take the mild discomfort because tonight I won't be hungry.

The team files out of the cafeteria, and I go to the offices to meet with Coach Waters and Coach Ballistic. They explain the ins and outs of the program, that it works on a sliding scale, like BJ said, and that for a good number of players, it's fully subsidized. Coach Waters is Canadian, and they've modeled the program so it aligns with the way they grew up, including their healthcare. I don't know much about how Canada works, just that it's cold in the winter and they love hockey and maple syrup. Evidently they have good insurance too.

"I don't know if I'll be able to make all the practices with my work schedule."

"Most of our players have summer jobs at local shops. Management is always good about working around practices and games. And Tracey Lynn at Boones has always been more than accommodating," Coach Waters says.

I bite the inside of my cheek and decide to be honest. "I need to maintain my hours at Boones so I can afford to pay for college classes." I'll also have to figure out how to keep up with my online class this summer and all the assignments.

Alex nods, like he understands. "Where are you heading in the fall?"

"I take online courses, part-time so I can work."

"Can I ask what kind of grades you get?"

"Mostly Bs. I work hard to keep my average up." I fight not to bite my nails.

"A lot of our players are on scholarship. They play for the school team during the year and for us in the summer."

I tap on the arm of the chair, debating if I want to continue this truthful path. BJ's comment about divine intervention pops into my head. If we hadn't met the way we did, and if he hadn't been such a flirt, these new opportunities wouldn't exist. "I was offered a full-tuition scholarship at Monarch College, but I don't have a car, and I can't afford housing or books."

Coach Waters perks up. "Have you turned it down?"

"I have a few weeks before the offer expires." Though I've already given up on being able to go.

"Okay. That's good to know." He props his elbows on his desk and leans in. "Now I have two questions; the first will inform the second. Are you interested in a spot on this team?"

I nod and croak out a quiet *yes*.

"I was hoping you'd say that." He passes me a folder of information. "Second question, what jersey number would you like?"

I fill out a bunch of paperwork, including a contract with team rules and regulations, medical forms, and another with sizes for equipment and a jersey. Practice times rotate, but they're mostly in the afternoon. I'm given two copies of the schedule for the rest of the month, plus all the games. Those are on the weekends. I can give one copy to Tracey Lynn and keep the other for myself. There's also an online schedule for reference.

"We're excited to have you on the team," Coach Waters says.

"Me too. Thank you so much for the opportunity." I shake both his and Coach Ballistic's hand and leave the office, beyond elated.

The sun hangs low in the sky, pink threading through the clouds when I step outside. Parked to the right of the entrance is BJ's Jeep. BJ is sprawled out on the bench across from it, one arm tucked behind his head, the other resting on his chest, legs crossed over each other. He's wearing sunglasses, so I can't tell if he's just lying there or sleeping. I unlock my bike from the rack before I poke his shoulder, and he startles.

"I'm ready to roll!" He sits up in a rush, and his phone clatters to the ground.

"I'm sorry. I didn't realize you were asleep." I stoop to grab his phone and hand it to him. "I hope you haven't been waiting a long time."

"I can fall asleep anytime, anywhere. It's a gift." He removes his sunglasses and checks the time. "I picked up a skating lesson at seven with a player from the junior boys' team. Then Mav and I hit the food truck." He points across the parking lot. "Mav left about ten minutes ago, which is when I made myself comfortable. I assume I've been out for nine of those." He pushes to a stand. "How'd practice go?"

"I said yes to joining the team."

"Fuck yeah, you did. They're so excited about you." He clips my bike to his roof rack while I toss my bag in his trunk.

It's considerably lighter since I left my pads behind for cleaning. "Thanks for sticking around and driving me home."

"Totally self-serving since it means I get to hang with you." He closes the trunk and follows me to the passenger side, opening the door and offering me his hand.

I don't need the help but take it anyway because I like the contact. Once I'm settled, he rounds the hood and gets in on the driver's side. We buckle up, and BJ drives toward the exit.

"Why does it feel like I've known you for way longer than two days?" I muse.

He looks at me for a moment before he refocuses on the road and turns right out of the parking lot. "I don't know, but I feel the same way. We run on the same frequency, maybe? Like, even though I was shitting my pants because I almost hit you, the moment our eyes met I felt this...*need* to know you. Makes me think of Shakespeare and the humors and laser beams shooting out of our eyes."

"You lost me at humors and laser beams."

"Back in high school, I had this teacher who talked about the four humors and how people were connected. Like, you look at someone, and they look at you, and bam—the world aligns. Mostly I thought it was hilarious, hokey shit that only made sense in books, but now... I think I know what she meant."

We pass through town and head for the road that leads to the cottages and homes that dot the lake. "It's easy to forget myself with you," I tell him.

"Is that good or bad?"

"Both maybe, but leaning strongly toward good."

"What would make it bad?"

"It's easy to turn me into a project."

He taps the steering wheel, contemplating maybe. "Is that what you're used to? Being someone's project?"

"It's something I strive to avoid."

"Makes sense. I wouldn't want to be anyone's project either. I hope you don't mind blatant honesty, but from the moment you gave me shit and called me an asshole—which I admittedly was when I almost took you out with my steel baby —my main goal has been to find ways to hang out with you. Getting on the ice together seemed like a natural way to make that happen. Hooking you up with the Hockey Academy means you'll be at the arena a lot, and that will make it exceedingly easy to run into you."

"Do you take anything seriously?"

"I reserve my seriousness for skate practice and school. The rest of life needs a good dose of who gives a fuck."

I'm disappointed when we reach the T-intersection, but instead of pulling over, he turns down the road. "You should stop here."

"Don't worry, I won't stop in front of your place."

My anxiety makes my throat tight as we pass my driveway. "What are you doing?"

"This road is a dead end. Only people who live down here pass your driveway, and if your dad is coming or going, he won't see me from up the road." He passes the Kingstons' and the Winslows' and starts back toward my place, but stops at the bottom of the hill so we're still out of sight. Then he cuts the engine and his lights.

"Can I finish my story now?" At my questioning look, he smiles and taps his temple. "About how that whole almost-kiss was supposed to unravel."

"Right." I hide my smile behind my fingertips. "I can't believe I forgot about that."

His hand goes to his chest. "Ow. That's all I've been able to think about since it almost happened, and you're telling me you didn't think about it once?"

"That's not what I said. And the whole emotional-boner part is pretty unforgettable."

He cringes. "Not my best invented phrase, although it is accurate."

God, I like him. Probably too much for my own good, and far too quickly. "Are you gonna tell me the story now or what?"

"Do you remember where I left off?"

"We were going to have fun on the ice, and every time I smiled you'd get an emotional boner." I shift in my seat. The sun has dipped below the trees and shadows dance across his face.

"And that happened, which was awesome. I must be psychic or something." He stretches his arm along the back of my seat, hand close to my shoulder but not touching. "We'd share those fritters, which also happened. And I kind of love how you savor everything, and you make these little contented noises when you're eating something you enjoy."

"I do not make noises when I eat!" My ears and cheeks heat.

"You totally do, and it's fucking adorable. Anyway, as I was saying, we'd eat fritters and have that ice cream date I was hoping for. Except I didn't plan for it to be in the staff room, which is incredibly lacking in romance and ambiance. Although it meant we could heat up the fritters, and they're way better warm with ice cream."

"You're making me hungry again."

"Sorry, I'm meandering. I'll get back on track. So I'd convince you to go to that practice, which you did, and I'd wait for you, which I did." He runs the hand that isn't slung over the back of my seat over his thigh, like maybe he's nervous. "And then I'd drive you home, but I'd park far enough away that you wouldn't worry about getting caught with the tattooed bad boy from the other side of the lake—as an aside, I'm not a bad boy at all, and most of the time I'm in bed by eleven at the latest."

"How much longer is this story?"

"Not much. I'm getting to the climax. I promise."

When I don't say anything, he takes it as his cue to continue. I consider shoving my tongue in his mouth to hurry things along.

"So, we'd end up here." He motions to our surroundings. "And then I'd ask if you're still interested in skating with me tomorrow afternoon."

I hold up a hand. "I have a question."

"Do you not wanna wait for the end of the story before you ask it?"

"Actually, it's not a question."

"I see. And it can't wait until I'm done with the story?"

"This story better end with one hell of an amazing kiss."

"Are you saying you *want* me to kiss you?"

"Well, yeah, obviously. Otherwise I wouldn't still be sitting here listening to this endless fucking story. I'm over here waiting for something to happen, and you just keep talking and talking and talking."

"It's a slow burn." He runs his hand over his thigh again.

"Are you nervous? Because if that's the issue, I can help." I grab the front of his shirt and pull him forward. This would be fine if he wasn't wearing a seat belt and I hadn't yanked him aggressively, causing the belt to do its job and prevent him from getting more than six inches from his seat.

"Oh, for Christ's sake." I jam the release on my own seat belt and reach across to do the same for him. Once we're no longer at the mercy of restraints, I mash my lips against his.

He has the audacity to smile. "My version had a little more finesse."

"Shut up and kiss me."

He cups my face in his hands and pulls back, his expression suddenly serious. "Did you not like my story?"

"You are *killing* me, BJ. Put me out of my misery and kiss me. Please."

"How can I say no when you're being so polite?" He angles his head and brushes his lips over mine. Soft. Sweet. His tongue flicks out, skimming my top lip.

I lean in, glad the center console isn't an impediment. I tug the spiral tie out of his hair so it's loose and run my fingers through the gloriously satiny strands. He has great hair. I angle my head and part my lips, tongue pushing past his. That soft sweetness lasts for all of three seconds. BJ groans, the sound making all my hot spots light right the hell up. Then he does this twirl thing with his tongue that curls my toes. And suddenly it's a battle. I can't get close enough, can't get enough of the feel of his velvet tongue tangling with mine, or the way he sucks my bottom lip and uses exactly the right amount of teeth. BJ turns kissing into art, and I can't wait to find out what other talents he has.

I keep trying to drag him across the seat, but there isn't room. I abandon his hair and run my hand down his chest. When I find the hem of his shirt, I slide my hand under, meeting warm, bare skin. Before I can move to shove my hand down the front of his pants, he breaks the kiss and laces our fingers together.

He's still cupping my cheek with his other hand, and he brushes his thumb along the edge of my jaw. "Fuck, Snowflake, you're everything I'd hoped you'd be."

"Why are you stopping then?" My chest heaves, breaths coming fast and shallow. I'm light-headed and worked up.

"I like you," he says softly.

"Uh, yeah, that kiss told me that."

He smiles, his tongue sweeping out to wet his bottom lip. "I have a bad habit of rushing into things, and I'd like to try to break it with you."

"Huh?" I'm so confused.

His grin turns wry. "I want to get to know you before I try to get into your pants."

"Oh." I don't know what to say to that. I've spent most of my life avoiding relationships because bringing someone home to meet my family is on par with playing chicken with a guard-less circular saw. But I did have one long-term boyfriend in high school. He wasn't the best choice, but high school is mostly about making mistakes and hopefully learning from them.

"Can I pick you up tomorrow?" BJ asks.

"I'll probably come straight from Boones to the arena," I say.

"Okay. Can I pick you up from Boones?" His thumb is still sweeping along the edge of my jaw.

"It's a ten-minute bike ride, tops."

"I'd still like to pick you up."

"Can we make out in your Jeep if I say yes?"

He grins. "We could."

"Yeah. Okay." I fight a smile of my own. "You can pick me up tomorrow."

"Excellent. Let me help get your bike off the roof rack." He hops out of the Jeep.

I blow out a breath. Based on the throb between my legs, I'll need to take care of my situation when I get home—which is a hell of a lot easier now that I have a bedroom with a door. By the time I peel myself out of the passenger seat, BJ has already unclipped my bike, dropped the kickstand at the front of the Jeep, and circled around the back to get my hockey bag.

"We don't need to strap it to the bike. It's light and I can carry it," I say as I close the passenger door.

"Okay." He sets it on the ground.

I don't know what I'm supposed to do or say now. Mostly I want to suction my mouth back to his and feel his hands on me again. But I don't want to seem desperate.

It's darker now, the sun having set. The only streetlights are at the end of the road, between the Kingstons' and Winslows' driveways. Their properties are also gated.

BJ tucks a loose tendril of hair behind my ear, his eyes dropping to my mouth. "Can I kiss you good night?"

Looks like I'm not the only one stuck on the idea of making out. "Are you going to tell me a long-winded story that doesn't have an ending first?" God, I'm so salty.

He chuckles. "You're turning into my favorite person real fast." He leans in to brush his lips over mine.

I slide my hands up his chest and curve a palm around the back of his neck. I'm fairly tall for a girl, but BJ is well over six feet, so I have to tip my head back. And just like the first time, it starts off slow and gentle, but quickly turns into a tangle of tongues. I find myself pressed against the side of the Jeep.

One of his hands slides into the hair at the nape of my neck, and the other eases down my side until it reaches the hem of my shirt, slipping under the fabric to skim my waist. I press my hips into his, feeling the hard length of him against my stomach. I moan into his mouth, wishing for friction, for anything to ease the ache building between my thighs. A kiss shouldn't do this, shouldn't make me feel like this, but here I am, turning into a wanton, needy mess.

I hook one of my legs around his and shift until it settles between mine. I roll my hips, moaning at the delicious friction and the feel of his erection against my hip. I let one hand drift down his arm and move the hand resting on my waist over my ribs until his fingers reach the underside of my sports bra. I push it up until my breast pops out and move his hand to cup it.

He breaks the kiss. "This feels like the opposite of taking things slow."

"I never said anything about taking it slow. That's all you."

He chuckles, but this time it's a dark sound that sends a thrill rushing through me. He sucks my bottom lip and sweeps a thumb over my nipple.

I moan and arch into the touch.

He rolls the tight peak between his thumb and finger.

"Oh fuck." I shamelessly grind on his leg, looking for more friction.

"I think we're going to have a lot of fun together, Snowflake," BJ whispers against my lips.

"I think you should put your hand down my pants."

He pulls back again, gaze moving over my face like a caress that echoes through my body and pings between my thighs. "The environment is lacking in romance."

I point to the sky. "The stars are all starry, and the crickets are being cricket-y. How much more romantic does it need to be?"

"How about we make a deal?" He rolls my nipple between his fingers again.

I dig my nails into the back of his neck. "This is highly unfair. I'm too horny to think straight."

He ignores me and keeps on with the nipple attention. "We hang out for the rest of this week, and if you still want my hand down your pants on Friday, I'll make sure we have privacy and don't have to use the back seat of my Jeep."

"But we can still make out between now and then?" I kind of love that he's negotiating for ambiance.

"Absolutely."

"Okay. Deal. Fingerbang Friday is on like Donkey Kong."

He laughs, kisses me one last time, and moves my sports bra back into place. "I'll see you tomorrow."

"Looking forward to it." I pick up my hockey bag and slide my arms through the straps, then hop on my bike.

He waits until I reach my driveway before he drives away.

My dad's car is sitting at a wonky angle in front of the cabin, which makes me wonder if he stopped at the Town Pub before he came home. I leave my bike and hockey bag in the garage, grab the backpack I keep inside the hockey bag, and turn off all the lights before I enter the cabin. My dad is passed out in the lounger, the TV droning in the background. I assume my mom is already in bed since she has to get up at five to be at the diner by six.

I tiptoe across the kitchen and disappear into my bedroom, locking my door. I unzip the front pouch of my backpack and retrieve today's tips—fifteen dollars. Not a lot, but every dollar counts.

I lift up on the handle of my dresser drawer and pull to the right. The drawer sits askew on the track. It's hard to open, and if done wrong, it makes a horrible squealing sound. I could fix it, but it's where I keep the things I don't want my dad to know about, including my tuition money.

I remove the book-shaped lockbox, unlock it, add my tips to the roll, wrap five ones around the outside, secure it with an elastic, lock the box up, and shove it to the back of the drawer.

My fingers brush over the thick envelope, the other thing I don't want my dad to know about. What I wouldn't give to be able to accept the offer of admission and the scholarship. Until today it felt like an impossible dream. But now...I have hope.

I understand why my mom cautions me against dreams, though. Because the only thing worse than not having them at all is getting close enough to touch them, only to have them snatched away.

9

Embrace the Change

WINTER

AS AGREED UPON, all week BJ picks me up after my shift at Boones—but at the library since I'm done between one and two in the afternoon, and he's on the ice until three. We make out for a handful of minutes before we get on the ice and he helps me strengthen my weak areas. We talk and skate and laugh and flirt.

I find out that BJ and the rest of his friends all go to the same college I have a scholarship for: Monarch. I haven't mentioned the letter to him. I don't want to get ahead of myself. He lives off campus with his friends, and he's in his senior year with a major in psychology. I'm working on a degree in social work, but because I'm only part-time and online, I'm a sophomore when I should be a junior.

Later, when practice is over, BJ drives me home, and we spend a good twenty minutes making out. But he keeps stalling us at second base. As frustrating as it is, BJ is an amazing kisser, and if I'm honest, I kind of like not rushing things.

So far I haven't said anything to my parents about the Hockey Academy, using homework from my online summer course and internet access at the library to explain my late nights and missing dinner lately. It's not a complete lie. With daily hockey practices, my homework is allocated to later in the day now. After the first practice, I started filling the takeout containers with items that could be from Boones, so they were easy to explain away if I didn't polish them off before I got home.

I feel bad about keeping it from my mom, but she's a terrible liar, and I don't want to get her in shit for hiding things from my dad. I also don't want a lecture on hanging out with the people from the other side of the lake, and how it'll make me want things I can't have. Eventually I have to say something, but I've only attended a handful of practices. I don't see the point in stirring up drama when I can't be sure how long this will last.

On Friday after practice, I'm extra giddy. I skip Iced Out to meet up with BJ and find him sitting on the picnic table beside the bike racks. His back is against the edge of the table, his long legs stretched out in front of him, one crossed over the other. He's wearing a faded black Depeche Mode T-shirt from the Ultra album, and the vibrant artwork on his arm is in full effect. His hair is pulled back with a rainbow spiral tie, but a piece has slipped free, and it rests against his cheek.

His eyes move over me on a hot sweep. "You're done early."

"It's Friday."

He grins. "That it is."

I practically skip to the passenger-side door. Along with brand-new equipment and skates that fit perfectly, I have a new hockey bag. It stays at the arena with my gear, and all I bring with me these days is my backpack.

BJ pushes off the bench and lopes over, hitting the unlock button when he's a few feet away. As always, he extends a hand and I take it, climbing into the passenger seat. He doesn't make a move to kiss me. We save that for when we're alone and there's no one watching.

He takes his place behind the wheel. "I forgot to tell you to bring a bathing suit. Can we stop by your place to grab one?"

I glance at the dashboard clock. It's after six. Friday nights my mom often stays on for the dinner shift, and my dad usually goes to the Town Pub after work for a few pints.

There's a chance I could grab a suit without running into my dad, but if he skips the pub and goes to his buddy's place to play poker, he might come home first to shower. It's dicey. "Better not to risk going home in case my dad is there. He's liable to give me a list of chores. I can always swim in my sports bra and shorts."

BJ nods. "Or you can borrow a suit. Lovey probably has half a dozen in the pool house."

I give him a look. "You can't offer me your friend's bathing suit."

He shrugs. "She's got more clothes at my house than I do. But it's whatever you're comfortable with."

We drive past the cutoff to my house and continue to the other side of the lake, where the biggest, most amazing cottage houses are. I've only ever seen them from the water, or passed their driveways on my bike.

BJ's place is designed to look like a rustic, albeit classy, massive cabin in the woods. It's stunning on the outside, and I can only imagine what it looks like inside. A few cars are already parked in the driveway, one of which I recognize as Rose's. "Uh, who's all here?"

"Rose, probably Lovey, and it looks like my roommate Quinn is in town." He pulls in next to a truck. Everyone around here has cars that are worth almost as much as the cabin my family lives in.

"Right. Cool." I drum on the armrest.

He stretches his arm across the back of the seat and caresses my cheek with a knuckle. "Don't worry. I haven't forgotten the deal we made."

I fully expect him to lean in and kiss me. Instead, he unbuckles his seat belt and gets out of the Jeep, leaving me with no choice but to do the same. I follow him around the side of the house and down a set of graduated stone steps, lined with beautiful, manicured gardens and built-in lighting. On the dock are Lovey and Rose, but I don't recognize either of the guys seated across from them.

Rose waves and arches a knowing brow. She's been relentless with her questions, particularly since BJ has come in more than once while I'm working and he picked me up the other day.

"Hey!" A grin lights up Lovey's face. "Winter! Yay! BJ said you were coming to hang out tonight." She pulls me in for a hug. "I don't think you've met my brother or Quinn, have you?"

I shake my head. "I've only met Logan so far, I think. And Lacey once." She was working at the foodbank, and I mistook her for Lovey. I felt bad, but she brushed it off with a smile and said it happens all the time.

"Quinn, Laughlin, this is Winter. She just started playing for the women's hockey team, and she works with Rose. Winter, Quinn is BJ's roommate, and Laughlin is one of my many older brothers."

I wave. "Hi, nice to meet you."

Laughlin raises his can of beer in salute, but doesn't respond with words.

The corner of Quinn's mouth tips up. He has hair the color of fire, green eyes, and an abundance of freckles. "Is your last name Marks?"

"Uh, yeah." I'm suddenly nervous. Who knows what they've heard about my family.

"So you're the new blood our dads can't stop talking about. They're flipping out over you," Quinn says.

Laughlin's gaze moves over me in an assessing way.

"Oh, uh, I haven't even played a game yet. The first one is tomorrow, so let's hope I don't choke." I laugh, but it comes out with a nervous lilt.

"You're gonna kick all the asses, no doubt," BJ says.

"Fingers crossed, anyway."

Lovey's still standing beside me. "Do you have your suit? Wanna get changed? We were just talking about taking the boatercycles for a spin."

"Boatercycle?"

She points to the personal watercrafts lining one side of the dock.

"Oh, that's my new favorite name for them. I didn't bring my suit, but I can go like this." I motion to my current attire of T-shirt and bike shorts.

"There are always spares in the boathouse. And usually there are a couple of new ones because I have an issue with online bikini shopping in the summer." She wrinkles her nose, like she's embarrassed by her admission. "Come on." She doesn't give me a chance to argue, just pulls me along the interlocking stone path to the three-slip boathouse.

I gawk as we pass a huge outboard motorboat, and a smaller one, as well as a barge, and step into a room with hooks, benches, and a double vanity. Towels are piled on shelves, everything organized and pristine. Lovey crosses over to a cubby and rummages through a bin, tossing a few bikinis onto the bench beside her. "You're what? A medium?"

She's narrower than I am, and willowy, but I don't want to be rude, and going home in wet clothes would raise questions.

"Most of the time, but bottoms always fit a little different. Most of the time I wear a size up."

She checks the tags on a royal blue bikini with a galactic print. "This one should be perfect!" She removes the tags and tosses it to me.

"Are you sure? It's never even been worn."

"Positive. We always have extras around because someone's bound to forget theirs."

"Okay. I'll be out in a minute." I head for the changing stall.

When I open the door, Lovey is adjusting her ponytail in front of the mirror. Her eyes widen. "Holy wow. You fill that bathing suit way better than I could." She runs her hands over her lean hips and nods her approval.

"It's the hockey butt. It's a blessing and a curse."

"I'm not seeing the curse part. Baby got back." She wiggles her hips.

"It's almost impossible to find jeans that fit in the thighs and the waist." This is why I own more leggings and athleticwear than I do pants.

"Oh. Yeah. I can see how that would be an issue." She taps her lip and smirks. "BJ is going to lose his mind when he sees you."

I frown at my reflection. "Because I'm wearing a bathing suit?"

She laughs. "Because you're rocking the hell out of a bathing suit, and I've never seen him like this with anyone before."

I don't know how to feel about the way that makes my stomach flip-flop. "How do you mean?"

"He's smitten." Lovey bites her lip. "I've been friends with BJ since we could blow spit bubbles. He's usually a dive-in-head-first-let-the-hormones-take-the-reins kind of guy, but you're different. He really likes you." She hands me a plush beach towel. "Anyway, I'm glad you came tonight. I've been bugging BJ to invite you to hang out and not keep you all to himself."

"I'm glad too," I say, and I mean it. Since the move, I haven't had much of a chance to see friends, and even before that, most of the time if I wasn't working or playing pick-up at the old rink, I was studying. My social life has been pretty lack-luster until this week.

It's closing in on seven. The sun is moving toward the hori-zon, but we still have more than an hour of daylight left. When we return, BJ is sitting on one of the many Adirondack chairs placed in a semicircle on the wide dock. His head is tipped back, sunglasses shielding his eyes. He's lost his shirt, and I can finally see the extent of his artwork. The tattoos that cover his right arm continue across the right side of his chest and down his ribs, disappearing into the waistband of his bathing suit shorts, a wash of vibrant watercolor. I take it all in—the way it curves around his long, lean limbs, how it seems to follow the dips and ridges of his abs. Maybe that's one of the reasons I find BJ so appealing. I know he's strong—I've seen him lift his partner—but nothing about him is imposing or intimidating.

"Who wants to take the boatercycles out?" Lovey shouts as we pad down the stone steps.

Three are tied to one side of the dock. It blows my mind that there's close to a quarter of a million dollars in water toys attached to this property. Will these fragile bonds of friendship expire with the summer? I'm already getting caught up in this world, tangled in the vines.

"Dibs on—hot damn." BJ pulls his sunglasses down, and I

can see his eyes as they rove over me. "Excellent bathing suit choice, Snowflake."

Lovey nudges me with her elbow. "Told you."

"Oh my God!" Rose grabs the arms of her chair. "You already have a pet name for Winter, and it's so cute, it makes me want to vomit rainbows and hearts."

Quinn snorts and BJ shrugs, but he's grinning while I'm over here blushing.

"Ignore the noise. You ride with me." BJ stands and holds out his hand.

I take it and let him lead me over to the black boatercycle.

Laughlin lazily pushes out of his chair. "You're mine, Rosebud."

Her mouth drops open and then clamps shut. She fires the double bird at him. "Fuck you, Laughlin."

Everyone stills for a moment. I don't understand what's going on.

"You don't think my nickname is cute?" Laughlin approaches her slowly, sort of like a panther sizing up his prey. His hair is dark like the night, and his pale blue eyes are almost iridescent. It's a little unnerving. Everything about him is. He has a vibe, like he's a powder keg waiting for an excuse to blow. "As much as I enjoy Quinn's company, I'm not interested in being that close to him unless one of us is checking the other into the boards, and Lovey is my sister, so it looks like you're stuck with me. On the upside, I have it on good authority that one of your preferred Butterson brothers is on water patrol this evening. Seems like the perfect opportunity to create some tension, wouldn't you agree?"

Rose rolls her eyes and uses her foot to push him back so she can stand. "I'm driving."

I give BJ a questioning look.

He shrugs and passes me a life jacket.

I put it on and buckle up, adjusting the straps so it fits while everyone else does the same. Rose and Laughlin are first to leave the dock with Rose sitting in front, Laughlin's body bracketing hers. They're followed by Quinn and Lovey, who wave as they speed off.

"I've got my boater's license, but I've never been on a boatercycle before," I admit.

Obviously I've seen them all over the lake. Been annoyed when they circle relentlessly, the drone and pitch of the motors as irritating as a mosquito buzzing around my ear. Felt that deep pang of envy followed by the longing to have the wind whipping through my hair. And now I get to ride one with BJ. It's a double win.

If my admission surprises him, he doesn't show it. "You can sit up front and I'll give you a quick lesson. They're pretty easy."

"Yeah. Okay. Sounds good." I climb on and scoot forward to give him room.

The watercraft rocks gently as he takes his place behind me. His legs frame mine, and his chest presses against my back. "Hi." His lips brush my cheek, and he pushes us away from the dock with his foot.

"Hi."

"You ready to ride?"

"The boatercycle or you? Because frankly, both."

He laughs and nuzzles into my neck. "Patience, Snowflake. I promise I'm not going back on the deal. But first, you learn how to ride this." He taps the watercraft. "Then—"

"Fingerbang Friday?"

"Exactly." He starts the engine and shows me how to steer, accelerate, and slow down. The controls are simple, so I catch on quickly and steer us in the direction everyone else went, but BJ guides us away from them.

"I want to show you something cool." He takes over steering, and for a moment I think we're about to run right into an island, but he slows down and cuts the engine as we pass through a narrow opening and end up in an alcove. A beam of sunlight shines down in the center.

"This place belongs on a greeting card."

"Right? This is my favorite spot on the lake. Most people miss it because it's tucked behind that." He points in front of us, to the tiny island that obscures the view of the lake.

"How'd you find this place?"

"By paying attention to the things other people don't, I guess." He kisses the side of my neck.

"That's kind of your thing, isn't it?"

"Seems that way." He laces his fingers with mine. "How has this week been for you?"

"What do you mean?"

"Lots of new people in your world. Lots of change. It isn't always easy." He rests his chin on my shoulder.

I lean into him, oddly at ease, despite his question. "I keep waiting for the bottom to drop out. I'm so used to disappointment that I've learned to expect it," I admit.

"Hmm..." He lifts our twined hands and presses his lips to the back of mine. "That's a hard mindset to rewire, I imagine. Here I am telling you wishes are hope with wings, and you're used to having yours clipped."

"That's an astute and unfortunately accurate observation," I murmur.

"Hope is an invasive emotion. It's difficult to control once it starts to grow."

"All of this, the Hockey Academy, you, Rose and Lovey, my job... It all feels so fragile, like a bubble that could burst at any moment." It's terrifying that I could blink and it would all be gone. And it truly could. "It's hard to step outside of my world and into yours. They're so different. I have this taste of what it's like on the other side, quite literally."

I trace one of the watercolor flowers on his forearm. "I know this is just a snapshot of your life. That you work hard on the ice. I see that. But I also get these glimpses of possibility. That life doesn't have to be an incessant grind of work, come home, work some more, take care of people who can't or won't take care of themselves. Wash, rinse, repeat." I tip my head until my temple meets his lips. "I know your perceived advantages come with disadvantages. There's no good without bad. But I've spent my life conditioned to stay inside my box of less. And then you come along, and suddenly there are opportunities, and I want to take them all." I blow out a breath. "Fuck. Why did this get so heavy? This is the perfect make-out spot, and I'm over here being a total rain cloud."

"You're just being real, which I appreciate." He wraps his arms around me. "I know I can't see it through your lens, but you're not wrong. Money doesn't buy happiness, but it can buy comfort, and sometimes it buys complacency. We get used to our own reality and forget what's on the other side. You make me want to look outside myself."

I tip my chin up. "You make me want to be selfish."

He brushes my cheek with his fingertips. "You're allowed to want good things, Winter. More than that, you deserve them." He slants his mouth over mine, and I sink into the kiss. This one is different. It's not just fueled by hormones and lust. There's more, and it scares the hell out of me.

But then BJ unbuckles my life jacket. "Thank you for opening up to me. I know it's not easy." He kisses me again, soft and slow, in no hurry to move things along.

Lust is a much easier emotion to deal with. And maybe he knows this too. He breaks the kiss so we can take off our life jackets and drape them over the handlebars. His arm comes around my waist, and his fingers splay across my stomach. His warm chest presses against my back and his other hand trails down my thigh. The hand on my stomach moves to cup my breast, thumb sweeping over my nipple through the fabric.

Desire pools low in my belly, and an ache flares between my thighs. "This is my new favorite spot on the lake."

"Mine too, for a very different reason than it was a few minutes ago." He nips at my neck and tugs one cup of my bikini top to the side, exposing my nipple. He rolls it between his thumb and finger, then tugs.

I moan and arch, wanting more of his touch, of his lips on my skin.

He bites my earlobe. "I fucking love that sound, Snowflake." He shifts his other hand, cupping me through the bikini bottoms.

I make another needy sound. "Touch me, please."

"I am touching you." He rubs over the fabric. His index finger finds my clit and circles it.

I roll my hips and do us both a favor by shoving the fabric to the side and guiding his fingers back to my bare skin. I sigh. "That's so much better."

He pinches my clit between his index and middle finger. Then rubs slow circles. Sensation rockets through me, need and desire taking over.

I let my head fall back against his shoulder. "Good fucking Christ. All week long I've been waiting for this." The sun sinks toward the horizon. The beam of light we're sitting in flickers like a bulb that needs to be changed.

"You and me both," BJ murmurs. "So goddamn sexy."

"You better not take us back to second base after this." I cover his hand and guide it lower.

"It was hard enough to hold out this long. The only reason we'd take a step back is because you ask for it."

"Not gonna happen."

He eases a single finger inside me, curls it, then adds a second.

I open my eyes and glance down to where his tattooed hand moves between my thighs. "That's so hot," I mutter, more to myself than to him.

"What's hot is the way you're getting off watching me finger-fuck you." He pulls the other cup down so both my breasts are bared.

He withdraws his fingers and circles my clit again, my pussy clenching, the throb between my thighs expanding. The pressure builds, and then he's sliding three fingers inside, pumping hard and fast, his palm adding just the right amount of friction against my clit.

"Don't stop. Don't stop," I chant as I roll my hips, chasing the high and feeling his erection pressed against my lower back.

"That's it..." He bites the edge of my jaw. "So fucking sexy. The next time I make you come, I'll be fucking you with my tongue."

The filthy, hot words coming out of his mouth are a surprise, although they probably shouldn't be, and they absolutely do the trick. "Oh shit."

I clamp my hand around his wrist and grind against his fingers on a low moan. And then I'm coming so hard, the world is washed with white and stars burst in my vision. I ride it out, wave after wave of intense pleasure. I don't think I've ever come this hard in my life.

I sag against BJ, breaths shallow and uneven. He doesn't say anything, doesn't move his hand, but he places soft kisses along the edge of my jaw.

Eventually I unclamp my hand from around his wrist and watch as he slowly withdraws his fingers. I fully expect him to rinse them in the lake, but instead, the hand on my breast slides up to cup my chin, and he turns my head so our lips almost meet. And then he drags his wet finger along my bottom lip.

"What are you—"

I don't get to finish my question because he sucks my lip between his. His groan makes everything clench all over again. He pulls back, eyes hooded with lust, and then he sucks the fingers that were inside me into his mouth.

I can't even begin to imagine what my expression must be. "You're a dirty fucker, aren't you?"

He grins. "A little, yeah."

I awkwardly turn around on the watercraft, nearly tipping it in the process, but BJ steadies us so I can climb into his lap. The top of my bikini is still askew, and the bottoms are pulled to one side, half my ass and crotch exposed, but I don't give a flying fuck.

I tug the spiral tie free from his hair and almost toss it in the water, but remember where we are and slide it on my wrist instead. Then I fuse my mouth to his, moaning at the taste of myself on his tongue. His hands go to my ass, and he squeezes when I roll my hips. And then I feel him, hard and thick against me.

"Fingerbang Friday is my favorite," I mumble.

"Just wait. Tongue-Fuck Tuesday is gonna blow your mind."

And that's the moment another boatercycle comes into the alcove and sends a wave splashing over us.

10

The Things We Want

WINTER

"EVERYONE BETTER BE—OH SHIT." The voice echoes into the alcove.

My stomach drops when I realize it's a police watercraft, and the officer holding a megaphone happens to be Lovey's brother.

BJ shifts my bikini top back into place so I'm not flashing Logan my tits. I slide off BJ's lap and adjust my bikini bottoms, so half my ass isn't on display either. Not that Logan can see it, but still. My face feels like it's on fire.

Logan's eyes flare with surprise, and he rubs his chin, like he's hiding a smile. "Hey, BJ, Winter. Sorry about that. I thought you were Mav and Clover. I'm trying to get him back for the shit he pulled on me last week." He looks at me. "You okay?"

"I'm fine. Just wet." In more ways than one.

"Mav and Clover are on a date, I think. What shit did he pull last week?" BJ gives me an apologetic look.

"Uh, just...uh, making things awkward."

"Right, okay. Well, Lovey is out there somewhere with Quinn, and Rose is with Dracula."

Logan's brows pull together. "Laughlin? What's he doing hanging out with your crew?"

BJ shrugs. "Dunno, but he was on my dock when I got home."

"I'm gonna go make sure Rose and Laughlin haven't tried to drown each other." He salutes us and starts his machine. "Sun goes down fast these days. Might want to head back soon," he adds before spinning around and speeding off.

"Sorry about that," BJ says.

"Not your fault. Kinda glad he didn't see my come face, though." I bite my lip. "I was hoping I could return the favor. For equity's sake."

"Why don't we save that for later? He has a point about the sun setting."

"Aren't you uncomfortable?" I trace the flower on his chest and let my fingers drift lower.

He catches my hand and brings it to his lips. "I've been dealing with nearly constant erections all week while I'm around you. I can handle waiting a little longer. And now that Logan knows we're back here, it's only a matter of time before someone else comes looking for us."

"I didn't think about that."

"We've got nothing but time, Snowflake. No need to rush through all the fun parts." He reaches around me and passes me my life jacket. It's wet, and so is his, but we shrug back into them and buckle up.

We do a circuit around the lake, and he shows me where all the retired hockey players live. "The Kingstons and Winslows are just there, down the road from you." He points to a huge A-frame and a two-story cottage set into the side of the hilly terrain. It boasts a beautiful view. Although most of the hillside cottages have great views.

We're close to the shore, and I let my gaze skip across it, my stomach dropping when I spot our decrepit dock less than fifty feet away. Sitting in a folding lawn chair is my father, a six-pack of beer beside him, a cigarette in his hand, a pair of binoculars around his neck. Sometimes my mom likes to bird watch. Sometimes my dad likes to be a giant skeeze and watch people —namely women in bikinis—but I expected him to be out tonight, not at home, and certainly not on the dock. He lifts the binoculars, following us. Even as BJ turns us and heads for the center of the lake, I know Dad saw me. I feel it in the way the hairs on the back of my neck stand on end.

"Fuck," I mutter.

"You okay?" BJ either heard my curse or feels the sudden tension in my body.

"We should head back," I say.

By the time we reach his place, I'm anxious to go home and deal with the consequences. I hate that my dad's potential anger so easily wipes out everything good about this day.

But I don't want my dad to take my lie out on my mom.

I let BJ guide the watercraft to the dock and jump off as soon as he has it tied up.

He climbs off after me. "Was that your dad on the dock?"

"Yeah. I need to get home." I struggle to free all three buckles, nerves making my hands shake.

"Will you get in trouble?" He runs a hand through his hair, his eyes concerned.

"I'll be in less if I'm home sooner." I shrug out of the jacket and hang it on a hook, re-clipping the buckle so it doesn't blow into the water and disappear down the lake. That's how my grandma inherited a few life jackets over the years, based on the names Sharpied inside them.

"Aren't you allowed to hang out with friends?"

"Yeah, I can hang out with friends. It's just...complicated." My dad has a grudge against everyone who has more than we do.

"Do they know you're here?"

I sigh. All that truth I laid out earlier is biting me in the ass. "I told my mom I was going to the library. My dad for sure saw me on the lake with you, so he'll know I lied."

"It's not okay that your plans changed?"

He seems genuinely confused, and I guess if I were him, I'd feel the same way.

"It's just different for me, BJ. I gotta get changed and go." I start toward the boathouse, and he falls into step with me.

"I'll drive you."

"You can't drop me off at home." My dad will lose his shit, especially if he's already downed a six-pack, and I definitely don't want BJ to witness that. Dad gets mean, and it's embarrassing.

BJ's brows pull together, like he's reading between the lines. "Can I take you to the T-intersection?"

I can't let him see how bad my home life is. Right now we're having fun, and I don't want him thinking he needs to save me. But it'll take half an hour to bike home. That's too long for my mom to be alone with my dad without a buffer. If I get a ride, it'll take me five from the T. "Yeah. Thanks. That would be great."

I slip past him into the boathouse and quickly change. My stomach twists when I check my phone and find new messages from my mom. I can't read the tone, but they're short, and I imagine she's upset.

I shouldn't have lied. It was stupid. And now she's probably getting grief, my dad believing she hid this from him.

It doesn't matter that he knows she can't lie for shit; he loves to be angry. He just needs someone to direct it at. It's a miserable fucking existence to live with someone whose primary life goal is to make people feel like shit. Less than. Not enough.

I message back and tell her I'll be home soon and that I'm sorry. I don't offer an explanation. It's pointless. I'm in shit no matter what I say. Less is better.

I meet BJ in the driveway. "Ready?" he asks.

"Yeah. Thanks." I climb into the passenger seat, uncomfortable. The weight of today settles around me, including my admissions, and how despite it all, I seem to be right. I can't have nice things.

BJ buckles up and puts the Jeep in gear. "Will you be okay?"

"Yeah. I'll be fine. Just need to deal with the fallout." I stare out the window, unable to look at him.

He's silent for a few seconds before he asks softly, "Should I be worried, Winter?"

My knee is bouncing, and I press my palms against the top of my thighs. "My mom isn't like me. She's soft. And when my dad gets angry, he says nasty shit. I just don't want him getting pissed at her when I'm the one who lied."

"Does your dad get angry a lot?"

"He's reactive. My mom doesn't deserve his anger because I fed her a line of bullshit."

"I just don't understand why you're not allowed to hang out with friends."

"Well, you wouldn't get it because your family is basically hemorrhaging money." I cringe, hating my caustic words, frustrated that I'm defensive and that I sound a lot like my dad does when he's being his asshole self. "I'm sorry. That wasn't fair. It's not like we're given a choice as to what family we're born into, and I sound like a dick. Look, to you, it's just hanging out with friends, but to my dad, I'm shirking my responsibilities at home by not helping keep food on the table. It's me wanting things I can't have instead of being thankful we have a roof over our heads."

"You have a job, though, so you are helping, and you're taking college courses, so that's good too, isn't it?"

I sigh. I'm sure he's trying to make sense of it. To understand my life. But his dad is a stand-up guy, and his mom is his coach. He doesn't know what it's like to live with constant emotional warfare. "He doesn't see the value in college," I explain. "Not when I can get a perfectly good job at the ice cream factory and bring home a paycheck we could use."

He reaches the T-intersection and turns down my road.

"You should stop here. I don't want to add fuel to the fire."

He doesn't push, just pulls over so he's not in the middle of the gravel road. He helps get my bike down, and I sling my backpack over my shoulder.

I'm about to hop on my bike when he links our pinkies and steps into my personal space. I put a hand on his chest. "I don't need to be saved, BJ. I can handle myself."

"I know, but should you have to?"

I look at the sky. "I need to go. Thank you for tonight. Fingerbang Friday was totally worth the wait." I meet his eyes, imploring him to let this go. To let me walk away and deal with things. To not get involved.

His expression is somber as he takes my face between his palms. "You don't have to fight every battle on your own." He brushes his lips over mine. "I'm going to text you in twenty minutes."

"I'll be fine." I kiss him one last time, sling my leg over my bike, and pedal up the road, leaving behind my escape from this shitstorm I call a life.

When I reach my driveway, I take a deep breath, wishing I hadn't started today with a lie I can't get out of. I prepare for the coming argument, for the corrosive vitriol my dad will spew.

Words leave invisible wounds, the kind that won't heal no matter how much time passes. They fester and ooze and infect the heart. So anytime someone tries to get inside it, it infects them too.

11

One Step Forward
Two Steps Back

DJ

I WATCH Winter ride her bike up the hill and disappear into the murky darkness. It seems a lot like I've sent her into battle without armor. I tap on the steering wheel, not liking the feeling in my stomach. Something about this situation seems off —like her actions and reactions don't match the circumstances.

Instead of going home, I drive to the end of the road and park in our make-out spot.

I cut the engine and debate my options. I'm certain there's more to this than financial struggles and a dad who's a jerk. Winter is nineteen going on twenty, she works, she plays sports, and she stays out of trouble. Catching heat for hanging out with friends on a Friday night doesn't add up. It's not like we're getting wasted and causing mischief.

Sitting here doing nothing seems the opposite of helpful. As I reach for the door handle, my phone buzzes. I have messages from Lovey and the gang, probably wondering where Winter and I disappeared to, but the newest ones are from Adele.

She doesn't usually message after nine unless it's an emergency, but our practice today was rough. The triple twists were sloppy, and she struggled with the angle. Mostly it seemed like she was psyching herself out, and the more we practiced, the worse it got, so I suggested we end early. I also mentioned potentially switching to a double twist, which seemed to make her feel worse.

Her message is short, asking if we can talk.

I give her a thumbs-up, and my phone rings two seconds later.

"Hey. What's up?" I ask.

"Hey. Hi. What're you up to?"

"Just dropping off a friend. What's going on?"

"Did you have big plans tonight?"

"Nah, just hung out on the dock and took the boatercycles for a spin." And made out with the hockey player I'm crushing on. "You wanted to talk?" Sometimes it's hard to keep Adele on track. And sometimes I feel bad that I keep my skating and my personal life so separate. But Adele knows what happened with my previous pairs partner, and that I won't let it happen again.

"Yeah. Uh...I, uh... I wanted to apologize for today. I know I wasn't on point, and I was messing up the twists. I just got in my head and couldn't get out. I know how important this competition is."

"It's okay. We all have off days. Don't sweat it." I don't want Adele to stress about it all night and come to practice underslept and anxious.

"I just don't want to screw this up, and I know if we don't have at least one complicated combination, we'll probably get docked points. And if we don't place, that has a huge ripple effect, and then we could be looking at another four years before we'd be able to qualify for the Olympics. I know how much this means to you, and I don't want to put that at risk."

"Hey, hey, take a breath, Adele."

"Sorry. I'm sorry. I'm just... I'm worried I'm going to fuck this up."

"I get that, and I appreciate you wanting to nail this combination, but I think we need to look at this logically. We can't risk an injury because we're pushing too hard, too fast. My mom is coming up with a few alternatives."

"But I think I can get this one, BJ. I don't want to give up yet." She sounds like she's on the verge of tears, which won't help either of us.

"Okay. How about this, if things aren't working by Monday, and we haven't nailed the combination, we try swapping the triple twist and see if that works better? We still have time to get it down."

"Maybe we should add a practice tomorrow afternoon."

"We already have practice tomorrow morning. Both of our bodies need a break, otherwise we risk an injury."

"Right. Yeah, I know. But maybe after practice we can talk through some of the other lifts? Figure out what would be the best one to swap it with if it's not going to work? Not that I wanna plan for the worst but—"

I stop her before she can work herself up. "I get that this is stressing you out, but I think it would be better to sleep on it. We can look at it with fresh eyes when we're on the ice tomorrow."

She sighs. "You're right. I know you're right. I'm just...overthinking things."

"We'll get this sorted out, Adele. We always do. Remember last year when we struggled through that one routine and thought we weren't even going to place and won silver?"

"That combination wasn't as complicated, though."

"No, but we've improved as a team since then. Now you can do that routine in your sleep. This will be the same. Once you get it, it's yours. Don't stress, okay? Get some rest, and we can work through it tomorrow, when we're fresh."

"Yeah. Okay. Thanks, BJ. You always make me feel better."

"No problem. That's what partners are for."

I end the call and run a hand down my face.

With Adele handled for now, I hop out of my Jeep and walk up the hill toward Winter's driveway. I can't shake the feeling that there's more going on here than it seems. I stop at the mouth of her narrow driveway. Even though it's dark, I can see her cabin. The lights are on inside, and a single bulb illuminates the front door. It highlights the wooden steps that sit on a slight angle. To the right of the cabin is a small garage and her dad's rusted-out Buick. A recycle bin sits next to the door, empty beer cans littering the ground around it.

The cabin is run-down, but that's not a surprise or the part that concerns me. Even from the end of her driveway, I hear the yelling. The loudest voice is male, and I catch the occasional f-bomb, but not the content of the argument.

I wonder how often it's like this for Winter—and whether angry words are the only things being thrown around.

12

The Fissure

WINTER

"YOU WERE with that rich kid with the tattoos." Dad flicks his cigarette, and ash hits the table.

"I got invited out. I didn't think it was a big deal." Defending myself is pointless. Reasoning with the unreasonable gives me a headache.

They're both sitting at the kitchen table, a united front apparently. Mom holds a cigarette between her fingers so tightly, she's nearly crushing it. Her eyes flash with betrayal. I lied and put her at risk.

I'm suddenly so, so angry. Angry at her for never standing up to him. For putting me in impossible positions. For making me her unwitting shield.

It's not her fault, I remind myself. *She can't help the way she is.*

But that doesn't make it suck any less. And it doesn't stop

me from wishing my life were different, that my parents weren't the way they are.

"Better not get yourself pregnant or you'll be on your own." There's a slur in my father's voice, a tremor that indicates his anger is simmering, ready to boil to the surface. He can't hold it in for long. His impulse control is abysmal. Frustration mounts as my mother brings the cigarette to her lips, hands shaking, eyes anywhere but on me.

"I wouldn't do something that stupid." I never want to be like my parents. Even though the words are true, I hate them as soon as I say them.

My dad's lip curls with derision. "Hear that, Lucy? Your own daughter called you stupid. Guess it must be true."

I close my eyes and exhale through my nose, trying to find some calm, to not stoop to his level. "Can you just fucking stop? She didn't do anything wrong. And the last time I checked, it takes two people to make a baby. You're the one with the goddamn sperm."

My mother gives me a warning look.

Dad's chair scrapes across the floor as he pushes to stand. He sways, unsteady on his feet, and moves across the room, stopping in front of me. We're almost the same height. And weight. He's lanky, with Gumby arms, malnourished with a slight potbelly from all the beer. I'm cut, from all the hockey he doesn't want me to play.

"You think you're so fucking smart, don't you?" he sneers.

"Not smart enough, obviously, since I'm still dealing with your nonsense on a regular basis." I'm done with this shit. So tired of the verbal abuse, of walking on eggshells because my mother refuses to grow a spine and leave his useless ass.

"I put a roof over your head and this is the thanks I get? You're an ungrateful little cunt!"

I bark out a laugh, fighting the sting of his caustic words.

"You're giving yourself an awful lot of credit. I've worked a part-time job since I was fourteen, and most of it has gone to support you and your shitty, money-leaching habits."

His right eye twitches. "Well, that's a fucking lie, isn't it?"

"That you have shitty habits? That's a goddamn fact."

"Where were you supposed to be tonight?" He glances from me to my mother, who shrinks in on herself, a wilted flower.

"The laundromat and the library."

"And were you?"

"You already know the answer to that."

"Give me your phone." He holds out his hand.

"No. I pay my phone bill, not you."

"You live under my roof! Give me your fucking phone, girl. I wanna see the messages you sent your mother." He spins around and stalks over to Mom, grabs the back of her chair and gets in real close. "You're a fucking liar! Telling me one thing and doing another. Hiding shit from me. You're both hiding shit from me!" She cowers and puts her hands over her ears, folds in on herself.

I hate this so much. I hate that for years when our neighbors have called the cops, she always says everything is fine, that Dad just had a bad day at work. That it was her fault.

"Hey, fucker!" I snap my fingers and take a step toward him. "You wanna get pissed at someone, get pissed at me. I lied to both of you. I told Mom I was at the library, but I was playing hockey. It's where I've been every single night this week. You wanna verify that shit, you can ask one of my coaches."

"Tell her," he shouts at Mom. "Tell her what you told me."

Mom doesn't look up, just stares at her hands folded in her lap. "Your coach came to the diner today."

Well, shit. That's a complication I didn't anticipate.

My father's eyes gleam with hatred. He pulls a rolled-up

wad of paper from his back pocket, tears it in two, and slams the pieces on the table, upsetting the ashtray and rolling cigarette butts into Mom's lap and then the floor. "You really think you're smarter than both of us, huh? Going behind my back, applying to college."

Dread turns my stomach. If he has my acceptance letter, he's been in my bedroom. Hopefully that's all he found.

"When'd you really tell your mother? How long has this been going on?" He grabs her arm and shakes her. "I know you're covering for her. I fucking know it!"

I shove the chair aside, and it clatters to the floor as I stalk over to him, rage leaching out of me in poisonous rivers. "Don't you fucking touch her."

He smiles, teeth stained yellow and gray. "She's my wife. I can do whatever I want to her." It's a taunt as much as a promise.

Less than half an hour ago I was zipping around the lake with a hot guy who's all about taking care of people, and now I'm dealing with this nightmare.

I grab his wrist and twist, forcing him to release my mom.

Her chair falls over, and she lands on the floor in a heap. "Winter, don't," she pleads.

But I'm done. So, so done. "You wanna flex your muscles, big man, do it with me. At least I'll fight back." I grab the front of his shirt and haul him toward the screen door leading to the deck. He's apparently not expecting this, so he stumbles over the lip and falls on his ass. His hands hit the ancient deck boards, and I can guarantee his palms are full of splinters. Serves him right.

He crab-walks backwards until he hits the rickety railing. He tries to pull himself up, but it creaks and groans ominously, so he lets it go.

"Winter, you need to stop this. Winter, honey," Mom calls from the doorway.

I hold a hand up. "Stay where you are, Mom."

"Please, Winter."

I hate the tremor in her voice. The fear that makes it unsteady.

I lean over my father, wishing I could be as ruthless as him. That I could choke the life out of him. That I could set my mother free. But she's a caged bird, too scared to spread her wings and fly. "Remember what happened the last time you put your hands on my mother?"

His jaw cracks, and he glares at me with such deep loathing I almost flinch. Almost. "Shoulda taken her to the doctor when I found out she was pregnant with ya and got rid of the problem. Then you wouldn't be here to ruin our lives."

His words are blades, and my armor isn't quite thick enough to keep them from cutting. But I'll be damned if I ever let him see that he's hurt me. "I think you do a pretty great job of ruining your life without my help, but feel free to keep blaming me."

"You're an ungrateful little bitch."

"So you keep saying." I give him a tight smile. "You should go for a drive. Maybe visit your friends at the trailer park and bitch about me there."

"This is my fucking house."

"It's not, actually. It's in Mom's name, not yours. And based on the will, it's stipulated that I'm to inherit it once you're gone. I know that's probably a lot of big words that are too difficult for you to understand." I hate myself for stooping to his level with the insults. "But you need some time to calm the fuck down. You can be as mad at me as you want, but Mom has nothing to do with any of this. I kept her in the dark for this exact reason."

He gets to his feet, stumbling back a step. The railing

sways, and for the briefest moment, I think the unthinkable—
that it might give way and I'll be rid of him. But he finds his
balance and steps away from the edge, forcing me to step back
too, so he's not breathing his rank smoke-and-booze breath in
my face.

He rolls his shoulders back. "I've had enough of this shit
tonight." He shoves his hand in his pants pocket, his grin malev-
olent. "You'll never get out of here, Winter. Not so long as your
mother is still breathing."

He shoves by me, and Mom shuffles back as he passes
through the kitchen. She grabs for his arm, apologizing, and he
shakes her off, telling her it's her damn fault. All of it. And then
the porch door slams shut. Gravel pings as he revs the engine
and speeds down the driveway. Every time he gets behind the
wheel like this, I cross my fingers he makes it wherever he's
going. We can't afford the hospital bills if he ends up in an
accident.

When I turn back, Mom is wringing her hands. "You
shouldn't have lied about where you were going tonight."

"I didn't want to get you in trouble." I step inside and close
the screen door to keep the mosquitos out.

"Is that why you didn't tell me about the acceptance letter?
I didn't even know you'd applied to college." Accusation laces
her tone.

If my mom was the one who found the letter in my room,
everything else should be safe. I can deal with her hurt. I can
smooth it over. I take a deep breath. "There wasn't a point in
saying anything when I didn't know if I'd be accepted. And I
applied on a whim. It doesn't matter anyway, since I can't
afford to go."

She peeks up at me, looking like a scolded child, not a
mother. "That letter made it sound like they'd give you some
money. Is that true?"

"Sort of... But it doesn't matter. I can't go." Even if they'll cover tuition, I have to pay for books, housing, and food, and what I've saved will only cover half those costs. And I can't leave her alone to deal with my father. He'll break her. I can't live with that guilt. It's an endless loop.

"You shouldn't have sent him to the trailer. He's been drinking," she whispers.

"He's always drinking, Mom. And do you want to sleep beside him when he's like this?"

She looks away, fingers going to her lips before she picks up one of the half-smoked cigarette butts from the ashtray. It's crumpled, so she straightens it and lights it with shaking hands.

I try to see her through my coach's eyes. Does he pity her? Does he pity me? Is that why BJ seems so invested in spending time with me?

"I'm sorry," she whispers. "I should leave him. I should. I know I should. But I don't know how."

I cross the room, emotions warring. I wish my mom could stand up for us, could leave the man who continually hurts her, but she isn't strong enough. So I have to be strong enough for both of us.

"You could kick him out. You could get an order of protection. He could stay in the trailer." Even as I say this, I know she'll never follow through.

"I should tell him to stay there for a few days. Until things calm down. I'm sorry he tore up the acceptance letter."

And we're back to this. Her continued apologies are a red flag. "Did you find the letter or did he?" I move around her, my legs wooden and my mouth dry as I push open the door to my room. Her contrition makes sense now.

It's been ransacked. My things are strewn all over the place, binder lying open, papers scattered across my bed. My textbook for my class lies in a heap on the floor, but it's my open dresser drawers that incite the real panic.

"I didn't realize you had so much money in there." Mom's tone is equal parts apology and blame.

"It was from tips." I didn't put it in the bank on purpose, so it wouldn't go missing from my account, which is still connected to theirs. I planned to drop it in when I needed to pay for my fall courses.

"It would have helped with the expenses."

"I know. That's why I put it aside, so I could help when we needed it."

The bottom three drawers are pulled out, the contents vomited over the sides and onto the floor. But the top one is missing completely. My underwear and sports bras are all over the floor.

My stomach sinks and rolls. I don't know what I expect to find as I drop to my knees and comb through the contents. It's like my mind is resisting the truth: that he found it and took everything. That my mom didn't stop him. We both have a secret stash, but she didn't know the extent of mine. We called it the just-in-case fund. It was supposed to be enough for emergency groceries, or gas for the car, or a bill that couldn't wait to be paid.

"No, no, no." The metal lockbox has been jimmied open, and the contents are gone. I almost had enough saved for an entire semester of online college courses. And the deadline to pay tuition is coming up. There's no way I'll make enough in the next few weeks to replace it. I can't afford a single class now.

Tears prick at my eyes. My dad is a master at ruining good things.

"Why did you tell him where to find it?"

"I-I-I didn't know there would be that much money." Her

hands strangle each other. "I thought you only had a couple hundred dollars in there. And then he found the acceptance letter. You shouldn't have hidden those things. Or that much money. He was so mad." Her fingers go to her lips again. "And then you were with that boy with the watercraft. You have to be careful, Winter. Those rich boys put ideas in your head. Like that coach. I'm sure he means well, but what happens when the funding for that program runs out? Or you can't make the grades and keep the scholarship? And then all your hope would be taken away again. Remember when that happened before?"

She's referring to when I played for the girls' team in high school. I always had to work on weekends and after school, I couldn't afford the equipment fees, and I missed too many practices, so I lost my spot on the team—and just before the scouts came to watch the playoffs.

"This is different."

"I know you're upset, but it's better this way," she says. "Better the money is gone. Now you can just focus on your job and take more hours at Boones."

"I'm not quitting hockey, Mom."

She sighs. "Your dad isn't going to like that."

"I don't give a fuck what he likes." I'm on the verge of tears, which I hate, or lashing out, which will make me feel like a bag of shit.

I shove down the emotion. Tears won't make it better, and they won't change the fact that I'm back to square one. I should have opened a second bank account, one my parents don't have access to, but I thought it was safer to keep cash, in case of an emergency. So stupid. So fucking stupid.

I stand, step around her, and head for the porch.

"Where are you going?"

"To get some air before I say something I can't take back."

She follows, but I leave her standing in the kitchen, looking as lost as I feel as I step out into the night. I flinch when the door slams closed behind me.

"Fuck my life." I kick an empty beer can across the driveway, and it hits the side of the garage. I press the heels of my hands against my eyes. Crying won't solve anything, but I'm so damn frustrated. The acceptance letter isn't the issue. They sent an email as well. But the tuition money is a different story.

If it didn't make me look needy and desperate, I might ride over to BJ's, just to escape for a while. But I have no idea how long my dad will be gone, and leaving my mom alone after a fight like this won't make things better.

I tip my chin up, working to keep my emotions in check as I look at the stars.

My phone buzzes in my pocket. I pull it out and check the messages.

Rose started a group chat with me, her, and Lovey after I skated with them. She sent a message saying she'd ask where BJ and I disappeared to, but they ran into Logan and his beet-red face told her everything she needed to know. She expects details the next time we're on at Boones together, if we don't see each other before then.

Another message pops up as I'm reading, this one from BJ.

You okay?

Rustling in the bushes drags my attention away from my phone.

The sun has set, and the only lights are over the door and on the side of the garage. The last thing I need is a confrontation with a bear. Although I wouldn't be surprised if a family of racoons had nested nearby, since my dad leaves empties all over the place.

"Hey, bear, you can fuck off!" I call out as I step backwards toward the cabin.

"Bears need love too," a voice replies.

"BJ?" I scan the area for him. "Are you out here?"

"Yeah." He steps out of the treeline by the garage, his expression reflecting his chagrin.

I glance over my shoulder. My mom is standing by the screen door, smoking a cigarette. I rush over and grab his arm, leading him around the side of the garage. "The hell are you doing? Why are you still here? My dad didn't see you, did he?"

"Was that him driving off?"

"Yeah."

"I was hiding in the bushes." He thumbs over his shoulder. There's a twig caught in his hair, proving he's telling the truth.

"What about your Jeep?"

"I parked in our make-out spot. I was going to leave, but I had this bad feeling, and you were sketchy about getting home, so I got out and walked up to your driveway. I didn't really have a plan, but then I heard yelling, and I wanted to stick around in case you needed an escape or whatever."

"So you thought lurking around in the dark was the best option?"

"Like I said, I didn't have much of a plan. Are you okay?"

"That's a loaded question." I rub the space between my eyebrows. "I wasn't lying when I said my life was messy. I guess one of my coaches talked to my mom at the diner today and spilled the beans about the Hockey Academy. I hadn't told my parents because I knew it would just cause a fight. And it did. And then my dad ransacked my room and found my acceptance letter to college and the money I'd been saving for tuition for the fall. He took all of it."

"What the fuck?" BJ's lip curls.

I think it's the first time I've seen him angry.

"Maybe I can help you get it back."

I put my hand on his chest and shake my head. "No. You can't. It's too late. He's gone, and he'll spend it all on nothing. I should have opened a second bank account, but I didn't, and that's on me."

A door opens and closes, and Mom calls, "Winter? Did you go down to the dock?"

"Shit. Stay right here and keep quiet, please. My mom can't know you're here," I whisper. I move toward the cabin. "I'm out back, picking up empties," I yell. "Remember to stay away from the railing. It's not safe!"

The sliding door opens and closes again, and a few seconds later, my mom pokes her head out the back door. "I'm really sorry."

"I know, Mom. It's not your fault."

"I'm going to lie down. Don't stay out here too long. Someone reported a bear sighting a couple weeks back."

"I'll be in soon."

"I love you," she says softly.

"I love you too, Mom." It's bad enough that my dad is blaming this on her. I can't do that too. It'll keep her up all night, and tomorrow will be twice as hard.

Once my mom disappears inside, I go back to BJ. His lips are mashed in a thin line. I sigh. "You weren't supposed to see this side of my life."

"You wanted to feed me a curated version of you?" He tucks a hand in his pocket.

"I liked that we were having fun, and spending time with you is a break from this. I'm not a damsel in distress."

He tilts his head. "I know you're not a damsel. But it seems to me like you're fighting a lot of battles on your own. I think the bigger question you need to ask yourself, Winter, is who are you really protecting when you hide your truth from people who care about you? 'Cause from the outside looking in, it sure doesn't seem to be you."

"I appreciate that you're concerned or whatever, but I've got things handled." I kick at a stone on the ground. "You should go. I don't know how long my dad will be gone, and I don't want you to get mauled by a bear, because that would make future Fingerbang Fridays hard."

"Okay. Hint taken. Dropping it for now." He pulls me in for a hug, then cups my cheeks between his palms and kisses me. It's soft and sweet, and I get lost in it for a few long seconds, until he steps back. His gaze moves over my face. "You don't have to fight every fight with an army of one, Winter. Just remember that, okay?"

"It's all I've ever known."

"It doesn't have to stay that way." He drops his hands and steps back. "I'll see you tomorrow at the game."

I watch him disappear down the driveway before I go back inside.

BJ's words stick with me as I clean up my room and climb into bed. Because he's right. The only person I'm protecting when I hide the abuse is the abuser. And how fucked up is that?

13

We All Fall Down

BJ

I WAKE ON EDGE, which isn't a surprise after last night. I messaged Winter when I got home and she hearted it, but she's been quiet since.

I check again this morning, but it's just the usual in the group chat. Lovey's working at the foodbank this morning, and Mav is coaching the boys' team with Lovey's dad and Darren Westinghouse. Clover has the literacy program, but Mav said she's hoping to make the second half. Rose is working at Boones.

I have new messages from Adele, promising she'll be on time and saying she's determined to make the triple twist work. I scheduled us early so I can be there to watch the game. I want Winter to feel supported, because from what I've witnessed, she doesn't have much from the people who count.

I eat breakfast on autopilot and compulsively check my

phone for new messages. Still nothing, though. Adele messages once I'm on the ice to tell me she's on her way.

She shows up fifteen minutes late, which is a heck of a lot better than her usual half hour. She's dressed in a black leotard and a black skirt. Her makeup is done as if she's ready for an actual performance, not just a practice skate. She'd probably be on time if she left it at mascara and lip gloss, but I keep that to myself since there are zero good reasons to make her feel shitty.

She falls into stride next to me. "Sorry I'm late."

"You're good. I can only stay until nine forty-five, though." I booked the ice until ten, but then saw she'd added an extra hour.

She frowns. "Oh, I thought your schedule was open today."

"My friend is playing her first game today, and I want to be there to support her."

"Oh." She does a two-foot turn so she's facing me. "What friend is that?"

"Winter. I've been giving her lessons. You met her at the beginning of the week."

"The girl with the long, dark hair?"

"Yeah, that's the one."

She chews her bottom lip. It's a little raw, like she's been doing this a lot. "You've given a lot of those girls lessons, and you've never bailed on practice for a game before."

I cross my arms. "You're chronically late and you're on me about cutting a Saturday practice short so I can support a friend?"

She props a fist on her hip. "I just want to get this combination right so we don't have to switch up our routine!"

Fighting isn't how I want to start practice. "Let's just make the most of the time we have." I cue up the music and end the argument before it escalates.

I reach for Adele's hand, and she slips it into mine, letting me lead, because Adele is more comfortable following cues than giving them.

She starts out strong, but as soon as we reach the triple twist, she misses her cue and we get the angle wrong. This happens on repeat for the duration of practice.

At nine forty-five, I call time. "I need to hit the shower soon if I'm going to make the first face-off."

"Can we try a couple more times? I know I can get it, BJ." Adele wrings her hands and gives me doe eyes.

I'm trying my best to be patient. I'm aware that this competition is a lot of pressure, especially since we need to place to move forward. But we can't spend every practice struggling through combinations that might be too difficult, and this is two days in a row that she's having trouble with the same element. It's the common denominator, and we need to fix it while we still have time. But I concede so she doesn't get upset.

"We can try it twice more. Then I gotta go."

"Okay. Twice more through."

She fumbles on the first attempt, but the second time she gets it. And of course, because she had success, she wants to try again. But it's better to end on a positive note with her feeling good.

I rush through my shower, but by the time I'm dressed, I've missed a few minutes of the first period. I take a seat behind the bench. There's a good crowd; the local hockey lovers are all about supporting their teams. I knock on the plexiglass barrier and my dad excuses himself to come talk to me for a second.

"How's it going?" The scoreboard indicates our team is up by one goal.

"They're playing tight." Dad doesn't take his eyes off the ice.

I scan the rink and find Winter heading for the opposition's net. The puck slides behind the crease, and she hits the boards before she can stop herself.

"Shake it off," I mutter. "You got this."

"She's off today," Dad says quietly.

"First-game jitters?" I ask, even though I know it's more than that.

"That's what I thought initially, but she's...on edge."

I worry about the ramifications of last night. I don't know how much money she had saved for tuition, but I can guess that any amount going missing would be a major setback.

Winter recovers and makes a nice pass, but her teammate misses the opportunity to score. My dad returns to the bench when Winter gets called off the ice and leans in to talk to her as she takes a seat. Her eyes stay locked on the game, and her jaw tics, but she nods, as though she's agreeing with whatever he says. I wonder if this is something she's used to doing—being agreeable so she doesn't rock the boat. Not to mention being afraid to lose this opportunity. Winter glances over her shoulder and gives me a small smile, but she looks tired and anxious.

Her knee bounces a few times as she turns back to the game, and she keeps pulling at the chinstrap of her helmet, like it's too tight. One of her teammates pats her shoulder, maybe in reassurance.

Winter rotates back onto the ice as our team gains control of the puck. She passes to her teammate and skates behind the net, staying in control in the crease. It's a great setup, but I see what Winter can't, and that's the opposition coming up from behind, looking to get between Winter and the boards. The player moves in tight to Winter, causing her to lose her focus and her balance. One second the puck is kissing Winter's blade, the next she's sprawled across the ice, taking the opposition down with her.

Winter gets to her knees, gloved hand going to her face. Red spatters her white and black jersey and dots the ice under her. She touches her chin, face contorting in a grimace.

"Shit, she's injured." I start to stand, but realize I can't do anything. Besides, she's not the type who likes to be fawned over, especially under these circumstances.

The refs call the play, and the buzzer sounds.

Winter yanks off her gloves and spins around, as if she's looking for someone to go after. Thankfully the ref and her teammates have surrounded her. Fern Harmer, the team captain, steers her toward the bench, and the opposition gets a penalty for interference. Blood drips from Winter's chin, leaving a trail on the ice. A thin stream travels down her throat and soaks into her jersey. Her eyes are on fire.

Once she's on the bench, my dad is there, helping unclip her helmet while the action on the ice is paused.

Winter takes the wad of tissues Uncle Alex hands her and dabs at her chin while he and my dad inspect the wound and the team doctor steps in. I can't hear the conversation, but all my time spent at an arena means I'm pretty good at reading lips. Winter's body language reads tension and worry.

She tips her head back for the doctor. Even from here, I can see she needs stitches. When the team doctor echoes that thought, Winter's eyes widen. She shakes her head, but after more back and forth, she finally follows Dr. Fellows down the hall to the therapy rooms, where he'll presumably stitch her up.

Dad watches her leave, and his eyes catch mine. I have questions, but they'll have to wait until after the game.

Winter returns halfway through the next period with fresh gauze on her chin, but they don't rotate her into the game. She gives me a chin tip when the team heads for the dressing room, but doesn't acknowledge me otherwise. I have to guess she's upset about being benched after the injury. Our team won by one goal, which is awesome, but I'm sure Winter would have liked to be a bigger contributor to that win.

I stop by the offices so I can catch up with my dad once he's done giving the team a pep talk. I stretch out on the chair in the hall to wait. The next thing I know, he's shaking me awake.

"You waiting on me?"

"Yeah. Just wanted to make sure Winter's okay." I didn't tell him about last night, partly because it isn't my place. I don't want to betray Winter's confidence.

"She's all stitched up. Doc says no concussion, but she'll have a headache, and she'll need to take it easy." My dad rubs his beard. "She was worried about the cost of treatment. She didn't realize the medical forms she signed meant she has full coverage."

Healthcare is one of the biggest perks of being on the team. "Is that all she's worried about?"

"She's concerned about proving her worth to the team from the bench."

"She's used to opportunities slipping through her fingers, and she doesn't like to ask for help." And last night proved that her fears are valid.

Dad leans against the wall, his expression pensive. "I met her mother at the diner yesterday."

"I know. She hadn't told her parents she was playing for the women's team."

His brow furrows. "Well, that explains her mom's reaction when I asked if she was coming to watch Winter play today. Fuck. I wish I'd known that."

"It's a small town. They would have found out eventually."

"Still. She didn't say anything about it today." He strokes his beard.

"She holds her cards close to the vest." I tap on my knee, restless.

"What's going on, BJ? What aren't you saying?"

I bite my lip, debating. "I don't want to betray Winter's confidence, but financial constraints are only part of the problem. Maybe talk to Logan."

He strokes his beard again. "Is she in danger?"

"Seems like a lot of words are being thrown around in that house, but I don't know if that's where it ends. She can hold her own, but she shouldn't have to." And the whole stealing her tuition money says a lot about her dad.

He claps me on the shoulder. "I had a feeling things were tough in that house. You'll tell me if there's cause for concern?"

"Yeah. Of course."

He nods once. "This will stay between you and me. And I'll do my best to reassure her that her place on the team is secure when we take them out for lunch."

"Okay. Sounds good." Dad heads down the hall, and I check the time. I teach a lesson in half an hour, so I send Winter a message congratulating her on the game and asking if she wants to hang out later. But that heavy feeling in my stomach keeps growing. I worry that what happened last night is just scratching the surface.

* * *

AFTER LESSONS, I check my phone. I have a new message from Winter and a pic of her stitched-up chin. It's not the first time she's had chin stitches. The previous scar is jagged and messy, but this one is clean and neat.

bringing sexy back

:Justin T dancing GIF:

> Have house stuff to take care of 🙄 Team said they're going to the beach later. Might go if I don't catch heat for the chin. We could meet up there?

> You're a sexy badass 😏

> message when ur on ur way to the beach, I can pick u up if u want

The humping dots appear, then disappear, then appear again.

> Suck Face Saturday doesn't sound quite as appealing as Fingerbang Friday and Tongue-Fuck Tuesday.

It's hard to believe she's over last night already. Or maybe this is her way of escaping the bullshit. Regardless I want to see her, that way I can see for myself that she's really okay.

> How about Sweet Spot Saturday?

> I'm down. Tlk l8r 🍆

Quinn is heading back to Chicago tonight, so I spend a couple of hours hanging with him and Mav. Lovey and Lacey invite me to watch rom-coms with Rose, but I take a pass and a nap in the hammock overlooking the water while I wait for Winter to message.

My phone buzzes on my chest, waking me. The sun has set, and it's already after nine.

> At the beach.

Two photos follow. The first is a selfie of Winter dressed in an oversized T-shirt, braid hanging over her shoulder, chin covered with gauze, one brow arched. It looks like she's in the parking lot. The second is of the starry sky.

> It's ambiance central here.

> I wld have picked u up.

> Needed to get out of the house. We still on for SSS tonight?

> Hell yeah. omw

Several GIFs follow, including a cartoon hot dog thrusting.

Yeah, she's definitely deflecting and looking for an escape. I brush my teeth, change into jeans and a fresh T-shirt, pull my hair back, and hop in my Jeep. Halfway to the beach, I pull over so an ambulance and fire truck can pass. My heart lodges in my throat when those vehicles turn down Winter's road.

I slow as I approach the T-intersection, which is blocked by a cop car with flashing lights. Logan is standing at the mouth of the T, so I stop and roll down the passenger-side window.

He approaches, expression grim as he rests his forearm on the sill and leans in. "Sorry, BJ. The road is closed."

"Yeah, I figured. This an alarm activation or something?" The Winslows and Kingstons have systems that sometimes get tripped by curious wildlife. The squirrels are notorious for chewing through wires.

Logan shakes his head. "I wish it was just an alarm activation."

"That doesn't sound good."

His walkie-talkie crackles. "Victim is in her mid to late thirties. Multiple breaks. She's in and out of consciousness."

"Fuck." He blows out a breath. "You know where the Marks girl is?"

"She's at the beach. I'm heading there now. What the hell is going on, Logan?"

"There was an accident."

14

Somewhere Soft
to Land

BJ

WINTER IS in the parking lot when I arrive at the beach. I don't want to be the one to break her heart like this. But it's better me than Logan—or worse, her dad.

I pull into a spot, and she leans her bike against the low fence that separates the lot from the beach. She's on me the second I step out of the Jeep, one hand wrapped around the back of my neck, pulling my mouth to hers.

"Whoa. Hey. Hi." Half an hour ago I was all about Sweet Spot Saturday. Now everything is different. I'm about to turn her entire world upside down.

"Hey. I'm super glad you're here. Today has been a bag of shit, and you're the only person who can make it better." Her backpack clinks when it hits the ground. "I brought you a gift." She unzips the bag and holds it open.

"Vodka and gin, huh? Is it martini night, then?" I try to smile, but everything is off.

"This is what my dad bought with my tuition money. He didn't pay the car insurance. He didn't buy groceries or get someone to fix the broken washing machine. He bought booze and smokes and rubbed it in my fucking face."

"I'm so sorry, Snowflake." I hate that this is her life, her normal.

She smooths her hand over my chest. "I shouldn't have gone home after the game. I should have gone anywhere but home, but I had leftovers from the team lunch, and they had the best desserts, so I figured I'd just leave one in the fridge for my mom—even though she's the one who told my dad where the money was. It's so fucked up, BJ. She throws me under the bus all the time, and I still feel compelled to take care of her. Why do I keep doing this? Why do I keep putting myself in positions where I know I'm going to get hurt? It's so stupid. What's wrong with me?"

I tuck a loose lock of hair behind her ear. "Nothing is wrong with you, Winter. You're just trying to survive in a life that doesn't make a lot of sense."

"You know what he said when he saw the stitches? He didn't ask if I was okay. He didn't even ask what happened. He told me my face was the only part of me worth looking at, and now I'd fucked that up too. I don't want to do this anymore. I can't keep doing this." She pinches the bridge of her nose. "I need to stop talking. You've already seen what a mess I am. I'm too much of a hassle."

"Hey. Stop." I cup her face in my palms. "Take a breath."

She looks like she's on the verge of a breakdown.

Kissing her won't solve her problems, but it's a distraction from the shit I'm about to pile on top of her already bad day. I press my lips to hers. "You deserve better than this, Winter. I will tell you every damn day that you're gorgeous, inside and out. A few stitches won't change that." I stroke her cheek, wishing I could make her life better, hating that I'm about to make it so much worse. "You can love the person and not love their actions."

"I just want out, BJ. Of this life. Of my head." Her chin trembles. "I just want to feel something other than hopelessness."

"I know. I'm sorry. I wish this wasn't so hard." I wrap my arms around her, and in that moment, I think I finally understand what it means to hate someone. Really and truly. Because I hate her dad for what he's done to her. Hate that she's stuck in a life she didn't ask for, hate that she feels compelled to protect someone who's so deep inside the abuse she lets her daughter be her human shield. Hate that the only thing her father does is cut her down.

I hold her for long minutes, wishing we could stay inside this bubble. What's coming next will hurt so much worse than what she's already been through. And I can't protect her from it.

"I want to escape my life for a little while." Her hands slide up my chest, and she curves her palm around the back of my neck. I let her pull my mouth to hers, and I get lost in the kiss right along with her, wanting to postpone the inevitable, but knowing I can't.

When her hand starts to travel down my chest again, I catch it in mine and break the kiss.

Her gaze roams over my face. "Should we go somewhere else?"

Dread fills me. Noxious. Toxic. I wonder if this is how Winter feels every time she goes back to that prison of a home. "I need to tell you something."

She frowns and drops her hand. "Your expression and tone aren't reassuring."

"I know. I'm sorry." I squeeze her hand. "Your mom had an accident."

The color drains from Winter's face. "No, she didn't. She's fine. We were texting half an hour ago." She pulls her phone out of her pocket, hands trembling as she taps on the messages. I catch a little of the content. Mostly it's her mom begging her to apologize and make it easier on everyone.

Winter's last message to her mom is that she needs time to cool off.

It still reads as unread. She sends another one, but it too will remain unread. I just don't know for how long.

"The ambulance had just arrived when I drove by. They were taking her to the hospital."

Even as she shakes her head, she asks, "What happened?"

"I think she fell, but I don't have a lot of information yet."

A look of horror crosses her face. "No." She shakes her head and steps back, bumping into my Jeep. "No, no, no." Her hand goes to her mouth. "This is because of me. This is all my fault."

"You didn't do anything wrong."

"I made him angry, and now she's in the hospital." She grabs my arms, nails digging in. "I need to see her. I need to see if she's okay."

"I'll take you to the hospital." I guide her around the hood and open the passenger-side door. She climbs in, hand over her mouth, eyes wide with worry.

I zip up her backpack and toss it in the trunk since it's full of liquor bottles. Once I clip her bike to the rack, I rush around to the driver's side. I turn the engine over and adjust the volume on the stereo so Robert Smith isn't belting out "Pictures of You," and instead, it's just soft background noise.

"I'm scared, BJ," she whispers.

I set my hand palm-up on the center console. "I know. I wish I had more information. We'll be there soon, and then we can find out what's going on."

She laces her fingers with mine. "I shouldn't have left her alone with him."

"I know you're used to holding the blame, but you had every right to get out of there. Parents aren't supposed to rip their kids apart for making mistakes."

"I just need her to be okay. She has to be okay," Winter murmurs.

I don't tell her everything will be fine, because I don't know if that's true. When we get to the hospital, a nurse tells us Winter's mom is in surgery.

"Surgery? What kind of surgery? What happened?"

"She took a nasty fall and broke her arm and her leg in multiple places. They're putting in pins and plates."

"Is she going to be okay?"

"The doctors will be able to update you in a couple of hours. I can show you to the waiting room, if you'd like. Your dad is already here."

She turns to me, eyes wide.

"That'd be great," I tell the nurse. "I got you, Snowflake. You don't have to do this on your own."

We follow the nurse down the hall.

"I don't know how we're going to afford this. I don't know what my dad's plan at the ice cream factory will cover," she whispers.

My mom is Canadian and so is my uncle Alex, so health-care has always been a huge part of the Hockey Academy, especially since so many players are subsidized. "The Hockey Academy has a family fund. It's specifically for situations like these. My dad will be able to help."

"I hope we don't lose the cabin," she murmurs.

"You won't. They won't let that happen."

When we reach the waiting room, the nurse tells us she'll be back with an update as soon as she can. Winter's dad is stretched across three chairs. He's wearing worn, grass-stained jeans and a holey T-shirt. The room smells like an ashtray and a brewery. One of his shoes is on the floor, and his big toe pokes out of a hole in his sock. A pack of smokes peeks out of his jeans pocket, and his mouth hangs open. He's fast asleep.

Winter grinds her teeth as she unlaces our fingers and pokes him in the shoulder. "Dad. Wake up."

He startles and sits up in a rush. "The fuck is wrong with you? You don't wake me up when I'm sleeping." His eyes dart around as he takes in his surroundings. For a moment he looks confused, but when he sees me, his eyes narrow. He scrubs a hand over his face. "'Bout time you finally got here. I left you a voicemail a long time ago."

Her hands ball into fists and her voice shakes with barely restrained fury. "I thought it was more of you telling me how useless I am and not to come home, so I didn't listen to it. What happened to Mom?"

I hate this for Winter. I hate that she's here and scared and the person who should be comforting her is a complete loser of a parent. And I hate most that she blames herself for this nightmare that she had no hand in creating, but is forced to live with.

His eyes shift to the side and he mumbles, "She took a fall."

"How? From where?" Winter presses.

His eyes lift for a moment before they drop again. "She was upset. Worried about all the money your stitches were gonna cost us."

"I already told you it won't cost anything. *What happened?*"

"Don't you raise your voice at me, girl."

Winter's back expands on a deep inhale, and she pinches

the bridge of her nose. "Please explain what happened. Is Mom gonna be okay?"

"She went outside, needed some fresh air after all the drama you caused today. Winding everyone up. Only thinking 'bout what you want." He rubs at his jaw. "I been tellin' her to stay away from the railing, but she didn't listen."

I've only seen the front of Winter's place from the water, but it's high up on a steep incline.

Winter's knees wobble, and she clamps a hand over her mouth. "No."

His eyes dart away again. "The railing gave out."

Her body goes rigid. "You're a fucking liar!" I rush forward and grab her around the waist before she can launch herself at him. "Let me go!" She tries to pry my hands free, shouting at her dad. "You did this! You put her here."

Her dad holds his hand up like he's fending her off, like he's afraid. And maybe he is. He sneers and glares at me. "Be careful with this one. She gets like this. Bad temper. Lashes out. Causes her mom a lot of stress."

"Seems like maybe she has a right to lash out where you're concerned," I snap.

Winter's nails dig into my arms, but she stops struggling, and her voice is a broken whisper. "What did you do?" she asks him again.

"Come on, let's go for a walk." I guide her out of the waiting room. There's a stairwell across the hall. I push through it, the door closing with a quiet snick.

"He did this. He did this to her. I know it. I know he did." She slides down the wall, hands shaking, tears streaming down her cheeks. "I left her alone with him, and now she's in the hospital, BJ. I can't ever get out. I can't ever have anything good. He just takes it all away." She sucks in gasping breath after gasping breath.

My cousin Lavender used to have panic attacks when she was younger. And sometimes my roommate Kody did too, especially around exam time. He had strategies to deal with them, and I search my mind for a way to help calm Winter. But all I remember is Kody doing breathing exercises, or naming the things he could see.

I crouch and wrap my hands around her calves. "Hey, hey. Breathe with me, okay? Take a breath. Slow and steady."

She does as I say, timing her breaths with mine. It takes a couple of minutes, but she gets herself under control. "He's lying about what happened," she whispers.

"Can you explain that to me?"

"You know we got into it on Friday after you dropped me off, about me playing hockey behind their backs." She curves her hands over her knees. "He was blaming it on my mom, saying she must have known. He got all up in her face and grabbed her arm, so I got all up in his."

I fight not to let my own anger bubble to the surface. She doesn't need more toxicity. She needs patience and softness and understanding. "What happened then?"

"I just needed to get him away from her. He does this. Takes my mistakes out on my mom because she won't fight back the way I will. The deck is in bad shape. The railing needs replacing, and I ended up cornering him right where it's the worst. Not on purpose. It just...worked out that way. But he knows how bad that railing is. What if he pulled the same move on my mom? What if he got her out there, but he didn't back off and the railing broke? It's a big drop, BJ. Like two stories up. And it's all rocks. What if she's not okay?" She dashes away her tears. "Every time I have something good, he ruins it. And now he's ruined her too. All because I'm selfish."

I thought I understood how hard Winter's life was, but I didn't realize it was like this. "You're not selfish."

"But I am. I knew how angry he was when I left tonight. I knew, and I went anyway. And now my mom is in surgery, and I don't know if she's going to be okay."

15

Break the Broken

WINTER

I DON'T RETURN to the waiting room. I can't face my dad now. Maybe not ever. Not when I'm sure he caused the fall. Instead, BJ and I wait in a room down the hall, close to the nurses' station. His parents show up an hour later, dressed like they've been on a date. BJ's mom is a petite woman with a dark brown, nearly black bob and a warm smile. BJ fills her in while Coach Ballistic takes me to update the medical information.

"We have a family fund with the Hockey Academy that will cover the deductible and we can help you with any other forms for supplemental insurance, okay? We'll get you through this," he assures me.

I hold onto the hope that he's right and that the Hockey Academy really can help, otherwise we'll end up back in the trailer. I don't want to think about what else that means.

It's one in the morning by the time my mom is out of surgery.

The doctor tells us she made it through just fine, but that she likely won't come out of sedation until morning. There are pins and plates in her right arm and left leg. She also has stitches in the back of her head and a concussion. That part scares me. Concussions are serious. They can change a person. My dad has had two. One was a forklift accident at work, and the other was a fall at the trailer park. He'd been drinking, as usual, so it's anyone's guess what happened. He was treated for the first concussion, but not the second. And it seemed to make him meaner.

I wait until my dad leaves before I go in to see her.

Even though I was warned, I'm not prepared for the sight of my mother lying in the hospital bed. Terror and guilt crowd for position with simmering anger. Her right arm is casted to her shoulder. Her left leg is in traction, casted past her knee. She's surrounded by medical equipment, beeping and monitoring her heart rate.

As I stare at her broken body, I can see what happened playing out—my dad cornering her like I did him, doing what he does best: intimidate, manipulate, insult, degrade.

The worst is when he's quiet with his anger, when he gets in close and whispers horrible, hurtful things—the kind of things that make Mom cry and me seethe. If this was an accident, it was an orchestrated one. All he needed to do was trap her against the railing. She'd have nowhere to go, a captive to his anger and spiteful words. Gravity did the rest.

"What if she's not okay?"

"The doctor thinks she'll make a full recovery, but it'll be slow," BJ's mom, Lily, says softly.

I always worried it would come to this. That one day I wouldn't be there to stop him. Now that it's happened, all I feel is overwhelming sadness. I couldn't be the hand that pulled her out of the darkness. I couldn't save her from him.

Every good thing is slipping through my fingers. And in its place is whatever comes of this.

"I can't go home. I can't go back to that." Panic hits me, along with stabbing blades of guilt that I can even think of myself when my mother is lying here broken, when I've failed her so completely.

But I don't want this to be my future too.

I can't walk this path.

I won't.

I'll go to the trailer. Stay at the shelter. But I won't live under the same roof as my dad. Not after this.

"You can stay with us until we get this figured out," BJ's mom says.

"What?" I wonder what BJ said to her while Coach and I were at reception so he could take down our insurance information.

"We have a spare bedroom. It's yours for as long as you need it." Her smile is warm and full of empathy.

BJ hooks his pinkie with mine.

I worry about the ripple effect. How this will impact what comes next. How it will change this thing with BJ. How hard it will be to keep my feelings for him locked down if we're living under the same roof. How nice it will be to have a break from the emotional warfare.

It's nearly three in the morning when we get back to the Ballistics'. I'm exhausted but on edge. Lily follows me and BJ upstairs, and she sets me up in the room across from his. Like every other part of their house, it's pretty and clean.

She turns to BJ, who stands just outside the door, one hand tucked into his jeans pocket, the other kneading the back of his neck. His eyes are droopy, like he's struggling to stay awake. He fell asleep a bunch of times in the waiting room. I wouldn't be the least bit surprised if he's got a neck crick.

"Why don't you give us a minute, Randall?" Lily says to BJ.

He nods once and crosses to his bedroom, but leaves the door open a crack.

"How you holding up?" Lily asks.

I lift a shoulder and let it fall. "I'm worried about my mom." Tears prick at my eyes, and I have to swallow all the emotions that threaten to overwhelm me.

She nods. "I'm sure you are."

"I shouldn't have left. I knew he was angry, and I left her alone with him," I admit.

Lily's eyes turn sad. "Oh, honey, this isn't your fault. It's a terrible accident, but you didn't cause it."

My chin trembles, and those tears I've been fighting leak out, because she doesn't realize I *did* cause it. I gave him the idea.

"Would you like a hug?"

I nod, and she wraps her arms around me. As I sink into the comfort, I realize this is what it's supposed to be like. The way I have to protect my mom from my dad isn't normal. I shouldn't be taking care of everyone else all the time. And that knowledge makes me cry harder, because the bubble I've been in for the past week has burst, and everything good feels like it's hanging in the balance, waiting to drop.

I don't know how long we stand there, BJ's mom holding onto me while I fall apart, but eventually my tears run dry. I'm so tired. So hopelessly exhausted.

Lily squeezes my hands. "Why don't you try to get some rest, okay?"

"Thank you, Mrs. Ballistic. For everything you're doing for me."

"It's Lily, honey. And we're here to help." She crosses the hall to BJ's room, and I notice my backpack is sitting just inside the door, which means BJ saw me snot-sobbing all over his mom. I don't even have the energy to be embarrassed.

The booze has been removed, so I'm guessing BJ tucked it away. I rummage around and find my toothbrush, then head for the bathroom. I always keep one with me for post hockey practice, so my mouthguard doesn't get funky. I cringe when I get a load of my reflection. My skin is blotchy, and there are huge, dark circles under my puffy, red eyes. I look as bad as I feel.

I use the bathroom and pull a fresh shirt from my bag. The dryer sheets inside don't mask the scent of stale cigarettes. But there's nothing I can do about that.

When I open the bathroom door, BJ is sitting on the edge of the bed. He looks tired and worried. He motions to the nightstand. "I brought you a glass of water." He extends his hand, palm facing up.

I cross the room and slip my fingers into his. He pulls me between his legs, settling a hand on my hip. He inspects my face.

"I look like shit."

"You look beautiful and sad and tired," he murmurs.

"I didn't want you to know how bad it was," I whisper.

"You've been fighting for a long time, huh?"

I bite my lips together. I don't want to cry again.

He wraps his arms around me. They're a family of huggers. "I can stay with you if you don't want to be alone tonight."

As much as I want the comfort, I don't want to give his parents a reason to send me home. "I'm a thrasher. I'll be okay on my own."

He stands and gives me a chaste kiss. "I'll leave my door open. If anything changes, you know where to find me."

"Okay." I climb under the covers, the sheets cool and soft against my legs. I'm used to being hot at night because we don't have air in the cabin. I grab one of the other pillows and curl around it, trying to calm my mind enough to sleep.

I get there, but bad dreams make it hard to stay that way.

I must be noisy, because eventually BJ raps on the door and slips inside. "I can't save you from the nightmares, but you don't need to suffer through them alone."

"What about your parents?"

"They'll understand." He climbs into my bed and curls his body around mine. "It's gonna be okay, Snowflake."

I want to believe him, but history tells me it probably won't be.

16

Open Your Eyes

WINTER

I GET a couple of hours of sleep with BJ wrapped around me. But I'm anxious and restless, so when six thirty rolls around, I climb out of bed, careful not to disturb him. I grab my backpack, change in the bathroom, and head downstairs. The house is quiet as I enter the kitchen. Huge windows offer a view of the lake and the sun cresting the horizon. The kitchen itself is bigger than our kitchen, dining room, and living room combined. The counter is white, polished stone. No empties litter the surface. There are no cigarette butts in the sink, no clutter on the counter.

My stomach rumbles as I fill my water bottle, and I glance at the pretty bowl piled high with fresh fruit. I won't snoop in their cupboards, but it would probably be okay for me to take something from the bowl. I grab a banana and a shiny, red apple. I eat the banana standing at the sink, trying to savor it. I drop the peel in the garbage and tuck the apple into my backpack. I leave a note so they don't wonder where I've disappeared to and hop on my bike.

I arrive at the hospital at seven thirty, half an hour before visiting hours begin, but the nurse at the desk lets me in to visit my mom right away.

A nurse is checking her vitals when I enter the room. She smiles when she sees me. "You must be Lucy's daughter."

"I'm Winter. The nurse at the front desk said it was okay that I'm early." I thumb over my shoulder and bite the inside of my cheek.

"Your timing is perfect. She's starting to come around again. She woke up for a few minutes a couple hours ago. She'll be groggy, and she might not remember what happened. That's normal. It can take anywhere from a few hours to a few days or sometimes longer for the memories to come back. Is your dad with you?"

"Oh, uh, no. I biked over."

"Ah, okay. Why don't you have a seat?" She motions to the chair beside the bed. "When she's alert, you can press this button."

"Okay."

The nurse leaves, and I take a seat in the chair beside the bed. Mom looks frail and small, machines hooked up to her battered body. I take her hand, noting the scrapes and bruises littering her non-casted arm. There's a round, blue spot on her biceps—maybe from where my dad grabbed her the other day. There might be matching circles on the other side, where his fingers dug in.

I catalog her injuries while I wait for her to come around. It's just after nine in the morning when she finally hums and her fingers twitch. A few minutes later, her eyes flutter open. She blinks blearily, like she's struggling to focus. That happens half a dozen times before her gaze settles on me. She opens her mouth, but all that comes out is a raspy croak.

"Hey. Hi, Mom."

Her eyes dart around, panicked.

"It's okay. You're okay. You're in the hospital, but you're okay." My voice cracks, and the tears start to fall. "I'm so glad you're awake. You scared us pretty bad." I run my thumb over her knuckles. "I'm gonna call the doctor, okay? Let them know you're awake."

She watches as I hit the button to call the nurse. "You've got a few broken bones and a concussion, but the doctor said you'll be okay," I assure her.

The nurse and the doctor arrive, and she introduces herself as Dr. Coule. She explains that my mom had a bad fall, and she required surgery to repair some of her broken bones, but that they expect her to make a full recovery. The nurse brings a straw to Mom's lips, and she takes a small sip, grimacing with the movement. They give her a moment before Dr. Coule asks the question I'm scared to know the answer to. "Do you remember how you fell?"

She tries to shake her head, but her brow furrows in pain.

"Take it easy. No sudden movements," Dr. Coule says. "You don't remember what happened?"

"No," Mom croaks.

Dr. Coule gives her a reassuring smile. "Event amnesia isn't uncommon with this kind of accident. The brain has to work hard to protect itself. It's possible your memory of the events will return over time. Your only job now is to rest and heal."

"Is there a chance she won't remember?" I ask.

"It's possible, but usually the memories come back with time." She tests Mom's reflexes and ability to follow a pen with her eyes. "Everything looks good. I'll be back before my shift ends to check in on you, Lucy." Dr. Coule turns to me. "Your mom will probably only be awake for short periods of time at first, but as she stabilizes, that will increase."

"Okay, thank you."

Once the nurse and Dr. Coule leave, I settle into the chair and take her hand again.

She clears her throat and whispers, "Clay."

"What about Dad?" I swallow past the lump in my throat.

"Is he here?" Her eyes shift toward the door.

I look over my shoulder, but there's no one there. I shake my head and bite my tongue.

"Can you call him?" she asks.

"You want him to come to the hospital?" My stomach twists and sinks.

She frowns, like she's trying to figure out my expression. "Time's it?"

"It's a little after nine. I can message him, let him know you're awake, if you want."

She starts to nod, but grimaces and croaks out, "Please."

My hands shake as I send a single message. Maybe seeing him will jog her memory. And it's better that I'm here when he comes. So I can keep her safe.

"How?" she asks.

"How did you get here?"

She taps her chin.

"What happened to my chin?"

"Yes."

"It was a hockey accident. I've been playing for the women's team at the Hockey Academy. I tripped and split my chin, but it's fine. The team doctor stitched me up. I'll explain, but one thing at a time, okay?"

"Okay." She licks her lips.

"Do you want some water?"

"Please."

I bring the straw to her lips, and she takes a small sip.

"You really don't remember what happened?"

She frowns and whispers, "I remember the college letter."

"That was the night before last. Dad found the letter and the tuition money in my dresser. He went to see friends and came back late. Do you remember that?"

She swallows. "Yes."

"I had a game the next morning. I didn't say anything because I knew it would upset Dad more. I split my chin during the game. He was drunk when I came home. You know how he can get when he's angry. He was really mean, and I just...was tired of feeling bad, so I left. I guess you must have gone outside on the deck. The railing gave way."

Her eyes widen, and she makes a sound, like a hiccup.

"Do you remember?"

She's quiet, as if she's searching for the memory. "Did I fall?"

"I don't know. But if you remember what happened, you can tell me. You're safe. Dad isn't here. It's okay to tell me the truth."

Her face falls, and she looks away. "I must have leaned on the railing."

I shake my head. "You knew how rickety it was."

She squeezes my hand and gives me a weak smile. "I always forget."

"No, you don't." I drop my head, more tears falling as I whisper, "You were knocked unconscious, Mom. You were in surgery for hours. It's going to take a while for you to heal. Probably at least a few months."

"I'm sorry you'll have to quit hockey."

That this is her solution to the problem is gutting.

I shake my head. "That's not fair."

"Then you won't hurt yourself, and your dad won't get so

upset." She smiles, like it's so easy, like she isn't dragging me right back into the hell I've been fighting to get out of my entire life.

I motion to the hospital room. "The Hockey Academy paid the insurance deductible, Mom, and they're helping me with the supplemental insurance forms so you can get the care you need. I won't quit."

"Knock, knock!" My dad's voice makes the hairs on the back of my neck stand on end.

I turn to find him in the doorway, holding a huge bouquet of wildflowers. Surprisingly, he's dressed like he gives a shit about his appearance. He's wearing a short-sleeve button-down shirt that's about two sizes too big, black dress pants that are an inch too short, and a pair of old running shoes that have been polished to hide the scuff marks.

The worst part is the way my mother's face lights up.

My dad's eyes skim over me, narrowing slightly before he plasters on a smile. "Hey, kiddo, it's good to see you here."

"Is it?" I glance between them.

He ignores me and rounds the bed, setting the flowers on the side table. He kisses my mother on the forehead. "How's my girl? Glad you're awake. Hopefully you'll be able to come home soon."

It's like I've entered the Twilight Zone. What if she never remembers? What if she does and she stays anyway? What if the next time she doesn't survive?

He turns to me. "You should come home too. Running off to your friend's house doesn't look good."

"Why? Because people might find out the truth about you? That you're an abusive asshole and the reason Mom is lying here?" My stomach twists into a knot of panic and anger.

His eyes flash with ire, and he glances toward the open

151

door. He lowers his voice to a threatening whisper, "You'd be wise to watch your mouth."

"Or what? What could you possibly do to hurt me? Especially here, with all these witnesses."

His gaze darts to my mom and back to me.

"Please don't fight," Mom whispers.

I don't have a chance to respond because a nurse knocks on the door. "Hi, Lucy. It's good to see you're awake. The doctor wants to run some tests this morning."

My mom's relief is palpable. And I get it. I really do. My dad's anger is a trigger, and she'll do anything to avoid it.

"What kind of tests?" I ask.

"Do you need to?" Dad narrows his eyes. "How much they gonna cost?"

"The doctor has ordered a CT scan, X-rays, and some bloodwork. It's all routine, but it'll take a few hours and most of it will be covered by your insurance policy. We have payment plans for the balance."

"The Hockey Academy is helping, too."

"We're not looking for handouts," Dad snaps.

"It's not a handout. They have a family fund and they're helping me with supplemental insurance forms. These tests are important."

He seems to realize fighting with me in front of a nurse over Mom's care probably isn't the best idea. "Okay. If she needs them, then."

I check the time. It's almost nine thirty. "I'll come back later, unless you want me to stick around, Mom."

"It's okay. The doctor and nurses will take good care of me." She smiles.

I lean over and press a kiss to her cheek. Dad does the same and tells her he'll be back when his shift is over.

I thank the nurse and leave. I don't wait for my dad. I just rush through the doors and take the stairs to the parking lot.

Panic hits me as I ride home. Hope is slipping through my fingers, fear taking its place. Worry that I'm going to end up stuck here forever, unable to escape this life, wraps around me like choking vines.

It takes me a little better than twenty minutes to bike home from the hospital. I don't know how long my mom will be there, or how long the Ballistics' invitation to sleep in their spare room will last. But I don't plan to stay in this cabin. Not with my dad.

I see this place through different eyes as I walk my bike around to the side, out of sight in case Dad comes down the driveway. There's a path that leads through the woods to the road, so I can leave without running into him again.

With my bike stashed, I open the front door. The smell of cigarettes seems stronger than ever. Empty beer cans litter the counter and the sink. My hands itch to clean up, but it's not my mess. I don't even glance at the deck, not yet. First I need to gather as much of my stuff as I can.

I fill a small duffle with clothes and slide my notebooks and the textbook for my online class into my backpack. Once both bags are stuffed to bursting, I leave my bedroom. My throat feels tight, and my stomach rolls as I open the sliding door and step outside into the hot summer morning. Guilt tears through me. An entire section of railing is missing, a gaping hole left behind.

If I hadn't lied, my mother wouldn't be broken.

17

The Scene of the Crime

DJ

I WAKE ALONE in the spare room. The clock on the nightstand reads ten thirty. A message from Winter lets me know she's at the hospital for visiting hours. It was sent at seven, so she hardly slept at all. Her backpack is missing, but a couple outfits are folded neatly on top of the dresser.

In addition to Winter's message, the group chat has blown up. Lovey heard about the accident from her parents, and because this community is small, and we're a tight-knit group, bad news travels fast.

My parents are at the arena according to my most recent message from Mom, but they plan to pop by the hospital later. Adele asked if I wanted to tag along to her costume fitting this afternoon. This is the third fitting for this costume, so I peace out.

I message Winter and get in the shower. But it isn't until I'm in the kitchen, making toast and packing food into an insulated cooler bag to take to the hospital, that Winter finally responds.

And the message has me abandoning my toast and grabbing my keys.

The drive to Winter's place takes ten minutes.

I park in the spot where we had our first kiss. It feels like a million years have passed since that happened. There's a narrow path leading into the forest about twenty feet from her driveway, so I duck under the branches, stepping over moss-covered fallen trees, mushrooms growing from their decaying shells. It smells earthy and fresh out here. The forest has no idea there's been a trauma recently. No clue that sadness and fear linger like heavy storm clouds.

I come out of the forest by a wooden shelter. I haven't seen Winter's place during the day before. It's an original build from the sixties. At the time, it would have been beautiful, a wood-sided cabin perched on top of the hill, overlooking the lake.

Most of the original cottages have been replaced by huge homes, but this one remains—run down and tired, in need of TLC.

Much like the people who inhabit it.

I hope her dad isn't here. If I run into him, there's a damn good chance I'll do something stupid and reckless. But I won't leave Winter to navigate this nightmare on her own. So I follow the narrow footpath, traveling the perimeter of the cabin. Her bike rests against a tree, her backpack and a small duffle beside it on the ground. Only a few feet of space separate the house from the forest, as though it wants to absorb the cabin back into itself.

The pillars that support the deck are made of old cinder

block. The poured cement is cracked and crumbling in places, and the punky wooden beams need replacing.

Splintered wood like giant toothpicks litters the ground. And sitting at the edge of the debris, her knees hugged to her chest, is Winter.

I cross the uneven terrain, following her line of sight to the empty space where a railing should be. It's a long way down. The landscape is rocky, patchy with grass and covered in deceptively lush moss that squishes under my feet. The landing wouldn't be forgiving. Every new piece of the puzzle provides clarity on Winter's bad situation. And how good she is at hiding it.

"How's your mom?" I sink to the ground beside her.

"She's awake. She doesn't remember anything yet. My dad came to the hospital, and I couldn't handle seeing her happy about him being there. The doctor ordered some tests this morning, so I'll go back in a couple hours." She runs her fingers over the moss-covered rock beside her.

"And this was the first place you thought to come?"

"I needed to get some stuff. And I wanted to see for myself what happened." She motions to the broken railing. "If I'd stayed home and dealt with my dad, she'd be okay."

Of course she's blaming herself. It's all she knows. It's what she's been taught. "You didn't choose him as your father. And you didn't choose to stay with an abusive partner. You have every right to feel sad and angry that your mom is where she is, but *you* didn't do this to her."

She plucks a piece of grass and rolls it between her fingers. "The worst part is that I keep thinking about what will happen to me. What I stand to lose," she whispers. "I'm just so fucking selfish."

"You're a lot of things, but selfish isn't one of them." I put an arm around her, and it takes a moment before her shoulders relax. She leans into me, succumbing to the need for comfort. "Your heart has too many cracks already, Snowflake. Don't go shattering it by carrying burdens you don't deserve."

"I'm not used to relying on other people, BJ."

"I get that, but it's never too late to flip the script and try something different."

She blows out a breath. "I don't trust stability. It's unfamiliar."

"That makes sense, considering what you've faced. And you have valid reasons to be skeptical." I motion to the decaying cabin. "But all being here does is pull you back down to places that hurt. It's an emotional sinkhole. Once you step in, it's hard to get out on your own."

"I was a mess before this happened. I'm going to be an even bigger mess now," she says softly.

I thread my fingers through hers. "I guess it's good I like messy, then, huh?"

She huffs a laugh. "Why aren't you running in the opposite direction yet?"

"Why are you so married to that potential course of action?"

She motions to our surroundings. "This place is a huge step up from where we were living before. You and I are just so different. We don't make sense."

I shift so I'm sitting in front of her, blocking her view of the broken railing. "I like you. Full stop. I like hanging out with you. I like that we both live and breathe for time on the ice. I like that you're a badass and a fighter and you don't back down. I like that we're the same in a lot of ways and different in so many others." I settle my palms on her knees. "I get that you're guarded, and that life hasn't always been kind to you, so I'm going to give you a free pass on this whole trying-to-push-me-away shit. Unfortunately for you, it's not going to work. I'm a tenacious fucker with a capital T, and I don't back down either. If you hate the box that's been made for you, stop stepping back into it."

She throws her hands in the air. "I don't know anything else!"

"I'm right fucking here, Winter. I'm the something else." I push to standing and hold out my hand. "Being here won't make things better."

She pulls her bottom lip between her teeth. "I'm scared."

"Of course you are. Everything about this situation is fucking terrifying, but you don't have to be terrified alone." I flip my hand over.

She takes it, and I pull her to her feet. And then I wrap my arms around her and hug the shit out of her. It only takes a second for her to return it. She melts like a snowflake on skin.

"Everything was going great until this happened," she murmurs.

"I know."

"I don't want to lose this good thing."

I press my lips to her temple. "Then stop visiting the places that make you feel like you will." I tuck a loose tendril of hair behind her ear. "You don't need to torture yourself like this."

"I needed to see it."

"And now you have, so it's time to go." I cup her face in my hands and wait until her eyes meet mine. "This is not your fault. *You* did not cause this. Playing hockey is not a crime, and neither is getting stitches or hanging out with a sexy, tattooed figure skater who gets emotional boners over you. That sexy guy is me, in case you weren't sure."

She shoves at my chest, fighting a grin.

"Come on. Let's get you out of Wallow World."

She lets me guide her toward the gap in the trees. I grab her bike on the way, and she takes her bags. When we reach the

Jeep, I clip her bike to the rack and unlock the doors. Winter tosses her bags in the trunk, then climbs into the passenger seat, and I take my place behind the wheel.

I turn the engine over and roll down our windows since it's humid and steamy hot today. "Want me to see if I can get us some ice time?"

She tugs on the end of her braid. "I should go back to the hospital."

"Honest question, is this so you can marinate in guilt that isn't yours some more?"

She lets her head drop against the rest and rolls it toward me. "I want to be there when she's done with the tests."

"How long will those take?"

"The nurse said a few hours. And that was around nine thirty."

"*A few hours* in hospital time is usually longer. If you're planning to sit for the rest of the day, getting on the ice first would help burn off some of your anxious energy." I tap the wheel. "How about this, I'll see if we can book a rink. If we can, we'll reset with a little ice time. Then we grab food, and I take you back to the hospital." I pull out my phone and check the schedule. "Rink four is open."

She pinches the bridge of her nose. "It feels selfish."

"That's because you're used to putting everyone's needs ahead of your own. Why don't we drive to the arena and see how you feel once we're there. If it's a thumbs-down, I'll take you to the hospital. If it's a thumbs-up, we'll stay as long as you're comfortable." This is probably the biggest hurdle for Winter. Putting herself first. Because she's been taught she should be at the bottom of the list.

"Okay. We can stop at the arena."

I shift into drive, and she stares out the window as I pass

her driveway. I turn up the radio, not to discourage talking, but so she doesn't feel compelled to fill the silence.

When we reach the arena, I pull into a parking spot, but don't cut the engine. "How do you feel about being here?"

"Like it wouldn't hurt to spend some time on the ice with you."

"Good. I was hoping you'd say that. Come on, let's do this." I turn off the Jeep, and we grab our backpacks from the trunk.

Winter stops by the women's locker room to get her skates, and then we head to rink four. We lace up, and I turn on the music, choosing something upbeat. I hold open the gate for Winter, and she takes my hand as we step onto the ice. We lap the rink a few times, finding our stride.

"Thank you. I needed this more than I realized," she says.

"Sometimes it makes sense to do something normal when everything else isn't." I pull her closer, my feet bracketing hers as I move us to the center of the rink. "It's okay to take a break from the trauma of it all."

And that's what we do. I spend the next half hour teaching her basic figure-skating moves, distracting her from the noise in her head.

I lace my right hand with her left and tap my shoulder. "Put your hand here."

She does as I ask. "What are you doing?"

"Teaching you something new." I guide her through the motions, adjusting her position so our bodies are close, one leg bracketing hers to help support her as I move us in a circle that tightens until we're in a slow spin.

"Pairs skating is intimate," she murmurs.

"It's mostly technical, and physically strenuous." I pull her tight against me. "But this is intentionally intimate." I drop my head and brush my lips over her cheek. "When I'm on the ice with Adele, I'm focused on the technical aspects, but when I'm on the ice with you, it's all about getting closer."

She tips her chin up, eyes searching mine. "Now would be a great time to kiss me. FYI."

I drop my mouth to hers and part my lips. Our tongues meet and tangle, our slow spin losing momentum until we stop altogether.

Eventually she breaks the kiss, but one hand stays curved around the back of my neck. "You make it easy to forget myself."

"Good. That was the plan."

Her fingers drift along the collar of my T-shirt. "I should probably hit the shower and go back to the hospital."

I finger the end of her braid. "Do you want help?"

She arches a brow. "Help?"

"In the shower. I give a mean scalp massage. But no pressure."

She's quiet for a few seconds, possibly contemplating.

"It doesn't have to lead to anything, Snowflake. I'd love to take care of you the way you take care of everyone else, whatever that looks like for you."

She bites her knuckle. "Okay. Yeah. I'd like that."

I smile and take her hand. "Come on, then."

We bring our backpacks with us into the locker room and leave our skates under the bench. I nab a few fresh towels from the linen closet and follow Winter past the communal showers to the private ones with plastic curtain dividers. I set the towels on the bench outside the stall and turn on the water, then pull my shirt over my head as Winter does the same. She looks over my chest and shakes her head. "God, you're beautiful. One day I want you to tell me the story behind all your art."

"It's how I memorialize the people and events that mean the most to me."

"Makes sense." She pulls her sports bra over her head, careful to avoid her chin. She hooks her fingers into her leggings and huffs a laugh. "Why am I nervous?"

"You don't have to get naked-naked. It's whatever you feel comfortable with." I keep my eyes on hers.

"I'm boxy," she mumbles.

"Says who?" I arch a brow. "I've already seen you in a bathing suit, so I'm hella familiar with your curves. You're strong and athletic, and you're damn well gorgeous, Winter. Everything about you is."

Her bottom lip slides through her teeth. "Can we drop trou at the same time?"

"Absolutely." I cock my head and wiggle my eyebrows, hoping to keep the mood light. "Pants only, or pants and panties?"

She laughs. "Pants and panties."

"On three?"

She nods. "On three."

I tuck my thumbs into the waistband of my joggers and count down. On three, we both slide our pants and underwear over our thighs and step out of them, hanging them on the hooks outside the shower stall. I pull back the curtain and step under the spray. Winter follows, pulling the curtain closed behind her.

When she turns to face me, her mouth drops open. "Holy fuckballs." Her gaze jumps from my eyes to my erection. "That's... Wow. That had to hurt."

"Probably less than you think. A Prince Albert piercing is surprisingly low on the pain scale."

"Well, that's a seriously unexpected surprise."

I hold out my hand and she takes it, letting me pull us under the spray. "How's the temperature?"

"Fine." She catches my arched brow. "I mean good." Her

eyes drop again. "Statistically speaking, you're already way above average. You didn't need to bling out your dick to make it more enticing."

I laugh. "It makes sex better."

"Does it now?"

"Mm." I nod.

"For you or your partner?"

"Both."

When she reaches out, I catch her hand. "How about you let me take care of you right now?"

"But you're hard."

"I'll calm down eventually." I spin her so her back is to my chest and pull the tie free on the end of her braid, separating the strands until her hair hangs in a curtain down her back, almost grazing the dimples above her luscious, very bitable ass. I squirt a generous amount of shampoo into my palm—the stuff at the arena smells nice—and run it through her hair before I massage it into her scalp.

"Oh my God, you weren't kidding about the scalp massage." She tips her head back, groaning as I knead tense muscles.

"When I was in high school, I took cosmetology."

"Because it was mostly girls?"

"Basically, yeah."

Winter laughs. "Figures."

"I learned some great skills though, this being one."

"Not gonna argue with that. I don't think anyone has helped me wash my hair since I was three."

"Anytime you want to shower with me, I'm in," I tell her.

When I'm done massaging her scalp, I rinse all the soap out, then finger-comb conditioner through the ends. I take my time, aware that once this is over, she'll likely stay at the hospital until visiting hours end. It's a short reprieve from the endless trauma.

Winter turns and runs her hands over my chest. She steps closer, and my erection, which has not chilled in the least, bumps her stomach. She looks down. "Doesn't seem like you're calming much."

"Eventually doesn't have a time limit."

She steps closer, until her warm, wet, naked body is pressed against mine. "Isn't that uncomfortable?"

"Sometimes connection is more important than gratification." I sweep her hair back over her shoulders. "Can I wash the rest of you now?"

She nods once.

I start at her arms, squirting body wash onto my palm and running it gently over her skin. I wash every inch of her, avoiding all the obvious parts, and focusing on those insidious erogenous zones that make her breath hitch. When I skim the curve of her ass, she whimpers.

"Please tell me this is going to end with an orgasm."

I cup her cheek and carefully tip her chin up until she looks into my eyes. "Is that how you'd like this to end?"

She runs her hands over my chest. "I figured getting naked in the shower together wasn't going to have a PG conclusion."

"Whatever you need, however you need it, I'll give it to you." I slip my fingers between her thighs. She sighs when I glide over her clit and moans when I ease two fingers inside. She grips the back of my neck and pulls my mouth to hers, rolling her hips with every curl of my fingers.

"You're so good at making me feel good," she moans against my lips.

"Anytime you need a distraction, I've got you."

Her palm curves around my erection, and my eyes roll up. I cover her hand. "Let me finish taking care of you first, please." I already know she's close. I can feel it in the way her legs tremble.

"I don't want it to end," she murmurs.

"It doesn't have to. I just want you to come before you mess with my focus."

She laughs and then groans when I stroke along the spot inside that lights her up. And then she's grabbing my shoulders, hips jerking as she clenches around my fingers.

"So fucking sexy," I whisper.

When her eyes flutter open, she reaches for me again, fingers wrapping around my length. She starts to stroke, slow and firm, thumb sweeping over the head and circling the ball at the ridge on the way down.

I plant a palm on the wall behind her and shift my hips forward. My fingers are still inside her, so I adjust my position, intent on making her feel good while she does the same for me.

"Oh good God." Her eyes flare, her strokes faltering when I hit the right spot.

It takes a moment, but she finds a rhythm, moving her hand in time to the pump and curl of my fingers.

"How are you—again." Her eyes roll up, and she shudders as another orgasm hits her.

I wait until I'm sure she's crested the wave before I withdraw my fingers and cover the hand wrapped around my erection with my own so I can help her keep the rhythm. "So damn good, Snowflake."

Her hazy gaze stays locked on mine as the orgasm rolls through me. Then she pulls me in for a slow, lazy kiss.

Eventually we break apart, and she grins up at me. "Thanks. I really needed that."

"Like I said, whatever you need, however you need it, Snowflake, I'll give it to you."

I turn off the water and grab our towels, tossing one to Winter.

"BJ? Are you in here? I thought you weren't coming to the rink this afternoon!"

I have just enough time to cover my junk before Adele rounds the corner.

18

Down Shift

WINTER

"OH! OH MY GOD!" Adele openly gapes at BJ, who's wearing nothing but a towel.

This is not ideal. At all.

Adele crosses her arms. "This is why you were too busy to come to the costume fitting?"

BJ seems completely unaffected by her presence. "Wanna give us a couple of minutes, Adele?"

She pokes at her cheek with her tongue, eyes shifting to me for a second before she whirls and stomps off.

"You didn't have to bail on a costume fitting for me." I don't want to be the reason for a fight between him and his partner, especially since they spend a lot of time with blades on their feet.

"This is the third fitting. I went to the last two. She keeps adding embellishments, and sitting there while they pin more sequins to her is a colossal waste of my time."

"Three fittings? Is that typical?"

"It is for Adele."

"Gotcha." I don't know much about Adele, other than she's his pairs partner. She seems a little high maintenance, but then, BJ is always striving for perfection on the ice, so maybe this is one way she tries to attain it too.

BJ glances at our sweaty outfits hanging from the hooks. "You got a change of clothes in your backpack?"

"Yeah." I'd like to avoid more awkward run-ins with Adele until I'm fully dressed.

"I'll grab your bag." He disappears around the corner and returns a few seconds later.

We rush to get dressed, and I stuff my dirty clothes in the large Ziplock I carry with me. It prevents my bag from smelling like sweat and dirty underwear.

"I'm sorry the afterglow bubble burst so quickly," BJ says.

"Don't apologize. You couldn't have known this would happen." I check my phone. It's after twelve. My mom should be back in her room soon.

I wipe down my skate blades and tie the laces together so I can sling them over my shoulder, then follow BJ out of the locker room.

Adele is in full skater gear, makeup and all, leaning against the boards. Her expression makes her look like she swallowed an entire bottle of lemon juice and chased it with vinegar. She tries to smile at me, but it's more of a constipated grimace. She did just walk in on us in the shower together, so I can't blame her for being unimpressed.

I turn to BJ. "My mom should be done with her tests."

"I'll give you a ride back to the hospital."

"It's cool. I'll bike over." I smile at Adele. "Your costume looks great."

Adele looks down at herself. "This is just a practice outfit."

"Right, okay." Clearly I'm not winning any points here. I turn back to BJ and make things even more awkward. "Thanks for—" I motion to the rink.

Adele scoffs.

Yeah. Time to roll.

"Text if you need anything." BJ's fingers brush mine as I pass.

"I'll catch up with you later." I force a smile for Adele. "Nice to see you again."

She makes a noise but doesn't respond with words.

I'm all about running away and leaving BJ to deal with the residual awkwardness. Unfortunately my water bottle is on the other side of the rink, so I glide across the ice in my running shoes to retrieve it.

Adele's voice echoes off the walls. "Seriously, BJ? You blew me off so you could what? Fuck your summer fling in the freaking locker-room shower? And you're on me about keeping my priorities straight."

"First of all, I didn't blow you off. You're the one who keeps having your costume altered. Me being there won't make you any happier with the way it looks. And secondly, my personal life isn't your business."

I step off the ice, grab my water bottle, and set BJ's on the sill so he doesn't forget it. Then I leave before I overhear any more of a conversation that isn't meant for my ears. I return my skates to my locker, unclip my bike from BJ's Jeep, and make the short trip to the hospital.

I've just locked up my bike in the hospital lot when Logan Butterson comes strolling out the front door, dressed in his police uniform.

I freeze in the middle of the sidewalk. "Is my mom okay? Did something happen?"

He holds up a hand. "Everything's fine. Nothing to worry about. I just stopped in to see Lucy."

"And ask her about what happened?" I fiddle with my backpack strap. Something hard is digging into the base of my spine.

He nods. "Yeah. I was hoping she might be able to fill in some of the gaps, but she's having trouble remembering."

"The doctors call it event amnesia. It's because she hit her head and has a concussion." I hate how on edge I am.

"Yeah, that's what they were saying." He rocks back on his heels. He has kind eyes that are so blue they remind me of tropical beaches. He looks like a Ken doll in a cop uniform, but with a rugged edge. "You mind if I ask you a couple of questions about what happened?"

"I wasn't home." I swallow down the guilt.

"Yeah, that's what your dad said last night. He mentioned you hadn't been honest about where you were, what you were doing, and who you were doing it with." He tucks his thumbs into his pockets. Casual. Easy. Open.

I bite back a scathing response and pinch the bridge of my nose. "He doesn't want me to play hockey, and he doesn't want me to hang out with BJ. I was doing both behind my parents' back."

"You're over eighteen, yeah?"

I nod. "I'll be twenty in the fall."

He hums and leans against the brick wall. "Are things a bit rigid at home?"

"Rigid?"

"You're an adult. You're playing competitive hockey, you have a job, and you seem pretty responsible, at least from where I'm standing. Doesn't make sense that your parents would keep you on such a tight leash."

I huff a laugh. "Well, it wouldn't make sense to someone

like you. And it's not my parents; it's mostly my dad." I cringe. "Fuck. Sorry. That was disrespectful, and that's not how I meant it."

A half smile quirks up. "Don't sweat it. You're under a lot of stress. Want to have a seat and explain what you mean?" He nods to the bench nearby.

"Sure. Okay." Saying no to a cop seems like a bad idea.

I fall into step beside him, his strides slow and measured.

"Your dad is a hockey legend," I note.

"Yup. He sure is."

"So you grew up comfortable, right? Lots of opportunities?" I shrug off my backpack and drop down on the bench, setting it at my feet.

"I did." He takes a seat beside me but leaves a foot of space between us.

"You've seen my house. It's the nicest place I've ever lived, which is saying something."

"Lots of people struggle financially." He crosses his legs, ankle resting on his knee.

"I know. But it's more than the financial struggle." What BJ said about not staying inside the box that's been made for me anymore is starting to make sense. Keeping these dirty family secrets isn't doing me any good. All it does is tether me to a life I don't want. "Hockey is expensive, so the money thing is an issue, but more than that, it costs me time, when I don't have much to spare. My dad thinks I should be working more instead of playing so I can help with the household expenses."

Logan shifts and rests his arm on the back of the bench. "Aren't you doing that with your job at Boones?"

"Yeah, but playing hockey means I'm not home to do the chores, like cut the grass, or make dinner, or make sure the garbage is taken care of and the house is clean. And in his eyes, hanging out with BJ is another way I'm shirking my responsibilities. Plus, he lives on the nice side of the lake."

"So do you," he points out.

"Yeah, but the cabin is falling apart. Hanging out with BJ and his friends, playing for the Hockey Academy, to my dad, it's me striving for something I shouldn't. He thinks I should be happy with what I have. And the worst part is, I get where he's coming from, even though I don't want to."

Logan frowns. "Can you explain that?"

"We got into a fight yesterday when I came home with stitches in my face." I motion to my chin. "A visit to the hospital is an expense we normally avoid. I tried to tell him it was covered by the hockey program, but he just...lost his shit. Accused me of..." I tip my head up and focus on a fluffy cloud floating in the sky, gritting my teeth against the prick behind my eyes.

"You're a useless fucking whore. You think that boy likes you? He knows you're easy. Gonna treat you like the trash you are. Just you wait and see."

"Mostly he was looking for a reason to fight, and he wanted someone to take his frustration out on, and that person is usually me or my mom. Playing for the women's team is a dream come true. BJ and your sister Lovey and Rose are all great. Everyone has been so nice, and it's hard to be part of that and then go back to the arguing. To see the other side is one thing, but to live in it..." I sigh and shake my head. "It makes me want to keep it."

He shakes his head. "You're talking like that's not possible."

I give him a look. "Come on, Officer Butterson."

"Just call me Logan."

"Okay, Officer Logan, even if things go great this summer and playing for the women's team opens doors, how will I walk through them? My mom won't be able to work for weeks, maybe even months, because of her injuries. She's got pins and plates in her leg and her arm. She's suffered a concussion, so who even knows what the lasting damage of that will be. Logically, working at the diner is probably out after this. It's too physically demanding. And she doesn't have her high school diploma. Neither of my parents does. So what kind of job can she get? She only qualifies for minimum-wage work, and her tips were a big part of how we got by, because at least we could hide some of them from my dad so he wouldn't blow everything on fucking beer and smokes." I raise a hand. "Sorry about the swearing."

"No apology needed. I'd be pissed too if the fridge was bare, and the garbage was full of death darts and empties."

"It's just so frustrating. And she's gonna need so much support when she gets out of the hospital. How will I work and take care of her, let alone make time for hockey or school or anything else? You see what I mean, right? How uphill this battle is? How hard it is to have all these great people trying to make things happen for me, and it's just one barricade after another."

"Not much has worked out in your favor, has it?"

"I try to enjoy the good things while they last, but this..." I shake my head. "The night before my mom fell, my dad and I got into it, which is obviously a pretty freaking regular occurrence. I told my mom I was at the library, but I was with BJ, and my dad saw me on the lake, which pissed him off because it meant I wasn't home doing chores or whatever. But it got worse when he found my acceptance letter to college, and the money I'd saved for tuition. I'm trying to take more than one course at a time so I can complete my degree faster. I kept the money in a lockbox in my dresser. I planned to put it in my account when it was time to pay for classes. But he took it all, and my mom just...let him."

His expression darkens, so I rush on, compelled to defend her. "I don't blame her. She can't take him on the way I can."

His cheek tics. "What does that mean, 'take him on the way I can'?"

I pick at a hangnail. "I think you know what it means."

"Can you spell it out for me, so I'm sure we're on the same page?"

I look away. "Sometimes he gets physical."

"Physical how?"

"He'll push her around. Or me. One time he went after her, and I'd been playing a lot of hockey—street and ice, lots of time slapping a puck around, and he's...wiry. I stopped him before he could do any real damage."

"How'd you manage that?" He's so calm, his voice even and gently inquisitive. But there's a tic in his right eye that gives away the undercurrent of rage. I appreciate it, even if I don't need him to defend me.

"To be clear, I know that violence isn't the answer, but he was hurting her, and I needed him to stop. So I knocked him out. With one punch." I'd been so scared. Afraid he would do something we couldn't come back from. Afraid I'd done just that. But he came around five minutes later. Washed down a couple of Tylenol with beer and went to the trailer park for a couple of days.

His jaw tics. "Seems like self-defense. Did it stop after that?"

"The physical stuff, yeah. But the other night when he took all my tuition money and found out I'd been lying, he got real angry and grabbed my mom's arm. She might even have bruises. It was only a couple days ago." It feels like a year has passed. I explain what happened, how I backed my dad into a corner to scare him, how I told him to take a drive and cool off, and how the next night my mom fell off the deck in the exact same spot. "I'm worried, though, because even if she does remember, she might still say it's her fault—and not because she's lying for him, but because she believes it's true. They've been together since she was in high school. She had me when she was seventeen. Twenty years is a lot of time with someone telling you it's always your fault. It's hard not to believe it's true, you know?" I bite the inside of my cheek and fight to keep my emotions locked down. "She's conditioned to believe she's the problem." And I'm conditioned to protect her from him. To take the heat off her. To absorb the abuse. But I'm so damn tired.

"It doesn't sound like much of a coincidence." Logan rubs his chin, his frown deepening. "I think you probably already know this, but I'm going to lay it out for you anyway. Without a corroborating story from your mother or some proof, like a video or photos, it'll be hard to prove he's at fault. But what I can do is take the information you've given me and start building a case."

I press my fingers to my temples, squeezing my eyes shut. "I don't know what I'll do if she doesn't remember, or worse, if she owns it."

"Sometimes people have to find the bottom before they start looking for a way back to the surface," Logan says softly.

"I don't want the bottom to be a grave." I dash away the stupid tears as they fall.

He pulls one of those little tissue packs from his pocket and hands it to me. "We're going to do everything we can to ensure that doesn't happen."

"But how?"

"You're hooked up with families who have a lot of connections. One thing at a time, though." His expression is full of empathy. "This hamster wheel your mom is stuck on, it doesn't have to be yours too. I know you want to protect her, but who's protecting you?"

"She doesn't know how to get out."

"Sometimes the best way to get someone to see what's possible is to save yourself." He pulls a card out of his pocket and passes it to me. "If there's anything else you think I should know, or if there's anything you need, just give me a call, okay?"

"Yeah. Sure." I slide the card into my backpack. "Thanks."

"Of course. You going in?" He tips his chin toward the hospital.

"Yeah. Thanks for the talk."

"No problem. You know how to get in touch if you need anything."

He stands, and so do I, and we turn in separate directions.

I take the elevator back to my mom's room. Her eyes pop open as I slide into the chair beside her bed, and she gives me a small smile. "You're back."

"You need anything? Something to drink? Eat?"

She flinches when she tries to shake her head. "I'm okay."

"How are you feeling?" There's a heaviness in the air, as if it's weighted down with questions that don't have answers.

"Tired and sore."

I nod. "Makes sense. It was a bad fall."

"That handsome police officer stopped by."

"Logan Butterson. I ran into him in the parking lot."

"He asked a lot of questions about what happened." She smooths her blanket.

"That's his job. What'd you tell him?" I know the answer, but I ask anyway.

"I told him the truth. That I can't remember." She glances at the nightstand. "Can I have some water? I'm thirsty."

"Sure, Mom." I bring the straw to her mouth, and she sips.

"Officer Butterson said you're a great hockey player, that

you have real promise. That must be true because you have that scholarship." She frowns again. "I'm sorry Clay ripped up the letter."

The scholarship has nothing to do with hockey, but that's not important right now. "It's okay, Mom. It's not your fault."

Her chin trembles. "He just gets so mad sometimes, and I don't know what to do."

I push her hair back off her forehead. "I know, Mom. It's okay. You don't have to worry about that."

She takes my hand in her uncasted one and whispers, "Sometimes I think about leaving."

Occasionally she'll make an off-hand comment about telling him to move out, but never when he's around, and usually when she's annoyed with him. But this seems different, like a guilty admission.

"Are you starting to remember?"

She looks away. "I don't know. It's all so confusing. I remember the fighting, but it's foggy."

"The doctor said it might take a while for it to come back to you. You should just rest."

"I am tired. Maybe it'll be clearer next time I wake up."

I smile. "Maybe."

"Will you stay for a while?"

"Of course."

She smiles. "You're a good girl, Winter. A real miracle."

"Thanks, Mom." I kiss her forehead and settle in the chair beside her bed.

Another seed of hope takes root. If she remembers what happened, maybe she'll finally do the one thing she's always been too afraid to: leave the abuse.

19

The Light

WINTER

WITH MY MOM awake and stable, I resume my shifts at Boones. I work from seven to one, Monday through Friday, then visit with my mom for a few hours before hockey practice. After that, I have dinner with the team at Iced Out before I spend a couple of hours at the library working on assignments for my course. BJ's house has more than one computer, but I like the library, and it gives me an excuse to see Clover.

When my homework is done, I return to the hospital and stay until visiting hours end. BJ picks me up, and we make out in his Jeep for a while before we go back to his place. Sometimes we jump in the hot tub or go for a late swim and make out some more, but sometimes we're both so exhausted, we go to our bedrooms and pass out.

A week after the fall, the doctors deem my mom ready to be moved from the hospital to a rehabilitation facility which is covered by the Hockey Academy's family fund. I'm beyond relieved that she doesn't have to go home yet, especially since she still can't remember what happened. BJ's parents assure me that she'll be able to stay in rehab until she's mobile again, and that their spare room is mine for as long as I need it.

Yesterday BJ and I stopped at the cabin to grab clothes for my mom while my dad was at work. The house was in even worse shape than before. Empties covered every surface, the sink was piled high with dishes, and ashtrays overflowed with butts.

We took my mom's clothes back to BJ's and washed them twice to get the cigarette smell out. I also grabbed a couple of family photo albums because she's been asking for them.

The hospital is transporting her to the facility in one of their vans, and I meet her there so I can help get her settled. The Sunshine Center is a beautiful, renovated house down the street from the library, and it's partially funded by the Buttersons.

I wheel my mom up the ramp, and we're greeted by Lovey. "Hey! Hi!" She abandons her post and rushes over, pulling me into a hug. "I saw your mom's name on the intake sheet, and I hoped I'd still be here when you arrived." She turns to my mom, her smile warm as she extends her hand. "Hi, Mrs. Marks. I'm Lovey, a friend of Winter's."

"It's nice to meet you." Mom smiles nervously.

"Lovey's dad is one of the coaches over at the Hockey Academy. Her brother is Officer Butterson."

"Oh, he came to visit me in the hospital and brought me this." She lifts the aloe plant in her lap. She refused to let me put it in a box. "He's quite handsome. Like a Ken doll."

Lovey laughs. "That's an excellent description. Come on. I'll show you around and we can get you settled in your room."

We're introduced to several staff members. There's always a nurse on duty, and a doctor on call, as well as nurses' aides to assist the patients. The center has a physical therapy clinic, a dining room with the daily menu posted, and access to a snack and salad bar all day. There's also a common room with a huge flat-screen TV, two shelves full of books, and a games and craft area.

"The daily schedule is posted here every morning. If there's anything you want to participate in, just let one of our staff members know, and they'll help you register. We also collaborate with the library, so if there are events you'd like to attend, we can arrange to get you there." Lovey points to a screen listing various activities scheduled throughout the day, including meal times, and a second schedule with the library's calendar of events.

When I start to push Mom's chair toward the hallway that leads to the patient rooms, she pats my hand. "Wait." She squints at the screen. "GED classes? Is that something anyone can sign up for?"

Lovey, bless her heart, doesn't even flinch. "Absolutely. Clover Sweet is the head librarian. She can get you enrolled if you're interested."

"That might be nice."

"Great. Once you're unpacked, we can work on setting that up."

Lovey shows us to my mom's room and gives us a quick tour. It's like a small, self-contained studio apartment, complete with a private, occupational bathroom.

"If you need anything, just let one of the staff know." Lovey winks at me on the way out. "I'll text you later, okay?"

"Yeah. Thank you." It comes out a little choked.

"We got you."

She closes the door behind her. Mom presses her fingers to her lips, on the edge of emotion. "It's so nice here."

"It really is," I agree.

"It'd be easy to get used to this, wouldn't it?" she whispers.

"The having help or the peacefulness?" I ask.

"Both."

OVER THE NEXT FEW DAYS, mom settles in at the Sunshine Center. Yesterday she attended her first GED class. Clover helps run the literacy component of the program, and this evening she offered my mom some one-on-one support.

The three of us are gathered at a table. BJ lent me his laptop so I can type up my assignments wherever I am. My mom and Clover are sitting beside each other, sharing a set of earbuds. Clover's introducing her to audiobooks, so my mom can listen and read at the same time.

My phone buzzes in my pocket, and I pull it out to check the message.

> lessons done, I can pick u up if ur still at TSC. Parents r out w friends. I need to make good on TFT, which still applies since it's Thursday.

I glance over at my mom and Clover, who are focused on the reading tablet in front of them. I snap a quick pic.

> at the library. How adorable is this?

> 💚 Mav is here so we'll head ur way in a bit

> sounds good

I slip my phone into my bag and finish the final question for my assignment.

"I like this narrator's voice," Mom whispers. "It's almost like I'm part of the story."

"He's a personal favorite. He could read a grocery list and I'd listen all day long," Clover says with a smirk.

"His voice really is lovely."

Clover and I share a smile. It's nice to see this side of my mom, one where she's not on edge, worried about pissing my dad off, or figuring out how to afford groceries and pay the bills.

I've just electronically handed in my assignment when the peacefulness is broken.

"Lucy! I know yer in here! Where r'you?"

I stiffen at the obvious slur in my father's voice. I haven't seen him over the past week, careful to avoid the Sunshine Center when he's visiting.

Mom yanks out her earbud, eyes wide with panic. "Is that Clay?"

I nod, and my mom's face falls, her voice dropping to a whisper. "He sounds drunk."

It's Thursday night, which is payday at the ice cream factory. He always stops at the Town Pub for a few pints before he comes home.

A buzz comes from my bag, but I ignore it.

Clover glances between us, as my dad stumbles around the corner. He bumps into the stacks and sends a pile of books tumbling to the floor.

His unfocused gaze settles on my mom. "D'er you are." He sneers. "The fuck you doin' in a li-berry?"

Another library employee comes around the corner, eyes wide, phone in her hand. She's a summer hire, a student returning to college in the fall. I remember her from high school.

I brace my palms on the table, ready to put myself between

my parents, but BJ and Maverick appear behind the library employee.

"Isn't this cute." Dad weaves a little. "Ya finally learnin' how to read."

"Clay, you're in a library. You can't be drunk, and you can't be noisy." Mom's voice wavers.

I stand as BJ and Maverick step in front of the poor girl I went to high school with. She brings the phone to her ear and takes a couple cautious steps backwards.

BJ's eyes meet mine, and instead of getting between my parents, I stay put. "Mom's right. You're intoxicated. You can't be here when you're like this, and you sure don't deserve to see Mom if all you're going to do is say mean, hurtful things."

"I'm just tellin' the truth," Dad spits.

"No, you're not. You're embarrassing yourself. You need to leave. Now."

"You gonna make me?"

I roll my eyes. "Really? What is this? Middle school?"

Maverick steps forward, and Clover scrambles out of her chair. BJ said she was married before she and Maverick got together. And that her ex was a problem when she moved to Pearl Lake earlier this summer.

"Mav, honey..." Her voice is unsteady.

"It's okay, sweetheart." He holds up a hand and shifts so he's between Clover and my dad. "Sir, I'm going to have to ask you to leave the premises immediately."

"I'm not leaving without my wife." He snaps his fingers. "Lucy. Come." Like she's a dog. Like she's his property.

Mom looks from Dad to me. Anxiety makes my stomach clench and my heart skip a few beats.

I see the moment she makes a choice, see the resolve settle behind her eyes as she crosses her arms and shakes her head. Her voice is a barely audible whisper, but her words bring so much relief. "You've been drinking, and you're being mean. I'm not going with you, Clay."

His face scrunches up. "You sayin' no to me?"

Maverick steps closer. He's usually all kindness and smiles. He has dimples and an infectious laugh, but right now, if looks could kill, my father would be six feet under.

Then Officer Butterson appears with the other library employee, his gaze skipping over the players in this scenario, zeroing in on the problem. He motions for the girl to stay put as he approaches my dad. Logan's eyes meet mine for a split second, and he nods. Seems like he's telling me he's on my side.

Dad looks from Maverick to Clover, then back to me and my mom, maybe finally cluing in that it's not just the three of us, and we're not at home where we can't escape his caustic words and abuse. "I see how it is. You're all brave because you got an audience."

"Sir, she's already said she's not going with you. It's time for you to leave," Maverick says.

"You can't stay away forever. You're gonna have to come home sometime, Lucy." It sounds like a threat.

"Clayton Marks." Officer Butterson's voice is loud and commanding.

My dad spins around. "You called the cops? I'm talking to my wife! That's not a crime!"

"No, but being drunk in public is. Do you own a beige Buick?" He rattles off the license plate number.

"So what if I do? You can't prove I drove it here," he slurs.

"Actually, Mr. Marks, I can." Logan rolls back on his heels. "Because there are cameras out front, right where your vehicle happens to be parked. You also ran over a bike and hit another car, which is gonna get you a ticket at the very least. Now I suggest you come with me and take a breathalyzer test, unless you want to be charged with resisting an officer."

Dad stands there for a few seconds, his eyes zeroing in on me. "This is your fault."

Officer Butterson shakes his head as he takes my father's arm. "Your daughter has nothing to do with you driving under the influence."

"Officer Butterson, wait," my mom calls out.

My heart sinks.

Tears pool in her eyes. "I remember," she whispers. "I remember what happened."

20

Another Step Forward

WINTER

I DON'T KNOW what flipped the switch. Maybe it was the taste of peace and the fear of returning to a life of abuse and hurt. Maybe being at the Sunshine Center showed my mom what life could be like when the person who was supposed to love her the most wasn't always dragging her down.

Whatever it was, it changed everything. After my dad was charged with a DUI and put in the drunk tank, my mom recounted her version of the events of the night she fell. Some of it was still murky, but she was clear enough to indicate that while my dad didn't physically push her over, he did hit her, and he used intimidation to corner her. And he didn't back off until it was too late.

After that he was also charged with assault and battery, and aggravated domestic battery, and we put an order of protection in place so he can't be in Pearl Lake anymore. He had to move to the trailer outside of town. A few weeks later, he was driving under the influence again and lost his license for a year.

All this feels like a win. But I worry about the ripple effect. Because there's always good with bad. And I fear the universe will balance it all out in the opposite direction.

After my dad was charged, Clover suggested that my mom and I attend a support group for battered women. During the first meeting, as we listened to women share their stories, I realized how we'd normalized the abuse. And it scared the hell out of me. I share half of Dad's DNA, and I don't want to be like him. I don't ever want to hurt the people I care about with words, or violence. And I don't ever want to go back to a life where every day is a battle.

So for now, I'm holding on to hope that this peace will last. And it feels like it could, especially when my mom gets a part-time job at the library. She's working behind the desk, checking out books and managing returns. She adores Clover, and Clover has a real soft spot for her too.

As July rolls into August, new fears bubble up. My mom is set to have her casts removed in a couple of weeks, and after that, she'll move back to the cabin. So will I. I could go now, but I don't want to be there on my own, and the Ballistics have continued to be great about me staying with them.

But beyond that, BJ will return to college in a handful of weeks, and so will most of my new friends, so I'm inclined to spend as much time with him as I can. Coach Waters and Coach Ballistic have mentioned the scholarship a couple of times, but with my mom on her own once she leaves the Sunshine Center, I can't see being able to go to Chicago.

IT'S a Saturday in early August, and we have a game this morning. I'm up early, along with Coach Ballistic. I can't get used to calling him Randy when we're off the ice, so I just call him Coach, and he rolls with it. We eat egg sandwiches for breakfast and hop into his truck.

"How you feeling about the game today?" he asks as we make the short drive to the rink.

"Good, I think. I don't want to get cocky because we've beaten this team before. But I watched their last couple of games, and their forward is still making the same mistakes. Their best defensive player is out with an injury, so unless something has changed since last week, we should be able to capitalize on their weaknesses."

He chuckles. "You sound like a true hockey player. Keep an eye on their right wing, number twenty-two. She's made a couple of questionable plays the past few games, and I'm worried now that we're getting close to the playoffs, she'll get chippy out of desperation."

"I noticed that too. I'll be careful. Don't want any more stitches to round out this summer." It feels like a year has passed, rather than a month since that happened.

We arrive at the rink, and I go to the locker room to change into my gear. Coach Waters and Ballistic give us a pep talk, and then we're clomping down the hall to the ice.

I scan the stands as we warm up and wave when I see my mom sitting with Clover. She's been coming regularly, and sometimes she even attends practices when she's not working, or in class, or having one-on-one sessions with Clover. Rose and Lovey are in the stands too. BJ is at his competition today, and his mom is with him and Adele in the city, but they'll be back tonight. They ended up adjusting the combination, so I'm crossing my fingers they still place.

Fern skates up and nudges me. "A couple of college scouts just took a seat at center ice, on our side."

"Are you serious?" I glance furtively in their direction.

"Sure am. They're from Monarch. I bet you a six-pack of fritters they're here for you."

I frown. "Why would they be here for me?"

She laughs. "Girl, you've been playing for the team for a little better than a month, and you have the fourth-best scoring record. The coaches want you on a college team, and I'm pretty sure they're looking to get you a sweet deal. I'll introduce you after the game if our coaches don't beat me to it."

"Jeez, talk about pressure," I mutter.

As we make another lap around the rink, she waves at them. "Just play like you always do, and you'll be fine."

I try to keep my head in the game, but by the middle of the second period, there are four sets of scouts from different colleges in the arena.

"Is this even normal? Isn't it kind of late in the summer to be scouting for players?" I ask Fern when we're rotated off after scoring another goal. This time I got the assist, and she made the goal, but earlier in the game, I scored our first goal.

"I already told you, they're here for you. And they probably know another college doesn't have you yet," Fern says, her grin wide. "I hope we're playing together in the fall."

"We'll see. They could be here for another reason."

"They could be, but they aren't."

We're called back onto the ice, ending the conversation. We win the game six-two. My teammates are buzzing because of the scout action, and when I leave the locker room with Fern, Coach Waters and Ballistic are waiting with the scouts from Monarch.

"Fern, great game tonight. Looking forward to seeing you

work your magic on our ice in a few weeks," one of the women says.

She smiles. "I can't wait. I think we're on track for an amazing season."

"No doubt." The woman turns her attention to me. "And you, Miss Marks, are just magnificent to watch. Your coaches tell me you're not playing for a college team in the fall yet."

"Uh, no, I'm not." I glance at my coaches, and they smile and nod encouragingly. "Not yet."

"I'll catch up with you later." Fern nods to me. "See you in a few weeks." She joins the other players on their way to Iced Out.

"Winter, this is Maxine Devereaux and Christian Cromwell," Coach Ballistic says. "Maxine is the head coach for the women's team at Monarch, and Christian is a scout. They'd love to discuss your plans for the fall."

"It's great to meet you. And yeah, that, uh, would be good. Can I just text my mom? She might be waiting in the lobby."

"We spoke to her, and she's waiting by the office," Coach Waters says. "We thought you might want her to be part of the conversation."

"Right. Yeah. Definitely." I don't know what to expect from her, but she's been a lot more supportive of my hockey ambitions since she made the decision to split with my dad. Clover is helping her with the divorce paperwork.

We find her sitting outside Coach Ballistic's office with Clover. They switched her to a walking cast, so she can get around with one crutch. Coach Ballistic introduces her to Maxine and Christian.

"Do you want me to be here?" she whispers as we file into the office.

I nod and help her into a chair at the round table.

Maxine smiles. "I know we're taking you away from the

team celebration, so we won't keep you long. But your coaches made us aware that there are a few other schools looking at you, so we wanted to meet with you personally. Your application essay was quite moving, and after seeing you on the ice, we approached the admissions office regarding a few amendments to the previous offer that we'd like to present to you."

"Amendments?" I look over at my coaches, and they smile encouragingly.

"Originally you were offered a need-based scholarship for tuition. However, we think we can do better than that. You would have a place on our women's hockey team, which includes tutors to help you maintain a three-point GPA. Tuition will still be covered in full for the duration of your undergrad degree, but we'll add a stipend for books, accommodations, and a meal plan, should you choose to live in the dorms. Or alternatively, we can offer a stipend to help with groceries should you decide off-campus life is better for you. We have a few houses off-campus for our players, as well as apartment options."

My mom, God bless her sweet heart, starts to raise her hand, but I catch it in mine. "It's okay. You can just ask the question, Mom."

"What is a three-point GPA?"

"It's a grade-point average," I tell her. "I'd need to keep Bs in all my classes to keep my scholarship."

"Oh. Well, you always get good grades, so that shouldn't be a problem. Would Winter start this fall? At the end of the month?" she asks.

"If she accepts our offer, then yes, she'll start at the end of August," Maxine explains.

"And you want to go." It's not a question. Mom squeezes my hand. "Don't worry about me. The casts are coming off soon, and I've got lots of support. If you want this, Winter, you should take it."

"Why don't we give you a few days to think it over? We can schedule a call on Wednesday, and you can let us know," Maxine suggests.

When I manage to nod, she and Christian thank us for our time and tell me they hope I'll consider joining them.

"We'll give you and your mom a few minutes," Coach Ballistic adds. "You can meet us up in Iced Out when you're ready. And Lucy, you're more than welcome to join us."

"Thank you, both of you, for everything you've done for Winter," Mom says.

"She's a talented player, and we want to give her every chance to shine." Coach Ballistic pats my shoulder and closes the door behind him.

Mom takes my hand, and her chin wobbles as tears fill her eyes.

"Are you okay?"

"I'm just so proud of you. Just so darn proud, Winter. Despite everything I've put you through, you've turned out to be this wonderful, kind, responsible young woman. And you're so talented. I had no idea how good you were. No idea." She chokes up. "I'm so sorry. I'm so sorry I put you through so much."

"You were just trying to survive."

She shakes her head. "No. Don't let me off the hook like that. This time with Clover, the group sessions we've been going to. They've helped me. I didn't see it before. I didn't see what I was doing to you, how unfair it was. How you were always standing up for me, and it should have been me standing up for you." Tears leak out of the corners of her eyes, and she holds up a hand when I start to speak, asking me to wait. She takes a deep, shaky breath and continues. "You took the brunt of so much of the abuse, and I...I should never have let that happen. That shouldn't have been our life. It took until this happened for me to finally see how bad it was." She shakes her head. "Why don't you hate me?"

"Because you're my mom," I say without hesitation. "We've always been a team, you and me against the world. Sometimes it was hard, but you were trying to keep the peace the only way you could. And you're out now. That's what matters."

"You need to take that scholarship, Winter. You need to go to Chicago and play hockey for that college team."

"I don't want to leave you on your own in that cabin." I bite the inside of my cheek and admit the thing that scares me most. "I can't keep you safe if I'm in Chicago."

"It's not your job to keep me safe, Winter. It's my job to keep you safe, and I failed at that a lot. But not anymore. Okay? I have people who want to help, and Clover, she's just so kind and helpful. She's been through a lot too, and look at how amazing she's done. She has a PhD, and she's a librarian, and she does all these wonderful things for her community. And that boyfriend of hers? He's just head over heels for her." She pats my hand. "What I'm saying is, I'll be okay. You need to put yourself first, Winter. Take the scholarship."

For a moment, I don't know what to do. I've never seen my mom like this. Will I blink and everything will be back the way it was? Seems very possible, but I want to believe she means this. That she's serious about leaving my dad for good and reclaiming her life. There's so much of it left to live.

As terrified as I am that the bottom will fall out, I want this. To be a college student, to play for a team, to get an education, have friends, be free. Hope is blooming. I can't help myself. "Okay. I'll do it."

She hugs me, and it feels like we're heading in the right direction.

21

The Safest Place

WINTER

MY MOM IS tired after all the excitement, so the Sunshine Center picks her up from the arena, and I meet the team at Iced Out, messaging BJ on the way. He's not scheduled to perform until this afternoon, so I don't expect to hear from him, but I wish him luck. I want to save the college news until he's home, because it doesn't feel like a text conversation.

My teammates bombard me with questions when I arrive. Fern decides my news about college is a reason to celebrate and invites everyone over to swim and hang out. Her place is small, like mine, but well maintained.

BJ messages at dinnertime with good news. He and Adele placed third overall, which means they're moving on. They're having a celebratory dinner in Chicago before they drive home, so I don't rush back.

At nine he messages that he's home, so I catch a ride with one of my teammates, but by the time I arrive, BJ is already

194

dead asleep, with the light on, holding his phone. I set the device on the nightstand and cover him with a blanket before flicking off the light and leaving him to sleep.

The last couple of weeks have been intense; he's been on the ice six to eight hours a day rehearsing, and despite his easy personality, the struggle to perfect that triple-twist lift was eating at him.

I work on an assignment for my class, but I'm exhausted from the high of today, so at ten I climb into bed. I wake at midnight to use the bathroom, and my brain turns on. Unable to settle, I go downstairs to get a glass of water and find BJ standing at the sliding glass door, eating a banana. He's wearing nothing but a pair of boxer shorts. His hair hangs down, freed from its usual tie, the ends barely reaching his chin. It's shorter than usual, because he had it cut right before the competition.

"Hey," I whisper as I move to stand beside him.

He turns his head, and I can see the five o'clock shadow on his cheeks. He had to shave his beard yesterday for the competition. It was a little startling to see him without facial hair. It makes him look more his age. But he has a strong, angular jaw, high cheekbones and full lips. I like both versions equally.

"You didn't wake me up when you got home."

I rest my cheek on his biceps. "You fell asleep with the light on. I figured you were exhausted and needed sleep more than anything."

"Mm... I was pretty beat." He wraps his arm around my waist, pulling me closer. "Yesterday was long. My dad said you scored two goals and an assist. I wish I could have been there to see it."

"And I wish I could have been there to see you compete."

"Maybe next time."

"Fingers crossed we can make that work." Although I'm not sure Adele will be all that excited to have me there. I slide my hands over his chest and let my fingers glide along the edge of his jaw. "College scouts came to the game."

His eyebrow lifts. "Oh yeah?"

"I got an offer for a full ride—tuition, books, accommodations, meal plan. Everything is covered as long as I keep my GPA above three-point-oh."

His face lights up with a smile. "That's great." Then it disappears and a flash of emotion I don't quite understand crosses his face. "What college?"

"Monarch. They amended their initial scholarship offer." My stomach flutters with nerves as I wait for his reaction. It's one thing to spend a summer having fun together, but going to the same college is different. We don't have a label. We're just BJ and Winter, figure skater and hockey player trading orgasms off the ice.

"Are you fucking kidding me?" He hugs me tight and lifts me off my feet. "Holy shit. That's awesome!"

"Shh! You'll wake your parents!"

"They sleep with a fan on. They're dead to the world." He sets me down. "Did you say yes? Does your mom know? Do my parents?"

"I haven't officially accepted, but I plan to. Yes, my mom knows. She sat in on the meeting with the scout and the coach from the college team, and she wants me to accept. And your dad and Coach Waters were at the meeting too."

"This is going to be amazing, Snowflake. We get to do college together." He cups my face between his palms and kisses me, long and deep. "I think this calls for a celebration of the orgasm variety. Up for a little middle-of-the-night Moany Monday?"

I chuckle. "Moany Monday sounds like fun."

He laces our fingers, and I follow him up the stairs to his bedroom. He closes the door and flicks a switch. The string lights at the perimeter of the ceiling blink on, basking the room in a soft, golden glow.

Normally we make out in his Jeep, or sometimes at the lake during one of our late-night swims. He's gone down on me a couple of times in the pool house. I have to bite the fleshy part of my palm to keep from making too much noise. But I don't sneak into his room at night. Not because I don't want to, but because I don't want to give his parents a reason to cut my stay here short.

Tonight feels different, though. Like things are changing. I've always assumed he'd go to college in the fall, and I'd stay here. What Adele said about me being his summer fling held some truth.

"For a second I thought you were going to some college upstate," BJ says. "I could have dealt if you were here and I was in Chicago, but this is going to be so much better." He brushes his lips over mine and one hand slides under my T-shirt, his warm fingers on my ribs. "Can I take this off?"

"Yeah. That would be awesome."

We part long enough for him to pull my shirt over my head. I'm not wearing anything underneath it. His eyes move to my bare breasts, nipples tightening in the cool air. He cups them on a low groan and circles the tight peaks with his thumbs as he kisses my neck. "I want to get naked with you, Snowflake."

"I'm not stopping you," I whisper-moan.

His fingers drift down my stomach, and he hooks one into the waistband of my sleep shorts. "Can I take these off?" His lips are at my ear. He nibbles the lobe and skims my cheek with his lips until they meet mine again. "This only goes as far as you want it to, okay? You're in control here."

I nod. It's not like we haven't been naked together before. It's just different when we're in a room with a closed door and a bed. "You can take them off."

"You're sure?"

"Positive."

He tucks a finger into the waistband at each hip and slides my sleep shorts and panties down my thighs. He sinks to one knee, eyes still fixed on mine as he presses his lips just below my navel.

I run my fingers through his hair. "You're so pretty," I murmur.

"So are you." He taps my right ankle.

I lift one foot, then the other, stepping out of my shorts and underwear.

He exhales a long, slow breath and runs his hands up the backs of my thighs. When he reaches the curve of my ass, he squeezes gently and nuzzles against my sex. "I want the taste of your orgasm on my tongue, Snowflake."

"I am definitely down for a tongue fuck, even though it's not Tuesday or Thursday."

He chuckles, and I suck in a breath when he nips my skin.

BJ pats the mattress beside him. "Let's get you comfortable, then."

I sit on the edge, then shift to the middle and stretch out. He lies next to me and props his cheek on his fist. His eyes are soft and warm, and he drags a single finger from my temple to the edge of my jaw, continuing down my throat, over my collarbone, and lower.

"You okay if I take a little time getting to the good part?" He circles my nipple, skims along my stomach, and keeps going.

"It's all the good part, but you're always about delayed gratification, so I know better than to expect you to dive right in." I bend my right leg and plant my foot on the mattress, giving him access to where I ache the most. "And I appreciate your attention to detail."

"The goal is always to make you feel good." His finger drifts across my skin, soft and gentle, skimming over my clit, circling, teasing, and delving lower.

"You do that well." I whimper as he eases a finger inside and clench, ready for more, wanting to drown in sensation, in connection, in desire. He curls his fingers, and I arch, eyes falling closed, lips parting on a sigh. I roll my hips when he does it again and groan when that delicious pressure disappears.

My eyes snap open, and I turn just in time to watch his glistening finger disappear between his lips. He makes a deep sound in the back of his throat. Primal. Feral. He looks like he wants to devour me. That familiar ache flares low in my belly.

"I couldn't wait." BJ's voice is low and rough, and I swear I feel it like a caress between my thighs.

I wrap my hand around the back of his neck and kiss him, pressing my tongue against his, tasting my own desire. I hook my leg over his and pull him on top of me. He braces his weight on a forearm, but his hips sink, and I feel his length against my stomach. I push his boxers over his hips until his cock springs free and I can feel that glorious steel ball rubbing on my skin.

BJ's lips find mine again, our kiss slow and deep. We grind against each other, skin hot and slick, desire building and pooling. Eventually he kisses a path along the edge of my jaw and over my chest. His stubble scrapes my skin in the most delicious way when he stops to devote attention to my nipples. And he keeps going, lower, over my stomach, past my navel.

He teases me with nips and kisses along the juncture of my thigh. And when I whisper *please*, he finally licks up the length of me. I bow off the bed and clamp a hand over my mouth to keep from moaning too loud—especially when he french kisses my clit and fucks me with his tongue, like he promised.

BJ's mouth is heaven. I grip his hair at the crown and roll my hips, wanton and desperate as he brings me to the edge of bliss again and again and keeps me hovering there. When he adds his fingers, I'm done for. That deep ache turns into waves of overwhelming pleasure, and I slap one of his pillows over my face to muffle my moans when I come.

I'm panting and sweaty, boneless, and I should be sated, but my body is empty, and I need more of him.

"Hey." He tugs at the pillow.

"Hey." I bite my lips together when his face appears in front of mine.

"How you doing?" His hair hangs down, skimming my cheek.

"You are a wizard with your mouth."

He grins. "Anytime you want a beard ride, I'm your man."

I laugh. "Literally the best gift you could give a girl." I wrap my leg around his waist again and pull him on top of me.

His shaft slides over my clit, and we both groan. We've been in this position more than once before, done the wet-hump thing. I've even braved a blow job, which wasn't easy, but watching BJ lose control was totally worth the awkward angle and fear I was going to chip a tooth.

I run my hands through his hair. "Do you have condoms?"

His eyes search mine. "We don't have to rush."

I shift my gaze to the side and remove my leg from his waist. "If you don't want to..." I'm going to die from embarrassment. "I can just return the favor instead." My voice cracks. Way to ruin the moment.

"Hey, hey. Can you look at me, please?" He strokes my cheek.

I side-eye him. The only thing that could make this worse is if I burst into stupid tears.

"I don't know where you're going in your head, Snowflake, but this isn't me saying I don't want the same thing. I do. It's basically all I think about. I can't tell you the number of times

I've thought about being in this exact position. It's my daily morning-shower-jerk-off fantasy. You're welcome for that overshare."

I bite back a nervous smile. "But?"

"There's no but." His swallow is audible.

I meet his gaze.

Emotions I can't pin down flash through his eyes. "I just don't want to mess this up." His thumb strokes back and forth along the edge of my jaw.

"How would you mess it up?" This is the first time I've seen BJ anything but confident. "I'm not worried that you're gonna fuck like you drive anymore."

He laughs, and I grin.

"I like you a lot, Winter." He licks his lips. "I just want this to be good for you."

"It's you. It will be." I trace the edge of his jaw with a fingertip. "But if you're not ready, it's okay. I can wait." I want him. I crave the connection that's at our fingertips, but I've been pushed into situations I didn't want to be in more times than I can count. I don't want him to feel pressured in any way.

His eyes stay on mine, searching for long seconds before he finally says, "I'm gonna get a condom."

"Are you sure?"

"I'm sure." He presses his lips to mine before he shifts and tugs the nightstand drawer open.

"I'm on the pill too. So we'll be double safe," I tell him as he pulls out a box.

"Safe is good." He folds back on his knees. The box is unopened, so there are a few awkward seconds where I'm lying on the bed with my legs spread and he's kneeling between them, but he finally gets it open and frees a foil square.

"I could put it on," I offer.

"Yeah. Okay." He holds out the square.

I sit up at the same time he rises to his knees. This puts me at eye-level with his cock. I take him in my hand, but instead of tearing the condom open, I lick my lips. My eyes find his as I lean in and brush my lips over the steel ball that rests just below the crown.

"Winter—Snowflake..." BJ's voice is gruff.

I part my lips and cover the head. The steel ball at one end slides over my tongue, and the other moves across the roof of my mouth.

BJ's brow furrows and his mouth drops open. "Fuckin' hell," he breathes.

I take a little more of him, then pull back and run my tongue around the head. I'm about to take him in my mouth again, but he cups my face between his palms.

"I cannot express how fucking much I love it when your beautiful lips are wrapped around my cock, but I'm gonna have to ask you to stop, because if you keep going, I'm not going to last very long, if at all, and I can't have that happen."

"Rain check?"

"Abso-fucking-lutely." He kisses me.

I tear the foil packet open, and BJ helps guide me through getting the condom on over the piercing. And then we're kissing and I'm pulling him on top of me. He lines himself up and pulls back enough to see my face as the head slides over my clit.

"You're sure about this?" he asks.

I nod. "I'm sure about you."

His smile is soft. "Good." He kisses me. "I feel the same."

And then he pushes in, filling me an inch at a time. His eyes stay on mine until he rests in the cradle of my hips, and then they close briefly on a soft exhale. "God, you feel so fucking good. So goddamn good." His eyes flutter open, and he strokes my cheek. "I knew it. I knew it was going to be like this."

He starts to move, pulling out, leaving me empty for one painful, suspended moment before he fills me again. Then I feel that insidious little steel ball hitting the spot that makes the ache inside me expand and swell.

This isn't like any sex I've had before. It's a different kind of connection. I can't escape his eyes, and I don't want to. It's as though I can feel everything he feels with every slow, purposeful stroke, and I absorb it in every caress and whispered word against my lips.

I fall. In lust, in more-than-like, into him.

"Right here, Winter, stay right here with me." He rolls his hips and hooks his hand under my knee, changing the angle, opening me wider, filling me deeper. And with every stroke, he takes me higher, gets me closer to heaven.

"I got you," he whispers. "Let go like you want to."

Fire rushes through my veins, lighting me up from the inside. A wave of pleasure radiates out from the center of my body, a ripple of bliss blanketing me. The world is a wash of black and then a burst of stars. And when my vision clears, I watch BJ come apart.

He doesn't roll off me or bury his face in my neck. He trails kisses along the edge of my jaw and comes back to my mouth. We kiss for long minutes before he finally pushes up on his arms.

"Give me a sec. I'll be right back."

He eases out, and I feel that emptiness echo in my chest. I don't understand it. He's just going to the bathroom, not sending me back to my room. But panic is already setting in. I said I was ready, and now I'm terrified this will change everything all over again. I'm halfway in love with him, and I'm moving to Chicago. Going to college. With him.

He pauses, searching my face. "You okay?"

"Yeah, fine." My voice cracks, and mortification makes me want to hide under a pillow.

He slides the condom off, ties a knot in the end, and tosses it in the garbage by his desk. Then he grabs tissues from the box on his nightstand and wraps them around his softening erection. "Fine is my least-favorite word in the world. Talk to me." He stretches out beside me.

"You're just going to leave it like that?" I motion to his tissue-covered cock.

"Yeah. Until we get to the bottom of fine, my cock is going to wear a tissue blanket." He skims my cheek with his fingertips. "Are you freaking out?"

I stare at the ceiling. "This won't change anything, right? We're still gonna be cool?"

"Why would we not be cool?" BJ pulls the sheet over us and taps my temple. "Where are you going up here? Worst-case-scenario-ville?"

"I don't know. I don't usually do sex and feelings, and I have feelings. About you."

"We're in the same boat then, because I don't usually do sex and feelings, and I also have them about you." He kisses the back of my hand. "It's okay to be afraid of whatever you're feeling. And it's okay to tell me that. But *fine* is not an answer I'll ever accept. That's probably going to be annoying, but you'll get used to it."

"You're uncomfortably real," I tell him.

"I know. It's part of my charm." He nuzzles my neck a moment. "You okay?"

"Yeah. Sorry. I sort of ruined the whole afterglow, didn't I?"

"You didn't ruin anything. Now we have a couple of options. We can snuggle and talk, or I can go to the bathroom, wash the tissue off my business, and if you're interested, we can do this all over again. But I'll understand if it's too much for one night."

"You can go again?" I bite my lip.

"I can go all night. It's about you and what you want. So if the feelings part is throwing you off, we can just chill out. But if you're down with all the feelings and more orgasms and more sex, we can take a short break. And if you go for option two, I would love you to be on top."

"Option two sounds good to me."

22

Oh Shit

BJ

THE POUNDING of a fist has me shooting up in bed. My door opens so fast the knob hits the wall and dents the drywall.

"Winter isn't in her room, but her bike is still here, and her phone is on the nightstand. Her bed isn't made, and that's not really like her. Do you know if something—" My mom stops short when she realizes I'm not alone. "Oh."

I'm shirtless. I'm everything-less. And so is Winter. Thankfully she's lying on her stomach, so only her bare shoulders and back are visible. Her long, dark braid contrasts with my light gray sheets. If my mom wasn't standing in my doorway wearing a shocked expression, I would appreciate the view a whole lot more.

Winter blinks groggily and mutters, "I'll make my bed." Then her eyes pop open and widen with horror as she processes her location.

After round two, I went down and got us water and a snack. I must have forgotten to lock my door.

My mom's mouth opens and closes a couple of times as her gaze shifts to the wall. "I'd like you two to be dressed and in the kitchen in fifteen minutes. We need to have a family meeting." She pulls the door closed with a quiet click.

Winter mouths, "Oh my fucking God." Followed by a panicked whisper. "They're going to kick me out. I'll be cut from the team. What happened to your alarm?"

"Hey, hey." I reach out, but she rolls off the bed, away from me. She's naked and gorgeous and totally freaking out. "Take a breath, Winter. They probably just want to talk about safe sex. It'll be embarrassing, but fine."

"I thought you hated the word *fine*." She nabs her discarded shirt from the floor and yanks it over her head.

I pull a fresh pair of boxers from my dresser and step into them, then grab a shirt from my closet and pull it over my head. My morning wood is a serious inconvenience, but apparently my dick is an insensitive ass and unconcerned with Winter's worries.

She's already got her shorts on. "I need a bra so my nipples aren't saluting everyone."

I grab her hand before she can open the door. "It's gonna be okay."

"Really? Because your mom just caught us naked in bed together, and I'm pretty sure that's the opposite of okay."

"They won't be mad at us." I don't understand her panic. But then my parents have always been pretty sex positive, and most of our conversations revolve around consent and using protection.

She swallows compulsively, eyes on the floor. "They gave me a place to stay so I didn't have to deal with my dad or stay alone in the cabin, and I go and disrespect them by having sex with you in their house."

"I'm twenty-one, and you're almost twenty. It's not really a secret that we're digging on each other. Sex is a normal part of life, and we're hormonal athletes. I'm pretty sure they expected this to happen eventually." She's still staring at the floor. "Can you look at me, please?"

She does, and her eyes glisten with tears.

"I don't know what kind of conversations you had in your house about sex, but here, it's about making sure we're safe and everything is consensual on both sides. Sex with someone you care about makes you human, and normal."

She blows out a breath. "I need to put a bra on."

"I know you're used to having the rug pulled out from under you, Winter. But try not to let your head go to the worst-case scenario, okay?"

She purses her lips but nods, then rushes to her room and closes the door. I'm not worried about my parents at all. They'll ask uncomfortable, but not unexpected questions. I'm worried about how Winter so easily assumes the worst will happen, or that my parents will somehow think less of her because we slept together. But who knows what kinds of crap her dad has said. He seems like a misogynistic douchebag. Undoing all that emotional damage will take time.

I grab a hair tie on my way to the kitchen. My parents are standing behind the island, holding coffee mugs.

"Are you being safe?" is the first question out of my mom's mouth.

"Absolutely. Yes." I shove my hand in my pocket. Yeah, better to get this part out of the way.

"Is Winter on birth control?" Mom sips her coffee.

So far my dad has said nothing.

"Yes. And we used condoms." I always use condoms,

mostly because until now, sex has been about feeling good. I've only been with one other person where actual feelings were involved, and that went so sideways it turned upside down. "I care about her," I blurt. "A lot."

My parents exchange a look. Mom smiles. "We can see that."

Footfalls on the second floor have us all looking toward the stairs.

Winter appears at the landing. Her hair is pulled back in a ponytail, and she's dressed in her work uniform. But the thing that makes my stomach twist is the backpack and duffle she has with her. Clearly I was right about her preparing for the cliff dive.

When she reaches the bottom step, she adjusts her hold on her duffle. "I'm really sorry." Her eyes flick to my parents and back to the floor. "I shouldn't have... We shouldn't have. I took advantage of your kindness. I can move back to the cabin now."

Mom motions to the chair across from her. "Why don't you put your bags down and have a seat, honey." If there's one thing my parents don't allow, it's running away from tough conversations.

Winter sets the duffle and backpack by the stairs. Her swallow is audible as she pads across the room. Her eyes meet mine briefly as she pulls out the chair opposite my mom and sits. I take the one beside her and skim the back of her hand, but she snatches it away and shoves it between her legs. Yeah. She's taken a right turn into Up-Shit-Creek-Ville.

"It's gonna be okay," I whisper.

She glances at me out of the corner of her eye. She's gone as white as a sheet, and her upper lip is sweating.

"Would either of you like some coffee?" Mom asks.

Winter looks confused by the offer.

"That'd be good, thanks," I reply. I turn to Winter. "How about you?"

"Um, okay. Yes, please?" Her knees bounce, so she covers them with her hands.

While my mom pours two coffees, my dad brings over the cream and sugar. "You have a chance to share the news about the scouts with BJ?" Dad says.

"Uh, yeah. I told him." Her voice is pitchy.

"Good. We can make that call whenever you're ready." He nods a few times, then looks to Mom, like he's waiting for direction.

"Okay." Winter seems extra confused by my dad's easy-going demeanor.

That makes sense. There probably weren't many discussions in her house. Just her dad losing his shit whenever he didn't like what was happening.

Mom sets the coffees in front of us. Winter's hands shake as she pours cream into hers and two heaping teaspoons of sugar. I take mine black.

"So, we have a few things we'd like to discuss, but in light of recent developments, we might need to adjust some of those plans," Mom says.

"What are you talking about?" I ask, worried for the first time that there will be backlash for this. "We didn't do anything wrong. I mean... We were safe."

Mom raises her hand. "I'm not talking about what I walked in on this morning. But while we're on that topic, I understand that you're both adults, capable of making adult decisions, so I hope those decisions will include continuing to be safe."

"I have no intention of ending up like my mom," Winter blurts, taking a huge gulp of her coffee.

Mom gives Winter a soft smile. "I was the result of an unplanned pregnancy, and my mom raised me on her own, with no support from my biological father. So I understand and appreciate not wanting to repeat history, Winter. However, mistakes happen, so I don't want either of you to think we won't be here to help and support. But doing your part and staying safe, especially with you both still in college, is important. Which brings us to the next piece." Mom looks to Dad.

Winter looks flabbergasted. She raises her hand. "I have a question."

"Okay." Mom smiles and waits.

"You're not upset with us?"

Mom tips her head, her expression softening. "Of course not. You two share a very real and obvious connection. You're being safe. That's what's important. Is that why you brought your bags down? You thought we were going to be so upset that we'd ask you to leave?"

Winter bites her lips together and nods.

Mom reaches across the island and gives her hand a squeeze. "In this house, we talk things through. You're not being irresponsible, or putting yourself at risk, and even if you were, it would be a discussion with a plan. Not us kicking you out, okay?"

"Okay. Thank you for being so understanding."

"Of course, honey. Do you feel a little better?"

Winter nods.

"Great. Well, now that that's handled." Dad claps his hands. "Lily and I were talking about the housing situation come fall. We know there are options for both dorms and off-campus housing and apartments, and that the revised offer from the college comes with a housing stipend—"

"Kody's room is still empty at our place," I jump in. "Quinn hasn't found anyone to take it yet. Winter can stay there. Then accommodations are covered, and Winter can use the housing stipend for something else." It's fucking genius, really. I can't believe I didn't think of it until now. Well, last night I was a little busy giving and getting orgasms, but now that my brain is mostly clear, I'm coming up with bomb-ass ideas.

Winter gives me a disbelieving look.

Mom arches a brow and fights a smile. "Originally that was our thought too. But considering recent developments, it would probably be best to make some adjustments."

"Why? This is perfect. And it makes the most financial sense. Why should Winter waste money on rent when we have an open room?" I argue.

"We don't—" Dad starts, but the front door opens, the alarm beeping once. A code is punched in, which tells me exactly who it is.

"Hello, second family! Rose and I are here to pick up our favorite hockey player!" Lovey calls.

They come traipsing down the hall and stop abruptly when they see the four of us gathered around the island. Lovey bites her lip, and Rose makes a face.

"I feel like we just walked in on something," Rose says.

"We're sorting out living arrangements for the fall," I tell them. I turn back to my parents. "I don't see what the big deal is. We'll have separate rooms. Winter swapping with someone from River's house isn't going to change anything. Lavender and Kody had the same setup last year, and you gotta know that one of their rooms was always empty."

"Are you talking about Kody Bowman? First-round pick for Philly?" Winter asks.

"Yeah. He's dating my cousin. They've been in love with each other since...forever," I explain. "Kody lived in the same house with Lavender for a while."

"Because your kitchen caught on fire. And that was for three weeks," Dad says.

Mom gives me a look. "Lavender and Kody have a very long

history, and not all of it was smooth, as you well know. And I'm very aware of what this"—she motions between me and Winter —"will look like when you're away from home and living on your own. However, there's merit in you two living in separate houses. It'll give you some space to navigate this new path you're on, and you don't want to make it awkward for Quinn."

Rose crosses her arms. "I feel like we're missing something."

"That's because you are," I say.

"I fell asleep in BJ's room last night, and his mom walked in on us this morning. You can fill in the blanks on your own." Winter's face grows redder with every word.

My dad looks like he's trying not to laugh. I really love my parents.

I don't know what my expression is, but Winter huffs and rolls her eyes. "They were going to find out anyway. And since it's the house they're living in that we're talking about, we might as well not beat around the bush." She addresses my mom. "I don't disagree with you about the living in separate houses. It's smart. But I don't think it's fair to anyone else to have to switch houses because of me. So as kind as the offer is, if living in one of the team houses would cause less disruption, I'd rather do that."

Lovey raises her hand. "I could live with BJ and Quinn."

Rose pulls Lovey's hand back down to her side. "I'll swap. I volunteer as tribute. I'll live with BJ and Quinn, and Winter can have my room at the Waters' house."

"That's kind of you, Rose, but we'll need to check with your parents first," Dad says.

"I'm seeing Vi, Char, and Sunny for lunch today," Mom says. "I'll talk to them, and we can work it out from there."

Those are my mom's friends. Vi is my half-aunt, Charlene is Rose's mom, and Sunny is Lovey's mom. They're part of our extended hockey family.

"I'm texting my mom." Rose thumb-types on her phone.

I glance at Winter, who looks like she has no idea what's going on. This is reasonable considering what happened this morning and the way my friends and family are basically taking over her life. It's a problem I'm partly responsible for. "Hey!" I whistle shrilly. "So I realize I suggested Winter move into Kody's room, and I appreciate that we're a family of problem solvers who like to solve problems, but this is Winter's decision, and maybe we shouldn't turn it into a family dilemma where everyone gets to say their piece and argue their side."

Rose's phone rings. "Uh, hey, Mom," she answers. "Yeah. I'm at the Ballistics' with Lovey. There have been some developments, but I might need to put a pin in my request, because I think we're actually steamrolling our friend." She pauses. "Hold on a second." She covers the phone and turns to Winter. "I'm just going to explain because not explaining is going to lead to a lot of unnecessary texting. Okay?"

Winter shrugs. "Okay?"

"I'll be quick." Rose goes back to her phone. "Long story short, you know that new player on the women's team that everyone is freaking out over? The one I work with at Boones?" Another pause. "Yeah, Winter Marks. That's the one. She's got a scholarship for hockey at Monarch, which is super cool, and we're trying to work out the living arrangements. She has the option to live with some of her teammates, but BJ and Quinn still have an open room at their place. BJ and Winter are a thing, though, and living together and dating in college isn't the easiest, so we were throwing out ideas, and I suggested I take Kody's old room at BJ's place and Winter take Lavender's old room. But that's when BJ pointed out that we're steamrolling Winter, which isn't cool. So we can put a pin in this for now."

Another pause. "Sure, you can talk to Lily, but like I said, this is Winter's decision." She holds the phone out to my mom. "She wants to talk to you."

Mom takes the phone, and they have a brief conversation that consists mostly of *yes*, *no*, and *we can talk more about it at lunch* before she ends the call and passes the phone back to Rose. "She said she'll hold off until we have more information."

"Seems reasonable." Rose pockets her phone, but a few seconds later it goes off with a siren sound. "Uh, we need to get to work."

Dad addresses Winter. "BJ is right. This is about what you want and what you decide is best for you, okay?"

Winter nods. "Okay."

"Can I get a minute with Winter before you go?" I ask, looking to my parents. "If we're done here, that is?"

"We're done for now," Mom says.

"We've got fifteen minutes, and it only takes five to get to Boones." Rose thumbs over her shoulder. "We'll wait in the car."

"I can drive Winter to Boones," I offer.

"Your dad and I want to have a conversation with you, so it's better Winter goes with the girls," Mom says.

Yeah. I knew I wasn't getting off that easily. "Let's take your stuff back upstairs." I tug on Winter's sleeve, and we grab her bags.

As soon as we're in her room, I close the door.

"What the hell just happened?" Winter rubs her temple.

"Welcome to family discussions at the Ballistic house. I'm sorry about the living-arrangement thing. The idea popped in my head and came out of my mouth without a lot of thought. I can totally appreciate that you might want to live with your teammates, and I see the validity in that option. You'd be on the same schedule, you'd have lots in common—maybe that's the better choice."

"So you don't want me living two doors down?" She arches a brow.

"I want what you want. And maybe that's a copout answer. But I want you to do what's best for you. And if that's living with your teammates, that's what you should do. If you'd rather live with Lovey and Lacey and River, that's cool too. But I feel like you've had enough of other people making choices for you, and I don't want to do that."

She pats my chest. "Thank you. I appreciate that, and I can see that everyone just wants what's best."

"Are you okay? I mean, besides figuring out where you're living in the fall."

She nods. "That was the opposite of what I expected. I honestly thought you had your head up your ass and I was going to get kicked out."

I laugh. "My parents are easygoing."

"Yeah. I'm learning that."

I run my hands down her arms. "Take some time to think things through, and don't let Rose pressure you either way. It's really whatever you feel most comfortable with, okay?"

"Yeah. Okay." She blows out a breath. "The last twenty-four hours have been a bit of a roller coaster." She runs her hands over my chest. "Last night was... You were... It was great. And then this morning happened, and I expected the worst, like you said, and that didn't happen at all. So yeah. Processing time would be good."

"Fair. We can talk tonight?"

"Yeah. Oh. Wait. It's my teammate Shawna's birthday, and I got invited out. Or maybe I shouldn't go."

"You should go. Definitely. They're your team, and you should celebrate with them. We've got time to figure everything out."

"Okay. Yeah. I should probably go. And I should go to work too."

"Can I kiss you first?"

She nods, so I wrap my arms around her and keep it mostly chaste.

She pulls away first. "I really need to go so we're not late for work on top of everything else."

"Fair. I'll text you later, okay?"

"Sounds good."

I walk her out to Lovey's car. Rose is sitting in the middle of the back seat, leaning forward as Winter sits in front. I don't even want to know what that conversation will be like.

My mom is in the kitchen, rummaging through her purse, when I come back down the hall. "How's Winter doing?" she asks.

"A bit overwhelmed, but okay."

"That's reasonable. She seemed shocked that we weren't angry."

I grab a banana from the fruit bowl. "I think there's some archaic belief systems in her house—very patriarchal and, based on what we've seen, highly misogynistic. It's going to take Winter some time to adjust her expectations and reactions. She's used to things falling apart."

Mom nods. "How are you handling all of this?"

"What do you mean?"

"It's not just change for Winter; it's change for you too. First girl I've seen you serious about since senior year of high school."

I blow out a breath. "Can we not talk about that?"

Mom arches a brow. "Not wanting to talk about something usually means you should."

"It's not the same."

"Doesn't mean it won't impact your choices and decisions."

Dad comes into the kitchen and kisses Mom on the cheek. He glances between us. "Everything okay?"

"Yeah. S'all good. We should get to the rink. I picked up a couple of lessons this morning and booked some personal ice time."

Mom frowns. "When did you do that? I thought you were taking the day off."

"I'm taking the day off from Adele, not from being on the ice."

"You need to give your body a break. And I'm pretty sure you didn't get much of one last night."

"Annnnnd I'm peace-ing out of this conversation. Dad, I'll meet you in the truck. Mom, I love you, but there are lines." I turn down the hall.

"If you'd locked your door, this morning would have gone a lot differently!" she calls after me.

I don't catch my dad's reply, but I'll be a captive audience on the ride to the arena, and I'm sure he'll have wisdom to impart.

A few minutes later, he sets two travel mugs in the cup holders and climbs into the driver's seat.

"I'm ready. Say whatever you're going to say," I tell him.

He's quiet as we pull out of the driveway.

I wait a minute, and then finally cave. "Are you upset with me?"

"No, son. Just gathering my thoughts." He taps on the steering wheel. "I see a lot of parallels between you and Winter and your mom and I when we were dating. Grandma Iris raised her on her own, and Iris didn't make the best boyfriend choices. She worried your mom would do the same. She sure didn't like me at first."

"Really? Why not?" These days Grandma Iris and

Grandpa Tim adore my dad. Tim loves to talk hockey and sports in general.

"Because your mom's biological father was an ex-hockey player who probably fathered countless children he never took responsibility for," Dad says darkly. "And your grandma Iris didn't want what happened to her to happen to Lily. She said a few things to your mom that left some marks. That was a long time ago, though, and they've worked all that out." He pauses. "But back when we were first dating, I didn't think I could be what your mom needed, mostly because me and your grandpa Randall are a lot alike, and he...wasn't a great dad or a great husband. He's cleaned up his act, and we have a better relationship now, but back then, it made me want to avoid relationships. And then your mom came along, and she turned my world upside down. I was such a fucking dumbass. Some of the stupid shit I did... I'm lucky she's such a patient woman." He shakes his head. "Anyway. Here we are. But back then, your mom was living in a tiny two-bedroom apartment in Guelph. Her life wasn't easy, and there I was making millions of dollars a year, getting all the chances I could to succeed. Your mom, she'd lost her opportunity to go to the Olympics and still looked on the bright side of things."

"You saw Mom in Winter, and you didn't want her to lose her chance," I say.

He nods. "If there's anything I regret with your mom, it's not pushing her to try for that dream again. I could have helped her get there, but she seemed so at peace with her choices." He clears his throat before he continues. "Winter's life has been hard—harder than I think either of us can realize or fathom. Your mom sees it very clearly. What I'm about to say...it comes from a place of perspective that you might not have yet. Although you're far more astute and self-aware than I was at your age." He glances at me. "Be careful with her, okay, son?

She's tough. And resilient. But she's been taught to sacrifice her own needs and that her wants should not be a priority, and that'll take some time to undo."

"I think I understand what you mean."

"Just check in with her to make sure the things she says yes to aren't because she feels a sense of obligation, but because it's what she genuinely wants." He pulls into his reserved spot and settles a hand on my shoulder. "It's the first time in years that I've seen you passionate about anything other than skating. I don't know what the future holds for the two of you, but I think you're good for each other."

"I think so too."

23

I Should Have
Thought This Through

DJ

WINTER MESSAGES later to let me know she'll be pretty late getting home. She's going to an escape room in Lake Geneva with a bunch of her teammates, and it doesn't start until eight. So when Lovey invites me to go to the movies with her, Lacey, and Rose, and promises we're not seeing a rom-com, I say yes. It's been a hectic couple of weeks, and Lovey's summer schedule is always ridiculous, as is mine, so we haven't had much time to hang out. I message Winter so she knows where I am, and I get a range of gifs in return, a couple with FOMO when she finds out what movie we're seeing, followed by:

> Have fun! Say hi to everyone for me 🤍

When the movie is over, I have new messages from Winter.

One sent an hour ago tells me she's home and suggests that if I'm still with Lovey, we should all hang out for a bit. I give her an ETA of half an hour because we have to drop Rose off first. Lacey has to work at eight, so I drop her off too.

It's after eleven, so the house is quiet when we arrive. Lovey isn't planning to stay long since she has to work tomorrow morning too, but when we get upstairs, Winter is totally asleep, like I was last night.

I turn off her light and close her door, then cross the hall to my room and shut my door behind Lovey so we don't disturb Winter with our chatter.

"She's had a day." I flop down on the bed and pat the spot beside me.

Lovey wrinkles her nose. "Did you change your sheets after last night?"

I laugh. "Yeah, I threw them in the wash this afternoon and put clean ones on. I have some class."

She stretches out beside me. "I don't know that my dad would be that cool about it if he found a guy in my bed."

"Ah, the old don't-touch-my-baby-girl double standard."

She frowns. "It's a thing, isn't it?"

"Unfortunately, yes. I'm just glad my mom was chill about the whole thing, for Winter's sake."

"Yeah. She couldn't believe they weren't angry." She side-eyes me, trying to seem nonchalant. "I didn't realize last night was your first time together."

"You're the one who said I should change things up."

"I know. But I didn't have a lot of faith in your ability to hit the slow lane and stay in it. You've boned your way through the past three years at college. You should have double-majored in one-night stands." She snort-laughs, but then grabs my arm. "Oh shit."

"Oh shit, what?"

"BJ, how many girls have you slept with over the past three years?"

"I don't know. Keeping track would be seriously douchey. They're not conquests, they're fun-time friends," I joke.

But she doesn't laugh. Lovey rolls her eyes. "A lot, though, right?"

I shrug. "I guess."

"Like one a week?"

"Why are you so focused on the number?"

She sits up. "For the sake of guesstimating, let's say one girl a week for each semester, which is sixteen weeks long, for the past three years, give or take a few."

I feel a little sick. "I don't think it's that many. There were a lot of weeks I didn't sleep with anyone."

"Sure, but some weeks there was more than one bedmate."

"Not often."

"Whatever. I'm trying to do mental math, and you're making it impossible." Her nose scrunches up. "Ninety-six." She makes a face like I just farted. "Oh, that's a lot."

"Are you sex-shaming me?" An uncomfortable feeling settles in the pit of my stomach.

"I don't think I need to. You've had a lot of meaningless sex, BJ. As your best friend, I love you, but that's a lot of orgasms without any connection. I'm super glad you've found someone you connect with, but you should consider giving her a heads-up about your prolific past. Because chances are, she'll run into one of your former flings in Chicago."

"Twenty thousand people go to that school."

"I need both hands to count the number of times some girl has come up asking if you want to hang out again."

"Yeah, but I'm with you all the time."

"News flash, BJ, label or no label, you and Winter are a thing, which means you'll be together a lot."

"I really don't think it's a big deal." I'm not sure I believe that as I say it.

"Which part? All the sex you've had with random hookups for the sake of getting off, or the possibility that Winter will run into one of them on campus?"

"She's not like that. She's easygoing."

Lovey sighs. "Last word on the topic, and then I'll drop it." She gives me her arched eyebrow. "Would you be easygoing if the tables were turned?"

I don't know what my face is doing, but her smirk tells me she's made her point.

I WAKE at five thirty in the morning. Lovey is wrapped around the body pillow next to me. We must have fallen asleep talking, which isn't unusual, particularly in the summer since her parents' place is just down the road. The body pillow became a necessary addition to prevent any awkwardness.

I shake her shoulder, and she makes a noise. "Hey, Lovey, you fell asleep."

She lifts her head and blinks blearily at me. "Time's it?"

"Five thirty. When do you have to be at work?"

"Seven."

"You should get a move on, then."

"Kay, kay," she mutters.

I hear footfalls on the stairs, but going down, not coming up. I throw off the covers and open the door, peeking into the hall. Winter's bedroom door is open, and a light filters up the stairs. My parents are early risers, but they usually don't start their day until six thirty.

"Hey, Lovey? Don't fall back asleep."

She raises an arm. "I'm up, I'm up."

"I'll catch you later."

She gives me the thumbs-up, and I pad downstairs and find Winter standing in front of the open fridge. She's wearing a pair of running shorts—the kind that only covers the most important parts—and a sports bra. She's all muscle and curves. Strong. Sexy. And a little more than twenty-four hours ago, we had sex. Great sex. Marathon sex. Thinking about that isn't helpful, particularly since morning wood is a thing and I'm wearing a pair of basketball shorts.

She pulls a container of pulpy orange juice from the door. For the first week she was here, she would only take food if it was on the counter, which means fruit from the bowl Mom always keeps filled, or baked goods like muffins that Dad would leave out. When I realized what was happening, I put out a bowl of energy and granola bars to test the theory. She's more comfortable now, but sometimes the number of choices overwhelms her.

I clear the gravel from my throat. "Hey."

Winter nearly fumbles the juice but recovers. "You scared the hell out of me." She sets the jug on the counter.

"Sorry. I didn't mean to scare you. You okay?"

"Yeah. Woke up to use the bathroom and my mind turned on and wouldn't shut up again." She taps her temple. "I passed out on you last night, didn't I?"

I round the counter and stop in front of her. "We didn't get a whole lot of rest the night before, and you've had a lot thrown at you in the past twenty-four hours. I figured you needed the sleep. I tucked you in, though."

"I still can't believe I'm going to college in a few weeks. I feel like I'm living someone else's life."

"It'll probably take time to get used to, huh?" Her hair is

down, falling in loose waves over her shoulders. I twirl a lock around my finger.

She nods. "I'm over here waiting for the axe to fall. Like, until I'm actually in Chicago, none of this is real."

"Did you get any closer to a decision about where you want to live? Lovey told me Rose was pretty Team Waters' House."

Winter laughs and rolls her eyes. "She made a spreadsheet, and I'm sure you wouldn't be the least bit surprised to find the list leaned heavily to the live-with-Lovey-Lacey-and-River side."

"It's okay if that's not what you want, though."

"I know, but it makes the most sense. They're already my friends, I'm comfortable with them, and financially, it's the best move."

"Lovey and Lacey are super responsible, and so is River."

"Yeah, I can see that about the twins. There's so much to think about. I've never taken a full course load, so that'll be new. And I've never lived with anyone but my parents, so that's freedom I haven't experienced before. I don't want to be one of those girls who goes to college and flunks out the first semester because I fell down a party rabbit hole."

"You're not really a huge partier, though, are you?"

She traces a petal of the lily on the back of my hand. "I don't think so, but I've also never had the chance. I don't feel like I'd intentionally do something stupid, but I've been going to those support meetings for battered women with my mom, and they talk about how hard it can be to break up with the abuse. The part that scares me is that I get what they mean. Look how I reacted yesterday when your mom caught us upstairs. The things my dad would have said if that had happened in my house..." She shakes her head. "The farther removed I get from it, the more I realize how toxic my home was. I'm scared I'll do something to fuck all this up."

"Are you worried you'll make it a self-fulfilling prophecy?" I settle a hand on her waist.

"Maybe?" She shrugs. "I'm so accustomed to being stressed out, I don't know how not to be."

"I get that your natural state is worry, and telling you to stop is probably pointless, but how does stressing about the things you can't control help you?" I release the lock of hair, letting it unfurl.

She gives me a wry smile. "It doesn't."

"I could take your mind off it for a little while, though." She doesn't start work until seven. We have plenty of time.

She glances at the clock on the stove. "Won't your parents be up soon?"

"We have over half an hour. That's more than enough time." I waggle my brows. "It's way better than starting your day in Worry World, don't you think?"

Her hands slide around my waist and down my back. I drop my mouth to her ear. "I can't stop thinking about the way you feel, Snowflake." I skim along her spine until I reach her lower back and press my hips forward, my erection nudging her stomach. "I just want to make you feel good."

She exhales an unsteady breath.

I kiss her cheek and lift her chin. "Will you let me do that for you?"

"You make it sound like I'm doing you a favor, not the other way around."

"Your permission is a gift, Snowflake. Never forget that."

Her eyes are soft. "We can make each other feel good again?"

"Whatever you want, however you want it." I brush my lips over hers. "Come on. Let's go upstairs."

I tug her toward the stairs and motion her ahead of me. But she comes to a grinding halt when we reach my door. I stumble into her back and settle a hand on her hip to keep from knocking us both over. Lovey is still sprawled out on my bed, sheets thrown off, body pillow hugged to her side.

"The fuck?" Winter spins around, her expression reflecting confusion, disbelief, and outright disgust. She points to my door and whispers, "Is that *Lovey?*"

I hold my hands up. "I can explain."

The color has drained from Winter's face. "What the fuck is even going on?"

Lovey bolts upright. "I'm awake! What time is it?"

I realize how bad this must look, especially after I convinced Winter to come upstairs so I could distract her with orgasms. Lovey is sleeping in my bed. I look shady as fuck.

Lovey's eyes go wide. "Oh. Oh, no. This isn't what it looks like, Winter."

"So you didn't spend the night in BJ's bed?" Winter turns to me, hands flailing. "And you didn't just offer me orgasms while Lovey is sleeping in your goddamn bed? That's *not* what's happening here?"

"Oh wow. Okay..." Lovey's eyes are frantic. "Well, I guess it's sort of how it looks, but not really. I'm not supposed to still be here. I was supposed to leave a while ago."

"Lovey, you're not helping," I mutter.

"We had sex in that bed last night." Winter shakes her head. "Or early yesterday morning. And now you're having a sleepover with Lovey? Why would you do that? Why would you fuck me and then let another girl sleep in your bed?"

I raise my hands. "You're jumping to conclusions."

"How can I *not* jump to conclusions?" She steps back, putting distance between us. "Is this a thing for you two? Like, is it a kink or something?" Winter seems completely shell-shocked. "Because I'm not into threesomes. Or sharing. Or open relationships or whatever the hell is going on between the two of you—not that I think we're a couple or anything, but this is like...really fucked up."

"Lovey is my best friend." I stay firmly planted in front of the stairs.

"With benefits? I knew this was too damn good to be true," she mutters.

"Can I explain?" I run a hand through my hair, scrambling to find a way to put her at ease.

"Oh please, this should be interesting." Her tone is laced with sarcasm, but her voice wavers.

Lovey is now standing in the doorway, wringing her hands. Conflict is not her strong suit.

"There's nothing going on between me and Lovey. She's like my sister."

Winter's nose wrinkles. "Is that supposed to make me feel better? Siblings of the opposite sex in their twenties don't usually sleep beside each other unless they're in a VC Andrews novel."

"I don't know who VC Andrews is."

"She writes forbidden romance," Lovey jumps in helpfully. "They're kind of incest-y. *Flowers in the Attic* was made into a movie. More than once actually. The brother and sister—never mind." She turns to Winter. "When we got back here, you were already asleep. BJ and I started talking, but we must have fallen asleep too. I'm sure out of context this looks really bad, but I swear, BJ and I are just friends. That's it."

"I'm so weirded out. How the hell can you sleep beside each other and not...do stuff?" Winter rubs her temple. "That would be like temptation nation."

"We've kissed twice."

"Seriously, Lovey?" I give her a what-the-fuck look.

"What? I'm trying to explain so Winter can understand. We need to work on our boundaries, because we clearly have none, and Winter deserves the truth—especially with every-thing else that's going on." She gives me a meaningful look. "Like I said, we kissed twice. But it was during a game of spin the bottle when we were fourteen. My brother Laughlin has a terrible sense of humor, and he thought it would be fun to play, but like, I have four brothers, and half of our friend group is related to each other. It got super awkward when we realized it was going to be all about cousins kissing. It *was* a VC Andrews novel."

Winter looks to be somewhere between disbelief and horror, and Lovey's face keeps getting redder. "Laughlin thought it was hilarious," Lovey adds. "And BJ and I ended up having to kiss twice because Lacey tapped out, which was smart of her, in retrospect. Anyway, it was super squicky and not good." Lovey makes a gagging sound. "Kissing BJ was like kissing one of my brothers. Or what I imagine it would be like, anyway. It was just...ew."

"Thanks," I mutter.

"You felt the same way. And we made a pact to never speak of it again, because it was one of those situations that seemed like a good idea until it wasn't." Lovey fiddles with her hair. "I know BJ is a good-looking guy, a little on the wiry side, and like, man pretty—"

"I'm a figure skater, not a jacked-up hockey player." I don't know why I'm compelled to defend myself.

"I know." She makes a general motion that apparently encompasses my wiry, man-pretty physique. "And what you have to offer is attractive to a lot of women, but—" She turns to Winter. "BJ and I have zero chemistry. He's like a brother, but less annoying."

"Really bolstering my self-esteem over here," I grumble.

"I'm being honest. And I don't do it for you either." She addresses Winter. "But you absolutely do. The way BJ looks at you is borderline NSFW. That look has never, ever been directed at me." She clasps her hands. "I swear we didn't mean to fall asleep, and I promise it won't happen again. I feel awful that I put you in this awkward position, and I don't want you to start your first semester at Monarch feeling like this is something you need to worry about." Lovey motions between me and her. "We're just friends. That's it."

She appears finished, so I decide it's time to wade in. "I'm really sorry, Winter. I swear what Lovey said is the truth. I wouldn't string you along like that."

Winter sucks her bottom lip between her teeth. She opens her mouth and closes it, then repeats the cycle. "I'm going to get ready for work."

"I can drive you."

She raises a hand. "I need time to process. Alone."

"Can I text you later?"

She purses her lips. "I'll text you. When I'm ready."

"Okay. Fair. I'm really sorry. This isn't how I wanted this morning to go."

"Me either." She walks into the spare room and closes the door behind her.

Lovey follows me into my bedroom, her hands on her cheeks. She doesn't say anything until the door is closed, and even then it's barely a whisper. "I'm so, so sorry. I really didn't mean to fall asleep."

"It's not your fault. I should've set an alarm or something." I run a hand through my hair. "We've been doing this for years. Until now, it never occurred to me that it was a problem." Part of that is because until Winter, my dating history consisted of one semi-secret relationship that imploded and a ridiculous number of casual flings that may or may not tally somewhere close to the hundred mark. Which isn't something I want to focus on.

Lovey shakes her head. "I feel awful. She just agreed to move in with us in a couple of weeks. We need to fix this."

"Hopefully she just needs time." This can't be the thing to derail her. Or us. My stomach twists. "I can't believe I didn't see the issue with this before now."

"We're used to being surrounded by people who know us. Our group is tight. They're accustomed to our brand of friendship, but I think we need to be conscious of how we are moving forward." The alarm on Lovey's phone goes off. "I have to go. I need to be at the foodbank. Can we figure out how to manage this later?"

"Yeah. Of course."

I follow her to the sliding door and open it in time to see Winter's bike disappear down the driveway. I worry that this one stupid mistake has the potential to taint everything we've built.

24

The Other Shoe

WINTER

"OKAY, you need to tell me what's going on." Rose blocks the door to the kitchen so I can't get by her with the tub of dirty dishes from the early-morning rush. We have half an hour before the second wave.

"Nothing is going on," I lie.

She props her fist on her hip. "Yesterday you were all smiles and giddiness and in love with BJ's peen, and today you're all frowny and serious and you've barely said six words since you walked through the door two hours ago—unless you were dealing with a customer, and then you were all forced-friendly."

"I'm having an off day." That part is not a lie. I'm definitely off.

Rose crosses her arms. "You were half an hour early for

your shift, and I know I'm awesome to be around, but no one willingly shows up to work early just to hang out with me."

Scottie peeks his head out of the kitchen. "I would come in early to hang out with your awesomeness." When he sees I'm holding a bin of plates, he skirts around Rose, giving her his best smirky smile, and takes them from me.

"That's because you're a walking hormone, and I flirt with you all the time. This conversation isn't for your ears, so go back to making sandwiches," she says.

"There's nothing wrong with dating a younger man," Scottie says. "Look at Maverick Waters and his girlfriend. He's like, what? Early twenties? And she's thirty."

I frown. "I thought Maverick was mid-twenties and she was late."

Rose shakes her head. "Nope. Mav turns twenty-two in the fall, and Clover is either almost thirty or already thirty. She was his professor last year."

"What? How did I not know this?" I never would have guessed there was that much of an age difference between them. Maverick has always seemed so together, but I guess I've only known him for a couple of months, and I mostly see him when he's coaching boys' hockey.

"I don't know, but we can come back to it later since it has nothing to do with why you're in a mood this morning." She arches a manicured brow. "Lovey has messaged three times to ask if you're okay, but she won't tell me why she's asking, so that right there tells me something happened. Might as well spill the beans. It's going to come out eventually. We're too tight-knit a group, and you're a member of our weird little family now, where everyone knows everyone else's business. Lucky you."

I sigh. She's not wrong, and I need a point of view that isn't mine, Lovey's, or BJ's on this really fucking weird situation. "Lovey slept in BJ's bed last night."

"And BJ slept in yours with you?"

"No."

Rose frowns. "Can you expand on this, so I understand?"

I explain what happened, glossing over our conversation in the kitchen and what we had planned to do when we went back upstairs, and fast-forwarding to the part where I found Lovey asleep in his bed. "What am I supposed to think? He was about to bring me back up to his room for fun times, and Lovey had just spent the night there." I drop my voice to a whisper. "And we had sex for the first time the night before. Tell me it's not fucked up."

"Yeah, it's fucked up." She sighs. "I didn't realize they were still doing this."

"Still doing what?" I hate the way my stomach twists.

"Talking each other to sleep."

"This is a regular thing for them?" I lean against the counter. I don't know how to deal.

"Keep in mind that I'm a few years younger than most of the crew, and I've only been around in the summers because I went to school out of state until I got kicked out—not that that detail is important or anything. But for as long as I can remember, they've been super tight. Sometimes they'd disappear down to the dock or wherever when we were having a campfire, or up to one of their rooms if it was a movie or hang-out night. I guess everyone assumed they were fooling around, but when we'd go to surprise them, they'd either be talking or they'd have fallen asleep—but not in any kind of compromising position. They'd just be lying there next to each other."

"So what? This is just something they do?"

Rose gives me a sympathetic smile. "They've always been really close. But as far as I know, they've never been more than friends."

"They told me they'd kissed twice. Both during a game of spin the bottle when they were teenagers."

"I can't believe they brought that up. It was supposed to be in the vault forever."

"You know about it?"

"Yeah. I was there. Laughlin came up with the idea, and I don't know why everyone jumped on board. He probably goaded them into it. It's totally something he would do. I must have been eleven or twelve maybe?" She thinks a moment. "It was awkward since so many of them are related. The Buttersons and Waters are cousins, and then the Waters and Ballistics are cousins or half-cousins—whatever. Blood is involved. People were tapping out left, right, and center. Lovey had to spin the bottle three times before it landed on someone who wasn't a direct relative, and obviously that was BJ. They both looked so freaked out afterward. We all agreed that it was a bad idea and we wouldn't talk about it again. And we haven't, until now anyway."

"So they really have no chemistry?"

She shakes her head. "I think there was good and bad in it for BJ and Lovey, because they didn't have to wonder if there was more to their friendship anymore. And we've all been exposed to it for years, so to us, it's just BJ and Lovey being BJ and Lovey. I think it ramped up a lot at the end of high school when all that shit went down with BJ's previous pairs partner."

"What shit is that?"

Rose chews on the inside of her lip. "Has he ever mentioned Caroline before?"

"In passing. This is the first time I've heard her name. When I asked what happened, he said it was a story for another day. And I got the sense it wasn't all sunshine and rainbows."

"It wasn't." Rose blows out a breath. "I think you should ask BJ what happened with Caroline. There's a reason his relationship with Adele is what it is. They only spend time together on the ice. Even if they meet to talk about their routine, it's always at the arena, and most of the time Lily is there, which makes sense because she's their coach, but BJ needs those boundaries." She taps on the edge of the counter. "Sometimes I wonder if BJ and Lovey are so close because it means he doesn't have to bother with anyone else. Except you came along and turned that all upside down."

"We're not a couple or anything."

Rose shrugs. "Label or not, you two are a thing. You're an anomaly where he's concerned."

At my confused expression, she continues. "BJ has always been this super-chill guy. And he *never* gets involved with anyone during the summer. All he does is skate and hang out with the crew. That's it. It's some unwritten rule he has. But from the moment he met you, he's been *all* about you." She gives me a small smile. "I know this summer has been a real roller-coaster ride for you, Winter, but BJ isn't stringing you along, and I guarantee he and Lovey both feel like shit about this morning. You have every right to be pissed off, and take whatever time you need to process it, but when you're ready, talk it out with BJ. And ask about Caroline when you do."

"You're being awfully cryptic."

"All I know is that he went through a rough time when he had to switch pairs partners before college. I can't pretend to know what it's like for you to have your world turned upside down like this. But I think you're turning BJ's world upside down too. And that's not a bad thing."

I SPOTTED BJ by the boards during practice, so I'm unsurprised to find him by the bike racks when I leave the arena that afternoon.

"Hey." He shoves his phone into his pocket and pushes to a stand. His stubble is already turning back into a beard—a short one, but it's dark, and it grows quickly. His hair looks like his hands have been in it a lot today. He runs his palms over his thighs. "How are you?"

"Okay. You?"

He lifts a shoulder and lets it fall. "Not gonna lie, today was fucking shitty."

I huff a laugh. "It was definitely that."

"Can we talk?" BJ is usually confident, so his uncertainty is surprising.

"Yeah. We can talk." I'm used to being unsettled, but it's better to just have the discussion and move forward.

"Should we go for a drive or a walk on the pier or something?"

We spend a lot of time making out in BJ's Jeep, so a drive is probably not the best plan. "The pier is good."

"Okay." He nods. "Want to put your bag in the Jeep?"

"It's okay. I can carry it."

He bites the inside of his cheek but doesn't try to persuade me otherwise. I fall into step beside him as we cross the open field that leads to the beach.

"I'm sorry about this morning, Winter. I feel shitty about what happened, and so does Lovey. I know it's not okay, and you have every right to be upset, but if there's a way I can fix this, tell me and I'll do it. Whatever it takes." He stops and turns to face me, running a hand through his hair. "I just... I really like you, and the thought of losing this, you... I've felt sick all day. And anxious. My stomach has been in knots, and my mouth has been dry, and I can't eat, and you're all I can think about. I don't want to fuck this up, Winter. So if there's something I can do to make this better, I will. Just tell me what to do."

He's practically vibrating with anxiety.

"I don't have a whole lot of relationship experience to draw on here, so I don't know what I should be asking for, but do you see how messed up that whole situation was from my perspective?" I ask.

He nods. "Yeah. It shouldn't have happened."

"But it did, and you can't take it back, so now we need to figure out how to move forward."

"It won't happen again. I promise."

"Don't promise things like that, BJ. You can fall asleep anywhere." I tug on his arm and lead him to a bench under a tree. I pull one leg up so my knee rests against the back of the bench. "I think it was the combination of things—going to college in the fall, possibly living down the street from you in a house with your friends, us having sex, and then you offering me orgasms and seeing Lovey in your bed. It was a lot. It's still a lot." I sigh. "I don't want to come between you and Lovey."

"You're not. She's my best friend. That's all."

"Rose and I talked today. She echoed the whole thing about you and Lovey being just friends, and I don't see why you'd lie since I'm most likely moving in with Lovey in a few weeks. But she mentioned Caroline."

BJ flinches, like her name causes him pain. "She doesn't have anything to do with me and Lovey, or you and me."

"I'd never heard her name before Rose mentioned it. You told me you skated together all through high school, right? That's a pretty significant span of time."

His knee bounces a few times. "Do we really need to talk about this?"

"Based on your reaction, yeah, we do. Why don't you want to? Because it's uncomfortable? Or it hurts?"

He's quiet for a moment. "Both."

"How do you think this morning made me feel?" I need this, I realize—something from him that shows me he has wounds too. That even people who seem like they have everything also have scars. I think this is his.

"Fair." He nods. "Caroline was my pairs partner during high school. She was super talented, a real natural. Skating with her felt effortless." He scratches at his beard. "We spent a lot of time together. If we weren't at school, we were on the ice. My mom wasn't my coach back then. That changed when Adele became my partner." He rubs his chin. "Caroline's family was strict. Super strict. She was only allowed out for school-related stuff and skating. I've always been driven when it comes to figure skating, so the more time we spent on the ice together, the better, you know?"

"It was her only escape." *He* was her only escape.

"Yeah. We were together seven days a week. We talked all the time—messaged in skating code sometimes because her parents monitored her phone. She didn't have a lot of friends because most of her free time was spent on the ice with me, so I was basically her only outlet. We were teenagers. Pairs skating can be intimate, and hormones are a thing." His cheek tics, but his smile is sad.

I can see where this is going. "You started dating?"

He nods. "Once I got my license, I'd pick her up after school and drive her to the arena. We'd practice for hours. She was the middle out of four kids. Her sister was a cellist, and her brothers both played soccer. They were busy all the time, and her parents trusted me. We kept it a secret, though. Her parents wouldn't have allowed it. We lost our V cards together." He swallows, eyes on his clasped hands. "We were great together on the ice, and we were on track to qualify for the Olympic trials. But I was a senior, and she was a junior. I started applying to colleges, because it was what you do, but it made things hard. Sometimes pairs who are involved shine on the ice. Their chemistry is palpable. But we were young, and things got complicated."

"Complicated how?" I'm aware this story has a sad ending, the kind that's impacted how BJ handles relationships.

"We had this huge competition, and there was so much pressure coming at us from all sides. Then her parents found out what was going on, and shit hit the fan." He pauses, his voice thick with emotion. "It was so fucking bad. They started coming to every single practice. Driving her. Picking her up. Monitoring every interaction. Then we had the competition." He runs his hands over his knees.

"It didn't go well?"

He shakes his head. "My mom thought maybe we should pull out, but Caroline was adamant that we compete. Neither of us was sleeping, though. We were too stressed. It was a complex routine—a lot of intricate combinations. God, we'd rehearsed it so many times. Executed it perfectly. We should've been fine. But she didn't land one of the spins and snapped the tendon in her ankle." He runs his palm down his face. "It was devastating, Winter. On so many levels. To recover from an injury like that, to get back on the ice, it was an uphill battle. She had multiple surgeries to fix the tendon and spent a lot of time in physical therapy. Her family moved away, and we lost touch. It was just too hard. There was too much guilt and blame." His gaze lifts, and I see it—the guilt he carries, the way it haunts him. "I wish I could go back and undo the damage, but it's already done."

"That's why you keep such rigid lines with Adele," I say softly.

He nods. "She knows what happened, and she understands why I want the boundaries we have. We set those up right from the start. I couldn't risk something like that happening again. All it caused was pain for everyone involved."

"How many relationships have you had since then?" I ask, puzzle pieces sliding into place, thanks to my conversation with Rose earlier today.

He rubs the back of his neck. "I'm assuming by relationship you mean one that's lasted more than twenty-four to forty-eight hours?"

"Oh, man." I huff a laugh. "Now what Rose said earlier makes sense."

I can see it in a way I couldn't before, how his relationship with Lovey helped keep a barrier between him and everyone else. They were never going to be a couple. She was always going to be a safe place for him, and after what happened with Caroline, it makes sense that he would guard his heart.

So many things line up now—the way BJ always tries to find the bright side, how he is with Adele, how dedicated he is to his craft, how willing he is to be my soft landing. Why we connect the way we do.

"Which was what?" he asks.

"That being close to Lovey means you don't have to get close to anyone else."

"That's not..." His brow furrows, and he runs his hand through his hair. "Fuck." He shakes his head and murmurs, "I turned her into a shield." He looks up at me. "How did I not see this until now?"

I shrug. "You didn't have a reason to see it."

"Fuck. I'm such an asshole."

"That's not true, BJ. I doubt it was conscious for either of you. You've been best friends your whole life—you lean on each other. It must have been hard to see you go through that. She would have wanted to protect you."

"Like the way you protected your mom from your dad," BJ whispers.

"Don't draw that kind of parallel, BJ. You're not an abuser."

"But I used my best friend as an emotional shield."

I squeeze his hand. "Everyone takes on roles, BJ. Some are good and some aren't. The important part is, now that you see it for what it is, you can do something to change it."

"I wish I would have realized this sooner. Then we could have avoided this shitty situation," he says.

"We all make mistakes. We learn from them and move on."

"Are we okay?"

"Yeah. We're okay."

"Can I hug you?" he asks softly.

"Yeah." I smile. "You can hug me."

He folds me into a tight embrace. "I hated every moment of today until this one."

I pull back. "But if it hadn't happened, would you have opened up to me about Caroline?"

"Eventually. Probably. Maybe."

I smile, and he ducks his head.

"Thank you for letting me in. I know it was hard, but I feel closer to you now. So yeah, today sucked, but we got past the bad part, didn't we?"

"Yeah. We did." He smiles. "Thank you for being you."

"Thank you for being brave enough to be vulnerable." I cup his face in my palms and kiss him.

I feel steady again. And like maybe this something good I've found is going to last.

25

New Beginnings

WINTER

LOVEY and I have a heart-to-heart to clear the air, and both of us end up getting emotional. She agreed that she and BJ needed some boundaries, and those would include not falling asleep together.

A few days before I'm scheduled to move to Chicago for college, my mom gets the all-clear to move back to the cabin. While she's been recovering at the Sunshine Center, a local, family-run company called Stitches Construction has repaired the railing at the cabin, and they've cleaned out the entire garage. They have some kind of plan for that, but I don't know what all it entails. They've also installed a security system, so my mom doesn't have to worry about unwanted visitors.

So far, my dad has been following the order of protection, although I have a feeling Logan is responsible for that. All I can do is cross my fingers and hope the work my mom has done will help her continue to make good choices and keep my dad and his toxicity out of her life.

I was nervous about Mom being alone in the cabin, but she met a woman in her GED class who has a job at Harry's Hardware and was looking for a place in Pearl Lake. She's a few years younger than Mom, but she's sweet and they get along well, so Clover and Sunny, Lovey's mom, and I helped get my bedroom ready for her new roommate. I can always bunk with my mom if I come home to visit during the school year. And it's worth it because for the first time in years, my mom has friends and a social life.

Mom has one of her GED classes the day we're driving to Chicago. I don't want her to miss it because it's math and that's never been an easy subject for her, so we plan for her to visit once I'm settled in. Coach Ballistic and Lily, and Rose's parents, Charlene and Darren Westinghouse, help us load their pickup trucks with our belongings. I don't have a ton of stuff, but Rose has enough boxes to fill a freaking warehouse, and we drive down to the city.

I've seen pictures of the houses, but they don't do them justice. I run my hands up and down my thighs, excitement setting in. "A few of my friends from high school went to college and lived in student housing," I announce. "None of those places looked like this."

BJ just smiles. Down the street is the house that's mine—well, that I'm going to live in. There's no old couch marring the porch, no sheets masquerading as curtains, no flags in the windows. The walkway is lined with pretty flowers.

"River likes to garden," BJ explains as we park out front.

"Really?" I haven't met him yet, but I've heard all about him. His twin is Lavender, and she's in New York. River has a boyfriend named Josiah and he works at a sporting-goods store.

He played for the school football team last year, but BJ said he's not sure if River plans to this fall.

"Yeah. He dresses like a black cloud, but he's a wizard with a rose bush," BJ says. "He's an interesting guy. He's low-key, serious about his studies, and not big on the party scene, so pretty much the ideal roommate. And he spends a lot of time at his boyfriend's because Josiah has his own apartment, so he might not be around much."

"Is he home now?"

Lacey waves as she opens the front door and carries a box inside.

"He's working, but he said he'd be home later."

"Cool." My hand is already on the door handle, waiting for BJ to put the Jeep in park so I can get out, but Lovey comes bounding up to the passenger side and yanks it open.

"Come on! I can't wait to show you your room!" She's practically vibrating with excitement.

"Just let me grab a couple of bags from the trunk." I give BJ an apologetic smile.

He tips his chin toward the house. "Go check it out. I'll be up in a minute with some of your stuff."

Lovey opens the door to the back seat and grabs my duffle and a plastic bin. I pull out my backpack and another bin and follow her up the front walk. I spot Rose two doors down doing a cartwheel on the front lawn, followed by a roundoff. She waves and skips up the front steps of the house, meeting Quinn at the door.

Lacey holds the door open for us. "Can I take anything?"

"We're good. BJ has more of Winter's stuff in his Jeep," Lovey says.

"I'll grab a tote." Lacey is the quieter of the twins, and her face is slightly more angular than Lovey's. She also has a small birthmark above her lip on the right side, which makes it easier to differentiate between them. Although their style helps with that too. Lovey is all pastel colors, and Lacey is a bit more funky.

"This is the kitchen," Lovey says as we pass through the spacious room.

It's eat-in, with white cupboards and gray countertops. It must be at least twice as big as the cabin's kitchen.

"Wow. This is amazing."

"It's great for communal dinners," Lovey agrees. "The living room is through there. I'll show you once our hands aren't full." She leads me up a staircase and down the hall, passing one closed bedroom door and two open ones—those belong to Lovey and Lacey. At the end of the hall, we climb to the third floor.

"It's a long way up, but it's private and has its own bathroom." Lovey elbows the door open and steps aside to let me through.

"Holy wow." I set down my load and take in the huge, open room with sloped ceilings. A sliding door leads to a balcony, which overlooks the backyard. "Are you sure you want me to take this room? Maybe you or Lacey would rather have it? Or even River?"

"River spends a lot of time at Josiah's place, so he already said he doesn't need the extra space. And Lacey and I are settled in the bedrooms on the second floor, so this is all yours."

"Every student house I've ever visited has been run-down and in need of a serious paint job," I admit. "I feel bad that I'm taking this from Rose."

The walls are painted a purple so pale it almost looks white at first. The floors are honey hardwood, and in the center of the room is a square area rug. The bed is set in the middle of the room, and I'm pretty sure it's a queen. Dark purple curtains frame the sliding door, pulled back and tied with white ribbons.

A huge white dresser sits across from the bed, and on the other side of the room is a pale wood desk, a combination whiteboard and corkboard fixed to the wall above it. Broadway play posters decorate another wall between two doors. The open one leads to the bathroom, and the other I assume is a closet. The spare room at BJ's house was nice, but this is so much different. It symbolizes freedom and new beginnings.

Lovey pats my shoulder. "Rose will be fine. Kody's room is huge and neat as a pin. Plus, it'll be good for Quinn and BJ to have a little estrogen in that house to balance things out. Rose is a neat freak, and BJ isn't. It should work well if they don't irritate each other to death."

BJ appears in the doorway, carrying a box and a bag. "I forgot how freaking many stairs there are in this house," he huffs, setting his armful beside the other totes and bags.

"I'm going down to help unload," Lovey says. "Rose brought everything except the kitchen sink."

"We'll be there in a minute," BJ says.

"Take your time."

She disappears down the stairs, leaving me alone with BJ.

"How do you like the space?" he asks.

"It's amazing. This room is almost the size of our entire cabin."

He comes to stand in front of me, the toes of his shoes touching mine. I look up at him. "It's a lot to take in, huh?"

I smile. "Yeah. It's a lot."

"My bedroom is smaller, and you're welcome to sleep beside me anytime you want."

"I don't know how much sleeping we'll be doing."

"Eventually we'll get to the sleeping part, but this week, it's all about showing you the fun side of college. And this room has lots of privacy." He wraps an arm around my waist and pulls me closer, his mouth covering mine.

I loop my arms around his neck and sink into the kiss, at least until I hear someone stomping up the stairs.

"Dad incoming!" Coach Ballistic appears in the doorway a moment after we break apart. "That's a lot of stairs." He's slightly out of breath. "I think there are only a couple more boxes down there for you." He sets down the ones he's carried, and his eyebrows pull together as he takes in the small pile that's accumulated next to the door. "Are we missing any?"

"Nope," I assure him. "I pack light. We should go down and help. Rose brought half of Pearl Lake with her."

He shakes his head. "No kidding. I think Darren and Charlene might be making a second trip later in the week."

"Is that because they forgot stuff or because they want to check up on Rose?" BJ asks as we follow his dad downstairs.

"Both, I think," Coach says wryly.

With everyone pitching in, we get all of Rose's boxes into her room. BJ's house is just as nice, with a big, open kitchen, a living room with a huge TV, and a main-floor bedroom that belongs to BJ.

Upstairs are two more bedrooms, each with their own bathroom. Quinn's room is across the hall from Rose's.

Once the vehicles are empty of boxes, the parents order food and we gather outside at BJ's. They have a hot tub and a big backyard with a hockey net and basketball hoop. After lunch, we're enveloped in a round of parent hugs as they prepare to leave. Charlene pulls Rose aside, and they have a whispered conversation while Darren rubs the back of his neck and frowns.

Lily approaches me while BJ talks to his dad. "We'll bring your mom up for a visit soon, okay?"

"That would be great. Thank you so much, Lily, for everything. None of this would have been possible without you."

"We just helped push things along. Remember that college is supposed to be fun, and it's okay to make mistakes along the way. Enjoy the freedom, be safe, and I promise your mom has a whole community to help her back home, okay?"

"Okay. Thank you." My eyes prick with emotion.

"Your mom is so proud of you, Winter, and so are we." She pulls me in for a hug, and we both shed a couple of tears.

Then I stand with everyone on the sidewalk and wave while the parents drive away.

The second they turn the corner, Rose shouts, "Party time!"

Quinn looks at his phone. "I gotta coach, but I'll only be gone a couple of hours. No parties until I'm home and able to play security guard."

"Come on!" Rose throws her hands in the air.

"You need to unpack anyway. We'll come help." Lovey links arms with Rose and Lacey. "And BJ can help Winter unpack."

"Unpack my ass," Rose grumbles. "But when we're done, we're having a party."

"Please don't burn the house down while I'm gone," Quinn says. "And please, for the love of God, Rose, do not invite five hundred people you don't know over by posting on social media."

"That only happened once, and it was an accident." Rose and the twins traipse across the lawn and disappear into the house.

Quinn turns to BJ. "Keep an eye on that one. I know Lovey thinks she'll be fine, but now that there's no parent supervision, I have a feeling the well-behaved Rose of the summer will give us a run for our money." He turns his smile on me. "I'm looking forward to shooting the puck around with you."

"Same here."

Quinn jumps into his truck, and BJ inclines his head. "Should we get you unpacked and then get naked?"

"Can we reverse the order?"

"I love that we're on the same wavelength."

26

The Other Side

WINTER

TWO HOURS, several orgasms, and zero unpacking later, our group chat starts blowing up. The girls want to swim. While BJ grabs swim trunks from his place, I dump my duffle in search of a bathing suit.

Quinn's already returned from teaching—he coaches a special-needs boys' hockey team. River's working until close this evening, so he probably won't be home until sometime after ten, but he's aware a few people are coming over.

When they say a few friends, I assume they're being literal. But by eight thirty, there must be twenty people in the backyard, and more keep trickling in. Most of them appear to be friends with Quinn, and based on their T-shirts, they play for the school team.

Along with the slew of hot guys, which Rose is super excited about, comes an equal number of girls in swimsuit coverups and bikinis. Everyone is drinking from red plastic cups or travel mugs. There's a huge sign on the fence by the gate that reads NO GLASS BY THE POOL. There's also a sign on the hot tub cover that reads CLOSED BECAUSE SOMEONE PEED IN HERE. In addition, padlocks keep it securely closed. Clearly they have some experience with backyard parties.

BJ is on the other side of the pool, talking to a group of people. No less than five girls have stopped to hug him. It's annoying.

"How often does this happen?" I motion to all the people in bathing suits milling around.

"Maverick used to throw parties all the time." Lovey twists her hair around her finger. "But mostly at the beginning of the year, before they shut the pool down and hockey season was in full swing."

"Although, he'd still throw the occasional midsemester party," Lacey adds. "Except last year. After the first month or so, he was all business. I can't believe none of us realized what was going on."

"You mean the part where he was trying to get Lavender and Kody to deal with their feelings or the fact that he was secretly dating his professor?" Lovey asks.

"I still can't believe Clover was his professor. Or that Maverick is only twenty-two. Or that she's eight years older than him," I mutter.

"They fit, though," Rose says.

"Agree." I sip my drink. It's some extra-sugary cooler that's bound to give me a headache. "What's this about Kody and Lavender, though?"

"That is a long, angsty story. But at the beginning of last year, Lavender and Kody were not on the best terms," Lovey says.

"Mostly because Kody thought he was bad for her," Lacey adds.

"But really, they've been meant for each other since Kody could say her name. They were adorable with each other as kids. He was in love with her right from the start." Lovey sighs and then smiles. "Anyway, Mav knew they needed a push, so he helped force them to deal with their shit. And now they're totally in love. It's the sweetest."

"Except for the duct-tape thing, that's not sweet." BJ appears out of nowhere. He's shirtless, wearing a pair of blue board shorts and slides. I let my gaze travel over all that ink. Despite having sex all over my new bedroom, I'm already thinking about the end of the night and how much I'm looking forward to another beard ride. It's grown back over the past few weeks, and his hair is longer again, pulled back with a baby blue spiral tie.

"What duct-tape thing?" Rose asks.

"Huh?" BJ turns to me. "How's your drink? You need a refill?"

I pull the lid off and check the contents. "I'm still good, but thanks."

"What about the rest of you? Need anything?"

"We're good for now," Lovey and Lacey say in tandem.

"Same, same." Rose gives him a thumbs-up.

He grabs the armrests of the lounge chair and leans down to kiss me. "I can't wait to get you back into bed."

"Give the PDA a break, BJ." Rose beans him on the side of the head with an ice cube.

He fires the bird in her direction. "Let me know if you need me for anything."

"I'm good, but thanks." I push on his chest, and he joins Quinn and a group of guys.

A minute later, a pair of definitely-not-sober girls flounce over. They look polished and color-coordinated. And like maybe their outfits intentionally match.

"Quinn said this is your house now. We were like, so sad that Mav wasn't coming back this year because he threw the best parties. But like, this is so great."

"So great," her friend echoes. "Are you guys like, identical twins?"

Lovey and Lacey nod in unison. I imagine that question must get old, and annoying. It's pretty fucking obvious they're identical twins.

"That's so cool," the girl on the right says.

"So cool," her friend agrees.

They turn to me. "I can't believe BJ kissed you," one of them says. "In public. That's like, my dream."

Her friend sighs. "Mine too."

"Uh..." I glance at Lovey, but she and Lacey are busy exchanging looks.

"Props, girl, for jumping on that early."

They giggle and stare at me, like they're waiting for something.

When I don't respond, the chattier of the two pipes up again. "Are you like, for sure, for sure hooking up tonight?"

"I need to go to the bathroom. Winter, come with me." Lovey hops out of her chair and pulls me out of mine. She pauses to address the girls. "And the answer is yes. BJ is out of bounds."

"Out of bounds?" The girls wear matching confused expressions.

"Off-limits. Unavailable."

"Right. Okay. That's what we thought, but we figured we'd check, just in case."

Lovey rolls her eyes and drags me along with her, skirting

around the side of the house because the sliding door is locked to keep randoms out.

"What the hell was that about?" I glance over my shoulder at the girls, now talking to Lacey and Rose, who look unimpressed about being left with them. "And why did they sound like Valley girl cutouts? They're like stock characters out of a bad nineties' movie."

Lovey stops at a side door I didn't know existed and punches in a code. When we enter, to the right is a small bathroom. She flicks on the light and pulls me in.

"Why didn't I know this was here?"

"It's the emergency bathroom."

"What are we doing?"

"Escaping the bunnies for a few minutes."

"I know there are hockey groupies, but there are figure-skater groupies too?"

"Sort of?" Lovey tugs at the end of her ponytail. "For four years, this house was where all Maverick, Quinn, and Kody's hockey buddies hung out. The girls who chase the players are still going to show up for a while, and River's football friends are a whole different story. But I don't know if we need to worry about them since River is on the fence about playing this year." She waves a hand in the air. "BJ is like, honorary hockey, I guess? I don't know, but he's friendly and flirty, and you've seen him."

"He's hot and looks like a bad boy with all the tattoos." And he has a peen piercing.

"Yeah. He's a bit of an anomaly. He's this tattooed, bearded —unless he has a competition—figure skater. It all sort of contradicts itself, you know? And these girls, some of them are nice, but others are status chasers. Sleeping with these guys is some weird rite of passage. It's fucked up. But that's how it is.

They come around at the beginning of the year a lot. We ignore them, for the most part."

"So I should ignore the fact that these girls are all over BJ?" We don't have a label, but we also don't fit in the fuck-buddy category.

"Not exactly. Sometimes you need to fight fire with fire."

"What does that mean?"

"Those girls curate themselves for parties like these. They're peacocks. You're stunning, and you have this rockin' body. I'm so jealous of your ass, it's not even funny." She holds up a hand when I start to interrupt her. "My ass is nice, but yours is like..." She does jazz hands and sings, "Ahhhhhh."

"What are you suggesting? Do I need to put on makeup? There's no way I'm getting those fake eyelash things. They don't mix with hockey." At least I don't think they do. And I have no interest in finding out. I'm a mascara and eyeliner girl. That isn't going to change.

Lovey shakes her head. "You don't need makeup, but your bathing suit is a little...understated."

It's a boy-shorts-and-black-top combo. It was the first bathing suit I found, hence the one I threw on. "You mean it's not sexy enough."

"Don't get me wrong; you look hot. But we can up your game a little."

"Do I want to play this game?" I genuinely have no idea.

"I love BJ. He's my best friend. But he can be a bit clueless when it comes to managing relationships."

I don't know that I have any more experience than he does. "So that's a yes? I do want to play this game?"

"I think he would benefit from a dose of his own medicine."

"Okay?" It comes out sounding like a question. I hold up a hand. "Wait. Is this a best-friend-sticking-up-for-her-best-friend test? Am I failing it?"

Lovey laughs. "It's not a test, and you're not failing. Let's just try a different suit and see what happens."

I nod, and she opens the bathroom door. Lacey and Rose are standing on the other side.

"We're staging an intervention." Rose holds up two scraps of fabric and a makeup bag.

"It's like we're telepathically communicating." Lovey presses her hand to her chest. "I was just telling Winter we needed a wardrobe change."

Rose smiles at me. "We also talked about how we needed to take you bathing-suit shopping this week because this black number, while very practical, isn't doing the body you're rocking justice."

"You were talking about my bathing suit?"

"Lacey and I were actually talking about how awesome your legs are, and then we got on the topic of bathing suits and how you make a completely functional suit look hot and how we needed to expand your bathing-suit game. Which we're doing right now, so BJ can get an actual clue. These fucking girls need to move along."

Rose tosses the bikini at me and pulls Lovey out of the bathroom. "Change into that. When you're done, let me know so I can give you dramatic eyes." She holds up her makeup case, then shuts the door in my face.

I stare at the scraps of fabric. There really isn't much to this bikini. Still... A lot of girls have been hugging BJ. And doing the hair-flip-giggle shit. I shuck off my shorts and pull on the pale pink bottoms. I'm grateful that they're held together by more than a string at each hip, but the crisscross half-inch bands leave a lot of skin exposed.

The top covers most of my boobs, but also gives me cleavage, which I don't have a ton of. I gotta give it to Rose—this is an infinitely sexier suit than the one I was wearing. And my entire ass isn't on display, so that's a bonus. I'll call this an acceptable compromise.

I open the door.

"Fuck, yeah. I'm a goddamn magician." Rose does jazz hands by her crotch.

"This is perfect. Lavender would be so proud," Lacey says.

"I miss her," Lovey sighs. "But you're right. She would be damn proud."

I clear my throat. "I have one thing I want to say before we move forward with this questionable plan."

"It's a rock-star plan, not a questionable one, but feel free to voice your concerns." Rose makes a go-on motion.

"We're all acknowledging that I'm basically asking for people to look at my body in an objectifying way?"

The three of them exchange looks.

"We're weaponizing your assets," Rose says. "BJ is out there shirtless, all his pretty muscles and tattoos on display. This is no different. And before you go defending your previous bathing-suit choice, or coming at me with more female empowerment, do-I-want-to-succumb-to-the-patriarchy nonsense, let me ask you this: Do you feel sexy?"

"Uh, yes?"

"Seriously, when you see yourself in the mirror, do you think: 'I worked hard to have an ass that's the envy of all my friends. As a strong, independent woman who believes in equity and freedom of self-expression, do I like the way I look in this hot-as-fuck bikini?'" She pauses. "The answer to that should be yes. And, yes, we're all acknowledging that you're showing off the goods. One day our boobs aren't going to hold themselves up anymore. We should give them a chance to be appreciated for their outstanding ability to defy gravity."

"Great speech, Rose. I vote you president of the bikini association," Lovey says. "Can we get Winter's eyes done so we can get back out there?" She thumbs over her shoulder.

All three of them cram themselves into the bathroom with me, and five minutes later I'm wearing dramatic eyeliner that's apparently water- and smear-proof and clear mascara. Rose undoes my braid, setting my hair free in kinky waves. She props a fist on her hip and shakes her head.

"What?"

"You're fucking gorgeous. Let's go turn some heads, ladies." She snaps her fingers, and we file out of the bathroom, our slides slapping an out-of-sync beat on the concrete.

"I feel ridiculous," I mutter to Lovey.

"You don't look ridiculous," she replies. "Let's consider this an experiment in cisgender straight male behavior."

We return to the pool, stopping at the cooler to refill our drinks. Our previous chairs have been taken by a new group of girls, two of whom hugged BJ earlier.

"Poolside, ladies." Rose sashays like she's strutting the runway. We all plunk our butts down on the edge of the pool, in the middle so we have the best view and are less likely to get hit by cannonball spray.

"Incoming, eleven o'clock." Lovey nudges Lacey with her elbow.

"Ah, shit. Who invited him?" Lacey grumbles.

"Hey, Lovey, Lacey, my favorite twins! How's it going? We miss you over at Kappa Pi!" A beefy dude with dark blond hair comes wading over, a smile on his face. He's drunk, based on the way he struggles to maintain a straight trajectory.

"Hey, Cooper. I'm sure whoever replaces us this year will keep you more than entertained." Lacey inspects her nails.

"It's a couple of freshmen in the engineering program. Those girls aren't much for a party, but we might be able to do a little corrupting."

"It is your favorite pastime," Lacey says with a stiff smile.

He turns to me and Rose. "Hey, I'm Cooper, and you are?"

"I'm Winter, and this is Rose."

Rose waves and takes a sip from her drink, looking anywhere but at the beefy guy.

"I haven't seen either of you around before. You freshmen?"

"Sophomore. I'm a transfer," Rose says, like she's bored and he's the reason.

"Same." I take another sip of my overly sweet cooler. I make a mental note to drink a bunch of water and take ibuprofen before bed.

"Oh yeah?" His attention returns to me. "Transfer from where?"

Two more guys join him. There's another round of introductions. I forget their names two seconds later. They *look* like dude-bros—thick, like they spend a lot of time at the gym doing bench presses and not much else. They all have gelled hair and straight teeth. If I run into them on campus, there's a good chance I won't be able to tell one from the other.

"Winter plays hockey for the college team," Lovey offers.

"Really?" One of the new guys looks me over. "I play rugby."

"Mm, that's a rough sport."

"I like it rough." He winks.

"Oh my God." Rose is in the middle of a sip, and she cough-chokes.

I pat her back, and she coughs into her elbow. "Sorry. Went down the wrong way."

I glance to the right, where BJ is standing with Quinn and a couple of girls. One of the girls is fully focused on Quinn, but his attention is on us. The other one is touching BJ's arm, probably asking about his tattoos. I smirk when I remember how I drove him crazy by tracing the one on his hip with my tongue earlier this afternoon. BJ's eyes flare when they find me, and his gaze flicks back and forth between me and the guys. He abandons Quinn and the girls and heads for the pool.

He steps off the edge, barely making a splash. He wades across the pool, skirts around the dude-bros, and makes a beeline for me.

"Mission fucking accomplished," Rose mutters, having recovered from her coughing fit.

"Hey, hey. You disappeared for a while. Where'd you go?" One side of BJ's mouth curves up in a knowing smile. He sets his drink behind me, then settles his hands on my knees and uses his hip to nudge his way between my thighs.

The guys who were chatting us up see someone else they know and move on.

"I changed and got a refill." I'm going for nonchalant, but fighting a grin. Mostly I find this whole thing somewhere between funny, because it's transparent, and irritating, because it's effective.

BJ bites his lip, hands sliding up my thighs. "When'd you get this bikini? I haven't seen it before."

"It's mine," Rose says.

"Maybe don't give it back." BJ doesn't break eye contact with me.

"We're going shopping this week," Lacey tells him.

"Excellent news. I look forward to the fashion show."

"Okay, job well done, girls." Rose clinks her travel mug against Lovey's over my head, and Lacey holds hers up in acknowledgment. "Let's leave these two to the poolside foreplay."

I purse my lips as BJ's grin widens, and the three of them get to their feet and abandon me. The dude-bros call after them, but they wave them off.

"Did I just fall into a trap?" BJ brushes my hair over my shoulders, skimming my arms with his fingertips.

"It was more of an experiment than a trap."

"What kind of experiment?" He takes my drink, sniffs it, and sets it aside.

"The successful kind." I drape my arms over his shoulders and link my fingers behind his neck.

"Does that mean I'm a good test subject?"

"The perfect one, actually."

"Oh yeah?" His hands smooth over the outside of my thighs. "Well, if you need to test other theories, I'm always a willing guinea pig." When he reaches my knees, he hooks his hands behind them and urges me to wrap my legs around his waist.

"We're not alone, BJ. There's a backyard full of your friends."

"Mm... Only a small handful count as friends. Maybe I should shout *cops* and make everyone leave." He brushes his nose against mine and pulls me into the pool with him. He cups my ass and lowers me enough that I can feel him hard between my thighs.

I unhook my legs and find the bottom of the pool. "Looks like you have to stay in here for a while." I step back, but he winds his arm around my waist, keeping me close.

"Whoa, whoa. You got my attention, now you're gonna leave me here?" He pulls me back into him. "That's what you wanted, right? My attention?"

We've been in a bubble, surrounded by his friends and family, cocooned in the comfort of the people he's closest to. This is the other side of his world, the one filled with parties and flirty girls. I suddenly feel out of my depth and out of his league.

I swallow hard and stare at his chest.

One of his hands slides up my back, under my hair to the nape of my neck, and along the edge of my jaw until his finger rests under my chin. He urges me to look at him. His eyes search mine, and I feel embarrassingly transparent.

He follows the curve of my lip with his thumb. "We marking our territory?"

I bite back a grin. "Seems like maybe, yeah."

"Gotta admit, I didn't love seeing those jocks chatting you up."

"Good." At least I'm not alone in this.

The right side of his mouth tips skyward. "You're sexy when you're territorial."

"So are you."

He dips down and captures my lips. I'm not usually one for PDA, but I'm not above giving those girls the clear message that BJ is off-limits. We get lost in a kiss, at least until someone cannonballs into the pool beside us.

Quinn pops up, a wry grin on his face. "You got bedrooms for that. Take it upstairs or down the street." He winks at me and swims across the pool, pulling himself out of the water next to where Lovey, Lacey, and Rose have snagged two loungers.

"I need a few minutes to calm down before I get out of the pool."

I grin. "I'm aware. I can feel you poking me in the stomach."

I try to step back, but he snags me again, both hands on my waist, and lifts me. I brace my hands on his shoulders, my hair falling in a veil around us. "What're you doing?"

"Keeping myself entertained until I can get out of this pool and convince you it's time for bed." He sets me back down. "When I say jump—"

"—I'm not saying how high."

He grins. "Never in a million years would I expect that to come out of your mouth. Indulge me. I wanna lift you."

"Lift me? Like, above your head?"

"Yeah."

"Uh, I weigh a lot more than Adele."

"I think she weighs more than you think. She's compact, but she's all muscle."

"And like five inches shorter than me. I'm also bottom heavy. The weight distribution is probably a lot different."

"Please?"

"You're going to annoy me until I say yes, aren't you?"

"Yeah."

"Okay. But don't be surprised when you drop me on your head."

"And if I don't? What do I get?"

"The knowledge that you're right and I'm wrong. Give me the lowdown on how to do this."

"Brace your hands on my shoulders. And when I say jump, you jump. When you feel like you have your balance, you can let go of my shoulders. I promise I won't let go of you. And when you're up there, imagine you're an arrow."

"Okay. I'm an arrow. Got it."

The first time he counts to three, I don't jump. But the second time he lifts me out of the water. It can't be easy. I'm not light.

"I got you. You can let go."

His words, while maybe unintentional, ignite heat low in my belly. It's what he says when I'm close to an orgasm and trying to stay in control. I release his left shoulder and he adjusts his grip. And again when I lift my right hand. Then I'm floating in the air, balanced in his palms.

I realize again the trust and connection he must have with Adele. How they rely on each other. How hard they work as a team. How intimate that relationship is. How BJ has worked to make sure they have clear boundaries. I wonder if it's difficult for her to have me in the way.

The partygoers hoot and cheer. Someone calls, "Ten out of ten," and someone else yells, "Do a swan dive!"

I glance down at BJ, his muscles corded, but still making it look effortless.

"I'm going in," I tell him, then tip forward.

He tries to correct us, but I'm already heading for the water. He bends his arms slightly, then pushes up, making me airborne for a second before I'm underwater. When I pop up, he's already there, tugging me to where Quinn and the girls are while everyone in the pool claps.

He doesn't leave my side for the rest of the night.

27

You Should Know

BJ

THE MORNING AFTER THE MOVE-IN/WELCOME party, I make Winter and me egg sandwiches on English muffins with bacon and cheese and bring them back to my bedroom with coffee. Quinn's already left for work, and I'm pretty sure Rose will be sleeping well into the afternoon based on the selfies she was sending to our group chat at three in the morning, but I have a couch and a coffee table in my bedroom, and this means Winter doesn't need to put on more clothes, since I plan to take off what little she has on once we're fed.

She's sitting cross-legged on the couch, wearing one of my T-shirts and a pair of black underwear. And that's all.

"I need to tell you something," I blurt.

She's in the middle of a bite of egg sandwich, so she covers her mouth with her hand and mumbles, "Okay."

I nod a couple of times and run my hands up and down my thighs.

She frowns and sets her plate down. "Are you okay?"

"Yeah. Fine. I mean, good."

Winter swallows her bite and gives me a skeptical look. "Everything about your body language says different."

I stop with the leg bouncing and stretch an arm across the back of the couch, adopting a more relaxed stance.

"You're making me nervous," Winter says.

"I'm making myself nervous," I mutter.

"Are you a serial killer?"

"What?"

"Serial killer." She makes an *ee-ee-ee* sound and accompanies it with a stabbing motion. "Are you?"

"No. I set spiders free, and junior year bio when we dissected the fetal pig was not my fave. I don't think I'd be a great murderer."

"Okay. So whatever is making you all sketchy and anxious over there can't be that bad. Just spit it out."

I drum on the edge of the couch, then wrap my fingers around it so I don't keep fidgeting. "Well, you know I haven't been in a relationship with anyone since my senior year of high school."

"Uh-huh. I haven't dated anyone since around the same time, so we're in the same boat. It gets kind of incest-y when the options are limited to local guys. At least in high school we were bussed into Lake Geneva, so it expanded the dating pool." She picks up her sandwich and takes another bite.

Maybe this isn't as big a deal as Lovey thought. Although last night was a bit of an eye-opener. "Right. So I've spent the past three years of college not taking much seriously, apart from skating and my classes."

"And?" She makes a go-on motion.

"And I've had a bunch of one-night stands."

Her brows pull together. "Yeah, you already told me this. After the whole Lovey sleepover when we talked about Caroline, I asked if you'd had a relationship since her. You asked if I meant one that lasted more than twenty-four to forty-eight hours, which I took as a no. Logically, that implies that you've had some meaningless sexual encounters. There's no shame in that. You're an athlete and a dude, basically a walking hormone. And you're exceptionally proficient with your tongue, your fingers, and your gloriously blinged-out cock. You didn't learn how to fuck like a champion by watching porn."

I clear my throat. "Right. Yeah. So that doesn't bother you?"

"Should it? I mean, I avoided relationships because there was no way I was going to introduce anyone to my dad, and half the time we lived in a trailer with zero privacy. It doesn't mean I never had sex, though. Sometimes you just need to feel something good."

"Yeah, exactly." I nod. I have a feeling Winter's number of one-night stands or regular hookups or whatever happened for her is a lot different than mine, but I don't want to keep beating a dead horse, or turn this into a thing when it doesn't need to be one.

She sets her sandwich down again. "Unless you're telling me this because you don't want to be tied down to just one person now that you're back at college."

"No. That's not—I want to be tied down. Not literally." I think about that a moment. "Or like, maybe literally—depending on the mood and the setting and maybe a safe word. Lavender and Kody use duct tape, but I feel like that would not be great for arm hair."

Winter half chokes and coughs into her elbow. "I'm sorry, what?"

"Forget I said that. It was supposed to be under the cone."

She shakes her head. "Oh no. You can't say things like 'Lavender and Kody use duct tape' and expect me not to ask questions. Are you telling me Kodiak Bowman, rookie NHL player for Philly, uses duct tape on his girlfriend? Isn't she like, tiny?"

"Yeah, she's tiny." I shake my head. "But, no. It's the other way around. Fuck. This is seriously cone. I'm not even supposed to know, but last year I found all this duct tape in his garbage and made some connections, so I'm about ninety-nine-percent sure she taped his arms to the chair. I don't know where it went from there, and I prefer not to think about it because Lavender is my cousin, but good for them that their kinks match."

Winter looks a little stunned. "I honestly don't know what to do with that information. I'm going to go ahead and say right now that I probably won't be into duct taping you to anything."

"I kinda like my arm hair where it is. And Lovey once took a wax strip to my leg, which hurt like hell and took weeks for the patch to fill in. I spent half the summer in jeans."

"What did you do to warrant a wax strip on the leg?"

"Why do you automatically assume I did something wrong?"

She gives me a look.

I debate how honest I should be and decide Winter doesn't need another bullshitter in her life. "I might have hooked up with one of her sorority sisters sophomore year. In my defense, I didn't know she was a sorority sister until afterward. I think the hookup part was less the problem, and more that her sorority sister felt the need to constantly share unnecessary details with Lovey—stuff she couldn't unknow."

"Ah. Well, that makes sense. You definitely deserved a wax strip for that."

"Yeah. I'd like to say I took it like a man, but I screamed and swore a lot."

Winter grins. "Hence your aversion to duct tape."

"I'd be open to silk scarves—much softer and far less likely to leave marks or take off hair."

"Yeah, because I have an abundance of those hanging around in my mostly athletic-wear wardrobe."

"A neck tie would work equally as well, and I have plenty of those."

Winter smirks. "Your hands are far too talented to restrain."

"Lots of other uses for a silk tie besides restraining, though." Winter has had enough of feeling powerless to last a lifetime. I can't see her ever wanting to be tied up.

"Such as?"

"A little sensory deprivation can heighten the experience."

"Like a blindfold?" Her eyebrows pop, and her voice drops to a whisper as her fingers drift along her cheek. "You or me?"

"Either. Both. Neither." I slide closer and move her empty plate to the coffee table, patting my thighs. "Come here. I have an idea."

She shifts to straddle me. "What kind of idea?"

"Close your eyes for me, please," I murmur.

Her eyes flutter shut, her hands resting on her bare thighs, lips slightly parted.

I take her hand and kiss each fingertip, then her palm, before I slowly make my way along her wrist and up her forearm until I reach the bend, my eyes on her face the entire time. She whimpers softly when I stop, and her eyes flutter open.

I gently close her eyelids and drag my fingers down her cheeks. "Keep them closed and focus on how you feel."

"I feel like you're doing a lot of teasing."

I set her palm on my shoulder and pick up her other hand,

271

grinning as my lips brush across her fingertips. "That's because I am."

She laughs and then sighs as I kiss a path from the inside of her wrist to the crook of her elbow. The fingers of my free hand skim along her thigh until I reach the hem of her T-shirt. "Should I take this off and keep going?"

"Yes, please."

"Can you raise your arms for me?"

She lifts them above her head, and I remove her shirt. Her breasts are at eye level, but I don't go for a nipple. Instead, I press my lips to the center of her collarbones. Then I work my way from one side to the other, her nipples brushing against the fabric of my T-shirt. "How does this feel, Snowflake?"

"Good. Nice. Like it's not enough."

I nip at the skin above the swell of her right breast. "Good. It's not supposed to be enough." I skim her ribs and follow the waistband of her panties with a single finger until I reach her navel. "Should we go back to bed?" I kiss a path to her neck. "I want to touch every inch of you, put my mouth where you ache the most." I circle a nipple with my finger, and she sucks in a sharp breath. "I could start here."

"Fuck, yes. Please." Her eyes pop open, and she slides off my lap.

Before she can make a beeline for the bed, I catch her hand and pull her close. I wrap an arm around her waist and cup her cheek in my palm. Her eyes fall closed again, lips parted in anticipation. I drop my mouth to hers, and she moans when our tongues tangle. Her hands slide into my hair, gripping at the crown, angling my head so she can deepen the kiss. We're both breathless when she finally breaks away.

"You could get a tie," she whispers.

"Why don't you help me pick one out?" I lace our fingers and tug her toward my closet.

It's a small walk-in, like all the closets in this house. Hanging on the back of the door is a tie rack with a half a dozen options. Winter brushes her fingers over the soft fabrics and chooses a black satin one.

When we reach the bed, she tosses the tie on the rumpled sheets and hooks her thumbs into her panties. I cover her hands with mine. "Why don't we keep these on for a little while longer?"

She tips her head. "You're really going to drag this one out, aren't you?"

I laugh. "We have limited days left before our schedules are full of classes and practice. I want to make the most of them."

"Hmm... Good point." She sits on the edge of the bed and shimmies back to stretch out. "Let the teasing resume."

I climb up after her and wrap the tie around my fist until only a foot of fabric dangles.

"Should I close my eyes?" she asks.

"Up to you." I brush the silk from her knee all the way to the top of her thigh. Placing one of my knees between hers, I drag the silk over her stomach, then lower, skimming between her thighs.

"Oh fuck." She gasps. "You're going to kill me softly."

"Mm..." I drag it higher, between her breasts. "We should get some feathers."

"Feathers?" Her eyes flick between me and the tie moving over her skin.

"Imagine how nice they would feel right here." I let the tie sweep over her nipple, then across her collarbones. "Or here."

She sucks in a breath. "Feathers would be a great idea."

Eventually I cover her eyes with the soft fabric, and she ties it behind her head. And then I kiss every inch of her, murmuring hot words against her skin, bringing her to orgasm with my fingers and then my mouth. It isn't until I'm about to fill her that I remove the blindfold. Her eyes meet mine as I push inside, and she comes in violent, glorious waves.

I wish we could stay here, in this perfect bubble of bliss, where it's just her and me. But it has to break eventually. I just didn't realize it had the potential to shatter.

28

The Bubble

DJ

THE WEEK before classes begin passes in a blur of sex, campus visits, time with friends, and ice time. Adele and I take a couple of days to settle in, and then we're back at it, practicing our new routine for our next competition later this fall. My mom suggested that I record some of our practices during the week so she can monitor progress.

Adele isn't the biggest fan of this strategy because she says it makes her nervous, so I often don't tell her when I'm recording—otherwise she'll overthink it and ask me to re-record. Or she'll want to watch them in the middle of practice, and that's not the best use of our time.

Hockey practices don't officially start until the first week of school, but Fern, who plays for the college team as well, has offered to show Winter around the facilities and invited her to play pick-up with some of the other women on the team. So far we're off to a good start.

On the first day of classes, Winter and I drive in together, but her schedule on Mondays is spread out, so she has big breaks between classes and doesn't finish until after five. I have practice with Adele in the afternoon at one of the rinks closer to her college, and Winter has hockey practice, so she brings her bike so she can ride home.

Our friend group plans to meet up in the quad at noon for lunch, since it works with most of our schedules. Winter, Lovey, Rose, River, Josiah, and Quinn have already nabbed a picnic table by the time I arrive with my chicken wrap combo from one of the school cafeterias. Lovey, Winter, and River have insulated lunch bags full of Tupperware containers. Quinn has a giant sub that's leaking sauce all over the wax wrapper, Josiah has pizza, and Rose is eating a muffin.

"Hey, hey! How was everyone's morning?" I sit next to Winter and kiss her on the cheek.

Everyone mumbles hello around mouthfuls of food.

Winter swallows a bite of her sandwich. "So great! I already know I'm going to love my social deviance class. In person is so much better than online. How was your morning?"

"My advanced behavioral and cognitive neuroscience course is going to be a shit-ton of work, but so far so good."

"Behari still teaches that, right?" Quinn asks from the other end of the table.

"Yeah, she does."

"I still have my notes and tests, if you want them."

"I will a hundred percent take you up on that." Having a roommate who's already finished his undergraduate degree means sometimes I can borrow his notes.

"Please tell me one of you has notes for statistics," Rose says.

Lovey and Quinn both offer theirs at the same time.

Lovey's cheeks flush. "You should take Quinn's. I used a lot of his notes, and he basically aced everything."

They're sitting across from each other. "Your grades in stats were solid last year," Quinn says.

"Thanks to you." She looks over at Rose. "Quinn's notes are super organized and color-coded."

"I have such jealousy that you can all share notes. I miss having Lavender in my class." Josiah's bottom lip juts out in a pout. "I need her to visit soon."

"She's supposed to come when Philly plays Chicago this fall," I say.

Lovey perks up. "We're all going to the game, right? How fun will it be to see Kody playing for the NHL?"

"Aren't tickets expensive?" Winter asks.

"They can be, but most of our dads played for Chicago at some point, and they're all still highly involved in hockey, so we have perks," I explain.

"Have you ever been to an NHL game?" Rose asks.

Winter shakes her head.

"Our parents have a box, but we should see about getting on-ice seats," River says.

He's already a huge fan of Winter. She's even convinced him to shoot the puck around in our driveway a couple of times, and usually he grumbles about playing hockey. Although part of his sudden interest in hockey might have to do with not playing football this year. He didn't want to be the front man for all gay college football players.

"A few rows up from the bench would be great," Quinn agrees.

"Are you guys serious?" A tomato slides out of Winter's sandwich and lands in her Tupperware container.

"Totally serious." Rose makes a circle motion around her face. "Why is this happening?"

"Why is what happening?" Winter dabs at her mouth with a napkin.

Rose taps her lips. "You look—"

"—shocked," Josiah finishes for her. "Which is super reasonable, considering you're all talking about having a box and the best seats at an NHL game like it's totally normal. For those of us who don't have parents who played in the NHL, it's a bit mind-blowing."

Winter nods. "What Josiah said."

"BJ! Hey! Hi!" A brunette comes bouncing over and throws her arms around me from behind. "It's so good to see you! How was your summer?"

"Good. It was good. And yours?" I search my mind for a name but come up empty.

"It was so great. I went to Spain for two weeks with my parents and then worked the rest of the summer. I missed the party you guys threw last week." She makes a pouty face. "Will you have another one soon?"

"Gotta buckle down now that the semester has started." I finally place her as a hookup from last year. Maybe second semester...

"You gonna introduce us to your friend, BJ?" Rose asks.

"Oh!" The girl's cheeks flush. "I'm DeeDee. Hi, BJ's friends." She waves at the table.

Everyone waves in return and mutters hi.

And because Rose clearly has it out for me, she asks the question I don't want DeeDee to answer. "And how do you and BJ know each other?"

DeeDee's cheeks flush an ever deeper pink. "Oh, uh... We hung out last semester." Her eyes slide my way, and she bites her lip.

Quinn coughs, and River makes a noise. I don't dare look at Winter.

Thankfully DeeDee has class, but she hugs me again and reminds me that I have her number before she flounces off.

"Well, that was spectacularly awkward," Rose says.

"Thanks to you," I mutter.

"You sure didn't help yourself out." Quinn arches a brow.

Lovey's looking at Winter, but all she does is purse her lips. I'll definitely hear about this later.

Then things get worse when it happens again, five minutes later.

The third time I try to put my arm around Winter, but she knocks it away. "Uh, no, dude. You don't get to use me as your post-hookup shield."

I realize I've done that a lot. I've used Lovey as a shield post-hookup, and even my cousin Lavender last year. I perpetuated the idea that Lovey and I were more than friends every time I threw my arm over her shoulder when a previous hookup came over to say hi. And how shitty was that for her? People probably believed we were on-again-off-again or in an open relationship.

When past hookup number three, whose name is Amy, leaves, Winter gives me a look. "You know, when you said you were a fan of the hookup, I didn't realize it meant you'd slept with half the female population on campus. I mean, I guess you don't earn your proficiency at oralgasms by practicing on a cut orange, but this is some next-level shit. Should I hand them all thank-you cards for helping you hone your skills?" She stands and starts packing up her bag.

Quinn bursts into laughter.

River slow claps. "You are my favorite fucking person in the entire world right now, Winter."

"Same," Josiah says.

Winter seems to be fighting a smile, but it's tense. "I should get to my next class."

"What building are you in?" Lovey asks.

"Sociology."

"I can walk you," I tell her.

She laughs. "Uh, thanks, but I need to get there on time, and you get stopped more often than a bus."

"Isn't this the picture of cozy?" Laughlin appears out of nowhere. He's wearing black jeans and a black T-shirt to match his sunny personality.

Half the table jumps in surprise.

"Jesus Christ." Rose presses a hand to her chest. "You're in direct sunlight. Why haven't you burst into flames?"

"I'm a day walker, didn't you know?" He tips his head and skims her bare shoulder with a finger. "You're burning, little Rose. Always so delicate, aren't you?"

"Always so creepy, aren't you?" she fires back.

"I'm going the same direction," Josiah says to Winter as he threads his arms through his backpack straps. "I'll walk with you."

"I'm coming with for no other reason than to escape this one." Rose pokes Laughlin in the hip, then elbows him in the thigh when he doesn't move.

Josiah kisses River on the cheek.

Winter gives me a chin tip and waves to the rest of the table. Josiah holds out both arms and the girls link elbows with him, laughing as they make their way across the quad.

"Why is River's boyfriend walking BJ's girlfriend to class?" Laughlin asks.

River and Quinn laugh, but Lovey just sighs. "I told you to talk to her."

"I did," I protest. "She was cool about it."

"I feel like maybe you played it down a bit."

280

Laughlin takes a seat beside his sister. When they're next to each other, the family resemblance is easier to see. "What are we talking about?"

"Why are you here?" I ask.

"Because I go to this school, and occasionally I decide that being a total recluse is overrated. Don't worry, it won't last long." He folds his hands together and settles his chin on top.

"I didn't try to play it down."

"But did you warn her that you might run into more than one of your previous hookups on campus?" Lovey asks.

I bite the inside of my cheek.

She sighs. "That's a nope."

"Ah. Your playboy ways are catching up to you." Laughlin chuckles.

His commentary is the opposite of helpful, so I ignore him. "Do you think she's pissed?"

"It's one thing to know something is true because you've been told. It's another to have it thrown in your face. Once would have been tolerable, but three times in an hour is a bit much. Reality can be a hard pill to swallow," River says.

"How do I fix this?"

"Eradicating your previous hookups would be one solution, but then you'd be the most notorious serial killer in history," Laughlin offers.

"Dude, tone your sociopath down a notch or five," Quinn says.

"Show her that you've changed," River suggests. "And flowers are a nice touch. I always get Josiah flowers when I've been an oversensitive asshole."

"I don't know if she's a flowers kind of girl."

"I don't think she's ever had the chance to be a flowers kind of girl," River replies.

"Good point." I nod. "Flowers it is."

ON THE WAY home from skate practice with Adele, I stop at a flower shop and call Lovey for help. Winter's favorite color is blue, so I pick out an assortment of pretty blossoms I think she'll like. I don't go too overboard, though, because she's not a fan of over-the-top. See my flashy Jeep for details.

When I get home, I park myself in the lounge chair in her living room. Lacey works part-time at the school bookstore, so she won't be home until later, and Lovey is at my place, helping Rose sort through Quinn's notes. River is at Josiah's, which is typical these days.

The sound of the alarm being punched in, followed by the door opening and closing startles me awake. I run a hand over my face and put the footrest down.

Winter comes to an abrupt halt when she sees me and the bouquet of flowers in the lounger. "What's this about?"

"Apology flowers."

She frowns. "What are you apologizing for?"

"Lunch today."

"We've already talked about this." She adjusts the strap of her backpack, eyes on the bouquet in my hands. "You didn't have to buy me flowers because your past hookups still have deep appreciation for your sexual skill set."

"Are you using sarcasm to deflect?" I ask.

She blows out a breath and looks at the ceiling. "I don't know. Maybe. I don't want to make a big deal out of this. What you did before we started this shouldn't matter."

"It's okay if it does, though, Winter. You're allowed to not like it, or the awkward position I put you in today. I know the crew made a joke out of it. But I didn't like the way it made me feel, so I'm pretty sure you liked it even less." My palms are sweaty.

"It kinda sucked," she admits.

"I'm sorry." I want to hug her, but I don't know if physical contact is welcome.

"It also would have been nice to have a heads-up that you'd slept with one of my teammates."

"Wait, what?"

She brushes past me and flops down on the couch. "I can't remember her first name. But her last name is Persaud. We were talking about where we lived off campus after practice today, and I mentioned that I lived here. Everyone on the team knows about this house because of all the parties, I guess. Maverick is kind of a legend. And you wouldn't believe the number of rumors flying around about his relationship with Clover. It's good they're in Pearl Lake being happy and not dealing with all that drama. Anyway, your name came up, and I'm sure you'll be unsurprised to hear that you've got quite the reputation."

I take a seat beside her, leaving some space because I feel like she needs it. "Yeah, I did a good job of having fun over the past few years." I could really use a glass of water. My mouth is so dry. I wonder if this is what Kody feels like before he gets on the ice, or how Lavender felt every time she was in a room full of people she didn't know. Even skate competitions don't make me feel like this. The opposite, actually.

"She had great things to say about your performance, so kudos on that." Winter picks at a loose thread on her jeans.

"You have every right to be pissed. I should have been honest about how prolific my sex life has been."

"I don't think I'm angry." She shifts so she's facing me, her smile a little sad. "Or maybe I am. I don't know. It's hard to feel secure that you want to be with me when that's so vastly different from your previous approach to relationships and sex. I don't know how I'm supposed to act or react when something like that happens. I get that you're flirty, and that this is college and we're supposed to have a good time, but what you were doing before seems a little...extra, to be honest. I can deal with it, though—mostly. What happened today—the way you only put your arm around me to ward off that girl when she came up—that's the thing that bothers me. It made this, whatever *this* is"—she motions between us—"feel like less. I've been a shield my entire life, BJ. I don't want to be yours too."

My stomach twists at her admission. I hate that I've made her question what we have. "That wasn't my intention, but I can see where you're coming from. Even apart from that, it's shitty and unfair, and it's worse that it made you feel that way. Until you came along, I didn't see the problem with my actions. I can't take them back, but I can handle things differently now."

"I'm living in your world, BJ. I'm surrounded by your friends, with all these people who are connected to you. It's tricky, especially under circumstances like this," she says.

I swallow past the lump in my throat. "Do you wish you'd moved in with your teammates instead?"

She sighs. "I weighed the pros and cons, and this made more sense. I look at things through a different lens than you. Financial motivation is strong when you come from the kind of home I do. And I try to avoid conflict because I've been conditioned to expect the people around me to get hurt if I engage in it or incite it. Living with my teammates could have been great, but there are so many unknowns with them. Lovey, Rose, and Lacey are my friends, and I'm comfortable, so I came into this with a built-in network of support. And River is great, and so is Quinn." She fiddles with the end of her braid. "But I knew you and I were going to be the trickiest part to navigate. Neither of us has a whole lot of relationship experience—not that I'm trying to define this or anything."

"Maybe we should."

She clasps my hand. "We have this amazing connection, BJ—one that's not just about sex, because if that's all it was, we wouldn't be sitting here, having this conversation. But labeling us because of what happened today won't change it or us. That's not what I'm asking for. Everything about this is new... And there's pressure on all sides for both of us. I'm used to the guy I met in Pearl Lake who flirted and then used skating lessons as a bargaining chip to spend time with me."

"I'm still that guy."

"I know. But you're also the guy who spent the first three years of college getting laid, a lot, and I'm benefiting from that extensive experience. But there's always a downside, and that happens to be running into some of those girls. It's a big shift. I just need time to digest and get my head around this."

"Do you want space?"

"I don't think so." She bites her nail. "But maybe we should put a pin in the physical stuff and just spend time hanging out together—not indefinitely or anything, because my restraint when it comes to you is pretty damn abysmal, and I already ordered feathers, and they should arrive next week. But maybe we get through this week?"

"We could go on a date. We *should* go on a date. We haven't done much of that. If at all, really."

"You don't need to take me on a date, BJ."

"But I want to. We should go on one now."

"It's, like, seven thirty."

"It's still early. There's this kickass ice cream place that's only a few blocks away. They have the coolest flavors—like Earl Grey tea and lemon, and lavender and pear—and their waffle cones are to die for." I stand and hold out a hand. "Do you want to go for ice cream with me?"

She smiles. "I can always eat ice cream."

"I know. That's why I picked it. Please, Snowflake. I know there isn't an instant fix, but I want to show you that whatever we're not calling this, I'm in. All the way."

Winter makes a face. "I'm trying really hard not to make a sex joke."

I laugh, and she lets me pull her to her feet.

I keep hold of her hand. "Can I hug you? A little affection without intention?"

She smiles. "Yeah. You can hug me."

I wrap my arms around her. "I hated this afternoon. I hated knowing I made you feel shitty."

"I know. That's what made it easier to have the hard conversation."

I tuck a lock of hair behind her ear. "You're an incredible person, Winter."

"So are you." She steps back. "Come on. Let's go get ice cream, and when we get back you can kiss me good night, and I can be annoyed that I'm sending you home to your own bed and sleeping alone in mine."

I nod and feel the tightness in my chest release a little. The problem isn't solved, but we're on the same page. Label or not, we're in this together.

29

The Up Before the Down

WINTER

I MAKE it until Thursday before I fold and BJ sleeps over. It's pointless to punish ourselves for things outside of his control. And honestly, I'm-sorry-for-being-a-playboy sex with BJ ranks as some of the best sex of my life. He pulled out the silk tie again, but this time I used it on him, which was way more fun than I expected. And empowering. I followed it with a beard ride. And then we had marathon sex that lasted until two in the morning.

I was spacey in my Friday morning class, and I ended up napping in the library between afternoon classes, which saved me from being a total mess during hockey practice. But it was totally worth it.

And if I'd realized how intense a full course load and daily hockey practice would be, I might not have taken that four-day sex hiatus. After the first week, spending time with BJ that doesn't involve sleeping has become increasingly difficult.

It's a Wednesday a few weeks into the semester, and I'm meeting BJ for lunch in the quad, but I've texted him three times with no reply. There's a decent chance he's fallen asleep somewhere.

In the summer, I often found him napping on the bench outside the arena, but here in Chicago, I've learned that BJ can truly sleep anywhere. And for reasons I'm unsure of, one of his favorite napping locations is the lounger in our living room. River says he's been doing it for as long as he can remember.

I pocket my phone and head to the quad. It's a beautiful afternoon, the sun is shining, and we're having an amazing September hot spell. It should break in a few days, but everyone is wearing shorts and tank tops, soaking up the sun, and drinking iced coffees.

I find BJ passed out under a tree, using his backpack as a pillow. Instead of waking him, I set a timer for twenty minutes, place my backpack next to his, and stretch out beside him.

When our fingers brush, he slides his arm under me and pulls me closer.

"We're not in your bedroom, in case you forgot your comforter isn't made of grass."

"So don't try to get you naked?" His eyes aren't even open.

"Not unless you'd like to become a viral video that might make getting a job in the future a serious challenge."

"Seems like something to avoid," he mumbles.

"I set a timer for twenty minutes. Stop sleep-talking and just sleep. I need the nap as much as you do."

"Nothing says romance like a lunchtime snooze." His breathing evens out a few seconds later. It blows my mind how quickly he can fall asleep. Sitting up, lying down, in a chair, in a bed, on a bench. In the middle of the quad. It's an art.

I close my eyes, not expecting to nap, but twenty minutes later, my alarm rouses both of us.

Lovey, Lacey, and Rose are now sitting cross-legged a few feet away, their lunches spread out between them. We have lunch-making parties every evening. We'll buy a huge baguette from the local grocery store and make one giant sandwich that we split between us. I've learned how to make some cool vegan sandwiches since Lovey doesn't eat anything that comes from an animal or has a face, and Lacey is a pescatarian.

I sit up. "How long have the three of you been sitting here?"

BJ hasn't moved yet.

"Long enough to take a bunch of pictures of you two cuddled together," Rose says.

"I wish I could fall asleep anywhere." Lacey pops a grape into her mouth.

"Same. I'm the worst napper in the history of the world," Lovey agrees.

"My mom said I gave up naps when I was a year old." Rose adds chips to her sandwich.

"That doesn't surprise me," BJ mumbles from his supine position.

I poke him in the side. "We have class in half an hour. You need to eat or you'll be hangry later."

He rolls onto his side and hugs me around the waist. "I'd take a bite out of you."

"No verbal foreplay in front of your friends." Rose throws a pinecone at him.

He drags himself to sitting.

Lovey frowns. "You look more tired than usual."

BJ pulls his hair tie free and his hair flops into his face. It's longer again, past his chin, and his beard is thicker than it was in the summer. He gathers his hair and refastens it. "Adele is struggling with one of the combinations again, and we can't afford to make changes to the routine. We need to spend more time on the ice until we get it down. A few more weeks and this competition will be done."

"You've been recording some of your practices, right? Has that been helping?" I ask.

"Yeah. It's been good—my mom can see the progress and give us guidance remotely. But I had to stop telling Adele I was doing it because it was psyching her out. The stakes keep getting higher. I can handle the pressure, but it's a lot to have a full course load and be on the ice three to four hours a day. Which you're aware of." BJ empties out half his backpack and starts shoveling food into his face.

I nod. "A few more weeks and then you get a break."

We finish our lunch, and BJ and I walk to class together. After the first couple of days, he started linking pinkies with me, which helped deter all the random huggers. People still say hi to him often, but they mostly don't throw themselves at him anymore.

"You have practice until six, right?" he asks when we reach the psych building.

"Yeah. What time are you and Adele finished?"

"Six thirty." He rubs his thumb along my knuckles. "Maybe when I get home, we can do dinner and jump in the hot tub."

"We could even get in some alone time when we're not passing out on each other."

He grins. "It's like we share a brain."

"Or our genitals are communicating telepathically."

He laughs and bends to kiss me. "Have I told you lately that you're my favorite person?"

"You have, actually."

He goes in for another kiss, but I push his chest and step back. "I'll see you tonight."

"It's a date."

"YOU'VE CHECKED your phone six times in the past fifteen minutes. What's the deal?" Rose asks.

Quinn is sitting in the wingback chair that looks like it belonged to someone's posh grandmother, reading a textbook. Lovey flips through notes for one of her classes, and Rose is complaining about stats.

"BJ and Adele were supposed to be off the ice at six thirty, but it's already quarter after seven." The arena is only a ten-minute drive. Even with a shower, he should be home by now.

Quinn looks up from his textbook. "Adele sometimes likes to book extra time on the end of their practices without telling BJ until they're already on the ice."

"I know she's struggling with one of the combinations again," I say.

"Yeah. It's interesting how that's been happening more often lately." Quinn flips his pen between his fingers.

"What do you mean?"

He shrugs. "I could be reading into things, but it seems like this year she's having a harder time than usual getting routines down."

"Do you think she's purposely having a hard time?" Lovey asks.

"I don't want to make Adele into a villain or anything, but it seems kind of suspect that the second BJ gets a girlfriend, Adele starts having more trouble with the routines. I mean, it's possible she really is struggling—the pressure is certainly a factor—but it seems suspiciously coincidental." He looks over at Lovey. "Remember how icy she was with you until she realized you and BJ weren't actually a thing?"

Lovey taps her lips with her pen. "Oh yeah. I'd forgotten

about that. It was a long time ago, though."

"Yeah, but let's look at this logically," Rose says. "BJ hasn't had a girlfriend all through college."

"We haven't put a label on it," I say.

All three of them give me a look.

"Label or no label, for the sake of simplicity, you're his girl-friend—even if in the Land of Denial, you're pretending you're not." Rose slaps her thighs. "As I was saying, BJ hasn't had a regular boning partner for a long time. Now BJ's spare time isn't just spent with his friends, it's spent with you. Keeping BJ on the ice is the only way Adele can get more time with him, because he's very clear that that's where their relationship has to stay."

"Does she have a thing for him?" I always assumed Adele and BJ were on the same page about their skating relationship, but maybe that was naive.

"I don't know. It's possible?" Quinn taps the arm of his chair thoughtfully. He looks like a redheaded godfather. "Until this year, ice time has been paramount for BJ, but now that you're in the picture, there's competition. He's always had a hierarchy, and skating has been at the top of that, followed by school, family, and friends. It's shifted because of you, and that's a good thing after what happened with Caroline. But Adele has been priority number one for a lot of years, so maybe this is her trying to maintain her position."

"I don't want to cause tension. I know how important this competition is to BJ."

"It is, for sure. But she might be manipulating him, and he's so focused on getting the routine down that he can't see it for what it is," Quinn replies.

"What should I do? Should I talk to him about it?"

Rose raises her hand. "I have an idea."

"You always have ideas, not all of them are good," Quinn

notes.

"Hear me out before you shoot it down." She crosses and uncrosses her legs. "I think you can be subtly not so subtle. It's already after seven. He hasn't had dinner yet. You love feeding people. Why don't you bring him a muffin? The ones you made this afternoon, not your lady muffin," she adds quickly, motioning to the kitchen.

The pantry is always stocked here, which makes it easy to try new recipes.

"Those were going to be my snack later," Quinn grumbles.

"I'll make more, don't worry." I look to Lovey. "What's your opinion?"

"I think Quinn is right about Adele. She's good at playing on BJ's competitive side. It wouldn't hurt to stop by the arena. I'm picking up Lacey from the humane society at eight. I could drop you off on the way," Lovey offers.

"Okay. Let's do it." I stand up.

"Uh, you're not going like that." Rose motions to me.

I run my hand over my stomach. I'm wearing athletic shorts and one of BJ's T-shirts. "What's wrong with my outfit?"

"Nothing if you're hanging with your friends doing home-work. Just give me five minutes to accentuate your assets."

TWENTY MINUTES LATER, Lovey drops me off at the arena. BJ's Jeep is still here. I'm dressed in a pair of skinny jeans and a baby blue tank that highlights my modest cleavage. Rose tried to get me into a skirt, but the last time I willingly wore a dress was prom, and that seemed too in-your-face.

When I find their rink, they're in the middle of their routine. The music is muffled by the door. They're moving backwards across the ice, Adele's back to BJ's chest, their hands linked. He spins her out and then back. The lift follows, and Adele's compact, narrow form arcs gracefully, BJ keeping her suspended in the air for long seconds before he lowers her and they part.

BJ moves into a spin and then they're converging again. But Adele must miss her cue, because BJ has to stutter step to avoid a collision. His expression pinches, and he skates away, maybe trying to shake it off. His frustration is obvious before he takes a breath and adopts a neutral expression. Adele catches up to BJ and links their arms, issuing an apology.

I decide now is a good time to interrupt, so I push through the doors.

The movement catches BJ's attention, and his furrowed brow smooths out. He unlinks their arms and skates to the gate.

"This is a nice surprise." He leans on the sill cap and uses the bottom of his shirt to wipe the sweat from his face. "Sorry. I'm kinda gross."

"I don't mind." I lean in for a kiss.

I mean for it to be a peck, but his hand curves around my nape and he parts his lips, stroking inside for a beat before he pulls back. "You look damn well delicious."

"I brought other delicious things." I hold up the Tupperware container. "I figured you might be hungry."

"Oh hell yeah, are those your banana muffins?"

"With chocolate chips."

He pops the lid and takes a giant bite out of one, barely chewing before he swallows. "What time is it?" he asks between bites.

The scoreboard is showing all zeros. "Closing in on eight."

"Shit. I'm so sorry. I completely lost track of time. I hope you didn't wait on me for dinner."

"I had a bunch of snacks, so I'm good."

Adele skates over, her smile tight as she loops her arm through his. "Sorry I've been hogging BJ lately. Our upcoming competition is a big one." She sounds about as sorry as I feel for showing up here unannounced.

"I get it. I just knew BJ hadn't eaten dinner yet, and you've been on the ice for hours."

"I would have called it quits a while ago if I'd realized the time." BJ starts on another muffin. He must be starving.

"Should we run through the routine once more?" Adele asks.

BJ shakes his head. "I almost rolled my ankle that last time, and my arms are tired. It's better if we start fresh tomorrow." He shoves the rest of the second muffin in his mouth.

"I'm sorry." Adele ducks her head. "That was my fault. I missed the cue."

"It's all right. It happens, but better to call it a day." He turns to me. "Can you give me fifteen? Just gonna shower real quick."

"Yeah, for sure. I'll wait in the lobby." I thumb over my shoulder.

He holds the gate open for Adele and follows her off the ice, kissing my cheek as he passes.

I take a seat on one of the benches in the lobby and check my messages. I'm unsurprised to find new ones from Lovey and Rose, asking how it's going. I tell them the plan worked and BJ's in the shower.

Rose sends back a thrusting gif followed by a cheerleader shaking her pom-poms. Lovey sends a slew of hearts and a *you go girl*.

Adele passes through the lobby before BJ. When she sees me, her expression flattens and she heads in my direction. "Look." She flips her hair over her shoulder. "I know you and BJ have this thing going on, but he's been my skating partner for four years. We have a lot of history, and this competition is important. We need to place if we're going to move on, and you showing up here is a distraction he doesn't need. Don't you get enough time with him already? Or are you pulling the jealous-girlfriend card?"

"Flip the mirror around, Adele. Maybe you should be asking yourself that question."

She crosses her arms. "This is about getting in enough ice time so we perfect our routine. If we don't place, we don't move on. I haven't spent the last four years *not* having a life for you to come in as a fun, new pastime and fuck it all up for us."

BJ enters the lobby, and I stand. I have a lot of height on Adele, so she backs up a step. "He's been exhausted lately."

"Whose fault is that?" she hisses.

"Running him into the ground won't help either of you," I mutter, smiling as BJ approaches.

"Hey, you ready to roll?" He kisses me before he turns to Adele. "I'll see you tomorrow afternoon, okay?"

"Yeah, of course." She adjusts her bag, looking unsure of herself now. "Have a good rest of your night."

"You too." He laces our fingers together and tugs me toward the exit. "Thanks for bringing me a snack. It really helped take the edge off."

"No problem. I know you don't like to fill up before you get on the ice, so I figured you'd be hungry. There's leftover pasta with homemade marinara sauce and meatballs at home."

"That sounds like magic. I need to carb-load like nobody's business." He passes me the keys. "Do you mind driving? My arms feel like Jell-O."

"Not at all."

I get behind the wheel, and BJ climbs into the passenger seat. "I hope it was okay that I stopped by. I don't want to interrupt your practice. I know this is a big competition."

"It's more than okay. I love that you showed up. I totally lost track of time, and honestly, I was getting sloppy. We weren't making progress. Maybe we can work it so you stop by once a week like that? We can even make a date out of it—go for dinner after so we get some hangout time. We've both been super busy lately, and I feel like all I get to do is sleep next to you."

"I could do that for sure."

"We'll pick a day a week so we get in us time. Sound good?" He sets his hand palm up on the center console.

"Yeah. That sounds great."

"Perfect."

When we get back to his place, I heat up the pasta and meatballs while BJ sets the table. Quinn's car is gone, and so are he and Rose. There's a note on the fridge saying they went on an emergency chocolate run.

BJ shovels food into his mouth like he hasn't eaten in days and slouches in his chair with a groan when he finishes. "That was freaking amazing. You are a wizard in the kitchen."

"I had loads of help." I love that meal-making around here can be a team effort. Everyone pitches in, and most of the time we try to eat together.

"Wanna cuddle in my bed?" BJ's eyelids are droopy.

"Are you hitting the food-coma stage of the evening?"

"I might need a ten-minute nap before we get to the good stuff."

I think he needs a ten-hour nap, but I don't argue. I follow him to his room and snuggle into his side. He falls asleep in seconds. I lie here for a few minutes, just enjoying the close-ness. There's no way I'll wake him in ten minutes though, so when I'm sure he's out cold, I slip out of bed, cover him with a blanket, and close his bedroom door.

I go back to my place and find everyone in the living room.

Lovey is sandwiched between Lacey and Quinn on the couch, and River and Josiah are crammed in the lounger together, looking damn well adorable. Rose is curled up in a beanbag chair on the floor. Laughlin, who randomly shows up these days, is lying on the floor, using the corner of Rose's beanbag chair as a pillow. It looks super uncomfortable.

Lovey frowns. "Where's BJ?"

"He fell asleep the second his head hit the pillow." I drop into one of the gaming chairs.

"After you boned?" Rose hands me a box of chocolates and the flavor map.

"Sadly, no." I find a vanilla buttercream and pop it into my mouth before I pass the box to Quinn.

"We vacated the premises so you could have the place to yourself." Rose motions to the TV. "And now I'm invested in this ridiculous movie, so I have to watch to the end, even though it's highly predictable."

"We're probably missing key plot points with all your moaning," Laughlin grumbles.

"Who even invited you?" She pokes him in the cheek with her toe.

"I would not recommend doing that again unless you want to be minus a toe. It's rather difficult to pirouette without them."

"Whatever, Dracula. I quit ballet, so my toes are no longer essential." She turns back to me. "Go back and wake him up."

"He's exhausted. He needs the sleep. He'll text if he wakes up."

But I have a feeling he won't. He's been burning the candle at both ends, and I don't want to be the reason something happens to him on the ice.

30

The Fall I Didn't Know Was Coming

BJ

WE WORK it so Winter drives me and picks me up from skate practice with Adele at least once a week. It means we get a little extra time together. And I've started setting an early alarm so we can have morning sex at least once a week. We also try to have breakfast together and meet for lunch often. Twice we've gone home for a little lunchtime fun, but we were almost late getting back to campus both times, so that's off the table.

Winter is settling into college life, finding the balance between school, hockey, and friends. My parents brought her mom to visit and see her play last weekend. They won the game, and we went out for a celebratory dinner. Everything seems to be going smoothly. Well, almost everything.

Adele has on days and off days, and it's tough to predict what version I'll be skating with. The closer we get to this competition, the more ice time she wants. The last few days she's been handling the complicated combinations, though, so that's good. I can't record all the time, and when I've managed to do so lately, I seem to get the sessions where she's nearly flawless, so I can't figure out where we're going wrong. And when my mom comes up on the weekends, Adele's skating has been on point.

Today is one of the days Winter is driving me in and picking me up. She has hockey practice in an hour, and I have to be at the rink in thirty minutes.

"You almost ready to roll?" I drop my bag on the floor as I scroll through the latest message from Adele. She's been slightly better about being on time-ish lately.

"Just having a snack first, but yeah."

I look up from my phone in time to watch her lips wrap around a banana. She's wearing a tank, no bra, and a pair of running shorts.

"Oh fuck me," I groan. "Come on, Snowflake. This isn't fair. I gotta be on the ice in thirty."

She looks down at her outfit. "I should probably find a bra and some pants, shouldn't I?" She moves toward my bedroom.

"Where's Quinn? And Rose?"

"Quinn went over to my place about an hour ago. I think he's helping Lovey with an assignment. And Rose is in class."

"So the house is empty?"

"It is." She tips her head. "Wanna see how fast you can make me come?"

"Fuck yeah, I do."

"I was hoping you'd say that." She pulls a condom out of the key pocket in her running shorts. I nab it from her and toss it on the counter before I yank her shorts down her thighs. She kicks them off, and I back her up against the island, wrap my hands around her waist, and lift her onto the counter.

"It's Thursday, isn't it?"

"One of my favorite days of the week." Winter groans when I squeeze her ass.

I drop to my knees, and she shimmies to the edge of the counter and parts her legs. There's no teasing, no working up to anything. I latch onto her clit and suck hard.

"Fucking Jesus, Randall. Oh my God." She frees the tie from my hair and shoves her fingers in it, rolling her hips in time to the swirl of my tongue. It only takes a few minutes to get her close to an orgasm, but I want to be inside her when she comes, so I stop when she starts to tremble.

"Why are you stopping? I'm right there!" she cries when I stand.

"I want you to come on my cock." I yank my shirt over my head and shove my joggers down enough to free myself from my boxers.

She makes a plaintive, frustrated sound, but wraps her warm fingers around my length, using it to pull me closer. I angle my erection down and rub the piercing over her clit.

Her eyes roll up, and she whimpers when I slide down, nudging against her entrance before I drag the head along the length of her slit. "You're so fucking soft."

She hooks her foot around the back of my leg, and I nudge against her entrance again. We both moan, and my eyes meet hers. I see the desperation there.

"I could go bare, just for a minute?" It's all question and no certainty.

She bites her lip. "Just for a minute?"

I nod. "Until you come."

"I haven't ever before," she whispers.

"Me neither. We don't have to. I don't want you to feel pressured."

"I don't. I want to." Her fingers drift along the side of my neck. "I don't feel pressured, I mean. I never feel that way with you. And I want to feel you."

"Me too." Our gazes focus down as I angle the head and the piercing disappears inside her.

"Oh fuck," she breathes.

My eyes lift to hers. "Is that a good or a bad *oh fuck?*"

"Good. It's good. This is so different. I feel your piercing, oh God." Her brow furrows as I push in another inch. "That's just... Don't stop, please."

"Anything for you. You know that."

I ease in, one slow inch at a time, eyes never leaving hers. She's soft and warm and wet and tight and damn well perfect. I get it now—the whole idea that sex without a condom is different. Because it is, although I feel like it's half about sensation and half about connection.

We're both panting by the time I'm buried inside her. She tugs me forward and claims my mouth. I wrap her legs around my waist and run my hands up her back, under her tank. She breaks the kiss long enough to pull her shirt over her head, and then we're kissing again. I rock my hips, staying deep, and Winter moans into my mouth.

Her hands are in my hair, fingers gripping the strands. Then her fingers wrap around my biceps, nails digging in. I want to move, to thrust, but I'm worried I won't last very long. Not like this—and not long enough to make her come the way I want to.

I break the kiss so I can get a hand between us and massage her clit. She cries out and throws her head back, hips rolling. "Next time we're alone like this, I'm going to bend you over the counter. How does that sound?"

"So fucking good," she groans. "So close."

Her arms tremble, and I feel it, the soft flutter—faint at first and then building. Every muscle in her body tightens and she moans my name, hips jerking as the orgasm rolls through her. Which is when I let go. I pull out until I'm at the ridge and push back in.

Winter's eyes go wide, and her mouth drops open. "Oh my God, yes. Do that again."

So I do. Over and over. Harder and faster at Winter's request. And she keeps coming, and I keep pumping—until I remember I'm not wearing a condom, and I'm about three strokes away from an orgasm.

"I gotta stop. I'm gonna come."

"So fucking come." Her legs are locked around my waist.

"I'm bare."

"Shit. Right." She unhooks her feet and pushes on my chest, somehow managing the coordination to wrap her hand around my erection as I come. All over her right thigh.

"Fuckin' hell," I groan. My legs are wobbly, and I'm unsteady on my feet. I brace a hand on the counter. "What a mess. That was the worst, best idea I've ever had."

Winter bursts out laughing. "Want to hand me a paper towel?"

I laugh and let my head drop to her shoulder, blindly reaching across the counter for the paper towel roll, or a napkin, or tissue, whatever is closest. "You have to drive me to practice. I'm too orgasm-stupid to do anything but breathe right now." I hand her a napkin.

"My pussy is that magical, huh?"

"So damn magical." I kiss her neck and back up so I can see her face. "I'm sorry that was close."

"It's not your fault. I got carried away too. And the condoms are a good additional precaution, but I just finished my period a few days ago, so I'm not ovulating. We're safe and smart, BJ."

"I know. Still, it was my idea."

"I have zero regrets, although it's going to be hard to go back to condoms all the time when I know how good it can feel." She pulls her tank back on.

"We don't have to. Not all the time, if you don't want. When it's safest, we could go without." I tuck myself into my underwear and nab my shirt from the floor. I pick up Winter's shorts and underwear.

"Okay. Yeah. That sounds good." She glances at the clock on the stove. "Shit, you're going to be a few minutes late."

"It's okay. Adele's always late anyway." I grab her hand before she can disappear into my bedroom to get dressed. "I have something I've been meaning to ask you."

"Do you want to wait until we're in the Jeep? I don't want to piss Adele off."

"Don't worry about Adele."

She tips her head. "Is everything okay?"

"Yeah. Everything is great. Better than great." I squeeze her hand, my stomach twisting a little. "I know you're not a huge fan of labels, but I feel like we're beyond the just-dating phase, and I'd really like to be able to introduce you as my girlfriend, if that's okay with you."

She tugs at the end of her braid.

I don't want her to feel like she has to say yes. "But it's also okay if you're not ready. I can wait, just know it's on the table."

"I'm ready for that label if you're ready for that label."

"Yeah?"

She smiles. "Yeah."

I take her face between my palms and kiss her, soft and slow. "You're my sexy girlfriend."

She laughs. "And you're my sexy boyfriend. But we need to get a move on if I'm going to get you to skate practice and me to hockey without both of us being late."

"Right. Yes. We'll celebrate later with more orgasms."

We clean ourselves up with a wet washcloth, get dressed, and hop in the Jeep. Adele's car is already in the lot when we arrive, so I give Winter a quick kiss. "Let's go for dinner later. I'll make a reservation. Just something low-key."

"Skinny-jeans low-key?" she asks.

"Yeah. I love you in skinny jeans. See you soon." I hop out so she can get to hockey practice on time.

I'm in a pretty damn good mood, so not even Adele's irritation over my being late—for the first time *ever*—can dampen my mood. Unfortunately, my being late, coupled with my good mood, seems to be throwing Adele off. She struggles, and after three hours on the ice, she's still not finding her groove. Winter will be here soon, and we haven't made it through the routine once today without a mistake.

"Can we go through it one more time?" Adele asks.

"You've said that three times." Or at least that's how it feels.

"This is the last time. I promise. I just want to get the angle right on the twist. Maybe you're overcorrecting."

I don't feel like fighting, so I just nod, even though the last time she almost kneed me in the face. "Once more through. Then we're calling it a night."

"One more time." She smiles, and I start the track again, setting my phone next to the portable speaker so I can record this one. I'm crossing my fingers that recording it means we hit all the right notes and end on a high. And soon my girlfriend will be here to pick me up. When we took a break earlier, I made a reservation at a restaurant. Nothing fancy, since we'll be fresh from practice, but I want to celebrate making it official.

I meet Adele in the middle of the rink. "Ready to rock this?"

"Yup."

I get into position behind her, and we start from the top.

Everything goes smoothly at first. We nail every spin, our

timing flawless as we move through the first complex combination and nail it, apart from a little stutter in the landing. I'm feeling great as we move into the second phase of the routine with the more complicated sequence—the one Adele sometimes manages and sometimes doesn't. But I feel like we've got it this time.

The spin is smooth, the timing on point, and then the lift. At first we're in sync, balanced, but then I see her hand lower, and her body tips forward. It's not a lot, but it's enough to throw us off. I correct, but so does she, and then everything goes sideways.

I don't want to drop her on her face, so I bring her down, and her knee slams into my chest, knocking the air out of my lungs. My feet slip out from under me, taking her with me. My head hits the ice, and my elbow jams into the unforgiving surface, making stars burst in my vision. But it's the vicious, searing pain in my left thigh that sends a wave of nausea rolling through me.

"Shit. Sorry." Adele rolls to the ice beside me. "Oh no, oh God!"

Black and white spots cloud my vision.

"BJ? Adele? What the hell happened?"

I must've hit my head pretty hard, because I swear that's Winter's voice.

I push up, but it sends a shock of pain through my right arm and an inky wave of darkness across my vision.

"What the fuck did you do? Get away from him." Winter's face appears in front of me, unclear and hazy, but present.

"Hey, Snowflake." I reach for her with the arm that doesn't make me want to scream in pain, and she catches my hand.

"Hey, hi..." Her voice is soft and unsteady. "Stay still, okay?"

"Call nine-one-one." She tosses Adele her phone. "Fucking

now!" Winter shrugs out of her coat and tucks it under my head. She unbuckles her belt and whips it through the loops. "Fuck, fuck, fuck," she mutters. "Babe, this probably isn't going to feel very good, and I'm really sorry, but I have to do it. I love you. I'm sorry."

I don't understand the apologies until she slides the belt under my thigh. The pain is brain-meltingly awful, and it becomes infinitely worse when she pulls the belt tight.

I'm pretty sure I lose consciousness for a few seconds because when my vision returns, with more black-and-white splotches, Winter's face is close again.

"What can I do? What should I do?" Adele's voice is high and reedy.

"Wait by the door so they know where to find us, and see if you can flag anyone else down."

"Snowflake?"

She strokes my cheek. "Hey. Hi. It's okay. You're okay. I'm sorry, Randall. I know that sucked, but I'm just trying to keep you here with me. Stay with me, okay? The ambulance is coming."

Her face gets lost in the white dots.

"Hey, hey." She presses her lips to mine. "I'm right here. Focus on me."

"I don't feel great."

"I know. We're going to do something about that. Just a couple more minutes and the paramedics will be here."

I try to lift my head, but she's right there, face inches from mine. "Just focus on me."

My body feels mostly numb, but every time I try to move my legs, a wave of pain hits me that makes it hard to breathe. I do what Winter says, focusing on her instead of the pain. "You're so fuckin' beautiful." I sound drunk.

"So are you." She brushes hair off my forehead. "I tried not to fall in love with you, but you made that impossible. You know that, right?"

"I'm charming."

She smiles. "So charming." Her fingers drift along my temple. "You're going to be okay."

"I hit my head."

"I know. Don't worry. It won't affect how charming you are."

"My leg feels like it's on fire."

"We'll get you fixed up. Not long now and the ambulance will be here." Her eyes glisten with tears.

"Is it bad?" My voice is hardly a croak.

"I've seen worse." She kisses me again, her chin trembling. "Eyes open. Focus on me."

I keep blinking, but it's hard to keep them open.

"I know you're tired. Tomorrow we'll lie in bed all day and watch movies. We can even watch that one about the hockey player and the figure skater."

"That's us. In reverse."

"It is. It's exactly us."

"You hate rom-coms." I sound far away.

"I don't hate them. They just make me feel too much."

"They're here. They're over here. Please, hurry, please," Adele shouts.

"I love you." Winter kisses me one last time, but before I can say the words back, I'm surrounded by EMTs.

"Lost a lot of blood..."

"Tourniquet kept him alive."

"He's crashing..."

"...oxygen..."

"Get him on the bus..."

"Radio ahead. Tell them we're coming in with a critical case..."

I'M IN A FIELD. The sun is shining down on me. So bright. A little too bright. I turn away from it, and behind me is a sunrise on the water. The water looks cool, and I want to go there. I want to dive in and stay there.

To my right, a figure appears.

"Great-Grandpa Balls?"

He rolls his eyes.

"You're dead."

"No shit, Sherlock. And here I thought you were the smart one." He scoffs. "Turn your ass around. It's not your time, yet."

"Am I dreaming?"

He gives me a look.

"Am I dying?"

"It's too soon. You have things to do. If you stay, you'll break her heart."

He turns around and walks toward the lake.

"Is this heaven?"

"Go toward the light."

"I thought I was supposed to stay away from the light."

"Christ, you're a pain in the ass. This time the light is what you need. Go back. You need each other."

I turn around, but the light seems so far away. I move toward it, though, because there's a pull I can't deny.

THE STEADY BEEP is the first thing I notice as consciousness returns, a slow tide receding, awareness seeping

309

in. My head aches. So does my arm. But my leg feels the worst. An aching burn grows with my alertness.

I crack a lid, but the light is too much to handle on top of everything else. Instead, I just breathe and try to figure out where I am and what happened.

Hospital.

The sterile scent, the beeping, the scratchy sheets.

How is the question. What happened to put me here?

As consciousness solidifies, I register the feel of warm fingers wrapped around mine. I know from the calluses it's Winter. Wanting to see her overrides my aversion to the light, so I open one eye again. It's not as overwhelming this time, maybe because I'm prepared. Maybe because seeing her is more important than anything else.

Her other arm is slung across the bedrail, her forehead propped on it. It can't be comfortable. Her arm must be asleep. Her neck will most definitely have a crick in it.

I give her fingers a gentle squeeze, which slices a ridiculous jolt of pain through my arm, and I suck in a sharp breath. Her head snaps up and her eyes find mine, wide and acutely alert. They're red-rimmed and swollen, as if she's spent a lot of time crying recently.

She mouths the word *hi* and bursts into tears, clamping a hand over her mouth. Her shoulders shake with silent sobs.

I can't do anything to console her. I'm hooked up to machines. There's an IV in one arm and a nearly empty bag of blood in the other.

As quickly as the sobbing started, it stops. Winter takes a deep breath and exhales slowly. She leans over to press soft kisses to my forehead and cheeks, and eventually my lips. My mouth tastes like I ate a bag of assholes, and I feel like an actual bag of smashed assholes, so I don't try to slip her the tongue. But I think about it, and that tells me I'm probably going to be fine. At least mentally. Physically is another story.

When she pulls back, her eyes are still watery and tears track down her cheeks, but she smiles. "I'm glad you're back," she whispers.

"Me too." It's a craggy rasp. "What happened?"

"You don't remember." It's a statement, not a question.

"Should I?"

Before she can answer, I'm startled by a loud snore. I turn my head and immediately regret the movement, because the pain that shoots through my head steals my vision.

My mom startles awake, and the second her eyes focus, she shoves my dad's shoulder and launches herself out of the chair she was awkwardly sleeping in. In fact, all three of them have been sleeping in chairs. Winter got the worst deal, though. Her chair looks like it was pulled out of a dumpster.

My dad jerks awake as my mom's hands move in the air like she's trying to take flight. And then, just like Winter, she bursts into tears. Hers are far from silent.

My dad shoots out of the chair and wraps his arms around her while she falls apart. I wish I could do that for Winter... My brain is sluggish, and I'm already so tired again.

"Here, take a sip." Winter lifts a bendy straw to my lips. I suck, and even that small thing takes monumental effort. But the cool wetness coats my tongue and slides down my throat. "He's only been awake for about a minute," she says to my parents. "I think it's all a bit overwhelming."

My mom's wailing quiets to soft sniffles, punctuated by hiccups. She takes a deep breath and lets it out slowly as she approaches the bed. She cups my face in her hands and presses her lips to my forehead. "I am so glad you're okay."

My dad's voice is gruff. "You scared the hell out of us, son."

"What happened?" I ask again.

Mom purses her lips, and her jaw tightens.

"You had an accident on the ice," Dad replies, pulling Mom against his side. He bends to kiss the top of her head.

I search my memory for the events I know must have taken place. I vaguely remember the knee to the chest. And then pain. A lot of it. "Bad lift. Is Adele okay?"

"She's fine," Mom bites out.

"Okay. Good. I didn't want to drop her." I remember that much. The overcorrection too.

My dad and Winter exchange a look.

"Lily, why don't you and I get Randall some fresh water?" Winter says.

She doesn't use my full name often—mostly when she's in the middle of an orgasm—so it's a bit of a shock to hear it now.

But Mom nods, and Winter wraps her arm around her shoulder. "We'll be back in a minute." She guides her toward the door. Always taking care of other people.

Dad pulls his chair closer and drops into it. He looks exhausted, like this has aged him a decade.

"Mom okay?" My voice is still raspy.

"Okay is a relative term." He folds his hands and drops his head, taking a couple of deep breaths. When his gaze lifts, his eyes are shiny. "It was a really close call, son." Another deep breath. "We almost lost you."

"I guess that explains why I feel like I went a round in the ring with death."

He gives me a look. "Not a good time for jokes."

"I'm not laughing."

"Winter saved your life. It's all on tape. What happened, how it happened. If she hadn't been there, you would have bled out in a matter of minutes. The ambulance wouldn't have made it if it wasn't for her quick thinking."

"Bled out?" I echo. The words feel like a punch to the chest.

His expression is somber. "Adele's blade sliced your leg and nicked your femoral artery when you tried to save her from falling."

"Jesus."

"—was absolutely present and watching over you."

"I think it was Great-Grandpa Balls, actually," I mutter.

"What?"

"Nothing." I was probably tripping balls, literally and figuratively. "This is a lot to process."

"Winter used her belt as a tourniquet. If she hadn't—" He chokes up, then clears his throat. "But you're here, and you're going to be okay, and that's what's important."

The statement feels unfinished, like it's weighted down with more, but I'm too foggy to ask questions. And tired.

Mom and Winter return with fresh water, and my mom fusses over me, running her fingers through my hair, unable to stop her tears of relief as she tells me she's glad I'm here with them. That it's going to be okay.

I wonder how true that is.

Because it sounds a lot like they're reassuring themselves, not me.

31

Curveball

BJ

STAYING awake proves to be a challenge, and the bliss of unconsciousness, where I'm free from pain and fear of the unknown, claims me again. The next few times I wake up, either Mom, Dad, or Winter is holding my hand. I'm not alert for long, though.

When I finally wake feeling clear, Lovey is at my bedside.

"Hey, bestie," I croak.

She startles, and her phone clatters to the floor.

"Hey. Hi." Her eyes well with tears, but she blinks them back. She takes my hand. "Fuck you for almost dying."

I laugh and then cringe, because everything hurts. "Sorry 'bout that."

Lovey's chin wobbles, and her shoulders shake.

"Hey, hey. It's okay. I'm okay." I squeeze her hand.

She fights to stay in control, but tears run down her cheeks and drop to her lap. "I promised I was going to keep it together, but you know how shitty I am about keeping my feelings from leaking out of my eyes."

I smile. "You cry every time we watch *Vet Rescue*."

"It's true. I'm so sappy."

"Don't ever change."

"I won't." She plucks a tissue from the box beside her and blows her nose. "We thought we were going to lose you. If it hadn't been for Winter—" Her voice cracks. "I thought I wasn't going to get to be the best woman at your wedding, and you weren't going to be co-maid of honor with Lacey for mine." More tears fall.

"Pfft. Like I was going to die and miss out on wearing a suit the same color as the bridesmaid dresses."

"Hey, look who's awake." Quinn appears in the doorway holding takeout coffees. "How you doing?"

"Alive, so that's good."

"Seems like you've got more than one guardian angel watching over you." He hands Lovey a coffee and murmurs something I don't catch.

"Lavender and Kody just arrived. I'll meet them in the waiting room and give you two a few minutes." Lovey releases my hand and stands.

"What are Lav and Kody doing here? He's not playing against Chicago for a few more weeks."

"They're here to see you, bro. Brushes with death make you popular." He skims Lovey's hand as she moves past him and leaves the room. "You need a drink or some food or anything?" he asks me.

"Water would be good."

He sets his coffee down and passes me the plastic cup with the lid. He helps me get the straw to my lips so I can take a couple of sips.

"Where are my parents and Winter?"

"Your dad is in the waiting room. They only allow two visitors at a time, and everyone is here. Your mom took Winter home to shower. She hasn't left your side since you got out of surgery two days ago."

"Two days ago?"

"You lost a lot of blood, my friend." He clasps his hands. "You scared the hell out of us."

"How's Winter holding up?"

"She puts on a brave face. Seems a lot like where you are now is an echo of where she was earlier in the summer. Sort of like how the Clover situation echoed Lavender's earlier in the summer for Mav. We'll all keep an eye on her for you," he assures me.

"Thanks. I appreciate that. She's spent a lot of years being the support instead of the supported."

"That's accurate. But her mom drove up here yesterday to support her, which is good. Her mom is a real sweet lady, started cooking up a storm the second she walked through the door. Guess we know where Winter gets her mad skills from, huh?" he says.

"She loves to cook, and bake, and grocery shop." I smile faintly. When the newspaper shows up every Thursday, Winter lays out all the flyers so she can price match and plans out the weekly dinner menu with everyone's input. "What about my parents? How are they?"

Quinn scrubs a hand over his face. "They're okay. Your mom is... It's been hard for her. But your dad is pragmatic. You're their only child, and they almost lost you, so it makes sense that they're pretty freaked out."

"What about Lovey?"

A small smile tugs the corner of his lips. "She's been vacillating between emotional and productive. Something like this makes us aware of our own mortality and how much we take for granted."

"I don't remember much of what happened yet."

"You got yourself a sweet concussion and some stitches in the back of your head, so that'll be a fun new scar to go with the one on your leg. I'm guessing things will fall into place over the next few days."

"How's Adele?"

His jaw works. "She's fine. Don't worry about her right now. Your focus should be on healing."

I remember asking about her before, and my mom having a similar reaction.

There's a knock on the door, and Kody's massive frame fills the open space. Lavender stands in front of him, her hair falling in dark auburn waves around her shoulders. She looks different but the same.

"Come on in. I'll give you guys a few minutes to say hi." Quinn moves toward the door. "You want me to get you anything? Food? Something else to drink?"

"We've been sent with nourishment." Lavender holds up a Tupperware container of muffins, and Kody has a ginger ale.

"I'll be back a little later," Quinn tells me. He stops to hug Lavender on the way out and gives Kody a hearty back pat. They have a brief, whispered conversation as Lavender approaches the bed.

"This is pretty dramatic, even for you, BJ." She shakes her head. "First your house almost burns down and now this?"

"Just keeping things fresh, I guess."

She sets the Tupperware on the nightstand, taking my hand between hers. "I'm sorry this happened to you. Don't let this define or derail you."

"God, I miss you this year."

"Same. So much same." She blinks a bunch of times and sighs. "I met your girlfriend."

"When?"

"In the waiting room a few minutes ago. She's a real badass. Tried really hard to keep it together when she met Kodiak." She smirks.

I chuckle. "She's all hockey all the time."

"Oh yeah. The two of them started talking, and it was like another language." Her smile is soft.

"She fits in well with our crew."

"She does. It's good you found each other when you did." Lavender knows all about the Winter situation because we have a group chat and our own private chat that we use often.

"Divine intervention at its finest." Winter is the reason I'm still here.

Kody appears behind Lavender. He seems bigger than when I saw him last—broader, thicker. He has a five o'clock shadow, and his hair is longer than usual.

"You're a good-looking fucker, you know that?" I say.

A smile tips his mouth, and his cheeks flush. "Yeah, but I'm an asshole, so it's all about balance. How you doin'?"

"Based on the number of visitors, I've been better. What day is it?"

"It's Saturday."

"Shit. Don't you have an exhibition game?"

"Yeah. I'm flying out later this afternoon, but I wanted to get Lavender here and see you first." He wraps his arm around her.

"I'm staying for a few days," Lavender says.

"That's great. You can take my room, if you want."

"Don't you worry about sleeping arrangements. We'll figure it out."

We chat for a few more minutes, and then fatigue slams

into me, thick like fog. Kody tells me he'll be back in a few weeks, and Lavender promises to visit later.

My parents and Winter return. I guess the visitor rules are different for them. Winter settles in a chair and slips her hand in mine. It's all the comfort I need. I close my eyes and fall asleep.

AFTER THREE DAYS, I'm able to keep my eyes open for more than twenty-minute intervals. Once I'm moved from the ICU to the regular recovery ward, my parents and Winter are no longer able to stay the night. Those hours are the longest. I'm used to sleeping next to Winter, to the sound of her steady breathing and the comfort of her presence.

On the morning of the fourth day, I ask Winter the question that's been bothering me. "Why hasn't Adele been by?"

My parents left a few minutes ago on a food run. My appetite is returning, and all I want is shitty fast food.

Winter's eyes grow sad. "She's not allowed to."

I frown. "Her parents won't let her?"

Winter lowers the bedrail so she can sit on the edge. She takes my hand. "What can you remember?"

I close my eyes on an exhale, sifting through the fog. "I remember you and the banana in the kitchen."

She chuckles. "Of course you do. And after that, I dropped you at the arena."

"I asked you to be my girlfriend first, though. And you said yes."

"I did." She smiles. "I probably should have waited until after skate practice to pull the banana move. Anyway, I dropped you off and went to hockey practice, then came back to pick you up."

"We were going out for dinner. I made a reservation, and we missed it."

"It's okay. We'll have plenty of opportunities once you're on your feet again." She swallows. "You were in the middle of your routine when I arrived. I watched from the door for a couple of minutes. You were flawless. It was perfect, but then Adele—" Her jaw clenches, and she clears her throat. "She messed up, and you tried to correct it, but she... She overcorrected. It was too late to stop the fall."

"I didn't want her to get hurt."

"I know." Winter plays with my fingers.

"What aren't you telling me?"

She looks away. "She messed up the lift on purpose."

"What? Why?"

"I don't know, but you were recording the run-through, and it was all on the video. That's why she's not allowed to visit. I don't think she meant for you to get hurt, but she was reckless, and it almost cost you your life." She cups my cheek, eyes full of sadness and empathy. "I'm so sorry, BJ. I can't imagine how hard this must be to hear. Whatever you need from me, I'm here, okay?"

Shock makes me numb. "It's on video?"

"It is."

"Can I see it?"

"I don't have it with me." Her thumb runs across my knuckles. "It's pretty graphic."

"So you've seen it?"

She nods.

"I want to see it. I need to see it."

"Shh... Take a breath, Randall." She presses her lips to

mine. "Give it a day. If you still want to see it tomorrow, I'll see what I can do."

THE NEXT DAY, I send my parents on another takeout run. Winter is sitting crisscross applesauce next to me, working on an assignment. The only time she's not here is when visiting hours are over, and yesterday she went to hockey practice, on my order. Her professors have given her permission to work remotely, unless it's a seminar, until the end of the week.

"I want to see the video."

She sighs. "I don't know if that's a good idea."

"Noted. I still think I need to see it."

She stares at me, and I stare at her. Her lips are pursed, and her eyes are tired. It's been a rough week. My parents want me to recover in Pearl Lake when I'm released. I would prefer to stay in Chicago where Winter is. Also, as cool as my parents are, and as awesome as our relationship is, my mother will smother the fuck out of me if I come home.

"It's now or later, Snowflake. One way or another, I'm going to see the video." I weigh my words carefully and admit, "I'd rather it be with you."

"Okay." Her jaw tics, but she flips open her laptop. It takes her a minute to cue it up. Her hands shake as she sets it on the tray that holds my water, a textbook, and a box of tissues.

"If it gets to be too much, just tell me." She hits play.

The video starts at the beginning of our routine. We're in sync, and like Winter said, we're nearly flawless, everything smooth and carefully executed. The first combination is perfect, but then the shift happens, and I see exactly where it all goes wrong. *How* it all goes wrong. The jump itself is fine, and at first Adele is a perfect, balanced arc in the lift. But what she does next doesn't make sense. The lift should be smooth, but she drops her head and her hand, and at the same time lowers her leg a few inches. I adjust, but the damage is done. A sense of déjà vu hits me. Adele has done this before. I remember the feel of her weight shifting in my hands, but usually it was just a minor adjustment. It's different this time, and much more obvious. She drops her hand and her leg at the same time. It's calculated and intentional. But this time the correction on my part wasn't enough to stop us from falling.

I'm not prepared for how violently I go down, how even as we're heading toward the ice, I try to break her fall. And I do, successfully, but when she pulls her knees in, it's the perfect storm for even more damage.

I was wearing dark gray sweats. They don't camouflage the quickly spreading stain on the fabric. And then Winter is sprinting across the ice, falling to her knees, and shrugging out of her coat, shouting at Adele as she tosses her phone to her.

A pool of red spreads across the ice under me, and Winter whips her belt free and uses it as a tourniquet. I close the laptop, cutting off the sound of my scream. My stomach rolls as reality hits me. My partner almost ended my life.

It makes me question a lot of things. First, I imploded a partnership of four years by getting romantically involved. Now my partner almost killed me because... I don't know why. Maybe I'm the common denominator. Maybe the problem is me.

"I would have died if you weren't there," I whisper, looking up at Winter. I've heard that several times over the past few days, but seeing it firsthand? How much blood there was. How fast it all happened. That's a mindfuck I'm unprepared for.

A tear slides down her cheek, and her smile is tremulous. "But I was, so you're here."

I inhale relief and exhale the pain of it all. "Nothing will ever be the same, will it?"

She shakes her head. "You can't beat death and view the world through a lens that no longer exists."

"I'm never going to skate with a partner again." The words sound wrong and right at the same time.

"Not with Adele." Her chin trembles, and the sadness in her eyes tells me more than her words.

There's another piece of this everyone has been dancing around. When they come to change the dressings on my wound, someone is always here to keep me occupied. "How bad is the damage?"

Her gaze drops. "I don't know. It's too early to say."

"That sounds like some real bullshit, Winter."

She lifts my hand to her lips. "Why are you making me do this with you?"

"Because you're the only person I trust to tell me the truth, even if it's going to suck." I'm right too. My parents will sugar-coat it. Lovey will downplay it and say everything will work out. But Winter won't.

Her tears land on the sheets beside our clasped hands.

"It's that bad?" My voice is a whisper.

"I honestly don't know, but it's a really deep laceration. You were in surgery for hours. Tendons and muscles were severed, and some nerves, but they reattached everything, as far as I know. It was touch and go, and I think the focus was on keeping you alive first, and putting you back together second. The healing process will be long." She sighs. "These are things I've heard the doctors say, but I don't have any timelines or defini-tives. I have pieces and not the whole picture." She flattens my palm against her cheek, her eyes full of pain. "I don't want to tell you lies, BJ, but I don't know what your future on the ice is going to look like. I'll be here, though, to help however you need."

I let that sink in.

All the things I've been working toward are no longer within reach. They've shifted, moved to a distant and indistinct future. For the first time in my life, I feel untethered. Uncertain. Like my path has been erased.

"I'm sorry I don't have more answers," she whispers.

"Don't apologize. I needed to hear it, and it's better coming from you than anyone else."

THE FIRST TIME I see the damage, I vomit and then faint. The second time I'm better prepared, but it's still a level of horrifying that's hard to handle.

I'm stuck in the hospital for a week. The first few days weren't that bad because I spent most of them asleep. But now that the fog has lifted, I'm stuck in my head, replaying the events that brought me here—especially at night when I'm struggling to sleep. That's the hardest, being alone with my thoughts, questioning everything. Feeling like this is my fault, like I should have seen it coming.

"I fucking hate being here," I snap on the morning of the seventh day.

Winter had to go back to class in person today, and I miss her. I miss her presence. I miss her face and her voice and her sass and the smell of her shampoo.

"You want out of here, you know how to make it happen," Dad says with an arched brow.

"It fucking hurts."

"You think I don't know that?" He leans forward in his chair and levels me with a challenging stare.

I want to tell him he has no idea how bad the pain is, but he sort of does. I know this because the whole teach-me-how-to-aim thing and using a urinal for the first time is some weird father-son rite of passage and I've seen his scar.

"Look, I know how difficult this is, son, but you make it to the bathroom on your own, and the doctor will sign the release papers. Then you can be in your own house, with your own bathroom, and you don't have to eat shitty hospital food."

"Fuck. Fine. Let's do this."

"I'll get the crutches."

Sitting up is fine. Getting my legs over the side of the bed sucks, yet I can breathe through the pain. But I stand up and sit down three times because of the wave of nausea and dizziness it produces.

"You got this, Randall. Just take it one step at a time, okay?" Dad says.

I pause between each step, worried I'll pass out from the pain. Halfway there, I want to quit. Twice I almost puke. But I make it to the fucking bathroom.

Reality comes crashing in when I see my reflection.

I'm standing in the hospital bathroom with my dad, crutches under my arms for support. I'm covered in a sheen of sweat from the exertion, my head swimming from the pain. My beard is a gross mess, and my hair is greasy. I probably stink. All I've had for the past seven days are wet-washcloth baths because I haven't been able to stay upright long enough to shower.

My dad is right in front of me, ready to catch me if I fall. "Just breathe, son. Just breathe through it."

"What if I can't ever skate again?" The question has been floating out there like a lost balloon.

"It's early, Randall. You're in the worst of it, and we won't have answers to that for a while." His tone is gentle, his words unsteady.

"Adele took my fucking future. I was supposed to do what Mom couldn't." My vision blurs. I've been fighting this emotion for a while now, not wanting to give in to debilitating sadness. But it's been waiting, ready to sink its claws in.

"Hey." Dad's hands come to rest on my shoulders, and his eyes reflect every emotion I feel—sadness, understanding, fear, and a helplessness I assume can only be understood when you're a parent trying to hold your child together while his world inverts. "If that's what you want, we will do the work to try to get you there. But you need to focus on your own goals, and not the ones you think you need to attain for someone else, okay? We're not going to conquer the world today. We're just going to take it one step and one breath at a time."

I can't form words, and I can't hold myself up anymore.

He wraps his arms around me.

"It's all right to fall apart, Randall. You're safe to mourn what should have been."

So I do.

32

Tough Love

WINTER

THE WEEK FOLLOWING BJ's accident, I barely slept, but his family and friends rallied in support, and I have never been so grateful to have so many people to keep me propped up, because the what-ifs are terrifying.

And my mom was right there with them, doing everything she could to help me through. She's stayed with me for a whole week. She's cooked and stocked our freezer with easy meals. She's baked and made me lunches and done my laundry. She adores River and the twins and thinks Rose is a hoot and Quinn is one of the sweetest guys she's ever met. She calls him a gentle giant.

And at night, when I wake up sweaty with nightmares, she's been there to save me from them.

"I just wish the nightmares would stop," I tell her when it happens yet again. I had them all the time when we were living with my dad—always afraid the worst would happen, and then it did. "I feel like I'm responsible for this somehow. Like it's my fault."

She brushes my hair away from my face. "Why would you think that?"

"You got hurt because I made Dad angry and left you to deal with him, and then BJ got hurt because I didn't love that Adele was manipulating him, so I started picking him up from practice once a week. Maybe I pushed her because I was taking his attention away from her."

She shakes her head. "Oh, honey, I know I've said this before, but what happened with Clay wasn't your fault. I stayed in an abusive relationship for far longer than I should have. And if it wasn't for you always defending both of us, far worse might have happened. You tried to get me to see how bad it was. I only wish I'd listened sooner." She sighs. "You've been conditioned to take the blame, and I'm at fault for that. I let you take that role for far too long, and I'm so, so sorry. I'm trying to make up for it, and I'm so lucky that you're as forgiving as you are." She looks at me a long moment. "You're not to blame here either. What happened with BJ's partner is not your fault. If you hadn't been there, the ambulance might not have been called in time. You saved his life, honey."

She hugs me and lies with me until I fall asleep again. In the morning, my mom calls Clover, and they set me up with a local counselor. It's compounded trauma, and I need a sounding board.

When BJ gets the all clear to come home, Mom fills their fridge with easy-to-reheat meals and promises to come back if I need her.

Just over a week after the accident, BJ's parents bring him home. Getting from the front door to his bedroom takes all his energy. It's hard to watch him struggle, to see his frustration over how depleting it is to walk fifty feet. He takes three breaks, and I can tell he's fighting to control his temper, which isn't typical for BJ. He's always even-keeled. But he's hurting and scared.

"You should really consider coming home, Randall, even if it's just for a couple of weeks." Lily crosses her arms, her lips pursed. BJ's lying on his bed now, covered in sweat, breathing heavy, his pallor somewhere between sheet white and pale green.

I actually don't disagree with her, though it's the last thing BJ wants.

"I want to recover here," he argues. "I don't want to lose my entire semester over this, and if I go home, that's what'll happen."

"We have to let him try, Lily," Coach says softly.

I can tell she doesn't love that, but she concedes. "We'll be talking daily, and the nurse will make home visits to help change your bandages."

"I know. The doctor said the same thing before I left the hospital," he grumbles.

"Can I have a minute with Randall?" I ask.

"Of course."

They leave the room, closing the door behind them.

I take a seat beside him on the bed. "I know this is hard, BJ. I know you're in pain and you're probably overwhelmed, but your parents are leaving in a few minutes. They're going to drive back to Pearl Lake, and they'll talk about how worried they are the entire way. Do not let them go without telling them how much you appreciate and love them. They almost lost you. I almost lost you. I know they're being overbearing, but give them a fucking break, yeah?"

He closes his eyes, and tears leak out of the corners. "I'm fucking terrified, Winter."

"I know." I brush his hair away from his face. It's finally

clean. They must have gotten him in the shower before they brought him home today. "And that's a totally reasonable feeling. But don't take that fear out on them."

"I'm sorry. My mom is a lot right now."

"Of course she is. You're her baby."

"You're right. I know you're right. I'm not trying to be a dick."

"Pain makes it hard to be nice. It shortens the fuse. Tell them you love them, tell them you'll send them regular updates, and if you can't manage, you'll come home."

"I'm not going home." He crosses his arms. It's pretty unconvincing with him lying here all broken and exhausted.

"Okay. But give them the peace of mind they need to walk out the door and not feel guilt or regret. Your mom is already struggling because she feels like she should have seen what Adele was doing. Give her the gift of your appreciation and an assurance that you won't tough it out like a testosterone-fueled idiot."

He stares at me for a few long seconds and uncrosses his arms. "Okay, point taken."

"I'm going to get them, okay?"

"Yeah. Okay. Thank you for not letting me be a complete dickhead."

"I know it's not intentional, and I don't want you to have any regrets."

I open the door, and his parents come back in. BJ lets his mom fawn and help him get comfortable, and I leave them to have some time before they go.

When they come out a few minutes later, they close his door behind them. "He's pretty tired," Coach tells me. "Just the drive home was a lot for him. It's probably going to be a tough few days."

"If you think it's too much, you can let us know," Lily

whispers.

I nod. "I'll keep an eye on him."

I walk them to the door, and Lily hugs me and thanks me for what has to be the hundredth time for saving her son.

"No way was I letting him go without a fight." Not when he has such a tight hold on my heart.

FOR THE FIRST few days BJ is home, expectations are low. He needs to get used to moving around with crutches and heal. But by the end of the first week, I'm not seeing much progress, and he's made zero attempts to attend class, citing too much pain and an inability to sit in the uncomfortable chairs.

Sure, he can get to and from the bathroom on his own. He'll even make the occasional trip to the kitchen when he's hungry. But he usually goes for easy things, like bags of chips, chocolate bars, and cookies. The empty boxes and bags are strewn across his bedroom floor.

BJ isn't a neat freak like River, or orderly like Quinn, who spent a couple of years in the army before he started college. But usually, BJ's lack of order is limited to a shirt thrown over the back of his chair or a stray pair of socks that didn't quite make it to the basket.

Currently, however, his floor is littered with discarded clothes, and there are empty pop cans on his dresser, along with crushed boxes and bags. It's seven on a Friday night, and he's sleeping, which is a new pattern. I've been staying at my own place at night because he watches TV in bed until late, and I can't sleep with the noise. I'm also a bit of a roller-arounder, and I don't want to bump his leg. But also? His room smells like the inside of a gym bag.

Communal dinner is at my place tonight. We're making personal pizzas and salad, one of BJ's favorite meals.

I knock on his door. "Hey, it's pizza night. You gonna come to my place and hang out?"

He grunts and pulls a pillow over his head.

"Is that a no?"

He mutters something.

"Sorry, I didn't catch that. Want to try again?"

"Can you just bring me something back?"

"Why don't you come over in half an hour. Or I can text you when the food is ready. You don't have to stay long. It would be good to leave your room, don't you think?"

"I leave my room."

"To go to the kitchen. When was the last time you stepped outside? You haven't even attempted class."

"Are you really going to get on me about this?"

I bite my lips together. I don't know what to do or say. I hate fighting. *Hate it.* "I'll text you in a bit." I close his door and trudge back to my house, feeling defeated.

The kitchen is bustling. Lovey is rolling out pizza dough, Quinn is making homemade sauce, River is grating cheese, Josiah is making salad, Rose is sautéing onions, and Lacey is chopping veggies.

"I need help." I prop my fists on my hips and tip my chin up, because I'm on the verge of tears.

Lovey, Rose, and Josiah drop what they're doing and fold me into a group hug. Lacey joins them next, and then River and Quinn wrap themselves around all of us.

"What the fuck is going on here?"

"Is that Dracula?" Rose's nose is smushed against my arm.

I can't see through the sea of bodies surrounding me. "It sounds like him."

"Group hug. Want in?" River asks.

"Physical contact is something I try to avoid, but thanks," Laughlin says.

Everyone steps back, and Lovey gives me a sympathetic smile. "Is it BJ?"

"I don't know what to do anymore. He's not leaving his room. He hasn't even tried to go to class this week. Not once. Not even behavioral psych, and that's his favorite. The only reason he leaves his room is to get food. I don't even know if he's showered."

"Ew." Lacey wrinkles her nose.

"His room smells like the inside of a hockey bag."

"That is accurate," Quinn agrees.

"I get that he's struggling, but lying around in bed all day is the opposite of progress. I don't want to start an argument. I hate fighting, but I don't know what I'm supposed to do."

Rose points a spatula at me. "You could use sex as a weapon!"

Quinn frowns. "Uh, I don't know that BJ is in any condition for sex. I've had a groin pull and a fucking hard-on is enough of a struggle. I know this isn't the same, but it's in the same area, and all those muscles are interconnected. And he's got a lot of stitches, both internal and external. The best you can probably do is rub the lamp."

"Or offer BJ a BJ," Josiah suggests.

Lovey's hand shoots up, then drops when she realizes it's unnecessary. "While I don't disagree with this tactic, I think you can up the ante." Her smile turns sly. "You need to remind him what he's missing."

"What do you mean?"

"BJ is always checking you out. That man is in *love* with your ass."

"It's a nice ass," Rose agrees.

River and Josiah nod. "Truth."

"I'm tapping out on this one since he's my roommate and you're my friend," Quinn says.

"BJ might not be able to kick my ass right now, but one day he will again, and I don't trust any of you not to throw me under the bus if I give my opinion on this particular matter," Laughlin says.

No one disagrees.

I roll my eyes. "Okay, so now that we have a majority consensus on the status of my ass, you want to tell me where you're going with this?"

"Offer him things he wants." Lovey motions to me. "And also threaten to call his parents if he doesn't start going to class. He doesn't want to be smothered, which is exactly what will happen if he goes back to Pearl Lake. He wants to be here, so tell him he needs to get his ass in gear and you'll help him. He's wallowing."

"She's right," Rose adds. "When your mom was in the hospital, he was right there, getting you on the ice and making sure you had some balance. You can do the same for him."

"And we can help get him to and from classes. We'll set up a schedule," Quinn offers.

"We have the same morning class on Monday, Wednesday, and Friday. I can make sure he gets to that one," Laughlin says.

"How did we not know you have a class together?" Lovey asks.

"Because I always sneak in the back a minute before class starts and leave the second it ends."

"Okay. That's one class taken care of," I say.

"His schedule is on the corkboard in the kitchen. If you grab it, we can figure out the rest," Quinn suggests.

I nod. "I'll see if I can get him over here for dinner. It might take a while, though, because he needs a shower."

"No problem. Dinner will be waiting when you get here,"

Lovey says.

"Go get 'em, tiger!" Rose calls as I head for the door.

I jog across two lawns and burst into BJ's room. He's traded sleep for bingeing TV. I grab the remote and turn it off.

"Hey! They were just about to solve the case."

"You can't keep doing this."

"Doing what?"

"This. Lying here in bed all day every day."

"I almost died!"

"I know! I was there, remember? I saved your fucking life!" The telltale prick of tears makes my eyes sting, but I won't back down. Not with him. "I know this sucks, BJ. I know you're in pain and nothing is the same, but I can't let you lie here and give up."

"What if I'm the problem, Winter? What if the issue here is me? I've had two partners, and both of those relationships ended badly. What if, after all of this, it happens again—or worse, the same thing happens to us?"

I see how all these hours alone have allowed those worries to grow and take over. I cross my arms. "Since when did you live in the world of black clouds of doom? I have no idea what's going to happen with us. I can't predict the future any better than you. We're both in our early twenties. It could go any which way, but locking yourself up and stewing in a pit of what-ifs won't make it any better. You didn't let me marinate in my guilt. You think I'll let you marinate in yours? Bad shit happens all the time, BJ. We both know that. You're here and alive. Take that gift and do something good with it. I'm here, and I want to help. Let me. Please."

He's quiet for a few moments, but eventually he sits up and shifts to the edge of the bed. He carefully lowers his injured leg to the floor and then his good one. He holds out his hand. "I hear you. I see you."

I cross over and settle my palm in his. He tugs me closer and parts his legs, inhaling short breaths as he works through the pain.

"Don't push me away," I whisper.

"I'm sorry. This whole thing is messing with my head. My path has changed, and I don't know how to handle it. My entire life I've been working toward one goal, and now I don't know if it'll ever be within reach again."

"I know, but isolating yourself isn't the answer." I cup his face in my hands. "You need to start physical therapy, and you need to start living again. Wallow World is closed for business."

He turns his head and presses his lips to my palm. "Thank you for being such a badass girlfriend and not letting me get away with this kind of shit."

"I gave you a few days. You've reached maximum wallow allowance. You need to come over to my place and hang out and eat pizza. Your lounge chair misses you, and so do all your friends."

"Okay." He looks up at me.

I wrinkle my nose when I get a whiff of him. "I would love to kiss you, but your breath smells like stale Doritos, and you actually stink in general—like sweat and jockstrap."

He chuckles. "I'm pretty gross."

"Yeah, you really are. You needed a shower three days ago." I take a step back and pull my shirt over my head. "It'll be a lot easier if you have help, though. And I'm absolutely willing to assist." I shove my yoga pants down my thighs and step out of them. "Does that sound like a good trade-off?"

He scrambles for his crutches. "That sounds like a fan-fuck-ing-tastic trade-off. And like I'm the clear winner of this deal."

I pull off my sports bra and let it fall to the floor, then slide my panties off and kick them in his direction. "Come on. Let's get you cleaned up."

33

The Hand in the Dark

BJ

NAKED GIRLFRIEND IS A GREAT MOTIVATOR. I manage, much to my surprise, to catch her panties before they hit the ground. They're basic seamless ones in navy. I toss them on one of the many piles of clothes on the floor and navigate my way around them, following Winter into the bathroom.

She's already turned the water on, and there's one of those special folding chairs that I associate with the elderly set up just outside it. On the counter are the supplies I need for bathing. The wound has to be covered with a waterproof wrap and taped around my leg so it doesn't get wet.

My erection is already at full mast. Taking care of my situation over the past week hasn't been easy, or high on my priority list. But with Winter gloriously naked, her long dark hair hanging in a braid over her shoulder, looking like everything I

337

need, my body is suddenly very aware and very excited. The tug around the injury isn't as bad as it was a few days ago.

The first time I woke up with morning wood, I thought my leg was going to burst into flames, the pain was so blindingly awful. But it's better now. Manageable.

"First things first. Brush your teeth, and then we can get you naked to wash the stink off." She passes me my toothbrush and squirts some paste on it, then does the same for herself.

Once my mouth no longer tastes like a sewer, we tackle clothing removal.

She holds my crutches while I balance on my good leg and remove my shirt, then she passes them back so I don't have to put all my weight on that leg for long. She tugs my joggers over my hips and kneels to carefully pull them down my legs. I'm not wearing underwear. They're too much work to get on and off, and they rub on the injury.

She pats my erection, which is pointing straight at her. "I'll take care of you as soon as you've been washed." She looks up when my pants are around my ankles. "Do you want to sit down so I can get them off, or lift one foot and then the other?"

Sitting down and standing up is its own challenge. I'm already upright, so I might as well manage. "I can lift."

We tackle the bad leg first, which is the easier of the two. Then I use my crutches to help take my weight for the other leg. Winter applies one of the patches to the wound site, tapes it down, and moves the chair into the shower. Then she helps me into it.

She uses the removable showerhead to wet my hair and lathers it up with shampoo, massaging my scalp.

"This feels damn well fantastic."

"As long as you're going to your classes, we can do it every day. Consider it a reward for good behavior."

I grunt.

"We're working out a schedule," she informs me. "Laughlin will take you to your morning class on Monday, Wednesday, and Friday, and I can cover your Tuesday and Thursday afternoon class. When we're done here, we'll bring your schedule next door and make sure you're covered for physical therapy as well. Your friends want to help, so let them."

She rinses my hair and washes it a second time before she lathers up a body pouf and starts at my neck, rubbing slow circles on my skin. Suds drip down my chest and arms. She takes her time, going over the same spots more than once, lingering on the places that make me groan, kneading the muscles in my neck and back that are stiff and sore from so much lying around. She's right. The only way forward is to start moving and stop feeling sorry for myself.

Eventually she comes to stand in front of me, drops to her knees, and starts working her way up my shins. I shift forward in the chair, parting my legs, anticipation building as she gets closer to my straining erection.

And then her soft, warm fingers circle the shaft. She squeezes gently and starts to stroke. I groan and soak her in, naked and gorgeous.

"Tell me if you need more pressure," she murmurs.

"This is perfect." I bite my lip. "The only thing that would make it better is if I could kiss you."

She rises, curves her free hand around the back of my neck, and leans down. I tip my head back, and her lips brush over mine. "I've missed you," she whispers. "I've missed touching you, hearing you groan my name. I've missed us."

"Me too. Thanks for forcing me to get my head out of my ass." I cup the back of her neck, parting my lips to invite her in.

Our tongues tangle as she continues to stroke me, steady and even, thumb sweeping over the piercing, circling it before she drags back down. I get lost in the sensation, in the feel of her tongue sliding against mine, in her soft, needy sounds. The orgasm hits me hard, tension causing a deep ache in my thigh, but the pleasure overshadows the discomfort.

She pulls back, a smile on her kiss-swollen lips. "Feel better?"

"So much better." I trace the contour of her lip with my thumb. "I want to take care of you now, though."

"You don't need to do that. I can take care of myself later."

"I'm sure you can, and at some point, I'd be more than happy to watch you, but I haven't made you come in two weeks." The last time was the day I had the accident. And it was the best sex of my entire life.

Her brow arches. "You'd be happy to watch, huh?"

She steps out of reach, then sits on the shower floor and parts her thighs.

"Come on, Snowflake. I want to help."

"I'm sure you do." She drags her fingers down her throat and circles a nipple. After giving her breast a rough squeeze, she smirks. "But that's a reward you'll have to earn."

"Whatever you want me to do, I'll do it." Any other time I'd launch myself across the shower and bury my face between her thighs. But I haven't done anything but hobble-groan my way to the kitchen and back the last few days. I'm sorely regretting that now.

"That's good to hear." Her fingers drift down her stomach and circle her navel. "I'm looking forward to sitting on your face in the near future."

"If you grab my crutches, I'll get back into bed and give you a beard ride."

She laughs. "Your sheets need to be changed, but thanks for the offer." Her fingers glide lower, circling her clit before she eases two inside. Her head falls back, and she moans softly.

"Fuck me." I'm already hard again. Obviously, I'm feeling better.

"It'll probably be a while before you're ready for that." She withdraws her fingers and circles her clit again, adding a third finger. "But I'm sure we can be creative."

"You're not playing fair, Snowflake."

"I know." She grins. "You give me what I want, and you get what you want, which is me sitting on your face later."

I stop pleading my case and enjoy the view. She's damn well magnificent, and she's mine. I murmur words of encouragement, telling her how sexy she is, how much I love the way she sounds when she comes, that I can't wait to have the taste of her on my tongue again.

Her soft whimpers turn into needy moans. I know she's about to come when her hips start to roll, and she bites her lip, head thrown back as the orgasm sweeps over her. I come again a few strokes later and sag in the chair. Winter leans against the tile wall, a grin spreading across her face. "That was fun."

"You should bring those fingers over here."

"Should I, now?"

"Little added motivation, just to tide me over until I earn the right to the real thing."

She withdraws her fingers from between her legs and moves across the shower to stand in front of me. She drags her index finger along her bottom lip, then leans in to kiss me. "How's this?"

I catch it gently between my teeth and suck softly. "Best motivation ever."

The water is starting to cool, so Winter turns the shower off and helps pat me dry before she hands me my crutches. She wanders around my room naked, grabbing me fresh clothes and helping me into my pants before she gets dressed too. She also changes my sheets and picks up all the random clothes scattered on the floor, tossing them into a laundry basket.

"I bet you're hungry now, huh?"

I arch a brow. "You offering a pussy-buffet appetizer?"

She laughs. "That can be dessert, if you're not in a food coma after dinner." She opens my bedroom door. "Come on, let's go hang out with our friends."

"Hey. Hold on." I grab her hand and tug her closer.

"What's up?" She settles a hand on my chest.

My stomach flips with nerves, but I need to do this. I stroke a finger from her temple to her chin. "I love you too. So fucking much. I didn't get the chance to tell you before," I explain. "I wanted to say it back, but I didn't get the chance."

She laces her fingers with mine, her voice a whisper. "I didn't realize you remembered that part."

"I thought I dreamed it at first."

"I needed you to know how I felt, just in case." Her eyes turn glassy. "I was scared it was the only time I'd get to tell you I love you."

"I couldn't go anywhere without making sure you knew I felt the same way."

I STOP BEING a mopey asshole and start going to class again. Getting around on crutches gets easier the more I move. The shittiest part is how damn itchy the injury becomes as it heals. And there's nothing I can do about it, because so much of it is internal. Thankfully, Winter proves to be excellent at distracting me when it gets particularly intolerable.

It's Tuesday morning, and Quinn has the pleasure of driving me to class. I'm sitting at the kitchen table, shoveling cereal into my face while he polishes off leftover pasta Bolognese.

"How are classes?" he asks conversationally.

"Eh. Okay. I'm still playing catch up, and I've fallen way behind in Advanced Research Methods. I don't know if I can recover enough to get the grade I need, but we've already passed the deadline to drop courses."

"Given the circumstances, I'm pretty sure they'd make an exception if you need to go down to part-time this semester." He sets his fork on the edge of his plate and laces his hands behind his head. "Your focus needs to be on recovery, not stressing about your grades. It's better to keep the classes you're doing well in and drop the ones you're struggling with."

I nod. "I'll make an appointment with my advisor, see if there's anything they can do."

"You won't know unless you ask, right?" He picks up his fork again, spins more noodles, and taps his temple. "How you doing otherwise?"

"Okay mostly. The doctor said I can move from crutches to a cane."

Quinn arches a brow. "I can actually see you rocking a cane."

I laugh. "Winter said the same thing."

"That girl is something else. You two seem solid."

"We are. She's been great about keeping me on track. Doesn't let me get away with shit." I duck my head and hide a grin.

Quinn chuckles. "You fit."

We're quiet for a minute and then he asks, "You got a timeline for getting back on the ice?"

I swallow past the lump in my throat. "I don't know. I guess once I'm past the cane stage? I'm not in a rush to get back out there, though."

"Any particular reason why?"

"First Caroline snaps her tendon, and then Adele almost ends my life. I feel...cursed, maybe?"

He nods. "I get that. I mean, I'm named after my uncle who was beaten to death in front of my dad. I get that they wanted to pay homage or whatever, and it was meant to be a good thing, but a heavy weight comes with it." He pokes at his pasta. "Accidents happen on the ice all the time. People get hurt. Caroline's family was a huge part of that problem. If she'd been allowed to have a life outside of figure skating, she might not have been so dependent on you."

"I feel like what happened with me and Adele is partly my fault because I set so many parameters around our relationship."

"Have you talked to her yet?" Quinn asks.

I shake my head. "She's left a couple of voicemails, but I haven't listened to them."

"You need closure on this, BJ. Otherwise you're just spinning worst-case scenarios in your head. You don't have to do it now, but when you feel like you can handle it, have that conversation so you can move on."

I run my hands through my hair. "You're right. I know you're right. I'm just...scared, I guess."

"We all play a part, BJ. It doesn't help to hold on to blame. Make peace with it, learn from it, and move on. The only way is forward."

34

One Step at a Time

WINTER

ONCE WE SET UP A SCHEDULE, getting BJ to and from his classes isn't a problem. After a discussion with his advisor, he drops Advanced Research Methods. It won't impact his ability to graduate, since he can retake it next semester and get the grade he wants.

We study together, do homework together when possible, and because he's not on the ice while he's healing, he comes to some of my hockey practices, and he's always at my games.

A few days ago, the doctor told him he could switch from crutches to a cane, so we went shopping for one. BJ even makes that accessory look badass. And the timing couldn't be more perfect, because tonight we're going to my very first NHL game. Maverick and Clover have come up for it, and Lavender flew in this afternoon. I'm staying with BJ tonight so she and Kody can have her old room. Although I stay at his place most of the time these days anyway, because three flights of stairs is hella ambitious for him at the moment.

We're congregated in the living room, just waiting on River, who went to pick up Josiah, and Laughlin. The latter has become a semiregular fixture around here over the past month. He shows up randomly, hangs out for a couple of hours, and then disappears.

"Lavender, catch!" Rose tosses something across the room.

Lavender screams and ducks, though the item doesn't land anywhere near her.

Lovey picks up the roll of tape with a candy cane pattern on it.

"Oh fuck," BJ mutters.

I remember when Rose was settling in her room and found that roll of tape. BJ told her to hold on to it and give it to Lavender the next time she visited. It isn't until now that I make the connection to the tie-me-down conversation BJ and I had, which led to the use of silk ties. I choke back a laugh.

Lavender flings her hand in the air. "Why would you throw something at me? You know I have the coordination of a newborn foal."

Lovey frowns. "Why are you giving Lavender duct tape with candy canes on it?"

"I found it in the closet in Kody's room when I was unpacking." Rose crams herself between the twins on the couch. "I thought maybe he'd want it back."

Lavender's face turns beet red, and she points an accusing finger at BJ. "You were supposed to take that to the grave."

"Take what to the grave?" Rose asks. She looks around the room, and most everyone seems like they're trying not to laugh. Except Maverick. He excuses himself to the bathroom.

BJ holds up his hands. "I didn't say anything to anyone."

"No one, huh?" Lavender points to me. "Why doesn't

Winter look surprised?" Then she points to Quinn, who's crammed into the corner of the couch beside a very confused-looking Lovey. "Or Quinn. Or anyone but Lovey, Lacey, and Rose!"

"I think you're forgetting that Kody was my roommate for a lot of years, and we played hockey on the school team together," Quinn says.

Lovey leans in and asks Quinn something, but he shakes his head. "I'll tell you later."

Lavender crosses her arms. "Is Mav out of earshot?"

"He's still in the bathroom," Clover says.

"Kodiak and I don't use duct tape anymore! We graduated to less conspicuous methods of restraint after BJ put two and two together last year and realized what was going on. Plus, it was ripping out his arm hair. Can we drop it now, please? Because there are some things my brother doesn't need to know, and this is one of them."

"I'm going to need more details on this later," Rose says.

Lavender waves a hand. "Yeah, yeah. We can talk about it when my brothers aren't around."

"When we're not around for what?" River asks.

"Great! Everyone is here! Let's roll out!" Quinn shouts, saving Lavender from answering.

We pile into vehicles and make our way to the arena. We have seats behind Philly's bench and access to a box with food and refreshments, but I've never been to a game before, so I want to be on the ice where the action is.

I end up sandwiched between Rose and BJ. The seats are amazing, giving us a perfect view of the rink and the action. While the crowd is dominated by Chicago fans, there are still lots of Philly jerseys dotting the crowd, and a startling number of fans appear to be college-aged women.

When Kody takes the ice, several girls scream and hold up

homemade signs professing their undying love. It seems to happen no matter where he plays this season. He's on every hockey blog, and the fact that he's otherworldly gorgeous increases his popularity.

When the team takes the bench, he removes one of his gloves and stops in front of Lavender. A camera homes in on them, projecting them onto the Jumbotron, but they're too wrapped up in each other to notice. Kody brings his fingers to his lips, then taps the plexiglass. Lavender does the same thing, and then they draw a figure-eight together and say, "I love you."

There's a collective sigh throughout the arena, followed by cheering. That's when they realize the entire hockey-watching nation has witnessed this. Their faces turn red, and Lavender slouches, pulling her hood over her head as she waves at the cheering crowd. Kody shrugs and takes a seat on the bench, cheeks flushed, but he's wearing a smile.

"Why do they have to be so cute all the damn time? They're like couple goals on crack, especially now that I know they're kinky freaks," Rose says.

The camera pans back to the rink, and the first shift is called onto the ice. Kody scores a goal and an assist during the first period, and Chicago ties it up in the second. But Philly recovers in the third with another goal by Kody, and they keep the lead, winning three-two.

After the game, we end up at the restaurant with Kody's team, and I meet a bunch of the players before we all go back to our place to hang out. We lounge around in the living room. Kody, BJ, Maverick, and Quinn talk hockey, and I'm sitting with the girls, making plans for tomorrow since Lavender doesn't leave until late in the afternoon. I'm half paying attention to their conversation, but also half listening to the guys, who are trying to get some ice time tomorrow morning.

Maverick and Clover rented a hotel room so they can see Kody in the morning.

"When do you think you'll be cleared to get back on the ice?" Kody asks BJ.

"Dunno. I'm not really in a rush, now that the Olympics are off the table," BJ replies.

"That's temporary, though. Maybe you're not looking at next year, but you could aim for the ones after that, can't you?" Mav asks.

"I'm not skating pairs again. Not after this." BJ's voice is tight, clipped.

"That's fair, but you skated solo before Caroline and Adele. You can go back to that."

"I dunno if it's what I want anymore."

"BJ just needs some time," Quinn says. "It's only been a few weeks since the accident. Being physically ready is one thing; being mentally and emotionally ready is something else. All those pieces need to line up." He points at BJ. "You can keep score for us tomorrow."

"That'd be good." BJ yawns loudly and stretches. "I can't miss my first-period class though, so I'm gonna hit the pit."

He welcomes a round of back-pat hugs from Kody and Lavender, and I excuse myself as well. We get ready for bed, and I slide under the sheets and stretch out alongside him.

"You have fun tonight?" he asks.

"It was amazing. So cool to watch a live game. Kody's a fantastic player."

"He really is. He's going to blow his dad's career out of the water."

"That's a lot of pressure, isn't it?"

BJ trails his fingers along my spine. "It is, but the only thing Kody's ever been obsessed with—apart from Lavender—is hockey. He used to play in his crib, so he was sort of born for the sport."

"Sort of like you were born to figure skate," I murmur.

"It felt that way for a lot of years."

"But not anymore?" I ask.

"I don't know. I worked so hard to get where I was, but if I get back on the ice, I'll be starting at square one, just like when I started skating with Adele. It took us years to get where we were, and that was without an injury. Walking up and down those stairs at the arena tonight was a challenge. My leg is achy all the time, and the nerve pain makes it hard to think sometimes. I just...don't know if the things I wanted are possible now." He brings my fingers to his lips and kisses the tips. "Can we put a pin in this? I had a great night, and thinking about this stuff... It just messes with my headspace."

I kiss his neck. "You want a distraction from the noise in your head?"

"You sure you want to get into that now? It's late, and I know orgasms aren't a sedative for you like they are for me." His fingers are already dipping under my sleep tank.

I run my hand down his stomach and slide my hand into the waistband of his boxer shorts. He's halfway hard. "I can handle a night light on sleep if it means I can help get your head out of bad places."

"I love you," he groans as I wrap my hand around his length.

"I know. I love you too." I press my lips to his and help him get lost in feeling good.

This conversation isn't over, but for now, we can put it on pause.

35

If You Want Me

BJ

"YOU'RE DOING great with your physical therapy. Mobility is good. We'll keep up with the weekly massage sessions to help minimize the internal scar tissue. You're cleared to get back on the ice."

"Already?"

The doctor nods. "It's been a month, and you've put in the work. I'm not saying start doing pirouettes and jumps, but putting your skates on and getting your body used to different types of activity will only help expedite the healing process," he explains. "It's okay if you're not ready, though. You're still seeing the therapist I referred you to?"

"Yeah. I'm still seeing the therapist." I've needed a perspective that wasn't one of my parents' or my friends', someone impartial to talk through all my fears with. To help me make sense of this.

"And that's going well?"

"Yeah, she's great."

He nods. "Well, when you're ready to take that step, the step is ready for you."

He also tells me I'm cleared for other physical activities, but to be careful of overexertion. That's one green light I plan to take full advantage of.

Mom is in the waiting room. She comes every week to take me to the doctor's appointments, and Dad usually attends physical therapy with me. I anticipate that they'll be more attentive than usual for a while. Mom is already talking about the holiday break and how glad she is I'll be home for a few weeks.

A small piece of me feels bad that I didn't go home to recover, but losing the entire semester wouldn't have been good for my mental well-being. I needed somewhere else to focus my energy, and Winter and my friends have really stepped up and helped make it work.

When I come out of the office, the doctor shares the good news with my mom.

"I can see about getting us some ice time this week. I'll make room in my schedule on whatever day works for you." Mom is giddy with excitement as we walk to the car.

"I'm not skating at that rink again. Not after what happened there." I have a giant pit of dread in my stomach.

"Of course not. Why don't you come home this weekend? That would be better, wouldn't it? To skate at the Hockey Academy?"

I'm quiet a moment as I navigate getting into the passenger seat. "Winter has a big game this weekend." They're playing the first-place team, and they're currently in third. If they win this game, they'll be in second.

"What about getting time at the school rink? I'm sure we could work something out there."

"I'm not ready, Mom. I don't want to get back on the ice yet."

Her expression grows concerned. "Are your pain levels still too high? Do we need to discuss it with the doctor?"

I shake my head. "It's not the pain. Things are better, less achy, and I'm getting my strength back, but I just... I don't feel ready to put skates back on. I'm not there."

She reaches over the center console and squeezes my hand. "Okay. We'll give it a bit more time."

THE SECOND WINTER walks in the door later that afternoon, I pull her into the bedroom and kiss her. "Feeling up for a gentle Fucktastic Friday?"

She breaks the kiss and blinks up at me. "Did you get cleared for sex?"

"Sure did."

"Oh my God. Oh, hell yes!" She yanks her shirt over her head and reaches for mine.

Clothes hit the floor until we're both naked. Before we stretch out on the bed, she pulls out the box of condoms that have gone unused for the past month. Then we slow it down, making out, touching, groping, fingers exploring sensitive places, building anticipation of what's to come.

Winter grips my erection, stroking from base to tip. "Should I be on top this time? Just so you don't have to do all the pelvic thrusting? That could be hard on your thigh and maybe distracting."

"Probably a good idea," I groan.

She carefully straddles my hips. "Okay. Tell me if anything is uncomfortable." She doesn't settle on my thighs, holding herself above me.

The injury is healed from the outside. An angry red scar slices across the top of my thigh, the staple holes still visible, although those tiny wounds have closed. But there's residual achiness and some neural pain the doctors said might take several months before it finally subsides.

"Do you want to put a condom on right away, or start bare? I finished my period two days ago," Winter tells me.

"I probably won't last very long without one."

"That's okay. I just want the connection. And we can always have sex again if one time isn't enough," Winter assures me.

"Start bare?" My erection kicks in her palm.

"I was hoping you'd say that." She rises and slides the head over her clit on a soft sigh. She positions me at her entrance, and the head disappears, up to the piercing.

We both groan.

"Yeah, I'm really not going to last long, Snowflake, and I'm sorry in advance."

"No apologies necessary. It's been a long time, and it's kind of an ego boost."

I laugh and groan again when she drops down, taking more of me inside her. When her ass touches my thighs, she leans forward and brushes her lips over mine. "I missed you."

"I missed you too." I kiss her, distracting myself from the overwhelming sensation. She feels so good. All I want is to roll us over and start thrusting, but that will end things far too soon, and possibly set me back, so I let her take control.

Winter rolls her hips, and her eyes flutter shut. I can tell she's getting close with the way her moans get deeper and her movements less fluid. I hold her hips, helping her keep her rhythm. Her gaze locks on mine as the orgasm rolls through her, muscles clamping down as she rides it out.

"I'm really close," I groan in warning. There's a pull in my groin that isn't particularly comfortable, and something the doctor warned me about, but like all physical activity, my body will get used to it over time. So the more we have sex, the better it will get.

Winter lifts off and strokes me to release, then cleans up my stomach with tissues and stretches out beside me. We're both sweaty, despite the complete lack of exertion on my part.

"God, I've missed sex with you." She kisses the edge of my jaw.

"Same. I mean, I've missed sex with you too."

"How was that? Everything feel okay?"

"Everything feels great."

She shifts so her palm rests over my heart and her cheek rests on my diaphragm. "If you're cleared for sex, that must mean you're cleared to get back on the ice."

"Did you talk to my mom or something?"

Winter frowns. "Uh, I love your mom—she's awesome—but I'm never going to casually bring up sex with her." Realization dawns as she puts the pieces together. "She took you to your appointment today, so she knows you're cleared for ice time. When were you planning to tell me?"

"I don't know. Later. After sex."

She arches a brow. "I can book us ice time."

"That's okay. You don't need to do that."

"Talk to me. What's going on in your head?"

"I don't know if I can handle getting back on the ice yet."

"You mean from a psychological standpoint?" Winter asks.

"Yeah."

"You come to my games all the time."

"That's different. That's me watching you, and you wear protective gear, so I don't have to worry about you getting hurt or anything."

She laces our fingers. "What's this about, BJ?"

"What if I can't get back to where I was? What if it's too hard or the injury has messed things up so much that I'll never be able to compete again?" I've been warned it's a possibility.

"You'll never know if you don't try." She sits up. "I get that it's scary, BJ. It was scary for me when I tried out for the women's team. All this hope and fear mixed together. What if I didn't make the cut? What if I made the cut and then screwed it up somehow? What if I got close to the dream and couldn't catch it? But you were right there, telling me to take the chance. You would never let me walk away from hockey if the roles were reversed."

"I have to start from square one."

"I know. But I'll get on the ice every day with you, if that's what you need, BJ. You can't avoid it forever. You love it too much."

"Not as much as I love you."

She smiles softly. "I love you too. Which is why I'll keep pushing you on this. You can't let fear hold you back."

MY AVOIDANCE of ice time ends abruptly the following evening.

I'm sitting at my desk in my bedroom, working on an assignment, when Winter comes in and closes the door. She crosses to the dresser and retrieves an all-black outfit. This means she might be planning to work out or something.

I abandon my reading and make it across the room by the time she's down to her panties. I wrap an arm around her waist, and she links her hands behind my neck, tipping her chin up for a kiss.

When I start to work my way down her neck, she covers my mouth with her palm and pushes back. "I booked us ice time at the school rink. We have it for an hour from seven until eight."

It's six thirty. "I can make you come first."

She shakes her head and steps back. She motions to her mostly naked body. "You can have me however you want me *after* ice time."

"That's not fair."

"Isn't it, though? I seem to remember you pulling the same thing on me when we first started spending time together."

"That was different. You didn't almost die."

Her expression softens. "You're still here, thank God. Still beautiful, still breathing, still living. I'm not asking you to spend an hour on the ice. I'm asking you to put your skates on and take the first step. If that's all you can handle, that's okay. But you can't know unless you try. And afterward, we can take care of each other, because that's what we do, BJ."

I sigh. "I'm really fucking nervous."

"I get it. And I'd be sorry that I'm using sex as a weapon, but we both know part of you wants to get back on the ice, so I'm not above using your hormones against you."

Twenty minutes later, I'm wearing skates for the first time in over a month. It feels weird, awkward. My thigh is already burning, and I haven't even stepped onto the ice, but Winter is right. I can't avoid this forever. And if there's one person I'd want to do this with, it's her.

She's already out there—wearing a pair of black leggings

and a fitted long-sleeve shirt that hugs every muscle and curve. The whole way here, she talked about positions and how much she's looking forward to a marathon sex day when I'm up for it. I gotta admit, it's a strong motivator.

She holds out a hand, and I slip my fingers into hers, putting one foot on the ice and then the other.

"How you doing so far?" she asks.

"I'm still breathing." Memories of the last time I was out here hit me with a ferocity I don't expect—how Adele and I had been on point, how clean the routine had been until it wasn't. How everything changed in a second.

And then Winter was there. I see now what I couldn't before—how scared she was at that moment, how bad the situation was. She wraps her arms around me. "It's okay if today is a struggle, BJ. I'm here."

I return the hug. I don't know how long we stand there, but I'm grateful for the comfort her presence brings. Eventually I pull back, and we link hands and do a slow lap around the rink. Everything is stiff at first, and the ache in my thigh makes me sweaty and nauseous, but I push through, and Winter is right there, encouraging me, telling me I'm doing amazing and that she's so damn proud of me.

After the first couple of laps, the sharp ache dulls, and the sick feeling in my stomach ebbs. We keep lapping the rink until I tell her I've had enough for today. We don't use the showers at the arena. Instead, she takes me home and we get into the shower together and have slow, easy sex. Then we climb into bed and make out some more.

"How do you feel now that you've been back on the ice?" She runs her fingers through my hair. It's a lot longer than usual, in part because I don't have a reason to cut it.

"Good. Better. Thank you for pushing me."

"I wouldn't have done it if I didn't think you were ready."

"I know."

"You've taken the first step."

"I just don't know what comes next," I admit.

"That's okay. Skate because you love it and it brings you joy. We can figure out the rest from there."

36

In it Together

BJ

OVER THE WEEKS leading up to the holiday break, Winter and I develop a new routine. We start with private ice time twice a week, and then we take advantage of the free skates at the school arena so our housemates can join us. Every time I step onto the ice, it gets easier. The path from here to wherever I'm going won't be easy, but Winter is right; I've taken the first step. Everything else we can figure out as we go.

The end of the semester is full of exam prep and hockey games for Winter. Because games are on weekends, she hasn't been back to Pearl Lake since the beginning of the semester. Our parents brought Thanksgiving to us this year, as Winter had an away game on Saturday and practice on Friday.

Once we finish exams, we head home for the holidays. Not sleeping beside Winter for three weeks sucks, but the down time will be nice. Winter has picked up some shifts at Boones, and the Hockey Academy has a few games scheduled for the players who return to Pearl Lake.

I'm on my way to the arena, but I make a stop at Boones on the way. I hop out of the Jeep, and as I walk toward the building, I spot Winter behind the counter, wearing the red Boones ball cap, looking as beautiful as ever. I wave and a smile lights up her face, but it drops as I hear my name behind me.

I turn to see Adele rushing across the street.

I knew this would happen eventually. Winter and I talked about it, especially when I started having nightmares about the accident last week. She didn't push it, but questioned whether it would be a good idea to get some closure with Adele. Quinn said the same thing weeks ago. And whether or not I'm ready, it looks like that's about to happen.

"Hey. Hi. Hey." She stops a few feet away and then takes a couple of steps back. "How are you?"

"Alive."

She nods, and her eyes go glassy. "Can we... Can I talk to you? Please."

The door jingles as it opens behind me. "You okay, BJ?" Winter asks.

I turn to her, and whatever the look on my face is, it prompts her to step out into the cold winter morning without a jacket. "Give him a second, please, Adele."

As Adele steps back to give us space, Winter settles a hand on my chest, over my heart. "Have the conversation so you don't have to carry the weight of this with you anymore."

"You always know the right thing to say." I cover her hand. "I fucking love you."

She smiles and laughs. "I love you too. I'm here when you're done. Okay?"

I kiss her, long and hard. It's probably borderline inappropriate, but I'm emotional and edgy.

When I release her, she turns back toward Boones.

"Winter," Adele calls.

She pauses.

"Thank you for saving BJ. I don't know what I would have done if—" She chokes up.

"Neither do I, and I'm glad neither of us had to find out." She disappears back inside, leaving me and Adele alone on the sidewalk.

"I'm so sorry," she whispers. "I didn't mean for that to happen. I didn't mean to hurt you."

I've had time to work through what happened, to sit with it, to unpack it. "I believe that's true—that you didn't mean for me to get hurt. But it doesn't explain why it happened in the first place. If Winter hadn't shown up, I wouldn't be here to have this conversation." It's a hard reality, but still the truth.

Her eyes dart away. "I know. And I'm so sorry. If I could take it back, I would."

"But you can't, Adele. I will carry this around with me forever. Every day I'll see the reminder of what happened and how it almost ended my life." I sigh and look up at the sky. I've rewatched that video a bunch of times, as well as some of the other ones I recorded. Hindsight is painful. Because when I went back and watched all those recorded sessions, a pattern emerged. One that wasn't obvious at first, and might never have been had I not ended up in the hospital as a result. Sometimes she could manage the combinations, and other times, I saw her adjust and lose form. It seemed harmless until it wasn't. "I don't understand why you kept intentionally screwing up. Were you afraid we weren't going to place? If it was too much for you, why not say something instead of doing something reckless?"

"I don't know."

"You don't know about what part? Being afraid? It being

too much? Some other reason I don't know about? You had to have some idea of the risk you were taking."

She wrings her hands. She looks tired. And like maybe she's lost some weight since I saw her last. "I just... It was a lot of things, I guess."

"Such as?"

"I knew when we started skating together, the goal was to qualify for the Olympics. You're dedicated and passionate, and I understood how important it was for you to keep boundaries with our relationship. That part never changed. But somewhere along the way, your dream and mine started to diverge."

I run my hand through my hair. "What do you mean?"

She exhales a long breath. "You're an incredible skater, BJ. You have so much natural talent."

"So do you."

She holds up a hand. "It's not the same. I wanted it to be. I wanted to reach the same level as you, and I believed that skating with you would help me get there. I know how careful you are, especially after what happened with Caroline. And you were always willing to stay on the ice for as long as it took to get the routine down. This year was different, and it wasn't that I didn't think you deserved to have a girlfriend, or a life outside of skating, but Winter changed things." She sighs. "I wasn't jealous of her; I was jealous of the fact that you could manage all the things—school, skating, friends, a girlfriend—and still be one of the best skaters out there."

"But you were doing the same thing." I'm trying to understand where she's going with this, but I'm lost.

She shakes her head. "I wasn't. I'm part-time in college because I couldn't keep up with a full course load. I was late for practice with you all the time because I spent extra hours on the ice trying to perfect everything. I didn't have any balance. And this year, the more challenging the routines became, the more time I spent trying to get it all right. I'm just not good enough, BJ. I wanted to be. I wanted to be the partner who could help you realize your dream, because if anyone deserves it, it's you. But I just...fell short."

My immediate inclination is to tell her she's wrong, that she absolutely has the skill set. But when I think about how hard the past year has been, how much time we've had to spend on the ice and how much she's struggled, it's hard to argue. "How much of the sabotage was intentional?"

"I've been struggling to keep up for a long time, BJ, but the past few months..." She drops her head. "The last two competitions, we barely placed third. I knew some of the combinations in the last routine were bordering on too difficult for me. Landing the second lift was always a challenge. It didn't matter how much I practiced. Executing it during a performance, I didn't feel confident."

"Why didn't you say something?"

"I didn't want to disappoint you. I didn't want to give up. I figured when I wasn't able to get it, you would eventually realize I wasn't good enough and move on. But you didn't give up on me, even when I messed up over and over again." Tears build in her eyes. "If I hadn't been such a coward, you wouldn't have gotten hurt." She dashes the tears away. "I'm so sorry. I wish I'd made different choices. I wish I'd told you how much I was struggling, but we'd spent all those years working so hard, and the thought of having to tell you... I couldn't do it." She shakes her head. "I didn't want to crush your dream, and then this happened. You were always so confident in my ability, but I could see where we were heading. I wasn't going to be able to hack it at the Olympics. I figured if I couldn't execute the combinations we would eventually pull out of the competition because you would see what I was afraid to admit."

"If you'd just talked to me and told me how you felt, we

could have avoided so much pain." I wish I'd seen it before now, how hard it was for her. How my encouragement only made it more difficult for her to tell me the truth. "I have to start all over again. Do you have any idea the damage you've done to my body? How much rehab I need? I have no idea if I'm ever going to be in the condition to compete again. A conversation could have changed everything."

"I wish I could take it back," she says softly.

"Me too." I'm reeling all over again—devastated that this is where we ended up because I couldn't see what was right in front of me, and Adele couldn't face disappointing me. I turn toward Boones. Right now I need comfort in the form of Winter.

"Do you hate me?" Adele asks.

I turn back to her. "I don't hate you, Adele. I hate how cavalier you were with my trust and my life." I push through the door and head straight for Winter.

"I'm going on break," she says.

"I got you covered," Rose replies.

Winter takes me to the employee break room. "Are you okay?"

I nod and wrap my arms around her. "You were right."

"About?"

"Needing the closure."

"Do you have it now?" She pulls back, her hands on either side of my face.

"I'm closer than I was before. I feel like I can start moving forward in a way I couldn't."

"Good. One step at a time, BJ. We'll get wherever you need to go together."

37

Pillars

WINTER

I DON'T EXPECT to get through the holidays without running into my dad. And just as BJ needed the closure with Adele, I need to end that chapter of my life on my terms. I get the opportunity on the 23rd, while BJ is doing a balloon pickup for the holiday celebration at the Sunshine Center.

I run into the pharmacy to grab my refill on birth control pills while BJ picks up the balloons. The plaza has a variety of stores, including a convenience store and one of the two liquor stores in town. On my way out, I slide my prescription into my bag, along with a box of condoms, and almost collide with another person. "I'm so—" The words get stuck in my mouth when I realize it's my dad.

His eyes widen. He's holding a brown paper bag, clearly full of alcohol. A pack of smokes is tucked into the breast pocket of his thin, worn plaid coat. His hair is longer, and he has about three days of stubble on his cheeks. His skin is sallow, and he somehow looks thinner. And like he's aged a decade since I last saw him. That makes sense because there's no one to take care of him anymore.

"Winter? What are you doing here? I thought you was up in Chicago at that fancy college."

"It's winter break. I came back to spend the holidays with Mom."

He looks away and nods. "How is Lucy?"

"She's good. Working on her GED." With the right support, Mom is getting close to being able to take the test. Math has never been her strongest subject, but she has a wonderful teacher who has been helping her get through the curriculum. And she's found a new love for audiobooks and sweet romance thanks to Clover.

"Good. That's good. She was always smarter than me. She feeling better too? Healed up okay?"

"She's got some new aches and pains, but otherwise she's doing well."

"Good. That's real good." He blinks a bunch of times. "I didn't mean for her to get hurt like that. I wasn't thinking clearly. Can you tell her that for me? That I didn't mean for her to get hurt? The police said I'm not allowed to talk to her or be near her or I'll go to jail, otherwise I'd tell her myself."

If I put up a filter and view him *not* as my father, but some sad man who lost his way, it's easier to find some empathy. I nod. "I can tell her that."

"Thanks. I'd appreciate it." He chews on the inside of his lip. "I tried to quit the drink, but, uh, it's not easy. I went to a couple of those meetings. I might try again after the holidays."

"I hope that works out for you." I can't remember a single day when my dad didn't have a beer in his hand. Alcohol is the other woman in his life, and I'm not sure he'll ever be able to leave her.

"You still playing hockey? How's college?"

"I am. And college is good, challenging, but good."

He nods. "That's good. You always had the brains for school." He exhales a long breath.

"I should probably go." This is the most interest my dad has ever shown in me, but it's too little too late, and it's getting awkward. Seeing him like this makes me both sad and angry. Even after losing everything, he still can't find a reason to turn his life around, and he's given up so completely.

"Yeah. Of course. You take care, Winter."

"You too." I dig around in my pocket with shaking hands for the key to BJ's Jeep.

"Winter?" My dad's voice wavers.

I really hope he doesn't ask me for money. I glance over my shoulder. "Yeah?"

"I'm sorry."

"For what?"

He looks away. "For the way I treated you and your mom. I know it's my fault she left. My temper gets in the way."

I nod to the bag in his hand. "You can fix that, if you really want to."

"I'm gonna try. After the holidays."

The door to the flower store jingles as it opens.

I feel BJ before I see him.

"Snowflake? Everything okay?"

My dad's gaze moves behind me.

"Yup, we're all good here." I offer my dad a small smile. "I really do hope you can kick that habit. Have a merry Christmas."

"You too, kiddo." He gets into the passenger seat of an old Ford. I recognize the driver as one of his friends from the trailer park.

BJ's hand settles on my shoulder as the car leaves the lot. "Are you okay?"

I nod. "Yeah. He apologized for being a shitty father and husband. He said he's going to try to kick the booze after the holidays."

"Do you believe him?"

I sigh and turn to face BJ. "I believe he wants to try. I don't know if he'll be successful, but I hope he is."

He wraps his arms around me. "That's all we can do, isn't it? Hope for the best."

ON CHRISTMAS EVE, BJ and I drive out to the trailer park with a care package for my dad. I don't tell Mom I'm going. She's doing so well these days, and I don't want to derail her. But I want to give my dad a piece of the hope the Ballistics gave me when I needed it most. Maybe it will inspire him to do better, to make the changes he needs to if he wants a place in either of our lives.

The trailer is in pretty bad condition, much worse than it was the last time my mom and I were here.

"He's living here?" BJ asks. "How does he stay warm during winter?"

"We had a couple of space heaters that kept it decent. But sometimes we'd stay at the shelter during a big storm. If he pays the electric bills, he should be okay."

"And if he doesn't?"

"He'll have to find somewhere else to stay." I worry about that, about him not having electricity or heat. About something bad happening. But it's out of my control. I can't force him to make better choices. I can only nudge him in the right direction and hope he'll choose that path. Before it's too late.

"You had to do that in the winter sometimes?"

"A few times, yeah." I squeeze his hand. "I try not to take what I have now for granted."

"Your life was so fucking hard."

"It could be, yeah. But it shaped me into the person I am, and the future is a whole lot brighter. That's what's important."

Dad doesn't answer when I knock, so I find the spare key and let myself in. The clutter is overwhelming, and the place needs a good cleaning, but that's not my job. I put all the perishables in the fridge and leave the nonperishables on the table, along with the card and a gift certificate to the local grocer's—the one that doesn't sell booze, so he'll use it for food.

Then BJ and I return to his house to celebrate the holidays with his family and all our friends.

My mom and I are used to small celebrations. Usually, my dad would take a shift at the ice cream factory because they paid double, and she and I would celebrate on our own with leftovers from the holiday dinners served at the diner. So the magnitude of the celebration with the Ballistics is something we haven't experienced before.

Mom and I spent the days leading up to the celebration making homemade origami ornaments with Clover to put in everyone's stockings. It's hands down the best Christmas we've ever had. BJ's parents invite us to stay the night, but my mom and I want to start new traditions of our own, so we go home with the promise that we'll return the following day for more celebrating, including a Christmas brunch.

The cabin is decorated for the holidays, and white lights frame the porch. Some work has been done since I've been away at college. The garage has new siding and a new door, which is a huge improvement.

The front steps to the cabin have been replaced, so they no longer sit at an angle. There's a new storm door, and the front porch has been cleaned out, no longer stuffed with empty beer cases. The kitchen counter is clear of empties, and it smells fresher inside, the scent of cigarette smoke almost gone.

There's a newer couch in the living room, and the old lounger has been replaced with two chairs. I know the Hockey Academy has been helping out a lot, and through her GED classes, my mom has learned how to create a budget, so she doesn't stress about the bills anymore. It's tight, but it's manageable.

Her new roommate is visiting family upstate for the week, so we have the cabin to ourselves. We put on *How the Grinch Stole Christmas* and snuggle on the couch, both of us falling asleep partway through.

In the morning, we make coffee and eat cookies while we look through our stockings.

"Your real present is a work in progress," Mom tells me. "It's not finished quite yet, but it should be ready when you move back to Pearl Lake for the summer, if that's still your plan." She wrings her hands with nervous excitement.

"Yeah, that's definitely the plan, as long as it's okay with you." I have a place on the women's team at the Hockey Academy and my part-time job at Boones, so moving home for the summer makes the most sense, even if it means I can't sleep beside BJ. We're not sure how it's going to work, but we have time to figure out where I'll sleep, even if we have to convert the front porch into a makeshift extra bedroom.

"I was hoping you'd say that." She stands. "Come on, I want to show you even though it's not quite ready yet."

We shrug into our winter coats and shove our feet into boots. She's practically bouncing with excitement when we reach the garage. "Close your eyes and keep them closed until I tell you to open them, okay?"

"Okay."

She takes my hand. "Watch the step."

I edge my foot forward until I hit the lip of the door, then step over it. The floor feels different beneath my feet, not the pitted concrete I remember.

She tugs me forward. "Okay. Now you can open them."

"Oh my gosh." I spin around. "What is this?"

"You know the Stitches, who own Stitches Construction? Well, I guess Lily and Randy know them personally, and they've been helping me turn this into an apartment, so you have your own space when you come home for the summer." She pulls me toward the framed wall in the back corner. "This will be the bathroom, with a shower." She motions to the wide-open space. "And you'll have a place for your bed, and over here is space for a couch and a TV. It'll have a kitchenette and everything. They're working on it between jobs, and all the materials are recycled from other homes. It'll be a bit of a hodgepodge, but it'll be yours."

"It's amazing." Tears sting my eyes. "Can we afford this?"

"Clover helped me apply for a special grant for housing improvements. I wrote them an essay as part of my English course. Got a real good grade on that one." Her eyes light up. "And they accepted my application, so here we are." She takes my hand in hers. "I know it hasn't been an easy road for us, Winter, and I made a lot of mistakes in the past, but I'm trying to do better. For both of us."

"I'm so proud of you." I throw my arms around her.

It's another step forward.

Another pillar of support to add to the foundation of our new life.

Built with hope and held together with love.

EPILOGUE

Go for the Gold

WINTER

FIVE YEARS *Later*

It's the third period, just over a minute and a half left in the game. We're tied. Overtime is coming if we don't score a goal. My stomach is tight with anticipation. Anything can happen.

I scan the arena and find BJ in the stands. His parents are here, too, and so is my mom. I never thought this would be my life. Never dared to dream this big until BJ came along and planted an entire garden of hope in my heart and made it bloom endlessly.

Nothing about the past five years has been easy, but every battle we fought to get here has been worth it.

BJ eventually decided to try for the Olympics as a solo skater. It took four years of rehab and hard work to get him there, but he made it to the trials. We both did. And this past year has been the toughest yet, because we had to spend so much time apart.

373

But we accomplished the goal, despite all odds, and he's made the best out of what has been a truly life-altering injury. There were so many times that he wanted to give up, months where it looked like competitive skating would never be an option for him again. He had some deep lows, but we battled through them together. I did for him what he did for me—fed his hope, held his hand, and held him up when he couldn't do it on his own. We've spent a lot of time on the ice together and even more time off it, planning, figuring things out, and growing as a couple.

Every day I fall more and more in love with him. With his resilience. With his patience. With his desire to overcome the obstacles in his path.

He didn't place, but he competed. For him, that was always the goal. And it was enough. His plan now is to go back to school and get his PhD in psychotherapy. I finished a degree in social work, but I have a place on the women's US hockey team, and it's been a dream come true.

And so much else has happened over the past five years. My mom completed her GED. Seeing her graduate was amazing, and then she took classes at a community college to become a personal care aide. She's working at the Lavender House now, which Clover and Maverick run with the help of our amazing hockey family. It's a place where battered women and their families go to get back on their feet. They help with everything from housing and therapy, to accompanying women and their families to court dates, or retrieving belongings from their homes so they can start fresh. It's exactly the right place for my mom, and she couldn't be happier.

I hope one day she'll find love again, but the good kind. The kind that builds her up instead of breaks her down.

I catch BJ's gaze from across the arena, and he presses two fingers to his lips and touches his heart, mouthing *you got this*.

A few seconds later, the whistle blows, and I'm back on the ice, heading for my teammate who has control of the puck. I see the opportunity, and so does she. She passes to me, and instead of taking the shot, I pass it back, skating behind the net and picking up the puck again as I come out the other side. Then I tap it in, the buzzer going off a few seconds later.

The roar of the crowd is deafening, and I'm swarmed by my teammates, my eyes lifting to the scoreboard as I watch our score move from two to three, giving Team USA the gold medal. Another goal accomplished. Another win. Another hope flower blooming.

Watching Winter kick ass on the ice fills my heart in a way no medal ever could. Making it to the Olympics was an uphill battle for both of us. But it's been worth every grueling minute to see Winter shine so brightly.

It's hours later before I can finally celebrate this huge win with her. And even more hours before we're alone in our hotel room. For the first time in weeks.

"You were magical out there tonight." I cup her face between my palms and kiss her, but don't make a move to deepen it yet. I want to revel in the closeness for a minute. To soak up her presence like a balm. "I missed you so much."

"I missed you too." She wraps her arms around my waist. "I'm all for love professions and long conversations, but can we save them for pillow talk? We haven't had sex in weeks, and I'm ready to explode."

I chuckle. "So you're saying you *don't* want me to tell you one of my long, meandering stories with no ending?"

"Later, after you've given me several outstanding orgasms and I'm too tired and sated to complain, you're more than welcome to tell one of your excessively long-winded, meandering stories. But for now, we have a lot of Tongue-Fuck Tuesdays and Sweet Spot Saturdays to make up for."

"Stop talking and let me kiss you then." I slant my mouth over hers and walk her backwards to the bed.

We kiss like the world is on fire, and Winter tries to tear the clothes off my body. "I'm not going anywhere, Snowflake."

"I need you. I missed you. The only reason I made it through was because I knew eventually I'd be right here with you again." She shoves my pants and boxers down and grips my erection.

We both groan as we climb onto the bed.

"What if I want to savor this experience? It isn't every day I get to have hot sex with an Olympic medalist."

"You can savor later. Right now, I need to fuck-ebrate."

"Fuck-ebrate? Did you come up with that on your own or—"

My words get lost when she pulls me between her parted thighs and guides me to her entrance. She wraps her legs around my waist, tipping her hips up as she pushes down on my ass at the same time.

Everything changes the second I'm inside her. All my stupid commentary dissolves into grunts of desperation and moans of need.

The sex isn't gentle or tender or sweet like I'd originally planned. It's weeks of pent-up desire unleashed. It's a frenzy of need, hot words, and promises of more groaned into each other's mouths. It isn't until we've both come twice that Winter finally takes stock of our surroundings.

She peels a pink rose petal off my chest and glances around

the room. "Oh my God, you tried to make this all romantic, and I attacked you like a starved wolf."

"I can't really blame you, though. I'm hard to resist, aren't I?"

She laughs. "Totally irresistible."

I caress the edge of her jaw. "I do plan to make sweet, sweet love to you. Soon—"

Before I can say anything else, Winter puts a hand on my chest. "I have something I need to ask you first."

"Fire away."

"I love you." Her hand rests over my heart. I've added new art over the years, including several snowflakes.

"I love you too. More than anyone else in the world."

"It's the same for me." She brushes her lips over mine.

"That wasn't a question, though."

"I know. I'm getting to it." She runs her hands through my hair. It's shorter again. And I'm beardless.

"The anticipation is real."

She smiles softly. "The last six years have been amazing, and challenging, and more than I'd ever dreamed they could be. The universe brought you into my life when I needed you most. You showed me what strength and perseverance are. I know my playing for Team USA means we're apart almost as much as we're together, but I feel like all it does is make our love stronger."

"Watching you live your dream has been totally worth it," I assure her.

"I want to face whatever challenges come at us together. I want to spend the rest of my life with you," Winter whispers.

I let my fingers drift down her cheek. I have a feeling I know where this is going. "Funny, because I've been thinking the same thing."

"I have something for you." Winter grabs her toiletries bag

from the nightstand. It's where she keeps her birth control pills and extra condoms. Her hands are shaking as she turns back to me. "I know this defies convention, but that's sort of how we roll." She reveals a small, blue velvet box, but before she can flip it open, I cover her hand with mine.

"Hold one second, please." I slide my hand under the pillow behind her and feel around for the box I tucked there earlier. I flip my hand palm up and show her the matching blue velvet box. "Looks like we're on the same page again."

Winter tweaks my nipple. "Are you stealing my thunder?"

I arch a brow. "Are you stealing mine?"

We laugh.

"I guess the sweaty palms are pretty pointless now, huh?"

"Seems like we're both sure things."

She grins. "Seems like."

"It might be a bit archaic, but in this case, ladies first seems appropriate."

"I had a whole speech prepared, and I can't remember any of it now," Winter admits.

"I'm planning to save mine for after we've made sweet, sweet love and you're too orgasm-sated to be annoyed by how long and meandering it is."

"Seems on brand." She takes a deep breath. "I know we're young, and we still have so much learning and growing to do, but you're my ride or die, Randall. You're the only person I want to experience this roller coaster called life with." She flips open the box. Inside is a white gold ring with a single snowflake etched into the band. "Will you marry me?"

"Absolutely and without question, yes." I flip open the box in my own palm to reveal a white gold band with tiny diamonds that form a snowflake pattern. "There is nothing and no one in this world that I love more, Winter. My heart belongs to you."

"And mine belongs to you."

We slip the bands on each other's fingers and lace them together.

"Whatever you need," I murmur.

"However you need it," she whispers.

"I'll give it to you," we say together.

"Just you."

She smiles and echoes, "Just you."

"Always."

She's one of a kind.

My Snowflake.

My forever.

THE END

OTHER TITLES BY HELENA & H. HUNTING

SHACKING UP SERIES

Shacking Up

Getting Down (Novella)

Hooking Up

I Flipping Love You

Making Up

Handle with Care

SPARK SISTERS SERIES

When Sparks Fly

Starry-Eyed Love

Make A Wish

LAKESIDE SERIES

Love Next Door

Love on the Lake

CLIPPED WINGS SERIES

Cupcakes and Ink

Clipped Wings

Between the Cracks

Inked Armor

Cracks in the Armor

Fractures in Ink

STANDALONE NOVELS

The Librarian Principle

Felony Ever After

Before You Ghost (with Debra Anastasia)

FOREVER ROMANCE STANDALONES

The Good Luck Charm

Meet Cute

Kiss my Cupcake

A Love Catastrophe

ABOUT THE AUTHOR H. HUNTING

NYT and *USA Today* bestselling author, Helena Hunting, lives on the outskirts of Toronto with her amazing husband, fabulous daughter and emotional boy kitty who's favourite place to sleep is her laptop. She writes contemporary romance and romantic comedies, and when she wants to dive into her angsty side, she writes new adult romance under H. Hunting.

Scan this code to stay connected with Helena

Made in the USA
Columbia, SC
22 October 2023

24719725R10220